## "ISABELLA, I AM BETROTHED."

"There is one thing I must know," she replied. "All my life I have wanted to be with you. I would be your mistress . . . anything . . . I, a queen, my lord Count, love you still. I had to see you. I had to know if I still loved you . . . wanted you for my lover. Hugh, you owe me this. This night. Tonight. And if you find you do not love me, I will go away."

"I am betrothed to your daughter," he said hoarsely.

She laughed softly and slipped the robe from her shoulders. "Come Hugh," she said, "I command you . . ."

# JEAN PLAIDY

FAWCETT CREST • NEW YORK

First American Edition 1981
A Fawcett Crest Book
Published by Ballantine Books
Copyright © 1978 by Jean Plaidy

Library of Congress Catalog Card Number: 80-24739

ISBN 0-449-24565-9

This edition published by arrangement with G.P. Putnam's Sons

Manufactured in the United States of America

First Ballantine Books Edition: December 1982

# Contents

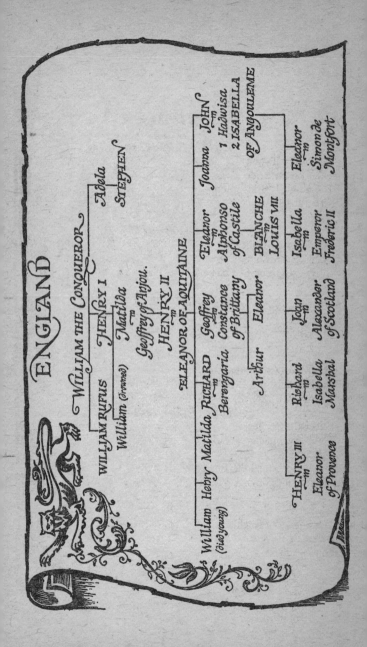

# ENGLAND

**WILLIAM THE CONQUEROR**

WILLIAM RUFUS · HENRY I · Adela
William (crowned) · Matilda / STEPHEN
m
Geoffrey of Anjou.
**HENRY II**
m
**ELEANOR OF AQUITAINE**

William · Henry · Matilda · RICHARD · Geoffrey · Eleanor · Joanna · JOHN
(died young) · m · m · m · m · m
Berengaria · Constance · Alphonso · 1 Hadwisa
of Brittany · of Castile · 2 ISABELLA
OF ANGOULEME

Arthur · Eleanor · BLANCHE
m
LOUIS VIII

HENRY III · Richard · Joan · Isabella · Eleanor
m · m · m · m · m
Eleanor · Isabella · Alexander · Emperor · Simon de
of Provence · Marshal · of Scotland · Frederic II · Montfort

# FRANCE

LOUIS VII
m

1 ELEANOR OF AQUITAINE — 2 Constance of Castile — 3 Adela of Champagne

Mary    Alix                                    PHILIP AUGUSTUS
m                                               m

Henry of Champagne        1 Isabel of Hainault — 2 Ingeburga — 3 Agnes
                                                    of Denmark    of Meran
Thibaud III.
m                          LOUIS VIII.                Philip    Mary
                           m
Thibaud IV
le Chansonnier             BLANCHE OF CASTILE

LOUIS IX. — Robert    Alphonse   John   Philip   Isabella   Charles
m            of Artois  of Poitiers     Dagobert            of Anjou
Marguerite
of Provence

# BIBLIOGRAPHY

| | |
|---|---|
| Appleby, John T. | *John, King of England* |
| Ashley, Maurice | *The Life and Times of King John* |
| Aubrey, William Hickman Smith | *National and Domestic History of England* |
| d'Auvergne, Edmund B. | *John, King of England* |
| Barlow, F. | *The Feudal Kingdom of England* |
| Bémont, Charles Translated by E. F. Jacob | *Simon de Montfort, Earl of Leicester* |
| Brooke, F. W. | *From Alfred to Henry III* |
| Bryant, Arthur | *The Medieval Foundation* |
| Davis, H. W. C. | *England Under the Angevins* |
| Funck-Brentano, Fr. Translated by Elizabeth O'Neill | *The National History of France The Middle Ages* |
| Guizot, M. Translated by Robert Black | *History of France* |
| Hume, David | *History of England from the Invasion of Julius Caesar to the Revolution* |
| Labarge, Margaret Wade | *Simon de Montfort* |
| Norgate, Kate | *England Under the Angevin Kings* |
| Pernoud, Régine Translated by Henry Noel | *Blanche of Castile* |
| Powicke, Sir Maurice | *The Thirteenth Century 1216–1307* |
| Stenton, D. M. | *English Society in the Middle Ages* |
| Strickland, Agnes | *Lives of the Queens of England* |
| Stevens, Sir Leslie, and Lee, Sir Sidney | *The Dictionary of National Biography* |
| Wade, John | *British History* |
| Young, Denholm, N. | *Richard of Cornwall* |

# ENGLAND
## 1216—1223

# Death of a Tyrant

THE long summer was over. From the turret window the Queen looked disconsolately beyond the moat to the forest where the bronzed leaves of the towering oaks and the copper of the beeches splashed their autumnal colours across the landscape. Mist hung over the marsh where the sedge grew thickly; listlessly she watched a pair of magpies, vivid black and white against the October sky.

And she thought of Angoulême where, looking back, the days had seemed always full of sunshine and the halls of her father's castle inhabited by handsome troubadours whose delight it was to sing of the incomparable charm and beauty of the Lady Isabella. And understandably so, for there could not have been a woman at the courts of the Kings of England or France whose beauty could compare with hers. There are many handsome women but now and then there appears one who is possessed not only of obvious physical charms but some indefinable quality, which would seem to be indestructible. Helen of Troy was one, Isabella of Angoulême such another.

She smiled reflecting on this. It was a comforting thought for a prisoner—and prisoner she was. The King, her husband, hated her and yet at the same time could not resist her, for having once come under her spell he could never escape from it. Nor did she intend him to.

Where was he now? In trouble, deep deep trouble. That was inevitable. There could never have been such a foolish monarch as King John. Many of his subjects were in revolt against him and so deeply was he hated that Englishmen had invited the son of the French King to come over and take the crown. Consequently the French were now on English soil and John was losing England as he had lost all the Crown's possessions in France. His ancestors—mighty William the Conqueror, and the first Henry, that Lion of Justice, would curse him; and his father, great Henry II and his mother Eleanor of Aquitaine would have been in agreement for once and have declared that it would have been better if they had died before they brought such a creature into the world.

John was lustful, cruel, vain and unwise. He possessed not a single quality which could be called good, and from the moment he had taken the crown he had progressed steadily towards disaster.

Perhaps, she thought, I should have married Hugh. No! Whatever else he was, John was a King and Hugh could never have made her a Queen.

She had always wanted power and great honours and it had seemed only natural that her beauty should provide them for her.

How pensive she was today! It was as though something portentous was in the air. She sensed it. But was that unusual? Each day when she looked from this turret window she would gaze fixedly at the horizon, watching for a rider. It might be John, remembering her existence and perhaps the early days of their marriage when he was so enamoured of her that he would not leave their bed—not only throughout the night but during the day as well—much to the disgust of his barons, for, although they knew him for a lusty man, and of his scheming, after he had come by accident upon Isabella in the forest, to get her to his bed, they believed that, as the King, he should have remembered he had other duties than to get his wife with child and to indulge his voracious sexual appetites.

She knew that such memories would come upon him suddenly and he would ride to Gloucester, storm to her chamber and remind her that although she was his prisoner she was his wife. He might have cursed her for her infidelities—although he expected her acceptance of his—and he might have hung her lover on the tester of her bed so that when she awaked she found the corpse swinging there, yet he would lust for her and she was not entirely displeased, for her appetites were as keen as his in this respect, and this passion of hatred and desire amused and intrigued her.

Her youngest child, Eleanor, had been conceived in this prison and born a year ago. She was thankful that she had the children with her, but she must never let him know of this, for he might then seek to deprive her of their company. She had never been a doting mother, and perhaps that was why it had not occurred to him to rob her of them. He believed her to be as indifferent to them as he was.

Young Henry, now nine years old, would be the next king, provided the French did not conquer the country which, according to news which was brought in to her, they were on the point of doing. What next? she asked herself. Who could say? It seemed likely that there would be one among the invaders—perhaps Louis himself—who would not be insensible to the charms of the Queen. She would have to wait and see what happened; and considering the pass to which John had brought them, perhaps it would have been better after all if she had married Hugh de Luisignan. She had been only twelve years old but already mature when on their betrothal she had become enamoured of Hugh. Her ardent nature had set her dreaming of love-making with that handsome man, but he—though desiring her—had held aloof, fearing that she was too young and having romantic notions of waiting for marriage. Dear Hugh, during those wild orgies with John she had often remembered him and during the softer moments in her thoughts she had substituted handsome gentle Hugh for her violent husband and found delight in doing so, if only to contemplate how furious John would have been had he read her thoughts.

Always she had consoled herself: But he is a King and has made me a Queen which was a long step from being merely the daughter of the Count of Angoulême, even though she had been the only child and a considerable heiress. One thing she could say was that John had taken no count of her inheritance. His desire to marry her had been pure lust. And it had remained even through his dalliance with other women— on whom he had got several children—even through her own adventures which he had made her pay for by that terrible act. And paid she had for even now she could awake from a nightmare in which she was back in that fearful dawn opening her eyes to that grisly spectacle. But through all that, his desire for her lived on.

She had seen him throw away his inheritance, reduced to utter humiliation by the barons who had forced him to sign Magna Carta at Runnymede. Those same barons were now weary of his foolishness, his rashness, his ineptitude and his cruelty to so many. He had enemies everywhere.

And now the French. They had trumped up a claim to the English throne for Louis, son of Philip of France, because Louis had married Blanche who was the daughter of John's sister Eleanor and Alphonso of Castile. Eleanor was a daughter of Henry II—and with such a monarch as John on the throne his enemies were ready to clutch at anything.

William Marshal, the great Earl of Pembroke, one of the few loyal men in the country, had shown himself to be sick at heart by all that had happened and being the wise man he was he would know well at whose door the fault lay. But he had always stood for the king and the application of law and preservation of order. He had served Henry II well and had stood by him when all his sons came against him; he had fought face to face with Richard; but when Richard came to the throne he had had the good sense to make William Marshal the first of his advisers. Even John realized the need to listen to him. If only he had always taken the Marshal's advice he would not have been in this position now.

So the French were invading the country and John was in retreat and even the Marshal's eldest son had gone over to the French.

What next? Isabella asked herself, as she sat at the turret window waiting for the sight of a rider who might bring her news.

It was none other than William Marshal himself who brought it.

She saw him riding towards the castle at the head of a small party.

He was very old—he must be nearly eighty—yet from a distance he might have been a young man. For a while she watched his approach and then she came down to the court-yard to greet him.

With what dignity he sat his horse. He was very tall and his features were clear cut; his were the kind of good looks which age cannot destroy. His dignity was great and it had been said of him that he carried himself like a Roman emperor. In his youth he had been one of the finest horsemen of his day and had won great honours in the joust. His curling hair was still brown in colour and he held himself like a soldier.

He dismounted and kissed the Queen's hand.

'Ill news, my lord?' she said.

And when he answered bluntly, 'The King is dead,' her heart leaped with mixed emotions. She was surprised by a sense of desolation; but it quickly passed and excitement gripped her.

'What now?' she whispered.

'Prompt action,' he said.

'Then come into the castle.'

'There is much that must be done without delay,' answered the Marshal.

It was a tale of horror. He did not tell her immediately but she learned of it later. The tyrant, the foolish reckless King who had brought misery to thousands, who had placed his country in jeopardy, was no more.

She sensed the relief in the Marshal; it was as though he were saying: Now we may begin to plan.

'Where is the King?' he asked. She was startled. Then the truth came to her like a river that flowed over her, taking her breath away.

She answered firmly: 'He is with his brother and sisters in the schoolroom.'

The Marshal hesitated. He was a man for protocol. Instinct was urging him to go to the boy, dramatically to kneel before him and swear allegiance.

The Queen laid a hand on his arm. 'Later, good Marshal,' she said.

The Earl hesitated; then bowed his head in agreement.

'He knows little of what is happening,' said the Queen. 'I did not wish him as yet to despise his father. I must talk with you. Ale shall be brought. You have ridden far and need it.'

'As I have said, Madam, prompt action is necessary.'

'I know it well.'

'The King should be crowned as quickly as possible.'

'We will talk of these things . . . but in secret—for who should know what tales are carried? Your own son . . .'

The Marshal agreed. 'He had no love for the King. He believed that it was better to stand against him. I did not wish it, but I saw the reason in it.'

She clapped her hands and almost immediately ale was brought. She ordered meat but the Marshal was in no mood for food though he admitted a need to quench his thirst.

'Pray leave us,' said the Queen to her attendants who hovered awaiting further commands, and when they were alone, she said: 'How did he die? Ignobly I doubt not, as he lived.'

William Marshal did not meet her eye. 'It is uncertain,' he said, 'but there is talk of poison.'

'Ah! So someone was bold enough. You must tell me my lord, for depend upon it, I shall discover and would rather hear the truth from your lips than the garbled tales of others.'

'I can only say, Madam, that he paused with his troops at a convent on the way to Swinstead Abbey and there demanded refreshment. Rumour has it that he saw there a nun whose beauty was apparent in spite of her habit.'

'Oh dear God, no. So! Right to the end . . .'

'I heard Madam, that she had a look of yourself which amused the King.'

'And I doubt not that he declared it was in looks only that there could be a likeness.'

'I heard not that, my lady. But he sought to molest her and she fled. He did not pursue her. He did not seem to have the spirit for it.'

'And she escaped him. I am glad.'

'News of what happened may have gone ahead of him to the Abbey if this rumour be true, for his men declare that it was the peaches which were given him there which set him in violent pain. He was in agony all the way to Newark and when he reached the Bishop's castle there he lay on his bed and died.'

They were silent for a while. Then the Marshal rose and said: 'Now, Madam, I must see the King.'

'He is but a child, my lord Earl.'

'He is the King of England, my lady.'

'Grant me this,' she said. 'Let me go to them. Let me break the news. I must prepare him. He is a serious boy and will quickly learn.'

William Marshal saw the point of this. He had never greatly admired the Queen. That she was an exceptionally attractive woman he was aware and old as he was and strict in his morals, he could not help but be stirred by her unquestionable appeal.

He had thought often in the early days of her marriage to John that she suited the King. Her sensuality was immediately apparent. She wore it like a gleaming ornament and every man must be aware of it. John had been completely ensnared on that first meeting in the wood when she had been only a child. Hugh de Lusignan had remained a bachelor because, it was said, after having been betrothed to her, he could take no other woman. That she was a schemer, he knew. He had once remarked to his wife—another Isabella—that the Queen deserved the King and the King the Queen, but he sometimes thought that perhaps he had been a little harsh on her. There could hardly be a woman in the world who deserved John.

He was uneasy now. The new King a minor and a forceful mother in the background. He could see trouble ahead.

So he hesitated.

Then he said: 'The situation is fraught with danger.'

'I know it well. The French are here. There are many traitors in this country who would set Louis on the throne. He has brought foreign soldiers on to our soil.'

'Your husband the late King has done that too, my lady. His army consisted mainly of mercenaries from the Continent.'

She was silent for a while and then she said: 'I pray you, my lord Earl, give me a little time with my son, that I may tell him of this burden which has descended on him.'

'Go to him, Madam,' said William Marshal. 'And then I will pay my homage to the King.'

\*　　\*　　\*

Isabella went at once to the schoolroom where she knew she would find the three eldest children. Isabella aged two and Eleanor one, would be in the nursery.

The two boys and the young girl were seated at a long table drawing together, their heads bent over their work.

At the sight of their mother the children all rose, the little girl curtseying prettily and the boys bowing. The Queen always insisted on this homage; she often wondered whether they knew they were in captivity on their father's orders. They were aware that he came of course. Henry the eldest dreaded his coming even more than the others, for Henry was a boy who wanted to live in peace; his brother Richard was quite the reverse. Sometimes Isabella had thought that it would have been more fitting if Richard had been the elder of the two.

She took Henry by the hand and led him to the window seat, the others following.

Richard said: 'There are visitors at the castle, my lady.'

She frowned slightly. It was always Richard who spoke. Why did Henry hang back? The boy looked different in her eyes now. He was a king even though his subjects might decide not to accept him. She thought again: It ought to have been Richard. Fleetingly she remembered the day her second son had been born. It was at Winchester and young Henry was only fifteen months old at the time. There had been a long period before she had conceived her firstborn, and she had indeed wondered whether she was barren—for John had already proclaimed his fertility by scattering bastards throughout the country. And then the birth of Henry had been quickly followed by that of Richard; and Joan was not far behind.

She need not have concerned herself about being barren. Children were a blessing, particularly when they could wear crowns.

She drew Henry to her and he said: 'It was not my father who came, my lady.'

There was a note of relief in his voice. She knew the children cowered in their bedchambers when their father came. Henry feared he ill-treated her. Nay little son, she wanted to explain. I can give him as good as he gives me.

And now he was dead, and the world had become an exciting place.

'Grave news, my children,' she said. 'You saw the arrival of the Earl of Pembroke then?'

'From the window,' replied Richard. 'And we saw you go down to greet him.'

'He is an old, old, old man,' said Joan.

'Pray that you will be as hale and hearty when you reach his age, child,' said the Queen sharply.

Joan appeared to be fascinated by the idea of growing as old as William Marshal.

Her mother said: 'He has brought me news of your father.'

'He is coming here?' That was Henry. Concern showing in his sensitive face.

'No. He will never come here again. He is dead.'

There was an awestruck silence. Isabella took Henry's hand and kissed it. 'And you, my son, are now King of England.'

Henry's face puckered in horror. Richard cried out: 'He's Henry the Third, is he not, my lady, because our grandfather was Henry the Second.'

Henry was plucking at his mother's sleeve. 'Tell me, my mother, what must I do?'

'Only what you are told,' she answered quietly. 'Now,' she went on, 'there is no need for concern. I shall be here to help you and the Earl of Pembroke is waiting now to kiss your hand and swear allegiance to you.'

Joan went to her brother and touched his arm with an expression of awe on her pretty face.

'We must never make Henry angry any more, must we,' she said. 'If we did he could cut off our heads.'

Richard cried out: 'I'd cut off his head first.'

'That is no way to talk of your King,' said Isabella severely. 'And you should never have made Henry angry, Joan. That was wrong of you. Certainly now it will be well for you to remember that he is your King.'

She looked at her daughter with a certain dislike. Her feelings had changed towards Joan ever since John, with typical devious cunning, had decided that it would be an excellent idea to betroth her to Hugh de Lusignan. Isabella's eyes narrowed; she could hear that mocking voice. 'He didn't get the mother so perhaps the daughter will provide some consolation.' 'You must be crazy,' she had answered. 'Hugh is a grown man and Joan but a baby.' 'Let him wait,' was the reply. 'He's a waiting man.'

Hugh—the man she was to have married and about whom she had often been regretful because she had not, to be the husband of her young daughter! John had known that she preserved some feelings for him, and that was why he had done his best to humiliate Hugh at every turn. But it was not easy to humiliate Hugh for he had that innate dignity which a man like John—royal though he might be by birth—could never aspire to. He had known that she would hate her daughter to go to Lusignan there to be brought up in the household of the man she had once loved. For she had loved Hugh, though in a self-seeking way, which was all she knew herself to be capable of. Hugh was however the one person for whom she might have made a little sacrifice. And John had betrothed her daughter to him! She could not help it, but the child irritated her, and to see her growing prettier every day gave her no comfort.

She turned from Joan to Henry.

'Now, my son, I am going to take you to the Earl of Pembroke. Put aside those frightened looks. Are you a baby that you must be afraid of your crown? You should rejoice. Some have to wait years for what is yours in your youth. Come, look like a King. Act like one.'

She gripped his shoulder firmly and led him from the room. Richard watched him enviously, Joan with wonder; and Henry was wishing that he had been fifteen months younger than Richard instead of being his senior.

It was a strange sight to see the noble Earl kneel before the pale-faced boy. Yet in those moments Henry seemed to acquire a new dignity; and as William Marshal looked at the slender boy a new hope came to him that perhaps his accession could put an end to the torment of civil war in the land and might even result in driving the foreign invader from the country.

\*　　\*　　\*

The young King had retired to his chamber, for his mother said he was still her son and must do what she considered best for him.

Henry, rarely other than docile, obeyed her. He was glad to be by himself that he might contemplate the enormity of what had happened to him.

Meanwhile Isabella and William Marshal talked earnestly together.

'The King must be crowned without delay,' declared William. 'We must let the people see that a new era is about to begin.'

'With a King who is a minor!'

'With a King, Madam, who will have good advisers.'

'Yourself,' she said with a hint of wryness.

'I think that many would consider me fitted to the task. I have sent a message to Hubert de Burgh and I doubt not that ere long he will be with us.'

Isabella's spirits rose. With two such men to support her son, his chances were good.

'I do not think that the people of England want to hand over their country to the French,' went on William Marshal.

'It would seem that many of them were attempting to do just that,' she retorted.

'In desperation, my lady, seeing anything preferable to rule by John.'

She had no answer to that, for she knew that he spoke the truth.

'But now that we have a new king—a boy who can be guided—it could mean a turning point in this dire state of affairs.'

'I hope and pray so, my lord.'

'A King becomes a King when he is crowned. We must therefore have no delay in bringing about the coronation.'

'With what could he be crowned? John has lost the crown jewels in the Wash.'

'It is not the crown itself which is so important as the ceremony of crowning and the people's acceptance of their King.'

'But a King needs a royal crown. And that of Edward the

Confessor is in London. Is it true that London is overrun by the French?'

'To the shame of Englishmen—yes. But it shall not be for long. Let the people of England know that the tyrant is dead, that we have a new young and innocent king on the throne— with strong men to support him—and you will find that they rally to him. I doubt not that this time next year—if we act wisely—there will not be a Frenchman in this land.'

She could not but be convinced, for William Marshal was known throughout the country, not only for his bravery and loyalty but for his sound good sense.

'My lord,' said Isabella, 'the Archbishop of Canterbury should perform the ceremony.'

'Impossible. Stephen Langton is in Rome—whither he went to escape the persecution of your late husband.'

'And the Archbishop of York and the Bishop of London. . . .'

'My lady, a coronation does not depend on a Bishop nor yet an Archbishop. We will find someone to perform the ceremony. I have already sent a messenger to the Bishop of Winchester. He, being the only one available, must crown the King.'

'And the people. . . .'

'Ah, there is a greater problem. So heartily sickened were they by John's tyrannies that they might stand out against his son. We have to woo the people, Madam, and that is our greatest task.'

Isabella shrugged her shoulders. 'A hostile people, absent Archbishops of Canterbury and York, also a Bishop of London, no royal crown . . . and you would have a coronation.'

'Yes, Madam, I would, for I believe it to be the only way to save England for the rightful King.'

His eyes were on a gold throat-collar which she was wearing. Noticing this she touched it wonderingly.

'Could I see the ornament, my lady.'

She unfastened it, and gave it to him. He examined it and smiled.

'This could be the crown of Henry the Third of England,' he said. 'Methinks it would fit well on that young head.'

\*       \*       \*

Before the day was out Hubert de Burgh had arrived at the castle.

He was exhilarated by the turn of events. He was a loyal man; he had done his best to hold off the French; he had held Dover Castle against them until it had been no longer possible to do so. He deplored the fact that foreigners were on English soil, but he rejoiced in the death of John.

Perhaps he, as well as any, was aware of the villainy of that twisted nature. He had seen England lose the greatness which rulers like the Conqueror, Henry I and Henry II had brought, but no country could prosper when its King was so enamoured of military glory that he was scarcely ever in the land he was supposed to govern as King. Richard—whom they called the Lion-hearted—had been thus; and when such rule was followed by that of a depraved, cruel, unscrupulous man—whose folly was even greater than all his faults—England was doomed.

And now, the tyrant was dead and the Marshal had sent for him. The King was a minor. Could it be that they could take England out of the wretched humiliation into which she had fallen? If William Marshal believed this was possible, Hubert de Burgh was ready to agree with him.

There had been encounters with John which Hubert would never forget. All men now were aware of his villainies but what had happened between him and Hubert thirteen years ago would be a hideous memory for ever. Hubert often thought of the boy who had loved and trusted him and whose life he had tried to save. Poor Arthur, so young, so innocent, whose only sin had been that he had a claim to the throne of England which might have been considered by some to be greater than that of John.

Hubert would always be haunted by those scenes which had been played out in the Castle of Falaise where he had been custodian of the King's nephew, son of John's brother Geoffrey, poor tragic Prince Arthur. A beautiful boy— arrogant perhaps because of the homage men had paid him, but how pitifully that arrogance had broken up and shown him to be but a frightened child whom Hubert had grown to love as Arthur had loved Hubert. Sometimes in his dreams Hubert heard those dreadful cries for help; he could feel a hand tugging at his robes. 'Hubert, Hubert, save me Hubert. Not my eyes. . . . Leave me my eyes, Hubert.'

And in his dreams he would smell the heat of the braziers and see the men, their faces hardened by brutalities, the irons ready in their hands.

And for Arthur he had risked his life—for Hubert knew his master's rewards for those who disobeyed him; he had risked his own eyes for those of Arthur, dismissed the men, hidden the boy and pretended that he had died under the gruesome operation which was to have robbed him of his eyes and his manhood.

It had been as though fate were on his side for he could not have kept the boy hidden for ever. It was ironical that foolish John should have become afraid of the uprising of the men of Brittany and the constant whispers set in circulation by his enemies—the chief of them the King of France—that the King of England had murdered his nephew. So Hubert had confessed and been rewarded with the King's approval, for John, whose evil genius had ever made him act first and consider the consequences afterwards, realized that Hubert had done him a favour by saving Arthur's eyes. But it was not long before Arthur was taken from Hubert's care and murdered in the Castle of Rouen. At least, thought Hubert, I saved his eyes and death is preferable to one who has known what the green fields are like and then is cruelly deprived of the blessing of seeing them.

But often he had found John's eyes upon him and he had wondered whether the King was remembering that Hubert de Burgh was the man who had disobeyed his orders and refused to mutilate Arthur.

Hubert had been useful. Perhaps that was why he had outlived the King.

And now jubilation. John was dead and William Marshal was with the new King.

Could it be that a new era was coming for men such as himself?

He was in sight of the castle when he saw a solitary figure riding towards him. As the rider came nearer he realized with great pleasure that it was none other than William Marshal, Earl of Pembroke, himself.

Their horses drew up face to face, and the two men raised their hands in greeting.

'This is good news, William,' said Hubert, and William acceded the point. 'He died as he lived,' went on Hubert. 'Violently. It was inevitable that death would overtake him. Do you think it was poison?'

'Whenever a man or woman dies suddenly it is said to be due to poison.'

'No man could have been more hated.'

'He is gone,' said William. 'We need consider him no more. Long live King Henry III.'

'And you think, my lord Earl, that the King will be Henry and not Louis?'

'If we act wisely.'

'Louis is in command of much of the country.'

'Give them a King—a crowned King—and the people will rise against the foreigner. Within a few months we'll have the French out of the country. None could know better than you, Hubert, how difficult it is to invade a country which is protected by water.'

'Louis is safely landed here. . . .'

'But uneasily. Let the news spread through the land that John is dead, and that we have a new King.'

'A boy of nine.'

'With excellent counsellors, my dear Hubert.'

'Yourself?'

'And the Justiciar.'

'I am to keep hold of that office?'

'Assuredly. Hubert, we are going to make England great, and a land for the English.'

'Pray God it will come to pass.'

'Let us go into the castle. We must make plans. Henry is going to be crowned, even if it is only with his mother's throat-collar.'

Before the month was out the young King was crowned. The ceremony was performed by Peter des Roches, the Bishop of Winchester, and the crown used for the purpose was that gold throat-collar which had belonged to his mother.

After the King had been crowned the bishops and barons must pay homage to Henry.

Eager for action William Marshal, supported by Hubert de Burgh, summoned all loyal barons to Bristol where they would be presented to the new King.

It was comforting to the Earl to discover that more had assembled than he had dared hope. It seemed that now King John was dead they had no quarrel with the crown. A young monarch was always appealing though a matter for apprehension, for, surrounding the immature, there were usually too many ambitious men. But in this case there was a difference. Providence had rid them of the most hated most foolish King that had ever been known—and was ever likely to be—and if his son was a minor he was backed by one of the finest and most noble men England had ever known—a loyal servant to Henry II and Richard, and who had even tried to guide John to reason. That man was William Marshal.

So they came to Bristol and when they saw the pale boy, who could not have looked more unlike his father, so gentle was he, so eager for their approval, they were ready to swear allegiance to the crown. There was not a man among them who did not deplore the fact that there were French invaders in England; and they wanted to turn them out.

So they swore allegiance to the new King.

Henry, with his mother and brothers and sisters, spent Christmas in Bristol. William Marshal was with them and Henry found himself the centre of controversy. All the important men who came to the castle must be received by him and he was never allowed to forget for a moment the terrible responsibilities which had fallen on him.

Richard envied him while Joan watched him with a kind of awe. She took to calling him King, which in a way he liked, because now that the first shock had subsided and all he had to do at first was listen to the Earl and do what he told him, it was not difficult.

Their mother was with them more often than she had been and that pleased them. They were all conscious of her beauty and found pleasure in merely looking at her, as so many people did. Moreover she was a little more respectful to

Henry than she had been and he enjoyed this. He had been inclined to feel that Richard was much better liked than he was which made him hang back behind his younger brother, but now that he was King and Richard so clearly envious, all that was changed.

Isabella always liked to break news to them before it was formally announced by the council which assembled in the Bristol castle and which Henry had to attend whenever it assembled. At first this had frightened him, then bored him and afterwards he began to take an interest because they were discussing the affairs of the kingdom . . . his kingdom.

Isabella summoned the three eldest children to her because she had news for them.

'You know your new responsibilities, Henry,' she said. 'You have been crowned a king.'

'With your necklace,' giggled Joan.

Isabella gave her a light slap on her arm. Joan's frivolity was irritating and she was so pretty with her violet eyes and dark hair—growing like her mother, although of course she could never be quite so beautiful.

'Attend to me,' said Isabella sternly. 'The lords are going to choose William Marshal as Regent and they are going to put you in his charge.'

Richard grimaced and Joan looked at him, hunching her shoulders.

'Now, Henry,' said Isabella, 'we will take no heed of these foolish children. This is a matter of the King. You will have a tutor who will be Philip of Albini. He is a good man I know and a great scholar. You will enjoy learning with him.'

Henry was not alarmed. He was good with his books. Sometimes he wished that was all there was to kingship.

'You will have to study and be worthy of your crown. As for you Richard, you are leaving at once for Corfe Castle.'

Joan's face puckered. 'I don't want them to go.'

'Be silent, you stupid child. Richard has to learn even though he is not a king. He will be under the charge of Peter de Mauley at Corfe and his tutor is to be Sir Roger d'Acastre. The Earl of Pembroke has chosen the men he considers best for these important tasks.'

The boys were a little dismayed but Joan's lips were beginning to quiver.

'I like it as it was when our father was the King . . . instead of Henry.'

Isabella looked at her coldly. 'Do not imagine that *you* will be here for ever.'

'What will happen to me, my lady?'

The Queen smiled slowly. 'You are betrothed, you know.'

Joan nodded. 'To an old man.'

'Oh come, he is not as old as that. I knew him once . . . well, very well.'

'So he is as old as you, my lady.'

'Older,' she said sharply. 'But he was then a very handsome man. I never saw a handsomer in all my life.'

'People don't stay handsome,' said Richard.

'Some of them do,' retorted Isabella.

'Is he still the most handsome man?' asked Joan anxiously.

'That you will discover . . . soon I think.'

'Oh, am I going away, too?' Joan looked round the room as though she were seeking something to cling to.

'Yes, you will go away.' Isabella smiled secretly. 'You will have a governess to conduct you to your bridegroom. You will not be entirely alone, you know. Who knows . . . I myself might decide to take you to him.'

The Queen began to laugh and her children joined with her, without quite knowing why.

Throughout the country there was rejoicing because the tyrant was dead, but all must realize that being rid of John did not solve their difficulties. Many of them had welcomed Louis to England, certain that any ruler was preferable to John; but now that there was a new King supported by men such as William Marshal and Hubert de Burgh, they were eager to turn out the aliens. This was easier said than done. Louis was young; he was anxious to prove his valour and skills to his father, and he was as determined to succeed as many of the English were to turn him out. Moreover he had a foothold in England and his men were already in London.

It was disturbing to Louis to find that since young Henry had been crowned, the English who had supported him were now slipping away to the other side. Louis understood. The whole world had been aware of the misfortune which had overtaken England in such a King as John and, distracted by his injustices, the English were determined to be rid of him; now a higher power had intervened and mercifully for England, the tyrant was dead. It was naturally the time when Englishmen were asking themselves: What are we doing with foreigners on our soil? Why are we welcoming England's enemy? The need to do so is miraculously removed. We have a young King supported by great men. Let us drive out the invader . . . no, they could not call him that. He was the guest, invited by many of them. Come rid us of this John and in return you shall have the crown of England. How they hated John! But he was dead, and that changed everything.

Yes, Louis was very uneasy.

He returned to France to spend Christmas with his wife, Blanche. Because of the deep love and trust between them—rare in royal marriages—she was a wife with whom he could discuss state matters. That she was anxious about the English expedition, he was in no doubt; and he had agreed with her that now a new King had been crowned, it was time to make the final settlement. They must raise a new army—a force which the English would not be able to resist. Louis must capture the young King and hold him as prisoner—hostage, while he himself was acknowledged as King of England.

It was April before Louis had perfected his plans and returned to England, full of confidence that this would be the final phase and that England was ready to fall into his hands. He and Blanche had even made plans for their coronation in England but Louis did not know that during his absence in France loyalty to the crown of England was growing fast. Men were now talking disdainfully of the foreigner on English soil, forgetting that many of them had invited him there. There were some who were asking themselves how England could ever have come to such a pass and were determined to drive the French from the country.

Louis's first setback was at Lincoln, where the castle was in the hands of Nicole da la Haie, a Norman woman of forceful character, said to be as good and better than any man in her determination to save England for the English. Already she had sent out a proclamation that any of those barons who had rebelled against John were invited to her castle if they now were eager to be loyal to John's son, that they might discuss plans for restoring England to its rightful King. The boy was not responsible for his father's sins, she declared; and the spirit of the great Conqueror and the two Henrys would haunt them for the rest of their lives if they allowed the country to pass into the hands of the French. Nicole was eloquent. Under John the country had been humiliated beyond endurance, but those days were over and they must start to rebuild an England which would be as great as it had once been.

What an undignified defeat that had been. It had begun well enough with the French on the point of forcing an entrance when they had been nearly decimated by William Marshal's cross-bowmen, led by the Marshal himself, who in spite of his years, was in the thick of the fighting. There was about William Marshal that aura which comes to some men. The Conqueror had had it; so had Richard Coeur de Lion; men who were ranged against him lost their will for the battle because he was there. So many victories had been theirs that the notion had grown among the opposing armies that they were fighting against an irresistible force. When Marshal engaged the Count de la Perche—who was leading one section of the French—and the Count's followers saw the fleur-de-lis fall from the hands of the standard bearer and the Count dislodged from his horse, mortally wounded, they were certain that there was some magical quality in this man Marshal which was invincible.

And from that time it seemed the battle was lost and that God had determined to discountenance the French for at the vital stage of the battle a cow had become wedged in a narrow lane with a small opening leading into one of the courtyards and could not be moved, so that the soldiers could not pass; thus the men were trapped and four hundred prisoners were taken, which was near the number of those who had assembled to defend the castle.

So the French were utterly defeated at Lincoln and there was great rejoicing among the English, for those who had wavered and asked themselves what could be hoped from a boy King, saw now that with men such as William Marshal behind him he might learn to govern well.

When he heard of the defeat at Lincoln, Louis was very melancholy. He could see the campaign ending in disaster for him if he did not act promptly. He knew he could trust Blanche. She had the blood of the Conqueror in her veins and she would not fail him.

Nor did she. Within a short time he had word from her. She had toured the country raising men and money for him and her enthusiasm, her energy and her determination to serve her husband brought about excellent results. In England great consternation spread through the army assembled to meet them and even the heart of Hubert de Burgh quailed when he realized the number of men and the amount of ammunition the French were bringing in their fleet.

He immediately sought out William Marshal to discuss with him what was to be done. William was with the Bishop of Winchester when Hubert arrived and he listened with dismay.

'I need your help,' said Hubert. 'We must attack the fleet. If they make a landing we are lost.'

William Marshal pointed out that he was a soldier and the Bishop was a cleric, and he felt it would be unwise for them to take part in a venture of which they were entirely ignorant; but they implored Hubert to set out at once and do everything in his power to divert the French fleet. They were very worried men at that time; it would have been comforting had they known that Louis in London with inadequate forces was equally worried.

Everything depended on the successful landing of the fleet. Hubert knew this and that he had to match cunning strategy against the might of the French immediately. With all speed he rode to Dover and there assembled the ships of the Cinque Ports, not a large fleet by any means. He made sure of the defences of the castle and he chose the most stalwart guards to defend it. They must hold it with their lives, he told them. As for himself if he fell into the enemy's hands and they tried to ransom him for the castle they must let him hang and hold the castle till not a man was left of them. 'Depend upon it,' he cried, 'Dover Castle is the key to England. They may have London but while we hold Dover we command the sea.'

The French fleet was in the charge of Eustache the Monk, which in itself struck alarm in the hearts of loyal Englishmen; for Eustache was one of those seamen about whom a legend had grown. He had, in fact, taken orders in the monastery of Saint-Wulmar near Boulogne, but he had soon discovered that the monastic life was not for him and had left his monastery to take to the sea, which was much more suited to his nature; and the fact that he had been blessed with success allied with his earlier piety had meant that a legend had been built about him that he was a magician possessed of supernatural powers. Men flocked to serve under him because they believed that heaven had granted him some special dispensation from evil which would reflect on those about him. Here again John had shown his folly, for there had been a time when Eustache had worked for the King of England, but being unjustly treated by him he had retaliated by leaving him and offering his services to the King of France.

Some troubadour had made him the hero of a song which told of his brilliant and always victorious exploits and throughout England, Normandy and Aquitaine, and at the Court of France men sang the *Roman d'Eustache la Moine*.

And this man, who many believed could not fail, was chosen by Louis to bring the French fleet to England.

It was small wonder that Hubert was uneasy.

He talked to his men of the great Conqueror who would be looking down on them this day. They were descended from him and his Normans who had rightly come to England and succeeded. If they were brave and bold, if they were determined to succeed as he had always been, he would be with them this day. If they thought of him, took his example and prayed to God, they must succeed. They must remember that God would not be pleased with one who had deserted his monastery to become a pirate.

God was certainly with Hubert that day. Or it may have been that the Conqueror was really at hand to guide them to victory against the French. In any case it seemed that Hubert was endowed with a wisdom which outclassed the supernatural powers of Eustache. His fleet was small and that which Blanche of France had gathered together, great and powerful.

How Eustache must have exulted as he contemplated the task before him. So few English; so many French; the French ships were big and powerful; the English less so. Hubert had sixteen ships; the French had eighty; he had known he would be outnumbered but he had not thought it would be by so many.

Wily strategy was his only hope. The French fleet was, as expected, taking a straight course to Dover. Hubert commanded his captains to steer a slanting course, holding their luff, so giving an impression that Calais was their destination. It did not occur to Eustache that such a small force would attack, and he did not realize that this strategy enabled the English—well to windward while the French were running leeward—to attack the few ships at the rear and thus engage a smaller force than their own. By doing this Hubert was able to overcome the French in small sections, and Eustache, in the leading vessel, did not realize what was happening until it was too late.

Eustache was drowned, but his body was recovered from the sea, and his head was cut off that it might be shown to the people that the magician monk was a lesser man than Hubert de Burgh who had defeated him and destroyed the legend of his supernatural power for ever.

What rejoicing there was when Hubert landed at Dover, for news of his victory had already reached Dover and a great welcome awaited him.

Five bishops headed the procession which wound its way up to the castle—that very castle which not so long before Hubert was warning his trusted men should be held at all cost.

There was no longer need for anxiety. Louis was defeated. He had lost his ships and all they contained, and many of the spoils were now in English hands. Hubert was proud to hear that only fifteen had escaped and returned to France and as ten had been sunk that meant that over fifty had fallen to the English with all the treasure Blanche had gathered together for her husband's army.

Victory indeed!

This would be the end of Louis's hopes. How the Conqueror would be smiling on this day. He would say that Hubert de Burgh who by a simple strategy had saved the throne for Henry was a man he was proud to claim as a Norman, a man after his own heart.

John was dead. A new King was on the throne. There would be peace with France. It was a new beginning.

Isabella's women were dressing her in scarlet; this was a triumphant moment, for after Hubert de Burgh's masterly defeat of the French fleet the throne was safe for Henry; and a great deal of that disaster which had come about through King John's ineptitude could now be repaired and men of good will, nobility and intelligence could begin the task of rebuilding a kingdom.

William Marshal came to her. He was ready to conduct her to the ceremony.

As he bowed and took her hand he could not but be aware of her beauty; she seemed to be possessed of a new vitality which must be due to the fact that she had escaped from John. She looked, though, more like a woman setting out on adventure, than one who has just been bereaved of a husband.

Her eyes mocked him slightly. 'You think I am gaudily dressed for one so recently widowed? Nay, my lord, the last thing the people want to be reminded of is John. I have my son to consider. I do not wish that people should think of him as the son of John. 'Tis better if they forget that he is.'

There was something in that, Marshal acceded. But at the same time he thought it might have been more becoming for a widow to show some discretion.

'Come, my lord,' she went on. 'This is a happy day. Our good Hubert de Burgh has scored a marvellous victory. We are sending Louis about his business. England will be at peace and my son will learn to be a King when he has to guide him two of the greatest men this country—or any country—has produced. That is no reason for mourning.'

'You are right, my lady,' said William Marshal.

'Then shall we proceed?'

They went out to the barge which would take them to that spot near Staines where the ceremony would take place.

There, Isabella took her place on one side of the river with

William Marshal on one side of her and the Papal Legate on the other. Across the river were Louis and his advisers. Isabella noticed with satisfaction that Louis was crestfallen, as well he might be. She imagined his returning to his father, sly Philip the King, who had wanted the conquest of England but would have no part in it because he feared defeat; and he would return to his wife Blanche too. Isabella had heard of their conjugal bliss. So might it have been if she had married Hugh.

Louis was slender and had a look of frailty about him which she felt to be deceptive. His features were fine drawn and his thick blond hair gave him a youthful look which was not unattractive in its way but he lacked the virility of Hugh de Lusignan which even now she remembered.

But what would Hugh be like after all these years? Ever since he had passed out of her life she realized she had been comparing every man with Hugh. The lovers she had taken had borne some resemblance to him and John had known this. Perhaps it was one of the reasons why he had so savagely murdered one of them and hung him on the tester of her bed.

How she would love to see Hugh again! Perhaps when he was her son-in-law she would. The thought made her hysterical with amusement or rage. . . . Which? A mingling of the two of course.

But she should be concentrating on this ceremony which was going to make England safe for her son.

The solemn pledges were announced and spoken across a narrow stretch of water; and in the fields tents were being set up and in one of these a chapel was erected in which it would be necessary to make vows before the altar and Louis would swear that he would return to France and keep the peace for which William Marshal would promise that he should receive compensation.

The next day the French crossed the river and in the chapel set up in the tent, peace was agreed upon and Louis would return to France with a compensation, to be paid by the English, of six thousand marks which would help reimburse him for the costliness of the venture.

The Papal Legate and the leading men of London then went

with the King of France and members of his entourage to
Dover where Louis set sail.

As the ship disappeared below the horizon there were cries
of 'England is safe. This is the King's Peace. Long live
Henry the Third—England's King for the English.'

The Queen was feeling disgruntled. Neither William Marshal nor Hubert de Burgh had behaved in the manner she had
hoped they would. It was true that Marshal was an old man
and had always been one who would never adventure far in
the realms of erotic passion. He had married his Isabella late
in life and been faithful to her all the years they were together; they had had five sons and five daughters and he had been
the model husband, she the model wife—everything that
would be expected of William Marshal. So it was hardly
likely that now he was rich in years he would be so overcome
by the charms of Queen Isabella—not physically of course
but enough to make him ready to indulge her.

Hubert de Burgh—now he was of another type. His married
life had been very varied. Isabella had become interested in
him at the time of Prince Arthur's imprisonment; she remembered how John had summoned him and given him secret
instructions to put out the boy's eyes and castrate him—a fate
which had filled her with dismay for Arthur was a good-
looking boy and it was horrifying to one so aware of mascu-
line perfection to contemplate his mutilation. She had been
amused when she had heard that Hubert had disobeyed John—a
noble thing to have done—and despising her husband she had
admired Hubert, and had looked at him with favourable eyes
for he was of comely appearance; but she quickly realized
that although he was ready to risk his life, or worse still
hideous mutilation, for the sake of a young boy for whom he
had felt affection, he would not have been ready to indulge
any sexual appetite he might have felt for the Queen. She had
dismissed him from her thoughts then. Now she considered
him. He had had three wives . . . so far, for he was not old
and could well marry again should his third wife die. First
there had been Joan, daughter of the Earl of Devon; she had
died and he had taken Beatrice, who was the widow of Lord
Bardulf; he was now married to Hadwisa, which was an

extraordinary coincidence because Hadwisa had been John's first wife. This was rather amusing. Hadwisa had been far from beautiful but the greatest heiress in the country; that was why John had married her and that had been before it seemed he had a hope of wearing the crown. He had tormented Hadwisa and rid himself of her to make Isabella his wife. And now Hadwisa was married to Hubert de Burgh! Hadwisa had had another husband after John—Geoffry Mandeville, the fifth Earl of Essex. He had died but it had not been long before she found another husband in Hubert de Burgh—both embarking on their third marriages.

Well there was Hubert—a much married gentleman, wise and shrewd and in no mood to become the slave of a widowed Queen. It was exasperating, but if she wished she could find lovers in plenty. That potent sexual power in her had not diminished since John had seen her in the forest and been driven to desperate means to possess her, already affianced to Hugh de Lusignan though she was.

That brought her back to Hugh. Her first love. For her there would never be another like him. How she would enjoy seeing him again to test whether his charm had lost its potency.

But here she was—some would say in an enviable position—the mother of a King who was a minor, ten years old. Surely her place should be to guide him, to rule through him. That would be invigorating. People would come to her to ask favours. They would say: 'Oh it is necessary to approach the King through his mother the Queen.'

It was true that she had been present at the treaty with Louis near Staines, but somehow she felt that had been a mere formality. She had had no voice in any of the arrangements which had been agreed by the council, the head of which was Marshal and de Burgh. *They* had made the decisions; she had merely been there to represent the King.

It would not do. She had no intention of being forced into the background. Her best method she believed was to approach her son, and knowing that he was at Windsor with his tutor, Philip of Albini, she went there to him.

She was faintly disturbed to see a change in Henry's demeanour; then she laughed inwardly and told herself it was natural for a young boy who had suddenly realized that he was a king, and now of course the French were driven from the land his position was very secure.

She embraced him warmly and dismissed his tutor Philip of Albini who seemed reluctant to leave the boy alone with his mother.

'Ah,' she said, 'they are making a king of you, my son.'

He replied somewhat haughtily: 'I *am* a king, my lady.'

'Praise Heaven that the French have gone. You must be greatly indebted to William Marshal and perhaps most of all to Hubert de Burgh. His strategy was masterly.'

'He is a good servant,' said Henry calmly.

Isabella burst into laughter and taking her son into her arms she held him against her. Sensing his resentment as he stood stiffly in her embrace, it occurred to her then that it was not going to be so easy to rule him as she had imagined.

He drew himself from her and for a few seconds they regarded each other; Isabella's gaze was shrewd; his was wary.

'I trust, Henry,' said Isabella reproachfully at length, 'you will not forget that, King though you may be, you are my son.'

'It would be impossible to forget such a fact. All the world knows that you were my father's wife and I the eldest son of the marriage.'

Again she laughed, but uneasily. 'You are the same in many ways. You were always so serious. Tell me, do you miss your brother Richard and little Joan . . . and the babies.'

'No, my lady. I have matters of great import with which to occupy myself.'

'I'll swear *they* are missing you.'

'I think not, my lady.'

'Why Joan was speaking of you but a few days since.'

'Joan . . . Joan is little more than a child.'

'Not too young to be betrothed. We shall be finding a wife for you ere long, I doubt not.'

'The matter will be for me to decide.'

'Nay, my son. That will be a matter of such importance that you will have to listen to the advice of others.'

'My marriage will be of more importance to me than to any, and therefore I am determined to see that it suits me.'

'Why, Henry, what has come over you?'

'I have become a King, Madam.'

It had occurred to her then that there was a hint of hostility in his manner towards her. They had never doted on each other; she had never experienced that obsession with her children which some mothers felt, but she had perhaps taken it for granted that they must admire her for her beauty and that inherent gift to attract.

'Dear Henry,' she said, 'let us not lose sight of the fact that you are ten years old.'

'It is something of which Philip constantly reminds me. For that reason I must learn quickly. I must be wary of those who would seek to influence me. I must learn to form judgments and they must be wise ones. William Marshal is often here. It is likely that he will be here this day. He insists that I sit in council with him and other ministers that I may learn quickly; and indeed, Madam, I am determined to do so.'

'Let us hope that you will be able to spare a little of your attention for your mother,' she retorted with some asperity.

'As you see I am doing that now.'

'With not very happy results. And I see also, Henry, that you have grown away from me.'

'Was I ever near you, Madam?'

'My dear son, you know we were in captivity.'

'I know for what reason.'

'Your father's cruelty.'

'You had betrayed him.'

'My dear Henry—though you be the King—pray remember that I am your mother. You do not know what manner of man your father was.'

'I am learning and what I know best is that I must be as different from him as it is possible for one man to be from another.'

'Well, that is a good lesson to have learned. One day you will understand what havoc was wrought in this kingdom.'

'I have already learned. My tutors insist that I learn what has happened in this kingdom from the days of the Conqueror that I may profit from the errors of my predecessors. I know this: I must reign well, so that it will not be held against me that I am the son of John and . . .'

'And Isabella of Angoulême,' she supplied.

'I said of John, my lady.'

'And stopped in time. You do not appear to have a very fine opinion of your mother.'

He was silent.

'What do you think it was like, married to such a man?' she burst out. 'You know how he lost the crown possessions in France and came near to losing this kingdom. But that is not all. There are matters of which your clever tutors know nothing. I could tell you. . . .'

'Pray spare me,' said Henry coolly; and she thought: Is this my son—my ten-year-old who talks like an old man? How did we get such a boy, John and I? There is no laughter in him, no joy in living. He is a King—power stretches out before him when he is old enough to enjoy it, and he is like an old man already. She could see that there was no hope of his listening to her.

She shrugged her shoulders and left him.

Later she spoke with Philip of Albini—a man with a very serious mind who assured her that he, acting under the instructions of William Marshal and Hubert de Burgh, was determined to instruct the King in all matters pertaining to his role in life, while not neglecting his general education. He was happy to report that the young King learned quickly; indeed he had a taste for learning and was particularly interested in literature and the other arts. He was a pupil whom it was a joy to instruct. Philip of Albini could assure the Queen that the Earl of Pembroke was delighted and had even said that it might be an advantage that the King had come into their care while there was time yet to form his mind.

The fool! thought Isabella. He thought he was pleasing her by this praise of her son, when what he was saying was tantamount to pointing out that it was fortunate he had escaped from her care.

Hearing that the Earl of Pembroke would be visiting the castle the following day, she decided to remain to see him; she spent a sleepless night trying to face this turn about in events. It was not going to be as she had planned. She was not going to be there—the power behind the throne, whom all realized they must placate if they were going to find favour with her son. She was going to be the figure in the background, of no importance, the old Queen Mother to whose rank these powerful men would pay a certain homage and that would be the end of it. There was no one among them who would have given up everything to become her lover. They were a dull lot, concerned only with moulding the young King in the way *they* wanted him to go. It looked as though the future might be bleak for Isabella.

This was confirmed with the arrival of the Earl in the company of Hubert de Burgh. They were delighted with the application and progress of the King; his mother had reason to be proud of him; but both these gentlemen made it very clear to her that her guiding hand was to play no part in the young King's progress.

Fuming in her bedchamber later she asked herself if she was to accept this retiring role. She was thirty-one years of age, and with a woman who had cared for her appearance as she had, that was no great age. Her beauty was perennial; although she might have become a little mature that did not detract from her charms she was sure.

Hugh would never have treated her like this.

Hugh! How she longed to see him again. Would she be disappointed in him? What a bold man he had been! What looks! They and his great height had made a god of him. How different from John whose depravity had made him grow more and more hideous. John had hated Hugh—chiefly because he knew that she had loved him, but partly because Hugh was handsome and possessed of a nobility of character which made men respect him. The last time Isabella had seen Hugh was when he was chained hand and foot in a cart that was like a tumbril and drawn by oxen. He had been John's prisoner then—for Hugh had been fighting on the side of Prince Arthur—and John's one idea had been to humiliate the noble Hugh, and that Isabella should witness that humiliation. Foolish John, he did not realize that it was not Hugh she despised at that time but himself. John had known nothing of other people because he had been so deeply concerned with himself as the only person who could be of any importance.

How delighted she had been when Hugh was released—because John thought it was to his advantage to do so. What a fool that man was. It did not seem to occur to him that Hugh might hate him as much as he hated Hugh. She often wondered how much Hugh had contributed to John's utter defeat and loss of the French possessions.

And how she longed to see Hugh again.

Suddenly her mood of depression had passed and she was wildly elated.

Why not? It was feasible. It was the right thing to do.

She was thankful that William Marshal was in the castle: She would approach the matter tentatively the very next day. She spent a restless night and could scarcely wait to talk to the Earl.

'It is with great relief and pleasure,' she told him, 'that I watch the King's progress. I thank God that he is in such good hands. I think he is as different from John as anyone could be.'

The Earl looked well pleased.

'Hubert de Burgh and I have the utmost confidence in Philip of Albini.'

'And so have I. It occurs to me that I can serve no useful purpose in this country.'

'I trust the King will never forget that you are his mother.'

'He will never do that. But I can safely leave his upbringing in capable hands and turn my attention to other members of my family who need me more. Richard is well looked after by Peter de Mauley at Corfe and I understand that Roger d'Acastre is most excellent. My youngest daughters are as yet little more than babies, but my daughter Joan is betrothed and I believe it to be time that she went to the home of her betrothed where she will be brought up in his household as is the custom.'

The Earl nodded slowly. It was the custom of course for girls to be brought up in the country into which they would marry.

'I believe,' went on Isabella, 'that she should leave without delay. She is seven years old—an age when a child's mind begins to take shape. Do you agree with me, my lord?'

'I do indeed.'

'It will be necessary for her to make this journey in the care of someone who can be trusted.'

There was a short silence. The Earl was trying not to betray the hope which had come to him. He had consulted with Hubert de Burgh and they had agreed that the Queen would have to be watched. Mothers of kings who were minors could be tiresome; and there was no indication that Isabella was a meek woman who would listen to advice.

The Earl cleared his throat as though about to speak but Isabella spoke first. 'My two sons are in good hands; my two young children are well cared for. It would seem, my lord, that since I am scarcely needed here, I should be the one to accompany my daughter.'

William Marshal tried not to sound too elated.

'My lady,' he said slowly, 'the Princess Joan is indeed fortunate to have a mother who so cares for her welfare. . . .'

'Then you agree that I should be the one to accompany her.'

'I think we should first ask the King if he would be prepared to let you go.'

She nodded gravely. 'I think my son will want to do what is best for his sister,' she said.

Her spirits were rising and she felt more excited than she had since she had heard of John's death.

She took leave of the Earl and went to her bedchamber. She had to be alone.

'Hugh,' she murmured to herself. 'What will you think of me? What shall I think of you?'

And the thought of going back to the scenes of her childhood, of being reunited with her old lover—now to be her daughter's husband—filled her with a wild elation.

# The Chosen Bride

WHAT joy it gave her to ride southwards through the fair land of France, and the nearer she came to the Angoumois—the land of her inheritance—the happier she grew. It was seventeen years since she had ridden in those lanes and forests— an only child and the heiress of the Angoumois, the petted darling of her parents' household. Hugh, eldest son of the reigning Count de la Marche, had seemed a worthy bridegroom for her; and when she had been taken into his father's household she had thought so too.

The smell of the woods—different from those of England, she assured herself, the golden light in the air, the warmth of the sun . . . all these conjured up memories of those days of physical awakening when she had longed for marriage with Hugh and then had met John in the forest and been aware of a curious mixture of desire and repulsion while mingling with them was an ambition to wear a crown.

Her daughter rode beside her. Young Joan was apprehensive and that was understandable. A child seven years of age going to meet her bridegroom.

'Is not the country beautiful, daughter?' demanded Isabella. 'Think! When I was your age I used to ride through these woods. You will spend your youth where I spent mine.'

'But you did not stay here, my lady.'

'No, but it is a joy to be back.'

Joan looked wistful. It was clear that the poor child was wishing she were in Gloucester. Too much had happened too quickly to enable her childish mind to adjust.

Isabella softened a little. 'You are anxious, child. You need not be. You will be happy here, as I was. Have no fear of Hugh. I knew him well when I was your age and I can tell you this, there is not a more kind or gentle man in the whole world.'

'My lady, how long will you stay with me?'

She sighed and smiled. 'That, daughter, I cannot say. But I can promise you this: You have nothing to fear.'

And so they travelled down to Angoulême, in the dukedom of Aquitaine, once so proudly ruled over by the father of Eleanor, mother of John, a rich and fertile land watered by the sparkling Charente, extending from Poitou in the north to Périgord in the south, eastwards to La Limousin and westwards to Saintonge.

Isabella talked to her daughter as they rode. 'How different life was than in your father's court. Here we assembled at night when the fires were lighted and the candles guttered and the troubadours took their lutes and sang about the beauty of ladies and the valour of their lords. It was gracious. Men were chivalrous. Ladies were treated with respect. Oh, my daughter, you are going to bless the day I brought you here.'

Joan was becoming influenced by her mother's enthusiasm. The country was beautiful; the sun warmer than it was in England; and as they travelled through France they were welcomed in the villages through which they passed and spent their nights in inns or castles, and as they came south Joan found that her mother's description of the singing of the troubadours was indeed true. She would sit, heavy-eyed with sleep, listening to the strumming of the lutes and the singing of the songs which so delighted Isabella.

Especially she remembered their stay at Fontevrault which was particularly important to her family, she was told. The Breton preacher Robert d'Arbrissel had founded it nearly two hundred years before and there were four convents—two for men, two for women but an Abbess was in control and she must always come from one of the most noble families. Royalty had always taken a very special interest in the place.

With great solemnity Joan was conducted through the abbey church to walk under the cupola, which was held up by tall pillars, to the tombs of her family. Here were the burial places and effigies of her grandfather and grandmother— Henry Plantagenet and his wife Eleanor of Aquitaine of whom she had heard much, which made her think of them with awe and some relief that they were not alive today to demand great things of her. Her uncle was there with them—the one after whom her brother had been named. Richard Coeur de Lion they called him, because he was such a brave fighter. It seemed only fitting that his life should have been cut short by the arrow of an enemy.

'These are your ancestors,' Isabella reminded her. 'Never forget that you are the daughter of a King.'

'Perhaps my father would have liked to lie here with his father.'

The Queen laughed. 'Where did you get such a notion, child? Your father was fighting against your grandfather at the end. He at least would not want your father there.'

'Where lies my father?' asked Joan.

'In Worcester Cathedral. Before he died he asked that he should be buried there close to the grave of St. Wulstan.'

'Who was he?' asked Joan.

Isabella regarded her daughter intently. Poor child, she would have to grow up quickly. Isabella tried to imagine herself at seven. How much of the sad facts of life had she been able to absorb at that time? Joan would learn in due course that she was the daughter of one of the most evil men who ever lived.

She said: 'St. Wulstan was a Saxon Bishop who was most saintly. Your father thought that the bones of the saint might preserve him from the devil . . . when he came to claim him.'

Joan shivered and Isabella laughed. She put an arm about her daughter. 'Your father was not a good man. As you know the barons rose against him. All will be well now, for your brother will be taught to rule well and the kingdom will grow rich and powerful again. As for you, my child, you will know great happiness. You are going to be the wife of the best man in the world.'

Joan was relieved, but glad when they left Fontevrault which for her held the ghosts of her terrifying ancestors.

And so they came to Valence which was the cheif town of La Marche; and bordered on the Angoumois, Isabella's own country.

All that day as they came closer to their destination Isabella had talked to her daughter of the happy days of her youth and, although Joan believed that very soon she would see her aged bridegroom, her mother's conversation had its effect on her and she was beginning to believe that she was going to some paradise. Moreover there would be no wedding yet. She would live in that castle where for a time her mother had lived because twenty or so years before when her mother was a girl of eleven she too had ridden to this castle and looked with awe and wonder at what was to be her home. That was comforting. Her mother had loved Valence and so would she.

And here was the grey stone-walled castle. Serving men and women came hurrying to their aid, paying great homage to Isabella who had become a Queen and whom some remembered as the most beautiful little girl they had ever seen.

In the great hall a man was waiting for them. As her mother took her hand Joan was conscious of Isabella's tremendous excitement.

The man was old . . . very old . . . surely this could not be the one they had chosen for her husband. He looked closer to a funeral than a wedding—and that his own.

He had taken Isabella's hand; he was bowing low; his eyes glistening brightly and he looked as though he might weep at any moment.

'Isabella,' he said. 'Isabella.'

'My lord,' she began and Joan knew that she was looking about the hall for someone she missed.

'As beautiful as ever,' he murmured. 'Oh, it is long ago.'

'Let me present my daughter to you.'

'So this is the child.'

The old eyes were studying her. Joan tried not to look alarmed. He was so very old. Her mother had spoken of her future husband as though he were godlike and now was presenting her to this ancient man.

Then the old man said: 'I see that you did not know. My son is not here in Valence, nor in this land. It is a year since he left us. He is with the crusaders in the Holy Land.'

Joan was aware of floods of relief. This old man was not to be her bridegroom then. Of course he was not. But she had been afraid because she was old enough to know that sometimes little girls were married to very old men.

Then she was aware of her mother. Isabella had turned pale. She swayed a little before she steadied herself. Then she said: 'In the Holy Land . . . and he has gone a year since. . . .'

Young as she was Joan heard the bitter disappointment and despair in her mother's voice.

How silent Isabella was that night. Joan would never forget it. She seemed to grow up suddenly. He had gone away and none knew where he was. Even his father could not say except that he was somewhere in the Holy Land. She thought of the stories she had heard of her uncle Richard whose exploits there had been sung about in wondrous lays. Richard it seemed was a knight in shining armour with a red cross on his breast which meant that he had pledged himself to fight the Infidel. They had fled before him but for some reason he had not captured Jerusalem for the Christians—though that was something the writers of the songs preferred not to mention. There had been a Saracen called Saladin and he and Richard had fought each other, though who had won Joan had never really heard. Suffice it that Richard emerged from the songs as the greatest hero of the day—a man who had given up everything to carry the cross.

It was therefore only natural that this wonderful man whom she was to marry should follow in Richard's footsteps. He was a noble knight. Not only the most handsome and best man in the world, but also devout.

If Joan were truthful she would admit that she was not displeased. Whatever he was, he was going to be old. Her mother was old and Hugh was older than she was. So she was relieved and she hoped her mother would not be too unhappy. She supposed it was because since Hugh was not here and she could not leave her daughter she would have to stay until he came before she could return to England.

For a few days Isabella was with the old man who had received them when they arrived and they made plans as to what was to be done. It was at length decided that Isabella should go to her own estate in Angoulême and that her daughter should stay at Valence where she could learn the customs of the land and be educated in a manner which would prepare her to be châtelaine of that castle when the time came.

Angoulême and Valence were so close that Isabella could see her daughter frequently, but it would be as well if she left her so that the child could learn some self-reliance and she would be safe with the family of her future husband.

Joan was less disturbed than she had thought she would be as she watched her mother ride away. Isabella had never been exactly a fond mother; Joan did not understand her and she did not believe even Henry and Richard had either. Perhaps all the children had been a little afraid of their parents—they certainly had on those occasions when their father had visited the castle. So although she was left with strangers she did not feel unduly lonely. She had grown up a good deal since her departure from England.

Life became interesting. She had her lessons each day and there were special tutors for her. She must learn to speak her prospective husband's language fluently; and she must understand something of history and literature; she must be able to calculate, draw and be proficient with her needle. The last was very important, for all well-educated ladies must master the art of embroidering. She must dance nimbly and gracefully; she must play the lute and sing prettily and play chess with skill for her husband would expect her to be a good companion to him.

She applied herself whole-heartedly to these tasks. It helped to make her forget her home in England and her brothers and sisters and also the fact that one day her betrothed would return to Valence. She hoped he would not come for a very long time; and each night when she went to bed she would pray: Please God don't let it be today.

She was surrounded by attendants. They grew fond of her. She was such a pretty little thing. Some of them remembered her mother when she was a girl. 'You're almost the living image,' one of them said. It was always 'almost' and she knew they meant that although she was attractive she could never be the beauty her mother was.

Once she overheard one attendant say to another: 'I could almost believe it was the Lady Isabella. But of course there'll never be another like her.'

And another said: 'No. They used to say she had something no other had. Still has too. No, you're right. There'll never be another quite like her. Well it made a Queen of her, didn't it?'

'I'll never forget the day. I thought my lord would go quite mad with rage and grief.'

'Well, now he's going to have a young bride . . . and so like. . . .'

'I don't believe he ever forgot *her*.'

'Oh, you romantic old woman.'

'But he never married, did he?'

'Well, he's going to now . . . when he comes back . . . when she grows up.'

'When will that be?'

'When she's fourteen . . . perhaps before. He lost the lady Isabella by waiting too long. He won't do that again, depend upon it.'

And they laughed together and whispered what Joan could not hear. Fourteen, she was thinking. She was now eight. It was years and years away.

She liked to get them to talk of him and they were nothing loath.

'Count Hugh, my lady. Oh, he is the most handsome man you ever saw. There's not a man hereabouts that does not suffer in comparison. Brave, noble, kind to all those below him in rank and respected by his equals. In the joust who is always the victor? Count Hugh. And if anyone needs help who is the first to give it? Count Hugh, of course. If there is injustice, he is the one who will go to right matters. We of Lusignan are happy in our Duke.'

'But his father is the Duke.'

'Count Hugh is his heir and now that the old Count is so old it is Hugh who will rule when he returns from the crusade.'

'Perhaps he will come home soon.'

'If he knew his little bride were here he would be back, I promise you.'

'Even if he has not beaten the Saracen?'

It was so pleasant to talk of him. She found now that she loved above all things to hear stories of his exploits. He was always the hero of some noble adventure. They were constantly saying: 'When Count Hugh comes back from the Holy War . . .' as though everything would be transformed by his coming.

And she began to say it too, and look for him and instead of praying that he would not come she would say when she awoke: 'I wonder if he will come today?'

The weeks began to pass into months. Her mother came frequently to Valence to see her daughter, but Joan suspected there was someone else she sought. She would always ask eagerly if there was news from the Holy Land and show a bitter disappointment because there was not.

She wants to go back to England, thought Joan. Perhaps in a little while she will do so . . . even though he does not come.

Now she was growing up and still he did not come. Two years had passed since her father's death and she was nine years old. Not such a child now. She was beginning to understand something of the meaning of marriage for some of her women believed that it was unfair to send a young girl to her husband with no inkling of what would be expected of her.

She was at first repelled, then awestruck and finally came to the belief that perhaps it was not so bad after all. She had heard rumours of her father's habits and they had always filled her with a vague fear, but it had been impressed on her that the man she would marry would be a kind of god, not only handsome but benevolent.

Sometimes she sat with the old man in the sun by an ancient sundial—a spot he loved. He would be wrapped up in spite of the heat for he was growing very frail and he would tell her stories of past adventures, of battles in which he had fought and always his son Hugh would be the hero of the stories.

'Ah,' the old man would say in his quavering voice, 'you will come to reckon yourself fortunate to be the chosen bride of Hugh Le Brun, Count of Lusignan.'

And so it went on.

Then one day while she talked to the old man he fell forward in his chair and she ran into the castle to summon his attendants. He was carried to his bed and a message was sent to the castle of Angoulême to acquaint Isabella of what was happening.

She was soon with them and was in eager agreement with the family that news must somehow be sent to Count Hugh that his father was very ill and that his presence was needed with as little delay as possible in Valence.

There followed a time of waiting while the old Count lingered on. Isabella's visits had become more frequent and the first question she asked when she arrived was: 'Is there any news?'

There was tension throughout the castle and all wondered whether the messengers had found Count Hugh; they were certain that when he knew that his father was dying he would return to take over his inheritance.

Then the old man died and Hugh had still not come.

There was great fear then that he might have been slain in battle for so many who set out for the Holy War never returned.

Joan was ten years old. Sometimes she wondered when the change would come. If Hugh did not return there would be no reason why they should stay here. A new husband would be found for her. She was filled with apprehension and realized then that she had grown to accept Hugh as her prospective husband and that she was half in love already with the image they had presented to her. She would often sit at the turret window and watch for a rider and when she saw one she would be filled with elation and when it proved not to be Hugh a bitter disappointment would follow.

And so the days passed.

Then, one day he came. She was in the gardens so she did not see his arrival. There was a clatter of horses' hoofs and a great commotion through the castle; the bells started to ring; Joan heard the shouts of many voices.

She ran into the castle and there he was standing in the hall—tall, bronzed by the sun, in shining armour with a red cross on his breast. She knew him at once for none she was sure could look so noble.

For a few moments they stood looking at each other; then

she saw the blood rush into his face and he took several strides towards her, seizing both her hands in his, and she noticed that his eyes had a bewildered look in them.

She heard someone say: 'The Lady Joan, my lord.'

And he continued to gaze at her. Then he said: 'For a moment I thought I was dreaming. You are so like. . . .'

She herself answered: 'All say I bear a resemblance to my mother.'

She noticed that his eyes were misty. He kissed her hand and said: 'It delights me to see you here.' Then he asked to be taken to his father.

He was very sad when he heard that his father had died; and divested of his armour, he went to that spot in the chapel grounds where the old man was buried and knelt by his grave for a long time.

Without his armour he looked less godlike, but not less handsome; and Joan was quick to notice the kindliness of his face.

She sat beside him at the table and he fed her the best of the meat. He talked to her in a gentle and kindly fashion and she knew that all she had heard of him was true.

He said: 'I am many years older than you, my lady Joan, and you will have to grow up quickly. How old are you now?'

'I am ten years old, my lord.'

'It is a little young to be a bride. We must wait a few years.'

'They say three or four,' she answered.

'Well, that is not so long. Shall you be ready by then, think you?'

She looked at the dark curling hair which grew back from the high and noble forehead, at the pleasant curve of his lips and answered: 'Oh yes, my lord. Perhaps before.'

'We shall see,' he answered, smiling. And he asked how she had arrived and she told him her mother had brought her.

Then he was thoughtful and asked how her mother fared.

'Well, my lord,' she answered.

He nodded slowly.

'I heard of her widowhood,' he said, and fell silent. It did not occur to her then to tell him that her mother was close by at Angoulême.

He was thoughtful after that and when the meal was over he went away with his stewards and occupied himself in learning what had happened in the castle during his absence.

Joan went to her bedchamber, but not to sleep.

This was the most important day of her life. She had met her future husband.

A warm happiness suffused her. She was not afraid anymore. Indeed she was looking forward to the day when she would become the Countess of Lusignan. Sometimes she thought of her terrifying father and it had occured to her long ago, before she came to France, that it might one day be her lot to have such a husband. There could not be a man less like King John than Hugh Le Brun, Count of Lusignan, and that was a matter for rejoicing.

They rode out together; she wanted to show him how well she knew his forests, how she could manage a horse. She wanted to please him in every way.

They spoke in French together for she had become fluent in the language; he went to the schoolroom and examined her work. She told him that now he was home she would work harder because she was so anxious to grow up quickly.

He smiled gently and stroked her hair when she told him that, and she felt tears in her eyes but she was not sure why.

They played chess together and although she could not checkmate him she could come quite near to it.

'I can see I am lucky in my bride,' he told her.

And she answered: 'And I in my bridegroom.'

The ladies and gentlemen of the castle looked on indulgently.

'This will be a love match,' they said.

Isabella came riding into the castle.

'Is it true then?' she cried. 'The Count has returned?'

She was assured that it was true.

'Tell him I am come,' she said.

But the Count was hunting with a party in the forest and with him was the Lady Joan.

Impatiently she strode up and down the great hall.

Her cheeks were flushed; she had loosened her dark hair. Was it true that she looked like a young girl? She had borne five children; she had had many lovers; she had lived through twenty years of debauchery with the insatiable John. Could it really be that she looked like that young girl who had so enchanted Hugh that when he had lost her he had been prepared to go to war and had never taken another bride.

She believed she was as attractive as ever—more so for her experience. And he was no longer the young idealist he had been. He knew more of the world. He would want an experienced woman not an innocent young girl.

And what was she thinking? He was betrothed to her daughter. She laughed aloud at that. It was a trick of John's to upset her. Was it not characteristic of him that he should think of betrothing her daughter to the man he knew she still thought of?

Why did he not come? What was he waiting for?

One of the women came to her.

'You will be pleased, my lady,' she said. 'The Count is much taken with your daughter. They are often together and it gives us all great happiness to see them.'

Fool! thought Isabella and found it hard to stop herself slapping the woman's face.

'Is that so?' she answered slowly. 'The Count must be as gallant and courteous to ladies as he ever was.'

'Oh, he is, my lady; and the little Lady Joan has a look of you when you were her age.'

What is the woman suggesting? she asked herself. That I am old and decrepit!

'Leave me,' said Isabella coldly.

There was a fierce determination in her heart. He was going to be as enamoured of her now as he had been when she was his child-betrothed, before she had been snatched away by the rapacious John who had given her a crown.

It seemed a long time before the party arrived.

She stood in the centre of the hall, waiting.

And there he was—Joan beside him.

He strode towards her and said: 'Isabella.'

She laughed at him and held out her hand. 'You remember me then?'

'Remember you . . .!' The break in his voice excited her.

'It is so long. You have changed little, Hugh . . . since . . .'

He said: 'You have become more beautiful.'

She was exultant, triumphant. He had not changed at all. He was hers, she was sure of it. Her journey had not been in vain.

'And here is my little daughter. What think you of her, Hugh?'

'She bears some resemblance to you and therefore she delights me.'

Isabella held out a hand to her daughter and pulled her to her side.

'It pleases me. We have waited long, Hugh, for your coming.'

'I should have been here long since had I known,' he answered.

Isabella was aware of the watching eyes of those gathered in the hall, many of them old enough to remember. Hugh seemed suddenly aware of them too.

'I smell good venison,' he said. 'You will stay here with us . . . for a while.'

She bowed her head.

Then he left her and went to his chamber to wash off the mud of the chase and to change his garments.

Joan went to her chamber, slightly bewildered.

Her attendant said: 'The Count is happy that Queen Isabella is here.'

'I always knew they liked each other,' said Joan.

At the table her mother sat on one side of him, Joan in her usual place on the other. All the time they talked. There was an excitement between them.

They are so pleased to see each other, thought Joan, that they have almost forgotten I am here. It is good, she thought, when two families which are to be united are the best of friends.

There was a scratching at Hugh's door. He had guessed Isabella might come. She had implied it.

'There is so much we have to say to each other, Hugh. It is not easy to talk with so many onlookers.' She had said that while they ate. And there was a suggestion in her words. It was the reason why he had dismissed all those who would normally be in attendance in his bedchamber.

He opened the door and stepped back as she entered. Her beautiful hair was about her shoulders and she wore a loose robe of the shade of blue he remembered from the old days was a favourite colour of hers. It had been a favourite of his for the same reason.

He took her hands and said: 'Oh God, Isabella . . . you are indeed here.'

'I am no phantom. You may assure yourself of that, Hugh.'

He drew back a little. He was a man of honour and he remembered the appealing youth of his affianced bride.

'So now he is dead . . .' he said, in a vain effort to throw a cold douche of hatred on the fires which were rising within him.

'John. The brute. The lecher. You could not know how I suffered with him.'

'Yet . . . you went to him.'

'You know I had no choice. I was but a child. My parents forced me to it and so I did it.'

'You were there when. . . .'

'When he put you in chains and you rode in the tumbril drawn by oxen. Did you feel my hatred for him, Hugh, when you rode past . . . and my love for you?'

'I know that you were sad to see me thus. Because of your compassion I was almost glad of the humiliation.'

'You must have loved me a great deal in those days, Hugh.'

'Did you ever doubt that?'

'I never did. And now you love my daughter as you once loved me.'

She waited for him to deny it but he said: 'She is an enchanting child.'

'They say she is a little like me.'

'No one could be like you, Isabella.'

'Hugh, do you mean that?'

She had seized him by the arms and held her face up to him.

'No,' he said, deliberately avoiding her gaze. 'You must

go now, Isabella. You will leave soon and when Joan is a little older we shall marry.'

'There was one thing I wished to know, Hugh. Promise you'll tell me . . . truthfully.'

'I promise. What is it?'

'Hold me tightly, Hugh. Kiss me. And then tell me truthfully whether it is now as it was once.'

'Isabella, you must go. You should never have come here. If you were seen.'

'Oh, are you afraid of your servants?'

'I am afraid of your good name.'

'My good name! Married to that monster all those years . . . all the calumnies that he circulated about me to cover up his own vile doings! Do you think I have a good name to protect?'

'I will protect it with my sword,' he said. 'If any were to whisper ill against you. . . .'

'Ah, Hugh, my beloved, you have not changed. I feared you might. Let me tell you this, I have never forgotten you. When I was with him . . . I could only endure his embraces because I made myself pretend it was you, not him . . . the man I loved not the loathsome lecher who had taken me from you and made it so that I was a prisoner and could do nothing but submit.'

'Is this true, indeed?' he asked.

'I swear it. When I came here it was to see you, Hugh. . . .'

'It was to bring your daughter to be my bride,' he answered.

'I had to see you. I had to know for myself that you no longer loved me. And if you tell me you do not I will go to Fontevrault where my mother-in-law spent her last days and I will take the veil and never look on another man . . . though doubtless I shall go on dreaming of you in my convent walls.'

'You . . . a nun. Isabella!'

He laughed and she laughed with him. The tension was released. He said: 'I remember how you always made me laugh.'

'It is as it ever was. We were never lovers in fact. That seemed the tragedy of my life. I wanted you even as a child . . . and you wanted me. But you held off. You were afraid.

If you had taken me to the forest and seduced me . . . as I always wanted you to . . . I don't believe I should ever have allowed them to marry me to John. I used to dream how wonderful that would have been.'

'We must not talk in this way, Isabella. I am trying to look after little Joan. I am trying not to frighten her and let her grow accustomed to the idea of marriage.'

'As you did with me. And all you succeeded in doing was arousing my desire for you . . . my need for you . . . and then not satisfying it. Then he came . . . Oh my God, how I hate him; the terrible things he did to me. He would not leave me alone. . . .'

'I know. I heard. It was reported all over Europe.'

'How you must have hated me.'

'I could never do anything but love you, but my hatred for him knew no bounds.'

'So you fought for poor little Arthur and were captured and brought to him in chains. How he gloated! But he freed you. Do you know why, Hugh, because I persuaded him that it was best for him to do so. I said you would fight for him if he released you. What a fool he was! He believed me. But he is dead, Hugh . . . and I am here and you are here. . . .'

'Isabella, I am betrothed.'

'There is one thing I must know. All my life I have wanted to be with you. I would be your mistress . . . anything . . . I, a Queen, my lord Count, love you still. I had to see you. I had to know whether I still loved you . . . wanted you for my lover. Hugh, you owe me this. Tonight . . . this night . . . and if you find you do not love me, if the years have changed you, then I will go away.'

He said hoarsely: 'I am betrothed to your daughter.'

She laughed softly and slipped her robe from her shoulders. She held out a hand to him. 'Come, Hugh,' she said. 'I command you. Tomorrow you may tell me to go away . . . but tonight we shall be lovers as we should have been all those years ago.'

He turned from her and seating himself on a stool covered his eyes with his hands. But she was beside him, employing all those skills which life with the greatest sensualist of his age had taught her.

Hugh—who had dreamed of her for years—enamoured of her as he had ever been, was powerless to resist her.

After she had left him—and it was dawn before she did—he lay in his bed thinking of what had happened. He had never thought there could be such ecstasy even with Isabella; he had dreamed of her for twenty years; she had been an ideal in his life; he had never felt the inclination to marry any other woman. That had disturbed his family, since it was his duty to marry, to give the Lusignans their heir. He had brothers, he had excused himself. It was almost as though something had told him that one day she would come back.

And then when it had been suggested that he marry her daughter he had agreed to the betrothal. The marriage had seemed years away and like so many, such arrangements might never come to fruition. Moreover it was *her* daughter; and that had attracted him in some way. When he had seen the child—with a look of Isabella—and she had stirred his pity for she was a little afraid, he had determined to be kind and gentle with her and in due course do his best to make her happy.

Now Isabella had returned and everything had changed for him.

He must explain to her that he must marry her daughter. As the child had been brought here for that purpose, it was a matter of honour, and Isabella must return to England. He was determined that that which had happened last night must not happen again.

She was with the party which went out to the hunt. Little Joan was there too, so pretty in her riding cloak of red Irish cloth, tendrils of her hair straying out from under the matching hood. She rode beside him as she was accustomed to do, so proud because she sat her horse well and rode, as he had once told her, as though she were born to the saddle. Isabella had come up. Beautiful in her favourite blue. Poor little Joan, how insignificant besider her incomparable mother!

'I thought you would elude me,' she said reproachfully. 'And you know how I enjoy the hunt.'

'Nay, my lady,' he said. 'I give you good welcome.'

'Most gracious Hugh,' she answered softly. 'I thought I might not have pleased you.'

'You know how well you please me.'

Joan listened to their conversation. There was a note in her mother's voice which told the little girl she was pleased. In fact, Joan had never known her quite so pleased before. Perhaps it was because he was home and very soon now she would be able to go to England.

How beautiful it was in the pine forest—the lovely pungent smell, the glistening green and the excitement of the chase. Joan rode forward eager to show Hugh that she could keep up with the best of them. She was a little way ahead of him; on she went and the sound of pounding horses' hoofs went with her.

She caught a glimpse of the deer; she always felt a little sorry for them and did not greatly care to be in at the kill, though she told no one of this for fear she should be thought foolish. Once she thought that Hugh guessed, for he stayed with her and they rode back to the castle while the bearers brought in the deer. He had smiled at her very tenderly and she had loved him more than ever, because it suddenly occurred to her that he understood her thoughts without her having to express them and that he would keep her secrets, for he was going to protect her from the whole world.

She looked around for him, but he was not there. She could not see her mother either.

Isabella had whispered: 'Hugh, I must speak to you.'

She turned her horse and rode off while he followed. In the distance they could hear the baying of the dogs, and she rode on fast; he was close behind.

She pulled up and flashed her brilliant smile at him, holding out her hand. He took it and kissed it eagerly.

'We will dismount and tether the horses; 'tis easier to talk that way.'

'Isabella, I think we should return to the party . . . or to the castle.'

She laughed—it was the way in which she had laughed in the darkness of his bedchamber. She had already dismounted.

'Come, Hugh,' she said, 'or are you afraid of me?'

He leaped down and tethering his horse beside hers, turned to her eagerly. He held her fast.

'There is no doubt, is there,' she asked, 'no doubt at all. You and I belong together.'

'There is no doubt that we should have married years ago.'

'What is done is done. We are together now.'

She took his hand and they went into the thicket.

'You must never let me go again, Hugh,' she said. 'If you did, you would never have another moment's peace. I promise you that.'

'I know it.'

She slipped her arm through his and he kept a tight grip on her hand.

'We will walk through the trees and talk, Hugh. There is much we have to say.'

'There is only this, Isabella,' he said. 'I am betrothed to Joan.'

'A child . . . litle more than a baby. And my daughter at that. It was a sad sick joke of John's to betroth you. It was the sort of thing he enjoyed. He wanted to distress me . . . for he knew that I loved you. He always knew I loved you. It was the greatest emotion of my life and I could not hide it. You must not think that I shall ever let you go, Hugh. You do not know me if you think that.'

'My dearest Isabella, it is not for us to follow our inclinations.'

'You are wrong. How else should people live? Love should not be denied. Why should it? If you had a wife and I a husband, still I should stay with you. I would defy the world to do so. But you have no wife. I have no husband. You are betrothed to a child who knows nothing of the world . . . nothing of marriage . . . nothing of love. . . .'

'She has learned a great deal. She has lived ten winters and is old for her years. She cannot be sent back.'

'Then she shall stay here. She is my daughter. Oh Hugh, I have thought of last night. To be with you thus . . . it was a wonderful dream come true and so shall it be throughout our lives, for I shall never give you up. There is only one thing for us to do.'

'Nay. . . .'

'Yea, my lord. You shall have your bride. It is no child for whom you have to wait; it is your eager mistress who refuses to wait any longer for you. All these weary years have I yearned for you. I have caught you now, Hugh, and you are mine.' She stopped and drawing his face down to hers kissed him wildly. 'You shall never escape me. Never. Never.'

She watched him. He wanted her. He had never known such love-making. She laughed to herself. Cruel, wicked, ruthless, insatiable John had been a good tutor. Not that she had needed tutoring. Women such as she was were born with such knowledge. She could reduce him to such desire that he would be willing to promise anything. There was an innocence about him which had been completely lacking in John; she loved him for it. For if she was capable of love, she loved Hugh Le Brun. There was no self sacrifice in her kind of loving; a little tenderness now and then, a desire to give pleasure—but perhaps that was because she wanted to be thought supreme; there was a need to satisfy her own desires, a need to be loved and admired as no woman had ever been loved and admired before. In the first months of marriage with John she had believed she had brought him to a state of slavery, for he had given her all she asked in those days when he had shocked his ministers because he stayed in bed with her throughout the day. How wrong she had been! John could love no one but himself and she had quickly learned that it was an overwhelming sensuality in her which matched something similar in him which had made her imagine he was hers to command. It had waned as such feelings must—although he had never entirely escaped from it. Hugh was different. There was innocence and idealism in Hugh. Hugh would be her slave now and for ever.

Assuredly she was not going to allow him to escape her.

'It is not possible,' he said desperately.

'My dear Hugh, it *is* possible if we wish it to be. If you refuse me, I shall know that I was mistaken. All these years when I have thought of you have been a mockery. You did not love me after all. Perhaps it was as well I went to John.'

'You know that to be untrue.'

'I had hoped it, but now you spurn me. . . .'

'Spurn you!' He had taken her in his arms. And she thought: Yes, here in the forest . . . where some riders might come upon us at any moment. It will show him how great is his need of me, how his need and his desire takes from him the inherent inclination to conventional conduct.

'Nay, you do not spurn me,' she whispered. 'You need me, Hugh . . . just as I need you. You could never let me go. . . .'

He gave a cry of despair and thought of the innocent eyes of his young betrothed before he forgot everything but Isabella.


He had asked that he should first break the news to her.

'My dearest,' Isabella had cried, 'but why? She will hear of it in time.'

'Nay,' he had said, 'I wish this.'

She was a little put out but it seemed advisable at that time to give way.

He said he would ride out into the forest with his little betrothed because he thought it would be easier that way.

She was grave on that morning; it was almost as though she sensed some disaster. He found it difficult to tell her; he wanted to choose the right words, to explain that it was no deficiency in her.

She herself began it by saying: 'My lord, are you displeased with me?'

'My dear little Joan, how could I be?'

'If I had done something that you thought was wrong.'

'*You* have done nothing wrong.'

'Is it something to do with my mother?'

'Your . . . mother?' he repeated miserably.

'Yes, it seems that since she came. . . .'

He plunged in. 'You know that she and I were betrothed long ago?'

'Yes, I knew it.'

'Then your father came and took her away.'

'She has told me often.'

'Well, now she is here again and your father is dead . . . the truth is, we are to marry.'

'You . . . marry my mother. But how can that be? I am your affianced bride.'

'My dear child, you are very young and a much more suitable husband than I could ever be will be found for you.'

'*I* think you are suitable. You are kind and I thought you liked me and were happy about our betrothal.'

'I was, and I love you of course . . . but as a daughter. You understand?'

'No,' she cried. 'No!'

'Listen to me, little Joan. You have to grow up. There is much you have to learn. Your brother is the King of England.'

'Young Henry,' she said scornfully. 'He is only a boy.'

'He is the King of England and you as his sister are worthy of a great match.'

'I have a great match.'

He took her hand and kissed it. She said eagerly: 'You did not mean it. My mother will go back to England now you are home and it will all be as we planned.'

He shook his head sadly: 'Nay, my child,' he said. 'Your mother and I will marry. It was what was intended years ago. Fate has brought us together again but it is what was meant to be. Come, we will ride back to the castle. I wanted to tell you this myself . . . to explain.'

'I see,' she said, 'that you love my mother.'

He nodded.

'Far more,' she said sagely, 'than you could ever love me.'

Then she spurred her horse and rode forward. He kept a distance between them. He did not want to see her sad little face.

So they were married and Joan saw her mother take that place which she had thought would be hers.

She watched them but they were unaware of her; they saw nothing but each other.

There were festivities in the castle to celebrate the marriage. There was dancing and the singing of lays. Minstrels rendered their music soulfully, romantically, and it was all about lovers.

Isabella was as beautiful as she ever was, Hugh as handsome. The life of the castle seemed to revolve round them;

and the attendants whispered together and their talk was about the romance of two lovers, long parted, come together again.

Joan wondered what would happen to her. She supposed that when they emerged from this blissful wonder of being married they would perhaps remember her. Something would have to be done about her because she had no place in the castle now. Even the attendants looked at her as though she was something which a guest had left behind and must be set aside until she could be collected.

Even the bridegroom, kind Hugh, when they met, which she fancied he tried to avoid, seemed as though he were trying not to remember who she was.

She wept during the night when no one could see; and by day she wandered through the castle, lost and bewildered, but waiting with the certainty that something would have to happen before long.

# The Scottish Bridegroom

WILLIAM MARSHAL had gone to his castle at Caversham near Reading with the conviction that he would never leave it. He was old—few men passed their eightieth birthdays—and he should be grateful for a long life, during which he had been able—and he would not have been the honest man he was if he had denied this—to serve his country in a manner which had preserved her from disaster.

He could look back over the last four years since the young King had come to the throne and congratulate himself that England was well on the road to recovery from that dreadful malaise which had all but killed her and handed over her useless corpse to the French.

There was order in the land. How the people responded to a strong hand! It had ever been so. Laws and order under pain of death and mutilation had always been the answer; and if it was administered with justice the people were grateful. That was what John had failed to see, for he had offered the punishments without consideration of whether they were deserved. Praise God, England was settled down to peace; there had been a four years' truce with the French and he and the Justiciar, Hubert de Burgh, would see that it was renewed. England was rising to greatness and he could say *Nunc dimittis*.

Isabella, his wife, was concerned about him. They had grown old together; theirs had been a good union and a fruitful one. They had had five sons and five daughters and their marriages had often brought good to the family by extending its influence; and although his first concern was with his honour and the right, and he put the country's interests before his own, he could not help but be content that his was one of the richest and most influential families in the land.

But he had known for some time that his time would soon come; and he preferred to go before he lost his powers. Who—if he had been a man of action and sharp shrewd thinking—would want to become a poor invalid sitting in his chair waiting for the end?

His wife Isabella looked in at him as he sat thoughtfully at his table and he called to her.

'You are well, husband?' she asked.

'Come and sit with me awhile, Isabella,' he said.

She came, watching him anxiously.

'We must not deceive ourselves,' he said. 'I believe that I shall soon be gone.'

'You have the pain?'

'It comes and goes. But there is after it a kind of lassitude and times when I find my mind wandering back over the past and my King is another Henry, blustering, wenching, soldiering in the way of a wise general, using strategy rather than bloodshed. He always used to say that to me: "A battle that can be won by words at a conference meeting is worth thrice as much as that in which the blood of good soldiers is shed." I forget, Isabella, that it is the pallid boy who is now our King and not his grandfather who rules over us.'

'There have been two kings since then, William.'

'Richard . . . who forgot his country that he might win glory and honour with the Saracens . . . and John. . . .'

'My dear William, it upsets you to think of that. It is past. John is dead.'

'For which we must thank God,' said William. 'He has left us this boy King.'

'And you, William, have made England safe for him.'

William Marshal nodded slowly. 'We are at peace as we have not been for many years, but we must keep it so.'

'Hubert de Burgh is of your opinion and with two such as you to guide our affairs. . . .'

'Ah, my dear wife, how long think you that I shall be here. That is what sets me wondering.'

'We are going to see that you remain with us for a long time.'

'Who is this all powerful "We" which sets itself against the wishes of the Almighty? Nay, wife, when my time has come, come it will. And I want to be sure that England stays firm and that we continue in those steps towards peace and prosperity which we have taken these last four years. I am going to send a message to our son, William. I want him to come here with all speed as I have much to say to him.'

Isabella Marshal was alarmed. With that almost uncanny foresight of his William seemed to sense that his end was not far off. But she knew him well enough not to try to persuade him against such action. William had always known where he was going.

When she left him he went to a court cupboard and unlocking it, took from it a Templar's robe. Divesting himself of his surcoat, gown and soft white shirt, he put on the coarse garment.

He smiled wryly. It is what we all come to at the end of our days, he thought. When the end is near we turn to repentance.

He knelt down and prayed for forgiveness of his sins, and that when he passed on there might be strong men to keep the country peaceful and guide young Henry along the road to great Kingship.

Then he rose and wrote a letter to his wife in which he asked that when he died he should be buried in the Temple Church in London, for if his duty had not led him elsewhere he would have chosen to be a Knight of that religious but military order.

When William Marshal the younger arrived at Caversham he was shocked to see the deterioration in his father's condition. He had never known the old man other than healthy and it had never occurred to him that he could ever be otherwise. His father had always been the greatest influence in his life—although in recent years they had not always been in agreement with each other—and he was shocked to realize the reason why he had been sent for. As the eldest son he had been brought up to realize his responsibilities.

His father embraced him and young William looked searchingly into his face.

'Yes, my son,' said the elder Marshal, 'my time has come. I know it as surely as I stand here. My spirit is as good as it ever was but my flesh betrays me. Do not look sad; I'd as lief go a little sooner before my senses desert me. I am an old, old man, but I am mortal and mortals cannot live for ever. I have had a good life . . . a long life . . . and I feel it is crowned in success because I now see that the King is firm on the throne and with good government he will remain safely there. The country is free of the French and Hubert de Burgh is a strong man. I have asked him to come here, for I wish to see him before I go.'

Young William shook his head: 'You speak as though you are taking a journey to Ireland . . . or to France. . . .'

'It is not unlike that, William.'

'So you have sent for me to say good-bye.'

'Take care of your mother. Like mine, her youth is long since past. It has been a good marriage and I am happy in my family. Though . . .' he smiled wryly, 'there have been times when you and I were on different sides.'

'Father, there was a time when many Englishmen believed that there could be no good for England while John was on the throne.'

'Aye, and who could deny them? My son, all differences are over now. Serve the King. Honour your country.'

'I will do so, Father, when I can with honour.'

The younger William was referring to that period when Louis had landed in England and he had been one of those who had done him homage. It was understandable. He had been among those barons who had been present at Runnymede and he was well aware that disaster must come to England if John continued to rule. His father knew it too, but he could not bring himself to abandon his loyalty to the crown. It was young William Marshal who had seized Worcester for Louis. But a year later he had turned from the French Prince for he could not bear to see French nobles strutting through England and when John died it seemed natural that he should change his allegiance, so he had joined his father and became a sturdy supporter of young Henry.

He had been married at a tender age to a child named Alice who was the daughter of Baldwin de Béthune; but the marriage had never been consummated as they had been but children and Alice had died before they were grown up.

There was no doubt that young William Marshal was considered a man of great influence, not only through his father but because of his own abilities. Young as he was he had already caused some consternation by going over to Louis's side. Then he had fought beside his father and had taken possession of several castles which had been in French hands; but perhaps because of his one-time support of Louis he was watched rather closely by some of the older knights and in particular Hubert de Burgh.

He had recently been promised the hand of the Princess Eleanor—the youngest daughter of King John and at this time about three years old—because he was proposing to marry a daughter of Robert de Bruce, a prominent family of Southern Scotland who had some claim to the throne. The idea of a man's marrying into the North, which was a perpetual threat to England, was alarming—particularly when he had shown that he could shift his loyalty to the French. And it was for this reason that the greater alliance with baby Eleanor had been offered him.

Young William could be proud, for it was clear that he was regarded as a man who must be placated.

When his father died he would inherit great possessions; but the thought of a world without his father filled him with foreboding.

The old man saw this and grasped his son's hands. 'You will follow me, my son. You will be the second Earl of Pembroke when I am gone. I want you always to keep our name as honourable as it is at this day.'

William promised but assured his father that he had some years left to him yet.

His father shrugged this aside and said that he wished his son to send for Hubert de Burgh as there was much he had to say to him.

In due course Hubert arrived at the castle and spent some hours with the Marshal when they talked of the difficulties through which the country had passed and those which remained.

'There is not a man living,' Hubert told him, with some

emotion, 'who has made England's cause his own in the same self-effacing manner as you have, my lord.'

'And you will carry this on, I know,' replied William.

Hubert bowed his head and declared that he would do his best, though in his heart he doubted that he could match William Marshal. Hubert was a man whose emotions would always play some part in his actions; he often thought of his conduct with regard to Arthur for whose sake he had, at great risk, defied the King; and he wondered what William Marshal's actions would have been in similar circumstances. Honour was a fetish with William Marshal. He was the man who had defied Richard, when it was clear that his father was on the edge of defeat and Richard would soon be King. Fearless in honour—that was William Marshal and there were few like him.

Hubert said suddenly: 'My lord Earl, you must not expect the same degree of selfless service from other men as you yourself have given to the crown. The spirit is often willing, but self-interest creeps in—also the need to preserve one's own life. The service of kings is a dangerous one.'

'I know it well. I know you defied John when you saved Arthur from mutilation. You were not serving your King then, whatever your motive. But this gives you a quality which men perceive. I do not think they like you the less for it. Have you noticed how our young King turns first to you and with affection. He listens to me, but he cares for you, Hubert.'

Hubert knew this was true. The young King was fond of him . . . as Arthur had been.

'Serve him well, Hubert, and good will come to England.'

Hubert said he would do his best.

'There is a strong foreign interest in the land. Guard against it. The Legate Pandulf has too much power. It was necessary for us to have his support when the country was overrun by the French, but now England should be governed by the English. I regret I have to leave you to this task. But you are a strong man, Hubert, and you have the confidence of the King.'

They talked awhile of the country's affairs. The King was realizing his responsibilities and learning quickly. Richard was in good hands in Corfe and his future could be left for a while. The Princess Joan was safely in Lusignan, betrothed to Hugh Le Brun which was a good match, for it would keep Hugh an ally of the crown of England since his wife would be a member of the English royal family. Her mother Queen Isabella was safely in Angoulême and long might she remain there. It was well to have her out of the way, William declared, for she was a troublemaker and he did not want her too close to the King. As soon as Hugh de Lusignan returned from his crusade the marriage could take place; and the Queen should of course stay with her daughter until after the ceremony. The remaining children were young yet and could play their part later. It was always well to have a princess or two ready to contract a marriage which could be valuable or expedient. So it had been with the baby Eleanor, now betrothed to the younger Marshal. His loyalty would be assured if he married the King's sister. As for her slightly older sister Isabella, now five years old, she would have her uses in due course.

It seemed to the old man that the country's condition had settled down beyond his wildest hopes; and, having made his preparations for departure, and his peace with God—and most of all safeguarding his country's future as well as was within his power, he quietly slipped away.

No sooner was William Marshal dead than the peaceful progress of the country's affairs seemed to come to an end. Hubert de Burgh, in his role as Justiciar, took over control of the country; but he missed the firm hand of William Marshal. The foreign party—which had been subdued during William's lifetime—became more vociferous. This was headed by Peter des Roches, the Poitevin Bishop of Winchester, whose aim was to oust Englishmen from the major positions of power and put foreigners in their places.

Stephen Langton, the Archbishop of Canterbury, fortunately for Hubert was on his side; and when Peter des Roches, supported by the Legate Pandulf, wanted to appoint a Poitevin as Seneschal for Poitou, Hubert and the Archbishop stood firmly against them in favour of an Englishman's taking the post.

The controversy over this matter was significant, for Hubert, with the country behind him and the people beginning to take a pride in their nationalism—and perhaps feeling ashamed of having invited foreigners to rule them—were fierce in their denunciation of Pandulf so that his resignation was brought about.

While this was happening, news came to Hubert of the marriage of Isabella with Hugh de Lusignan and he hurried into consultation with the Archbishop.

'But this is monstrous!' cried Stephen Langton. 'And we are only told after the marriage has taken place.'

'It seems incredible,' replied Hubert. 'The Queen was betrothed to him years ago—and it seems they only have to meet to become lovers again. I have reports of their manners with each other and that it has been so since Hugh de Lusignan returned from the Holy Land. If that is not ill conceived enough, Lusignan is asking for her dowry.'

'He shall be told that there will be no dowry. The Princess Joan was sent over and he was pledged to marry her. This is a very different matter.'

'So thought I. I shall send messengers to the effect that the Princess Joan must return to England immediately and that there will be no dowry for the Queen.'

Messengers were sent off immediately to Lusignan.

It was shortly after that that Hubert began to wonder whether the marriage of Hugh and Isabella was perhaps fortunate after all.

Alexander the Second of Scotland—a young, warlike King of some twenty years—had soon after the death of John taken the opportunity to invade England; but when Louis had been defeated, a peace had been brought about with Scotland. The terms of the treaty were now being considered; the King of Scotland was eager to marry one of the English princesses. To wait for young Isabella who was only six was not so convenient, whereas Joan who was ten was much more suitable. In two years—perhaps one—she would be marriageable.

Hubert with Langton decided that he would ask for the return of the Princess Joan without delay while intimating to the newly married pair that there would be no dowry.

\*     \*     \*

Joan longed to get away from the castle. There was no one to whom she could explain her melancholy. She had been so frightened when she had first heard that she was to marry but Hugh had disarmed her and then charmed her, reconciling her to her fate to such an extent that she had come to long for it.

And it was not to happen. She was left to wander about the castle alone. It was true she had to take her lessons and her governesses would accompany her when she rode out. But she always tried to elude them. She wanted to get away, to be alone, to think of what had happened to her.

She supposed she had come to love Hugh.

He was kind whenever they met; he would look at her in a half apologetic manner if her mother was not with him; once he had tried to explain that the way in which he had behaved was in no way due to her. When her mother was with him he took little notice of her—nor did her mother.

She felt she had become a person who had to be looked after but who somehow had no right to be there, and that they were all waiting for a suitable moment to push her out of sight.

Hugh was obsessed by her mother. His eyes never left her when they were together; the timbre of his voice changed when he addressed her; his hands would caress her when he spoke to her.

'The Queen has bewitched my lord,' she overheard one of the serving women say.

It was true that he was like a man bewitched.

I came here to marry him, she thought, and now my mother has done that, so what of me?

She tried to ask her mother. 'Oh don't bother me, child,' was the answer. 'When the time comes something will be arranged.'

'Shall I go back to England?'

'I know not. Be thankful that you have me here to look after you.'

'But you do not look after me. And everything has changed now that *you* are Hugh's bride.'

'It was all so natural,' she said. 'Remember I knew him so well in the past. Now, why are you not at your lessons?'

'It is not the time for them, my lady.'

'Then you should ride with your women—or perhaps you should have your dancing lesson.'

She had turned away. It was clear that her mother did not want to be bothered by her.

She knew that Hugh's conscience worried him. Perhaps he knew that his gentleness and eagerness to make life smooth for her had won her love. A look of sadness would come into his face when he saw her, trying to overshadow the blissful expression which was there in her mother's presence. It never quite succeeded in doing that for Joan knew he only thought of her when he saw her and then did his best to forget that she had been his betrothed.

Once he said to her: 'You will go away from here one day, Joan. Your brother and advisers will arrange that. They will find a young husband for you. It is best for you.'

'No,' she had cried angrily, 'it will not be best for me. Please do not let us pretend.'

'Oh but it will,' he insisted. 'You will see . . . in a few years time.'

That was what he wanted, she knew. He must salve his conscience and he could best do so by promising her a handsome young husband—which would make it all for the best.

But it would not be for the best. She knew that. All her life she would remember Hugh.


Isabella was pacing up and down the bedchamber, her eyes flashing with rage. She looked magnificent of course but Hugh tried to calm her.

'So I am not to have a dowry! And this treatment from my own son! Of course he is not responsible, I know. He is in the hands of Hubert de Burgh and suchlike. He would never treat his mother so. No dowry! You married without my consent, he says. His consent! A boy of fourteen and I am to ask his consent.'

'He is the King,' said Hugh gently.

'Of course he's the King and might well not have been if I had not had the foresight to go ahead with his coronation. He was even crowned with my neck-collar. And he tells me that he disapproves of my marriage and therefore there will be no dowry.'

'We shall have to go carefully, Isabella.'

'Oh, Hugh, you are too mild. You always allow people to snatch what you want from you . . . when it pleases them. No dowry! Of course there is going to be a dowry. And what does he go on to say: The Princess Joan must return at once to England. You see, they order me! I, the Queen, am being told what I must do by Hubert de Burgh, because my silly little son is incapable of giving orders.'

'If they will not send the dowry what can we do?'

She looked at him with exasperation. 'What shall we do?' she mimicked. 'I will tell you what we shall do for a start. "Send the Princess Joan," they say. Very well I shall reply, "Send my dowry. And if one is not sent, nor shall the other be." '

'We cannot keep Joan here if they ask for her return.'

'Joan is my daughter. If I decide she shall stay with me, then she stays.'

There was a glitter in Isabella's eyes which Hugh had seen now and then. It filled him with apprehension, but being utterly her slave he made every effort to placate her.

So now she was a hostage. Joan heard about it—not through her mother, nor through Hugh—but by listening to the gossip of women and the chatter of servants.

Her brother wanted her to go back to England but her mother and her stepfather would not let her go until they sent the dowry her mother was asking for.

'They'll never send it,' was the comment.

Joan pictured herself wandering through the castle of Lusignan all her life, with the ardent lovers never far away; her mother indifferent to her, her stepfather trying to be, because the sight of her made him feel unhappy while she knew that as long as she remained, he would never be perfectly at ease.

She pretended to be listless but she kept her ears open for the whispers. They never told her anything. She was resentful of that. It was her life they were playing with and yet she was supposed to be the one who was kept in the dark.

She heard talk of the King of Scotland. Her brother was

making a treaty with him. It was difficult to think of Henry's making a treaty with anyone. It was four years though since she had left England and Henry had been only ten years old then—the same age as she was now. He would be fourteen years old now. Not very old for a king; but it was the age when a princess was considered marriageable. Now Henry was a king and making treaties.

It was a shock to discover that she was involved in the treaty.

'The Princess Joan will go away now,' she heard one of them say. 'She must because she is to be the bride of the Scottish King.'

Hugh did not want her, so she was to go to Alexander.

'I won't go,' she sobbed to herself in her bed at night. Yet did she want to stay here?

Her mother raged against Henry and his English advisers. Everyone had to be very careful how they treated her—even Hugh; because they must all remember that she was not merely the Countess of Lusignan but a queen. Once a queen was crowned she was a queen until the day she died and Isabella had been crowned Queen of England.

'I paid a big price for my crown,' she shouted once in Joan's hearing. 'All those years with that madman. And no one is going to forget my rank.'

The days passed and still Joan went on living the strange life in the shadows, knowing that they did not want her there and would have been happy to see her go, except for the fact that she was the hostage for the dowry which her brother's advisers would not send.

But Stephen Langton and Hubert de Burgh had the power of Rome behind them and one day there was great consternation in the castle, for messengers had arrived from the Pope himself with letters for the Count of Lusignan.

A terrible silence fell over the castle, for one thing which all men dreaded was that sentence from Rome and it was with this that Hugh was threatened. If he did not return the Princess Joan to her brother he would be excommunicated.

Isabella laughed aloud when she heard, but rather wildly for even she was afraid of the fires of hell. Of course she was young and, if all went as could be reasonably expected, would have years of healthful life before her, enabling her to slip into a convent for the last few years of her life to bring about the required repentance. But nothing in life was absolutely sure and if she died while under the interdict of excommunication she could expect to go straight to hell.

She was brazen though. She raged against her son who had called Rome into their dispute. She declared that they would snap their fingers at Henry and his ministers and at Rome too. They would hold on to Joan until the dowry was sent. Hadn't she a right to her dowry?

Hugh reasoned with her. She was prepared to face excommunication, she declared. It was not as simple as that, he explained patiently, for when a man was banished from the Church it was not only that he could not expect extreme unction and the services of a priest and so would die with all his sins on him, but the fact was that those who served him would lose faith in him. If it were necessary for him to go into battle he would have lost that battle before he took up arms because all believed that no man could prosper when the good will of God was turned against him.

Isabella remembered when John had been under a similar ban and how even he, irreligious and defiant, had in time realized that he must escape from it.

They would lose the dowry then; but at least they would be rid of Joan.

She listened to what Hugh had to say. Then she went to her daughter's bedchamber where Joan seemed to spend a good deal of her time. She found the girl looking listlessly out of the window.

Joan rose and curtsied as Isabella approached. Isabella said: 'Sit down.'

Joan obeyed, tense and waiting.

'You must prepare yourself for a journey with all speed. You are leaving here tomorrow.'

'Tomorrow!' cried Joan.

'Tomorrow, yes. You are going home. Don't tell me that does not please for I have seen how you have been moping here and longing to go. Your brother insists that you go and that with all speed.'

'But I thought that you wished me to stay here.'

'No longer.'

'Then you have your dowry.'

'The rogues still refuse it but you are to go. The Pope has joined in the battle and if your brother were here I would box his ears for his impudence. To call in Rome . . . against his mother, the ungrateful wretch!'

'You speak of the King, my lady.'

'I speak of a child. Well, you are to go. They have a surprise for you. A husband, no less. You smile. It amuses you.'

'I wondered whether he will be bestowed on someone else before I have time to claim him.'

'That could be. They are talking of betrothing him to your sister.'

'Isabella! She is but a baby.'

'Alexander wants a sister of the King of England. Eleanor has already been promised to the Marshal—so that leaves you and Isabella. It is you they want for there would be too much delay with Isabella.'

Joan began to laugh rather uncertainly.

'I am glad you are amused,' said the Queen.

'Is it not amusing, my lady, to be thrown from one to the other like a ball with little concern for its inclination.'

'Princesses do not have inclinations. They do as they are told.'

'Not always. You didn't.'

'I was betrothed to Hugh and John took me.'

'You wanted to go, my lady, I trow, or you would not have done so.'

She smiled slowly, as though remembering.

Then she looked at her daughter and said: 'No. I was forced by your father. My parents would never have dared go against him.'

'But you would, my lady.'

'Well,' she said, 'he held out a crown to me, did he not? I did not know then that he was a madman . . . the cruellest madman in the world. And in the end he died and I came back to Hugh.' She softened suddenly. 'Be clever, child. Yes, be wise and it may well be that one day you will be able to take what you want.' She was brisk suddenly. 'Now, be prepared. Tomorrow you leave. It must be so, for if you do not we shall be excommunicated and that is something your stepfather dreads. It could bring us great harm. So you must go.'

'I will make ready,' said Joan stonily.

The Queen's face softened as she laid her hands on her daughter's shoulders.

'Don't be afraid. Make the best of your life. Be clever and you should get something of what you want. I hear that Alexander of Scotland is a fine handsome young man.'

She kissed her daughter swiftly.

'You should rest,' she said, 'and be ready to set out at dawn.'

And the next day the Princess Joan set out for England.

The young king Henry was beginning to enjoy his position. The apprehension which had first been with him when he had heard of his father's death and realized what, as his eldest son, this would mean to him, had disappeared and the situation was proving to be far more gratifying than he would have believed possible. He could not help but feel some elation at the respect which was shown him even by people like the Archbishop of Canterbury and Hubert de Burgh. It was true that they expected him to do what they wanted, but being wise beyond his years he was prepared to follow them until that time when he was able to act with confidence without them. He had immediately realized that what he must do was learn quickly, for the sooner he was competent to make his own decisions, the sooner he would escape from the yoke. For the time being he would remain docile, listen avidly and agree to their advice.

The days were full of interest. When he was alive William Marshal had insisted that the young King attend meetings of his ministers. 'You may not understand their discourse,' he had said, 'but take in what you can, and in time you will learn how these matters should be conducted.'

Now William Marshal was dead and his chief adviser was Hubert de Burgh. He liked Hubert. He was not so serious as the Marshal had been. He was warm-hearted, more emotional, far less stern than William Marshal, who had given the impression that he was a man of such honour that all the little peccadilloes of normal people seemed like mortal sin to him.

Henry was far more in awe of Stephen Langton, the Archbishop of Canterbury—a man whose spiritual qualities set him apart from other men. He was intellectual, a man with a stern sense of duty which had brought him into conflict with both King John and Rome. As he had been suspended from office he had spent much time in writing—sermons, and commentaries on the Bible; he had many detractors, naturally, but Hubert had told Henry that he was a strong man and it was good to have such a man at the head of the Church in England.

A good man, no doubt, thought Henry, but an uncomfortable one.

He had recently come back to England to take up his office at Canterbury and Hubert had explained to him that this had brought at least one boon to England, for Stephen had asked the Pope that the Legate Pandulf be dismissed and that during his lifetime no Legate should take up residence in England.

Much to Hubert's surprise Pope Honorius had granted this request. 'Which means, my lord,' explained Hubert, 'that while Stephen Langton lives and reigns as Archbishop of Canterbury England is free of any Roman overlord the Pope may think fit to send.'

Now there was to be a coronation.

Hubert had explained the reason for this, 'True,' he said, 'you were crowned soon after your father's death. That was necessary. But you will remember that it was a hurried ceremoney and was not performed by the Archbishop of Canterbury. Moreover your crown was your mother's throat-collar. Now we propose that you be crowned in a fitting manner. A King's coronation is important. It is only when the people have seen him anointed and the crown placed on his head and the barons and prelates have sworn allegiance to him that he is, in truth, regarded as their sovereign. You are now of a more mature age.' Hubert grimaced. Fourteen was scarcely that, but of course an advance on ten. 'And, I may add, wise for your years. So there will be another coronation and this time it will take place when the land is free of foreign invaders.'

So on a May day in the previous year of 1220 he had been solemnly crowned at Westminster by Stephen Langton. It had been on Whitsunday—an impressive ceremony when all the leading barons of the land and all the dignified churchmen had kissed his hand and taken the coronation oath.

He had enjoyed the day and when at last he lay in his bed, physically weary but mentally exalted, he had eagerly looked forward to the future; and from that day he had begun to feel that he was in truth a King.

It seemed that those about him believed that the coronation had brought about some magic change and the young boy who had arisen from his bed on the morning of that Whitsunday had undergone a great spiritual and mental metamorphosis during the day. They talked to him more seriously than they had before. Apart from his lessons, which had never given him much difficulty, he had to learn of what was happening in the world.

There was one bogy which continually arose in the conversations with Hubert, the Archbishop and other ministers: the French.

'Let us not imagine,' Hubert had said, 'that because Louis realized that he could not keep a hold on this country once your father was dead and you proclaimed King that this means his ambitions regarding it have in any way diminished. We must be watchful of Louis and in particular his wily father. No country ever suffered more from its King than England did with John. You will have to face the truth, my lord, for your task is too important for it to be obscured by sentiments. John was your father and I praise God nightly that in you I see no sign of his nature. You are going to take after your grandfather—King Henry II, one of the greatest kings this country has ever known. England needs such a ruler— now as never before.'

So Henry learned of his grandfather and his grandmother Eleanor of Aquitaine. 'One does not often see their like,' said Hubert.

'My grandfather spent the greater part of his life at war,' said Henry. 'Was that wise?'

'Your grandfather fought only when he could not settle his affairs with words. He was one of the greatest soldiers we have ever known. He had wide territories to protect and when all was well in England, there was trouble in Normandy. Now your possessions in France are sadly diminished. Your father lost them.'

'We shall regain them,' said Henry.

'Let us hope this will come to pass.'

'Then I shall be as my grandfather—fighting all the time.'

Hubert shook his head. 'We will try to make peace in the land. Louis is not the man his father is and Philip . . . although not so far gone in years is not in good health. If Philip were to die and Louis be King then there might be a chance of regaining our lost possessions. Although the King of France has a very forceful wife, who is a descendant of the Conqueror.'

'Yes I know. She is Blanche. It was because of her that Louis laid claim to England.'

' 'Tis true. Philip was never the same after the Pope excommunicated him. It is a strange thing, my lord, that a man of great shrewdness, as is this King of France, should, when his emotions are aroused, forget his wisdom. You have heard of course of the Albigensians, that strange sect from the town of Albi in the South of France whose doctrines conflicted with Rome and whom Rome has determined to suppress.'

Henry nodded agreement.

'In his attitude towards them Philip Augustus has behaved with a wisdom which must be admired, applauded and emulated by every statesman. He never submitted to Rome, was never subservient, yet managed to keep on good terms with the Vatican without losing one iota of his independence. In a statesman's eyes it was a masterly performance, but then Philip Augustus is a great ruler. That is why what happened is so astonishing. There will come a time, my lord King, when it will be necessary for you to marry. Not yet, you are over young. But when that time does come we shall have to choose your bride with the greatest care. A King must marry in a manner which best suits his country—and it does not always happen that his duty and his inclination run side by side.'

'I know this well, Hubert.'

'Of a certainty you do. All royal princes know this. But to

return to Philip Augustus. He was married to Isabel of Hainault who gave him his son Louis. Isabel died and after three years of widowhood Philip Augustus decided he must marry again. The Princess chosen was Ingeburga of Denmark. He did not see her until the ceremony was about to be performed but his ministers had assured him that the alliance with Denmark was necessary. The ceremony went off as such ceremonies do and the royal pair were left together in the state bed. No one knows what happened during that night or what Philip discovered about his bride, but in the morning he was white and shaken and declared that he would have no more of her, that she must be returned to Denmark, the marriage must be dissolved and he would take a new wife—and this would be one whom he knew and loved *before* the ceremony took place.'

'And being King he could do this?' asked Henry.

'No, my lord, no. In spite of his happy relationship with the Pope he could not defy the laws of the Church so blatantly. There is a lesson to be learned here. The Pope had the power to apply the sentence of the Interdict, and this is to be dreaded by all—king or commoner. If a king is excommunicated all religious ceremonies and forms of Church practice are banned. In the case of a king, he and his country are cut off from all benefits of the Church. You can imagine the people's feelings over this.'

Henry nodded gravely. 'And did he rid himself of her?' he asked.

'He brought up the time-honoured excuse: consanguinity. His blood and that of his Queen Ingeburga were too close and as it is against the laws of the Church that people with close blood ties should marry, so the marriage was null and void.'

'And was this proved to be?'

'Philip Augustus was a king much feared by his people. If he told the council he had called together that the marriage was null and void it would need a brave man among them to declare otherwise.'

'So it was agreed.'

'In France, but of course there was Rome and Ingeburga herself had appealed to the Pope. Philip tried to send her back to Denmark, but Denmark would not receive her and the poor

Queen was taken from the palace crying aloud: "Oh naughty France. Naughty France. Help me, Rome, against naughty France." Which showed, of course, that she was not going to give in easily. While the decision was being awaited she was taken from castle to castle until Philip had the idea that she might be happier in convents and to these she was sent with the hope that she might develop a taste for the life, in which case she would be ready to relinquish her rights as wife to the King of France.'

'And did she?'

Hubert shook his head. 'Meanwhile Pope Celestine, who reigned at this time, studied the relationship of Philip and Ingeburga, and partly because there could be said to be a closeness but more because he did not wish to antagonize the powerful King with whom Rome had been on such good terms, he decided to annul the marriage but he added the injunction that Philip must not remarry. This did not suit Philip, who immediately ignored it and looked for a bride, finally choosing Agnes of Moravia with whom he became infatuated.'

'And the Pope said he must not marry again . . . yet he did!'

'Ah, that is why I tell you this, my lord. Kings and Popes have been in conflict through the ages. It is always well to live in peace with Rome. Philip realized this but on this matter of his marriage was determined to have his way no matter at what cost.'

'And this was unwise.'

'No doubt Philip thought that he could placate Celestine who was eager to be on good terms with France and that he could come to some arrangement with Celestine. But this is a matter on which Kings must be wary. Popes change, and what can be done with one cannot be with another. Innocent III had taken the place of Celestine, and Innocent immediately wrote to the Bishop of Paris saying that although Celestine had been unable to put a stop to the scandal, he was determined to obtain the fulfilment of God's law.'

'And so the King had to give way.'

'Philip Augustus was not the man to give way without a struggle. He would not wish his subjects to witness such weakness. Moreover he was becoming more and more enamoured of Agnes and declared he would rather lose half his domains than separate from her. Whereupon the Pope told him that if Philip did not give her up he would pass the dreaded sentence of the Interdict which should be pronounced throughout the kingdom of France.'

'And then?' cried Henry, who as one King considering another saw himself in the role of Philip Augustus, and was clearly hoping for the royal victory.

'Philip stood firm, though the Interdict was pronounced in the churches throughout France. Philip remarked that he would rather turn Musselman than agree to the Pope's commands. He added ominously that Saladin was a happy man and had got along very well without a Pope. He then turned all the prelates out of their sees because they had agreed with the Pope and had proclaimed the Interdict.'

'So the King won,' cried Henry well pleased.

'Nay, my lord. The country was plunged in gloom. When anything went wrong—as it did continuously—it was said that God had turned his face from the King of France because of his insults to the Church. For four years Philip held out and then he realized what was happening in the country and that his subjects believed he was ruining France. If he went to battle his armies were sure of defeat because they believed the hand of God was against them. Agnes, who truly loved the King, said that she would go into a convent and Ingeburga must return.'

'So the King lost the battle.'

'As all must against God. Your father realized that when he suffered the Interdict. So do all that is possible to remain on good terms with Rome while preserving your independence, which is what all Kings must learn.'

'Poor Agnes,' said Henry. 'So she truly loved the King.'

'The Pope was impressed by her virtue and although she must leave the court, His Holiness declared that the two children she had borne Philip should be considered legitimate. So she went away to a convent in Poissy and in a short time she died there.'

'And Ingeburga?'

'The King continued to hate her and banished her to Etampes.

And there she stayed for eleven years. But while he would not have her at Court, the Pope continued to show his displeasure and finally Philip decided that peace with Rome was more important than his prejudices, so Ingeburga was brought back to Court and given all the state of a Queen.'

'But Philip does not love her.'

'He is older now and doubtless feels that peace with Rome is more important to him than revenge on a wife who displeases him. I tell you this, my lord, because you must know of these matters. You must watch above all things your relations with Rome. There have been constant conflicts between the heads of States and the Head of the Church. You know the story of your grandfather and Thomas Becket, which ended in the murder of Thomas and his becoming a martyr. You know that your grandfather did penance for that murder, although it had not been committed by his own hands but by knights who misguidedly mistook his words. Never forget. Keep peace with the Church. We are fortunate in Stephen Langton. And another reason why we have talked at length is that you must know and understand always what goes on at the Court of France, for ever since William the Conqueror came to England and took the land he brought those two communities close; and since your grandmother brought Aquitaine to the crown, France has been important to us. We shall talk often of what is happening in France.'

Henry was wishing that all lessons were as entertaining as the marriages and excommunication of the King of France had proved to be.

There had been great consternation when news arrived of Queen Isabella's marriage to Hugh de Lusignan. Both the Archbishop and Hubert were angry. That the marriage between Joan and Hugh had been cursorily set aside might not in the circumstances be such a bad thing because now the country was settled, she might prove a good bargaining counter and a better match be found for her than with a French Count.

As for Isabella, she was of no great interest to them; and secretly they were glad to be without her. 'A trouble maker I am sure,' Hubert confided to the Archbishop. 'And if she chooses to return to her native land the better. But the demand for her dowry was sheer insolence and something which she would quickly understand was considered so in England.'

Henry was summoned and informed of what had happened.

'So my mother has a new husband,' said Henry. 'I wish her joy of him. I fear she had little with my father.'

'It is unseemly,' replied the Archbishop, 'that the Queen taking her daughter to the husband chosen for her, should marry him herself.'

'I think my mother and my father often acted in an unseemly manner,' observed Henry gravely, 'so we must not be surprised if she continues to do so.'

'When her unseemly behaviour concerns this country,' said the Archbishop, 'we shall express not only surprise but our objections.'

Making him feel like a child was typical of the Archbishop, thought Henry. Hubert would have put it differently.

'We shall send at once asking for the return of the Princess,' said Stephen Langton, 'and perhaps, Sire, you will inform your mother that she will certainly receive no dowry from you.'

Henry was sorry. He would have liked to wish his mother happiness and would willingly have sent her a dowry if he had been allowed to do so. He sighed. He was of course very young and not really a king since he always had to do what he was told. But it would be different one day.

The Archbishop explained to him that the country was settling down and thanks to the Church and the good will of Pope Honorious (another one since Celestine and Innocent who had played their part in the drama of the King of France and his marriages) the high offices in England were now being taken from those foreigners on whom John had bestowed them and were being returned to Englishmen. All the castles which had previously belonged to the King and taken from him by rebellious barons, were now being returned to the crown.

'It is necessary,' said the Archbishop, 'that you should visit these castles throughout the realm and receive them into your hands. It will be a good opportunity for you to meet your subjects and to receive the oath of allegiance from those who were not present at the time of the coronation. Hubert de

Burgh will discuss this with you and tell you what is expected of you. You must be firm, resolute and never forget your kingly dignity. You are hampered by your lack of years.' The Archbishop looked stern, as though this was due to some lack of zeal on Henry's part. 'But that is a fault which can be remedied. But remember, you must show no levity. The barons must realize that although you are so young, you intend to rule.'

'I shall do my best,' answered Henry.

'Hubert de Burgh will discuss the journey with you; and it would be well that it is undertaken without too much delay.'

So a day or so after the coronation, Henry set out on his journey northwards.

The ceremonies took place—one very like another. The young King with the strong Hubert de Burgh beside him rode from castle to castle, accepting the keys and the oaths of allegiance.

'When we reach York,' Hubert told him, 'there will take place the most important meeting of them all.'

Henry knew he was referring to the encounter with Alexander of Scotland. Hubert had explained: 'It is very important that we stop these perpetual wars with Scotland, and I am hoping we shall be able to make some sort of peace.'

Henry was enjoying this trip. He had never felt so much a king and he supposed it was due to the fact that he was growing up. The older he grew the more homage he could expect; and he was waiting for the day when he need not take his orders from the men who surrounded him. It would be interesting, too, to meet another young King, although he discovered that Alexander was old by his standards, being twenty-two years of age and having reigned for several years.

The meeting was to take place in York, a city of which any King could be justly proud. Henry was met at the Micklegate by the Archbishop of York and the leading dignitaries of the city, and passing under the Roman arch which supported the turrets was escorted into the castle which was said to have been built by his famous ancestor, William the Conqueror.

The meeting of the two kings took place within the great hall of the castle where Henry felt somewhat at a loss on account of his youth; Alexander seemed very mature, having been King of Scotland for seven years; he was shrewd, Hubert had said, and like all good rulers, ever alert for the advantage of his country. Of small stature, with reddish hair and light eyes, he had a foxy look which suggested a certain cunning.

Henry knew that when England had been figuratively on her knees through the bad rule of his father and the French had been on English soil, Alexander had taken advantage of the situation by attacking in the north and in the circumstances naturally achieving some success.

'It was a good opportunity for him,' Hubert had pointed out, 'and one which such a shrewd ruler would take advantage of.'

However when the French had been defeated and driven out Alexander had been forced to retreat behind the Border; and it was in the hope of bringing about a permanent peace that this meeting was taking place.

Hubert with other important barons sat with the Scottish King and some of his supporters. Henry was there in a chair of state but had been made to realize that he was, though a figurehead, a mere observer.

'It is important,' Hubert had told him, 'that you should learn how these conferences are conducted. Listen to discussion, watch, parry and thrust, and see how both sides juggle for advantage.'

So Henry listened, thinking what a long time must elapse before he was twenty-two years of age and put *his* views before men like Hubert de Burgh and was listened to with respect.

Hubert pointed out that a truce would be advantageous to both sides, for the English were eager to preserve the order they were beginning to experience after the lawlessness of John's reign and Alexander admitted that he would be pleased to have peace on the Border in order that he might divert his energies towards settling quarrels among his own chieftains. But he would expect concessions.

Hubert nodded gravely and said that the English would be prepared to consider these whereupon Alexander replied that he was in need of a wife and he would be happy with one of the English Princesses.

'The Princess Eleanor is betrothed to William Marshal,' said Hubert. 'That leaves Joan and Isabella. Isabella is but seven years old.'

'I knew well that Joan was betrothed to Hugh de Lusignan and that he married her mother,' said Alexander. 'Therefore as she is now free I will take Joan.'

'The King will tell you that he would derive great pleasure from the marriage of his sister Joan with you, my lord.'

Hubert was looking at Henry who said hurriedly: 'Yes, yes. It would please me to see you and my sister married.'

'I believe your sister is at this time in Lusignan,' said Alexander looking full at Henry who replied: 'That is so, but she is to return.'

'And that there is some trouble about that return,' went on the sharp-eyed King of Scotland.

Henry looked at Hubert who replied: 'My lord, the King has commanded the return of his sister and the Pope has threatened Hugh de Lusignan with the Interdict if she is not sent back at once. I think you may rest assured that ere long she will be your bride.'

The King of Scotland looked faintly sceptical.

'I am determined to have one of the Princesses,' he said. 'I do not wish for a mere child such as Isabella is, but by my faith I will take her if the other is not returned in good time. Marriage I will have—even with Isabella.'

'Marriage there shall be,' replied Hubert, 'either with Joan or Isabella. We will sign on that, my lord.'

'I have two sisters, Margaret and Isabella, and I want husbands for them,' went on Alexander.

Henry knew that Hubert was a little disturbed because King John had promised their father, William the Lion, that the two girls should have his sons—Henry, himself, and Richard. Henry knew though that the barons would not consider marriage with Scotland good enough for him now that he was the King. His wife would have to bring him a little more than peace with Scotland.

Hubert said: 'We will find rich and powerful barons for your sisters, my lord.'

For a moment Alexander hesitated and then, evidently so delighted was he to have a sister of the King for his own bride that he decided to settle for two noblemen for his sisters.

So the conference ended happily and it was clear to Henry that both sides were gratified.

Later there was feasting in the hall. Henry was seated beside the King and they talked pleasantly and in friendly manner together. He noticed that Hubert paid great attention to both the Scottish princesses and Margaret in particular.

It had been a long journey and a perilous one across France, and then the sea had been so rough that Joan had not much cared whether she reached the other side of the Channel or not. But at last she was home, and she kept thinking of how apprehensive she had been when she had set out with her mother and remembered the tales Isabella had told her of her childhood in Angoulême. She should have known that her mother loved Hugh; she should also have known that he would only have to take one look at her and he would be as much in love with her as he had been when they were young.

But that was all over now. Nothing was to be gained by brooding on the past. She had a new life to face and since she had failed to become Hugh's wife, they had another bride-groom for her.

A resentment flickered within her. They did not consult her wishes in any of these matters affecting her future. Princesses had to realize that their lives were governed for them and that they married men not because they would make good husbands or because the princesses loved them . . . no, it was only because it was good for the country to make an alliance with another country. Women like her mother, though, managed to get their own way; and sometimes Joan wondered whether if her mother had really loved Hugh in the first place she would have allowed herself to have been carried off by John.

She was not of her mother's nature; therefore she must accept what was prepared for her.

She arrived at Westminster Palace and was pleased to be greeted by her brother. He had grown in size and in dignity since she had last seen him. He was almost a man, being fourteen years old; and he was undoubtedly aware of being King.

He greeted her warmly and told her how sorry he was for what she had suffered. He did not mention their mother until they were alone and then he wanted to hear how she fared.

Joan told him that Isabella was well and happy in her marriage. Hugh de Lusignan doted on her and people said he was her slave. She did not add that she had heard the whisper that his devotion to his wife would be his undoing because he seemed to have no will but hers.

Henry told her that he had seen Richard at his coronation, that their brother was well content with life at Corfe, and that as soon as he was of an age to leave his tutors he would bring him to Court.

'The trouble with us,' said Joan, 'is that we are all too young.'

Henry admitted that it was a pity that they had not been born a few years earlier.

'Or that our father had lived longer.'

Henry shook his head. In his newly found wisdom he knew that if that had happened there would have been no inheritance for him.

Joan was able to see her sisters and was amazed how they had grown. As for them, they did not know her; four years was a long time in their brief lives.

Four years, thought Joan. When she had left she had been a child, and indeed knowing Hugh and learning to love him had given her a maturity beyond her years.

She must grow up; she must learn to shut out the past and face the future, for she was going to be married as soon as it could be arranged and instead of living, as she had believed she would, in the warm lush south of France, she was going to the bleak north of England to marry a man she had never seen.

Henry had said: 'He will be better for you than Hugh de Lusignan. He is not an old man. He is twenty-two, so he will be more suitable.'

She turned away. How could she explain to Henry that she had come to accept Hugh as the most suitable man in the world.

*    *    *

The cavalcade was on its way to York and beside the young King rode his sister. Outwardly she looked serene and she was surprised that she could appear so indifferent to her fate. Since she had lost Hugh it did not seem to matter what became of her, so perhaps that was just as well.

Henry was pleased with her. 'I had feared you would weep, sister,' he said, 'for you are young to marry. But you will be nearer home than you would have been had you married into France. We shall be able to meet now and then. I promise you shall join us when we travel in the North. It will be easy for you to come across the Border. And your husband will be pleased with you for you are very fair to look upon. I tell you this: you have a certain look of our mother and I have heard it said that there was not a woman in the Courts of France or England to compare with her.'

'I have heard that said too,' replied Joan.

'And you will have the satisfaction of knowing that your marriage has brought peace to England and Scotland. There is nothing that brings peace to countries like marriage between the ruling families.'

'I could believe that to be so.'

'It is so, Joan; and how happy we should be that it is in our power to bring peace to so many.'

'I hope you will feel contented when your time comes, brother,' she retorted. 'But it will be different with you. You are the King and I doubt not you will have more say in whom you marry than a mere princess does.'

'I intend to,' said Henry, smiling complacently.

She looked at the pines of the horizon and thought of riding in the forest of Lusignan with Hugh before she had known he was in love with her mother.

In due course they arrived in York, where people ran from their houses to get a glimpse of the bride. They thought her beautiful and called God's blessing on her. She thanked them quietly and graciously; and she heard one old beldame murmur: 'Poor wee child. She's over young for marriage.'

This time there would be no cancellation. This marriage would take place, she feared.

She stood in the cathedral, which was said to be the most

beautiful in England, only vaguely aware of the grandeur of its massive buttresses decorated with ornamental tracery, its elegant niches and clustered pillars, and beside her was the stranger—this red fox, as she had heard him called—young, eager to please her, not unkindly; her husband, and she must be glad of this marriage since because of it peace would be brought to the borderlands of England and Scotland.

The ceremony was over. She was a Queen—a Queen of Scotland. Alexander took her hand and led her from the Abbey to the castle and the bells rang out long and loud in the city of York for this was a day of rejoicing.

They sat side by side at the banquet and he took the most choice pieces of meat and fed them to her. His hand closed over hers and he said: 'You must not be afraid of me, little wife.'

She looked at him intently and tried to read in his face what manner of man he was, and because he smiled reassuringly at her, her fear passed away.

While the celebrations for the union between England and Scotland and the peace it would bring were in progress another marriage took place at York. Hubert de Burgh married Alexander's sister Margaret.

Alexander was clearly delighted for his sister to marry the most important man in England; as for Henry, he was so fond of his Justiciar whom he also regarded as his greatest friend, that he was absolutely delighted to give his consent.

Hubert was not exactly a young man but his warm open manner had always won him adherents among young people. He was shrewd and ambitious but there was just that touch of emotionalism in his nature which brought him friendship, as it had in the case of the young Prince Arthur and now Henry.

Alexander had further reason for satisfaction, for his younger sister Isabella would shortly marry Roger the son of Hugh Bigod, Earl of Norfolk; and this meant that his sisters would have for their husbands two of the most influential noblemen of England. It was true that John had promised the two girls to Henry the King and his brother Richard, but marriages with them would not have been celebrated for years and delayed marriages very often meant none at all.

So, Alexander was delighted. He had the Princess Joan for himself and his two sisters would represent his cause in England and bring up their children to have very special feelings for Scotland.

He could now retire behind the Border and deal with the quarrelsome chieftains who were always ready to rise and plague him whenever he found himself in difficulties.

Joan and Alexander rode north while Hubert with his bride and his King went south.

Hubert could be forgiven for a certain complacency. There had been those who had prophesied disaster when William Marshal had died, but this had not proved to be the case. He could say that England had been governed with the utmost skill in the last two years; and as the King grew out of his childhood, providing he was ready to listen to advice, the country would grow stronger and as the country grew stronger, its Justiciar would be more and more appreciated and more powerful.

Now riding along beside the King, his young wife on the other side of him, he could give way to a certain amount of exuberance, although he was too experienced not to know that a man in his position must be ever watchful.

He was perhaps the richest man in the Kingdom. Margaret had brought a good dowry and of course he would now have especial influence with Scotland. He remembered that once William Marshal had said that when a man was at the height of his power was the time when he must be most watchful.

Henry was smiling happily.

'I think Alexander will be good to my sister,' he said, 'and she to him.'

'I am sure of it, my lord,' replied Hubert. 'He would not dare to be otherwise than good to the sister of the King of England.'

'My brother is not a man to be influenced by fear,' said Margaret gravely. 'He will be good to his wife because it is his duty and inclination to love and cherish her.'

'Well spoken, my love,' cried Hubert. 'Is that not so, my lord?'

'It is indeed,' replied Henry. 'And it pleases me that we

have brought harmony to the two kingdoms. It will show people how I intend to rule.'

He is growing up indeed, thought Hubert. He takes credit for these marriages as though they were brought about by him. Well, that is the way of kings, and it will be well when he can be seen as the ruler—as long as he remembers to follow the advice of those who serve him well.

So it was a happy party that rode into Westminster; even the wily and experienced Hubert had forgotten that success—which fate had so bountifully bestowed on him—invariably provokes the envy of the less well endowed.

# The Rebels

ALMOST immediately there was murmuring throughout the court about the Justiciar. His enemies were asking each other: Who is this man? Is he the King? He is the man who decides who shall marry whom and he makes sure that his pockets do not remain empty while he pulls the King's leading strings. Is it not time the Justiciar was made to realize he is not quite the King of England?

John had sown a great many seeds of discordancy when— to further his needs of the moment—he had given land and castles to foreigners in exchange for money or certain concessions, and this meant that in spite of the efforts of William Marshal and Hubert to eliminate the foreign influence, a certain element remained.

This group was led by the Earl of Chester, that Randulph de Blundervill, who had married Constance the widow of Geoffrey (brother of King John) and therefore became step-father to Prince Arthur who had been murdered by his uncle John. Chester had hoped at one time to put Arthur on the throne when he, Chester, would have proceeded to rule through the boy. Constance however had hated him and fled from him taking Arthur with her and, declaring that their marriage had never been consummated and therefore was no marriage at all, had taken as her husband Guy de Thouars. Constance had not lived long after that and when John had murdered Arthur that put an end to Chester's hopes of ruling through the boy, so he had turned his attention to other ambitious schemes. Now that the power of Hubert de Burgh was ever increasing Chester was determined to bring the object of his enmity from his high place; so he gathered about him those as discontented as himself.

Chief of these was perhaps Falkes de Breauté, a wild adventurer, a man who was capable of any violent deed to gain his ends. He was a Norman of obscure birth and illegitimate, who had come to the notice of King John, and being of a similar nature—irreligious, unscrupulous, ready to commit any cruel deed and in fact relishing the undertaking—the King had found him amusing, a good servant, and as he enjoyed his company was ready to reward him. Thus the Norman, who was little more than a peasant, had sprung into prominence.

When the barons had revolted against the King, Falkes had been at John's side and as a general in the King's army he had enjoyed some success. As a reward John promised to find a rich wife for him and had decreed that he should marry Margaret, the widow of Baldwin, Earl of Albemarle. Margaret was horrified to be given to this crude man, merely in order that her fortune might pass into his hands, but the King had said the marriage must take place and Margaret, knowing the kind of man with whom she had to deal, submitted, though with the utmost reluctance. As in addition to being the widow of a rich man, Margaret was an heiress in her own right, being the only child of rich parents, Falkes was doing well, for John had bestowed on him not only Margaret but the custody of the castles of Windsor, Cambridge, Oxford, Northampton and Bedford.

With Chester he captured the town of Worcester for the King, but his treatment of the prisoners did little to help the King's cause for Falkes took a special delight in torture and he considered it a great sport to capture the rich and torture them with all kinds of methods which it was one of his delights to devise until they had given up all they possessed to save themselves from further torment.

He had a special hatred for religious orders—or it might have been that he greatly coveted their treasures; but it seemed that if he came upon an abbey or a convent he must desecrate it. Sharing similar urges the King made no effort to deter him and in fact enjoyed being given accounts of Falkes's adventures among the priests.

But even he could be alarmed by what he had done and the story was often told of his fears after he had sacked St.

Alban's Abbey. He had pillaged the town, mutilated and tortured the inhabitants but the abbey was his real objective. Marching into the sacred building, overturning treasures as he went, he demanded that the abbot be brought to him.

The abbot came, loudly demanding to know whether Falkes de Breauté knew that he was in a house of God. Falkes's reply had been to laugh aloud and tell the abbot that he wanted one hundred pounds of silver and if it was not given to him without delay he would help himself to the treasures of the abbey and burn it down.

Knowing well the man with whom he had to deal and that he was capable of such an act of sacrilege the abbot gave him the silver.

Falkes had then left, taking sly looks about the place, noting the treasures for his future attention. That night he awoke from a terrible nightmare. He sat up in bed shouting that he was dying.

Margaret, who must have been relieved at the thought of having the monster removed from her life, said: 'You have had a dream . . . a nightmare. But nightmares can have meaning. What was the dream?'

It was not often that de Breauté allowed himself civil conversation but shivering in his bed, with the terrible fear upon him, he was not the same man as the braggart who swaggered through towns terrifying all those who came near him.

'I dreamed,' he said, 'that I was standing beneath the top tower of the Abbey of St. Alban's church when it fell upon me and where I had been there was nothing but powder . . . nothing of me remained.'

'A dream full of portent,' replied Margaret. 'You desecrated the holy Abbey. It means God is displeased with you.'

De Breauté would have laughed her to scorn at any other time, but he was truly shaken at this time.

'You must go back to the Abbey,' she advised him, 'and ask pardon of the abbot and the monks.'

'You mean a penance. . . .'

'The King's father did penance for the murder of Thomas à Becket.'

'And you would ask me to do likewise?'

'I ask nothing of you,' she replied. 'Experience has taught me that would be useless. I merely advise. You have desecrated a holy place . . . many holy places . . . but St. Albans will have special favour in Heaven. You have been warned by Heaven. The meaning of your dream is clear. Unless you make restitution some fearful fate will overtake you.'

She was obviously amused to see her husband so frightened that he shivered with fear at the prospect of a fate which he had administered with such delight to others. However, so did she terrify him, while pretending to be fearful for him, telling him stories she had heard of the terrible ends which befell those who ignored warnings from Heaven, that he decided he would go to St. Albans with all speed, insisting that the knights who had taken part in the raid on the Abbey should accompany him. There he called for the abbot who, wondering what fresh outrage was about to occur, came in fear, but when he saw the dreaded Falkes de Breauté baring his back and declaring that he had come to do penance—as King Henry II had done for Becket—he summoned his monks, and it is not difficult to imagine with what relish they belaboured the backs of those men who such a short while ago had threatened them.

When the chastisement was over, Falkes de Breauté put on his doublet and shouted that he had only done this because his wife had begged him to, and if the monks thought that what he had taken from them would be restored they were greatly mistaken.

However, he left the Abbey and did not practice further sacrilege. He turned his attention to the French who at this time held firm positions in England. The death of John, the accession of young Henry and the defeat of the French had not entirely pleased de Breauté for it had meant the rise to power of Hubert de Burgh, who had demanded the return to the crown of many of the castles which John had bestowed on men such as de Breauté. He was disturbed as were the Earl of Chester and the Bishop of Winchester by the growing power of Hubert. A King who was a minor was a heaven-sent opportunity for ambitious men, and all these men were ambitious, so to see Hubert taking the most powerful position in the kingdom irked them and they decided that something must be done to curb it.

The three men met in Winchester: Peter des Roches, the Bishop of Winchester, Randulph de Blundervill, Earl of Chester, and Falkes de Breauté; and the subject of their discourse was Hubert de Burgh and how to curb his growing power.

'He thinks there will be nothing to stop him now,' observed Peter des Roches. 'Each day he grows more in the King's favour.'

'The King is a child,' growled Chester. 'It is a matter of whose hand he falls into. It is you, my lord Bishop, who should be his governor and controller.'

'De Burgh has ever worked against me,' murmured the Bishop.

'This cannot be allowed to go on,' replied Chester.

'Perhaps we could make the King our prisoner,' suggested Falkes. 'We could catch him when he was riding . . . surround him by our men . . . and then . . . he would be ours to command.'

The Bishop shook his head. 'If that could be, I doubt not it would be an excellent way of dealing with the situation, but to take the King by force would be called treason . . . rebellion . . . or some such name. The people would not endure it. They would want our heads on pikes over the bridge. We must work more secretly.'

Falkes de Breauté looked disappointed. He was fascinated by violence and he saw himself running his sword through the bodies of the guard while he told the young King that all would go well with him if he came quietly.

'It would seem,' went on the Bishop, 'that de Burgh is the richest man in the kingdom. He has done well through his marriages.'

'One thing I'll say for him,' added de Breauté with a smirk, 'the women like him.'

'He has an ingratiating manner,' murmured the Bishop, 'and this has won the heart of the King.'

'And those of his wives!' added Chester. 'The Scottish Princess is the fourth . . . his only virgin. The rest were widows.'

'He has a fancy for widows,' said de Breauté.

'A wise fancy,' put in Chester, 'for a widow will often have her husband's fortune as well as that which may come to her through her own family.'

'So it was,' said the Bishop. 'The daughter of the Earl of Devon, and widow of William Brewer, brought him wealth; then there was Beatrice, Lord Bardulf's widow, and then he had the temerity to marry John's cast-off wife Hadwisa of Gloucester, who by that time was the widow of the Earl of Essex.'

'John took a considerable bite out of her fortune but she still had much left to help fill the coffers of shrewd Hubert,' commented Chester.

'I wonder how she liked Hubert after John,' asked Breauté with a sly smile.

'By all accounts she found the change agreeable,' said the Bishop. 'But she died as all his widows did, and my point is that there was not one marriage which did not bring him benefit. Now he has made the best of them all—he is brother to the King of Scotland, being his sister's husband.'

'You may judge a man by his marriages,' said Chester. 'De Burgh's have shown him to be a wise man with a taste for wealth.'

'It would be well if the people realized this,' said the Bishop. 'At this time they are pleased with their young King and the Justiciar's rule. He has subdued the robbers and if his punishments are severe, he would say—and many would be with him—that this is the only way to keep the law effective. It will not be difficult, though, to rouse the people against him. He has served the country they might say, but it must be made known to them that in doing so, he has made himself very rich. You all know that the best way to arouse the mob against any one man is to tell them that he has so much more than they have. They will accept a man's lechery, cruelty . . . his acts of expediency . . . but arouse their envy and they will be ready to bring him down. The people want justice in the land; they want law and order; they want to rid the country of those they call the foreigners, and methinks, gentlemen, that we should all of us fit into that category. They hate all this but their envy will be greater than their love of their country. So we will rouse the people against de

Burgh. We will tell them that he is the richest man in England. He has just brought himself more advantage by marrying the Princess of Scotland. Arouse the people's envy and in due course they will bring him down.'

The three men looked at each other and nodded.

They knew there was truth in the Bishop's words.

In the taverns the people of London whispered together; they walked along by the river and talked of the influence the Justiciar had over the young King. The Justiciar was the richest man in England. He governed the King and lined his own pockets. The servants of Falkes de Breauté and the Earl of Chester mingled with merchants and apprentices and asked them and each other why the people endured this state of affairs.

It was always the same when there was a young King on the throne, they pointed out. Ambitious men sought to rule through them; and their rule was to fill their own coffers and the devil take the man and woman in the streets.

So the resentment grew against Hubert de Burgh and when he rode out with the King there was hostility in the silence which greeted them; there was an occasion when someone threw a stone at the Justiciar. One of Hubert's servants caught the man and his punishment was severe—the loss of the right hand which had thrown the stone.

A bitter reward, said many, for that which others would have the inclination to do had they been on the spot.

One of the principal citizens, Constantine FitzAthulf, called meetings in his house and there he with others plotted the overthrow of the King and planned to send a message to Prince Louis at the French Court asking him to come back to England where he would find the people of London ready to welcome him.

As a result there was rioting in the streets of London and Constantine marched at the head of a band of men shouting 'Montjoie. God and our Lord Louis to the rescue.'

But the majority of the people, while they wished to remove the Justiciar, had no desire to bring the French back to England. This had not been the intention of Falkes de Breauté and his friends. All they wanted was to keep the King where he was but change his advisers so that they could step into the shoes of Hubert de Burgh and in doing so rob him of his power and riches. For this reason there was little support for the rioters of London and in a short time they were routed and Constantine FitzAthulf and other leaders captured and thrown into prison.

Hubert was deeply disturbed. He must rid himself of Constantine and Hubert believed that he deserved to be condemned to the traitor's death for if ever a man was a traitor to his King that man was Constantine. Hubert paused though, for he knew how unwise it would be to anger the people of London even more so than they were at this time.

He kept the men in prison while he wrestled with the problem; and in the end it was Falkes—the very man who had provoked the rebellion—who came to Hubert and offered to hang Constantine, assuring all who would listen to him that the last thing he wanted was to depose the King. He took Constantine and his friends across the river and in a quiet spot hanged them.

This did not mean that Falkes and his friends had ended their attacks on the Justiciar. They had no intention of doing this until they had rid the country of him.

They met again and Falkes put forward a plan for seizing the Tower of London. The Bishop of Winchester stressed the difficulties of bringing this about; and suggested that it would be better if they formed a deputation and called on the King, when the Justiciar was absent and pointed out the true nature of Hubert de Burgh and the need for him to rid himself of him.

The Bishop thought this was an excellent plan. They would come to Westminster and there Henry would receive them. He would be unprepared for what they would say to him and they had no doubt that, since he was little more than a child, they could win him to their point of view and get a promise from him to turn Hubert de Burgh from his office.

They chose their moment and the Bishop's presence secured them an immediate audience with the King.

It was the first time Henry had received a deputation without having had either William Marshal, Stephen Langton or Hubert de Burgh beside him to tell him what he must do.

It was the Bishop of Winchester who addressed him and presented Falkes de Breauté and the Earl of Chester to him.

'Your humble servants, most gracious lord,' murmured the Bishop.

Henry inclined his head and bade them rise for they were kneeling before him which while it gratified him made him feel a little awkward. He told them they might be seated. They were so much taller than he was while they stood, which he found disconcerting.

'You have missed the Justiciar,' said Henry. 'He is not in London this day.'

'It was our purpose to miss him, my lord,' answered the Bishop. 'It was our King with whom we wished to speak.'

'Say on,' said Henry, beginning to feel more important with every passing second, which was exactly their intention.

'It has long been apparent to us,' said the Bishop, 'that you, our King, have been endowed with wisdom beyond your years, and we feel the time has come for you to take a more active part in affairs. You have no need to be constantly attended by your wet nurse.'

'My . . . wet nurse. . . . You mean Hubert. . . .'

'We are of the opinion that the Justiciar believes you still to be in swaddling clothes. He guides your tottering baby steps, does he not, my lord?'

Henry flushed. 'You are mistaken,' he said angrily.

'Do not imagine that we think you to be in need of such support, my lord. It is for that reason that we have come here.'

'I think you should state your business,' said Henry with dignity.

'You know, my lord, that we have trouble in London.'

'I know,' said Henry, 'that traitors were hanged for declaring themselves supporters of the French.'

'It is the Justiciar whom the people dislike,' said the Earl of Chester. 'It is their hatred of him which makes them revolt.'

'I think not,' retorted Henry. 'They were shouting for the French.'

'There has been much murmuring against Hubert de Burgh,'

the Bishop tried to explain. 'If he were removed, you would find the country in a very different mood.'

'Remove Hubert? He is my very good friend.'

'He is his own very good friend, my lord. Did you know how rich he has become?'

'I know full well that he has been rewarded and rightly so. I myself have given him castles.'

'And he has done very well with his wives,' added de Breauté slyly.

Henry conveyed by a certain regal manner that the man's coarseness offended him; and the Bishop signed to de Breauté to allow him to do the talking.

'My lord,' said des Roches ingratiatingly, 'out of respect for you and the Crown we have come to you in this way. We have seen with admiration how you have grown in stature since the crown was put on your head. You do not need such counsel. You are well able to manage your own affairs.'

'I am not forced to obey the Justiciar, you should know,' retorted Henry. 'I use my own judgment . . . frequently.'

'Which is the very reason why you can dispense with this man.'

'Dispense with him! You mean send him away, or would you like me to rob him of his estates? To send him to the Tower perhaps? To punish him in some way—to put out his eyes . . . to cut off a limb or two.' Henry was looking straight at de Breauté. 'I believe that you, Falkes de Breauté, oft times employ such methods. I will tell you this, my lords, you may go from here. I like not your words. I like not your manners and I like not you.'

They were taken aback. They had come expecting to face a boy of fourteen and they had found a King, moreover one who was loyal to his friends and would have none of their treachery.

The reaction of the King forced the conspirators to abandon hope of a quick victory. Peter des Roches was beginning to feel that it was time they shelved their plans for a while, but he had reckoned without Falkes de Breauté who had already summoned the malcontents of Northampton, with plans for marching on London.

Henry had quickly summoned Hubert who laid the matter before Stephen Langton and·as a result the Archbishops and Bishops—with the exception of Peter des Roches—stood firmly with the King, and threatened excommunication for the rebels.

Even Falkes had to see that his small troop of malcontents would have no chance against the King's army and if those who rebelled were excommunicated they could never gather together the necessary men to work with them.

It was defeat. Nor were they to be let off lightly. The leaders were summoned to Westminster where the Archbishops and Bishops invited them to lay their grievances before the King.

They met in the great hall of the Palace, the King since his encounter with the three rebels grown considerably in dignity. Hubert had told him that he had conducted himself like a king, and he would have said the same even if he had not been so completely loyal to himself.

Henry was seated on the chair of state, Hubert was on his right hand; and Stephen Langton, on the other side of the King, invited the Bishop of Winchester to state his grievance.

Peter des Roches, addressing the assembly, declared that he was no traitor and nor were those who stood with him. They had deplored the rising of the citizens of London who had been ready to invite the French into the land. One of their members, Falkes de Breauté, had actually carried out the hanging of Constantine FitzAthulf. Their grievance was this: the King was never allowed to act unless one man was always at his elbow. It was not Henry III who reigned, it was Hubert de Burgh. All he and his followers wanted was to see that man removed, and the King to engage a new minister in the place of de Burgh.

Henry said: 'I have spoken to you on this matter before, Bishop. I like not your tone. I am at this time very well served and have been so since I took the Crown.'

'My lord King, Hubert de Burgh has enriched himself. His policy is to pour gold into his own coffers and if by so doing the Crown should suffer he cares not.'

Hubert rose and asked the King's permission to speak.

'Pray do,' said Henry. 'Add your voice to mine and we will let these traitors know that we are of like mind.'

'I thank you, my lord,' said Hubert. 'You, Bishop, are at the root of this trouble. It is you who have incited these men. You want my position for yourself. I understand that well, but our King is no puppet to be jerked this way and that. He will choose his ministers where he likes—and I doubt very much that if I were removed from his service—which God forbid—that you would be chosen to take my place.'

Peter des Roches was white with rage. He shouted: 'I tell you this, Hubert de Burgh, I will spend every penny I possess to prove that you are unworthy of office and to get you turned out.'

Then he turned and stormed out of the hall.

There was silence. Then Henry said: 'We see what a malicious man we have in the Bishop of Winchester. I would have you know that I will no longer tolerate these rebellious subjects.'

Hubert said: 'My lord, if you give me your wishes with regard to them I will act upon them.'

'That I shall quickly decide,' said the King.

'In the meantime, my lord, we shall see that they do not have the opportunity to escape,' said Hubert.

Stephen Langton said that such dissensions were bad for the country and he believed that troublemakers should be put where they could make no more trouble.

The assembly seemed to be in agreement and all except the rebels were delighted with the King's show of strength.

The result was that shortly afterwards an assize was held at Dunstable and the castles of the men accused of treason were confiscated. De Breauté would not give in easily and he fortified himself at Bedford Castle and when the justices were on their way to deal with him they learned that he was waiting for them with men to capture them, and remembering his reputation for torturing his victims they decided to escape. There was one who did not succeed in this, Henry de Brayboc who was undersheriff of Rutlandshire, Buckinghamshire and Northamptonshire, and had at first supported John against the barons but later had seen the barons' point of view and had changed sides. When Louis was defeated he had

professed loyalty to Henry—as so many had—and consequently his lands were restored.

Brayboc was seized by de Breauté's men and dragged into the
castle where he was roughly treated. He was terrified, knowing the reputation of de Breauté, but fortunately for him one
of his servants was able to carry the news of his capture to his
wife and she lost no time in sending a message to the King,
who was then with the parliament in Northampton. She pointed
out that her husband, in his role of justice, had been arrested
by a rebel when he was on the King's business.

Henry was now realizing that he must take a strong hand
and how wise it was to let none say that he was afraid of his
subjects.

He suggested that he would march to Bedford and there
himself take de Breauté.

Falkes de Breauté was not the man to despair in such
circumstances. In fact they appealed to him. His colleagues
had dispersed and he was left to do lonely battle. All right, he
declared, the castle could withstand the King's army. If this
was battle let it be; and so the siege began.

It continued all through June and July and into August.
Falkes was excommunicated; and when his wife declared that
she had been forced into marriage with him and implored the
King to give her a divorce and free her from the monster she
loathed, the divorce was granted; but Falkes continued to hold
out against the King's army. Randulf de Blundervill, Earl of
Chester, had begun to deplore Falkes's methods. He was too
crude; he should have known that he was beaten temporarily
and withdrawn as Chester had, to fight another day. These
bold defiant gestures would bring him no good and he should
not have been such a fool as to imagine they would.

Chester joined the King and Falkes realized that he alone
was to bear the responsibility of the rebels, for Peter des
Roches had become very silent and was also content to wait
for a later opportunity to oust Hubert de Burgh from his
position.

The castle could not hold out indefinitely and on a hot
August day Falkes was forced to surrender. Eighty of the
garrison were hanged, but Falkes was held for trial.

He asked for an audience with the King which Henry granted. Then Falkes threw himself at Henry's feet.

'I have done wrong,' he told him. 'But you are a just King, my lord, and you will remember that there was a time when I fought side by side with your father. I served him well, and because you are a wise king you will remember that a man's good deeds should be taken into consideration when he is being tried for his bad ones.'

That appealed to Henry and he sent Falkes to the Bishop of London where he was to remain until it was decided what should be done with him.

He was imprisoned for some time before it was agreed that he should be exiled. Then he was sent to France.

'Let us hope,' said Hubert, 'that that is the end of this troublemaker.'

Then he told the King that he had shown himself fit to govern without a Regent; and with his permission he would send to the Pope and ask for his blessing, support and permission that the King from henceforth be the ruler of his people.

The King was savouring his triumph—for all agreed that he had shown himself to have the making of a strong ruler by the manner in which he had dealt with the rebellious Falkes de Breauté and his friends—when Hubert de Burgh came to him with news which he believed to be of the utmost importance to England and to the King.

'Messengers have arrived from France, my lord,' he announced. 'The King of France is dead.'

'So Louis is now King.' Henry's face hardened. He would never forget that for a short time Louis had been in England and was on the point of being proclaimed ruler of his country. If John had not died so opportunely, who could say what might have happened. Henry went on: 'Perhaps now he will have enough to occupy him in France and will no longer look to England—for I believe that he has never failed to do that since we turned him out.'

'There has always been conflict between France and England, my lord. It seems hardly likely that the death of Philip will change that.'

'I am aware that my ancestors knew little peace. They had

few opportunities of governing here because there was always trouble in Normandy. It almost proved the undoing of my father.'

'Your father proved his own undoing,' said Hubert soberly. 'You, my lord, will I doubt not regain much that he lost, and not only your possessions overseas but the dignity of the crown through honour and justice.'

'I pray God this may be so.'

'That is good, my lord. Now let us look at this matter overseas and consider what it can mean to England.'

'I can see only good in it. I do not have a great opinion of Louis.'

'Louis is an honourable man—a good husband and father. Such men do not always make the best kings.'

'He quickly relinquished his hold on England and went slinking back home.'

'He knew the country was against him and he took the wise though not the bold action.'

'Methinks, Hubert, he will want to stay within his own realms.'

Hubert was thoughtful. 'I was not thinking so much of the King as the Queen. I believe that Blanche, now Queen of France, is the one we have to reckon with.'

'A woman!'

'You are too wise, my lord, not to know that they should never be lightly dismissed. There are some—and many of them, thanks be to God—who are content to administer to a husband's needs, to work beautiful embroideries and decorate his house with their presence. But there have been some who have not been content so to remain. One of these I believe to be the Queen of France.'

'She is a kinswoman of mine. It was because of her that Louis laid claim to the throne.'

'She is your first cousin, being the daughter of your Aunt Eleanor who married Alphonso of Castile; her grandparents were therefore yours. It is difficult to imagine a granddaughter of Henry II and Eleanor of Aquitaine as being without spirit.'

'So you think we must be watchful of Blanche, though she is married to a weak husband.'

'I am sure you know, my lord, that it is a mistake to confuse a quiet demeanour with a lack of strength. Louis is not warlike. He does not wish to fight where it is not necessary and that could be called wisdom.'

Henry smiled to himself. He noticed how Hubert always prefaced his homilies nowadays with 'I am sure you know'. Before his defence of him when he had been confronted by the rebellious barons and the Bishop of Winchester, he had delivered them in the form of lessons.

Henry said: 'So you think we must be watchful of Blanche?'

'You will agree that the English must always be watchful of the French, and what is happening in France will always be of the utmost importance to us here. We can never forget that. So, now Philip Augustus is dead and Louis and Blanche are on the throne. Let us consider what this will mean to us.'

'What will it mean, Hubert?'

'We must wait and see how events develop.'

'And in the meantime,' added Henry, 'remember they are enemies, for that is what they must be. Louis and Blanche . . . and in particular Blanche.'

# FRANCE
## 1200–1223

# A Change of Brides

It was the first year of the new century; King John had been on the throne of England a year and Philip Augustus reigned in France. The affairs of these Kings seemed of little concern to the three girls who chatted together in their father's court of Castile where the sun shone throughout the long summer days and the greatest excitement was the arrival of a troubadour who would enchant them with new songs which in a short time they would all be singing.

Their father, King Alphonso VIII, and their mother Eleanor, daughter of Henry II of England, were a well-matched pair. They loved the sun and music, and delighted in their Court which under their influence was becoming one of the most cultivated in Europe. They enjoyed the company of their daughters, Berengaria, Urraca and Blanca, and took a great interest in their education. All the girls were handsome and intelligent; they were graceful, elegant and because music was of the greatest importance at the Court of Castile they were well versed in that art.

Contrary to the custom of the times Alphonso and Eleanor spent as much time as they could with their children; and they liked to pass their days in merriment and singing, dancing, and the telling of tales.

Eleanor had much to tell and she was determined that her children should not be brought up in the manner she herself had. Life in the nursery of Westminster, Winchester and Windsor had been fraught with tension and it had been no different in Normandy or Poitiers. Wherever she had been her life had been overshadowed by the conflict between her parents and she had quickly learned that this was due to her father's infidelities and her mother's forceful nature which would not allow her to accept these with equanimity. When her father had brought his bastard into the nursery that had really been the end of harmony between him and her mother.

Eleanor remembered their shouting at each other and the culmination of their quarrels when her mother had roused his sons against the King their father and as a result had herself been imprisoned for many years.

She was determined that her children should know a happy home and the Court of Castile should be far away—and not only in miles—from those in which she had passed her childhood.

The girls always wanted to hear stories of her childhood and she had thought it good for them to hear that they might appreciate the happiness of Castile and their kindly parents.

Alphonso was proud of them and there was little he liked better than to be in their company. His fond eyes would follow them, admiring, loving and he would smile affectionately at his wife and say God had been good to them.

It was scarcely possible that such a paradise should not have its serpent. When she was very young Blanca thought this was the Saracens, because there was a great deal of talk about them and the name was spoken with awe and fear. Her father had constantly to leave them to fight the Saracens—and alas, he was not always successful. Then there would be gloom in the palace and the sisters would talk about the wicked Saracens and wonder whether they would ever invade the palace and carry them off to be slaves.

None of this happened and when she was nine years old Blanca realized that there could be as great a threat to the peaceful days as the advent of the Saracens.

She was nine years old when, one day, as the girls were at their lessons a message came for Berengaria, the eldest, to go to their parents who had something of importance to say to her.

Urraca and Blanca were a little put out, for usually the girls shared everything. They knew that visitors had arrived at the castle and that their parents had given them a very warm welcome and Blanca immediately said that the summons for Berengaria must in some way be connected with the visitors.

What it could be, they could not imagine, but they were not left long in doubt.

Berengaria came into the schoolroom, her face blank as though something very bewildering had happened and she could not understand what it meant.

Her sisters immediately demanded to know whom she had met and what she had seen and why it was they were not invited to the meeting.

Berengaria sat down and blurted out: 'I have been seeing the emissaries.'

'What emissaries?'

'Of the King of Léon.'

'But why do you see them and not us?'

'Because I am the eldest.'

'But why . . . why?' demanded Blanca who, although younger than Urraca, usually took the lead.

'A terrible thing has happened I . . . I'm going to be married to Alfonso of Léon.'

'Married!' cried Blanca. 'You. How can you? You're not old enough.'

'They think I am.' Berengaria flung herself at her sisters, clinging to them. 'Oh, I have to go away . . . right away from here. I shall never see you again.'

'Léon is not so very far away,' said Blanca.

'We'll all come to see you and you must come here to see us,' consoled Urraca.

'You won't be here. It'll happen to you. You'll both have to marry too.'

Urraca and Blanca looked at each other in dismay. It would happen, of course. It happened to all. Their long carefree days would cease and their enchanted childhood would end.

'At least your husband has the same name as our father,' said Blanca soothingly, 'so he can't be so bad.'

'I wonder what the names of our husbands will be,' said Urraca.

At which Berengaria cried out: 'You are so young . . . too young to understand. What do *names* matter? I'm going away . . . right away. . . . It's never going to be the same again.'

\*    \*    \*

Nor was it, for understanding had come to them. Like Adam and Eve they had eaten of the tree of knowledge, and they were now aware that life could change.

In due course Berengaria went away and married the King of Léon. Their parents pacified her and told her that all would be well. She was going to be a queen and that was a very pleasant thing to be. She would help to rule with her Alfonso. Think how exciting that would be. And there would be occasions when the King and Queen of Léon would visit the King and Queen of Castile.

But Berengaria could not be easily appeased. She was going to a strange land and leaving the happy home of her childhood.

Her parting words were ominous. 'Your turn will come.'

They missed Berengaria but after a while they became accustomed to being without her and for three years nothing was said of marriage, but it was inevitable that it must come sooner or later.

This time both girls were summoned to their parents. Eleanor looked a little sad and as she drew them to her and held them close, a foreboding touched them, because what had happened to Berengaria had warned them.

Each girl was afraid—Urraca because she guessed it was for her the next husband had been found, and Blanca because she believed she would be the one to be left behind. They had missed their eldest sister, but at least there had been two of them—now she would be alone.

'This is really very good news,' said Eleanor. 'There could not be a grander match for you.'

She was looking at Urraca who began to tremble.

'Don't be afraid, child,' went on Eleanor. 'Your father and I assure you that unless this was the best for you we would never consider it. But we should be foolish indeed were we to refuse such an honour. Few princesses could receive a greater. Urraca, my dearest, the King of France has sent messengers to your father. He wants you as a bride for his son, Louis. We shall tell him that we are conscious of this great honour and when the settlement has been arranged there need be no delay in uniting our families.'

Urraca looked as though she would burst into tears and her

mother took her hands and cried: 'Why, my child, you should be rejoicing. Do you realize what this means? Berengaria is the Queen of Léon and that is very fine, but you will be the Queen of France. There is nothing better I could wish for you.'

'But I must go away and leave you all. . . .'

'Dearest Urraca, it is the lot of all princesses. You have been fortunate. You have learned how to make a happy home for the family you will have. I know, my dear daughter, that you are going to be so happy.'

'I'm not, I'm not,' sobbed Urraca. 'I want to stay with you and our father and Blanca.'

'I don't want her to go,' cried Blanca. 'I shall be all alone.'

'Not for long, my dear. Very soon a husband will be found for you and if he is as suitable as those of your sisters, your father and I will be proud and happy. Now listen to me. Your grandmother is so pleased with the match that she is coming here. She will take you, Urraca, to the Court of France and stay with you until you are safely married—so eager is she for the match and so important does she find the matter.'

'My grandmother!' cried Urraca in even greater dismay. It was bad enough to have to face a husband but in the company of that formidable lady it would be an even greater ordeal.

The redoubtable Eleanor of Aquitaine—eighty years of age though she was—made the long journey from Fontevrault, where she had hoped to spend her last days in peace and, it was whispered, repentance for a scarcely blameless life.

Great preparations were in progress at the Castile castle, for Eleanor of Castile was in awe of her mother now as she always had been; and Urraca and Blanca wanted to hear everything their mother had to tell about their grandmother.

They knew already that she had gone to the Holy Land with her first husband—another Louis who had been a King of France—and how she had come near to death in the midst of battles between Christian and Saracens. She had divorced Louis and married Henry, the King of England, and then had lived that wild and adventurous life with him which had culminated in her becoming his prisoner.

Their mother warned them. 'You must take the greatest

care of your manner towards her. If you offend her she will let you know it. Her temper was often a little uncertain and now she is suffering a great tragedy. Your Uncle Richard has died so lately and I can imagine what great sorrow this has caused her.' Their mother's eyes grew misty as she looked back over the past. 'Richard was always her favourite. How she doted on him. He was very handsome. She taught him to hate our father and he learned his lesson well.'

'That was not right, was it, my lady?' asked Blanca. 'Should a son be taught to hate his father?'

'My mother did what she considered right for herself. She never obeyed rules. Nay, my child, it would have been better for all if she had taught him tolerance. But she is a proud woman, the proudest I ever knew. She is very old now. Yet she comes here. I tremble fearing that she may not survive the journey. But when her family need her she will be there.'

'Why do we need her?' asked Urraca. 'Cannot the marriage be made without her?'

'It is a very important marriage.' Their mother lowered her voice. 'Far far more important than that of your sister. Your grandmother is eager that nothing shall go wrong, so she will take you to the Court of France and see you married herself.'

'Does she think the King would not let me marry his son if she did not insist?'

'In these matters, certain details can go wrong and this may spoil arrangements. Your grandmother wishes nothing to go wrong. She is very eager for this match. Therefore she will take you to the Court of France and see the ceremony performed perhaps . . . or at least make sure that it will be performed.'

'So I shall travel with her,' murmured Urraca.

'Be of good cheer, my child,' said her mother. 'Life will become wonderful for you. You are going to a great country. You have a wonderful destiny before you.'

Blanca asked: 'Shall I have a great destiny too, my lady?'

'I doubt it not, my love,' answered Eleanor. 'But Urraca's bridegroom will be the King of France and there are few greater destinies than that.'

Each day they watched from the castle turrets for the coming of their grandmother.

\*    \*    \*

When she came she was every bit as formidable as they had imagined.

She came riding at the head of the party and she called out as soon as she entered the courtyard: 'Where is my daughter?'

Eleanor the younger was there. The old Queen had dismounted and taken her daughter into her arms. She held her tightly and would not release her for some time. Then she drew back to look at her and declared she seemed in good health and turning to Alfonso she said in a loud ringing voice: 'And I should have wanted an answer from you, my lord, if my daughter had not been well cared for.'

'My lady mother has not changed,' said Eleanor; and she kept the old Queen's hands in hers as they came into the castle.

What feasting there was! Each day the hunters had brought in fine bucks and they had been baking in the kitchen in readiness for the arrival of the old Queen. Her daughter wished her to rest awhile but she would not hear of it; and she sat at the table while the troubadours played and sang their songs and she took a lute too and with the minstrels sang the songs she had sung as a girl; and it seemed she was very happy to be with her daughter.

It astonished the girls that she could be so tender; they had thought such a formidable old woman would never look so lovingly on any as she did on their mother.

She had eyed the girls rather sharply, and when they had both kissed her hand, they felt awkward under her scrutiny. She had asked of their mother: 'You have brought them up well, have you? Their manners must be graceful. You know the French.'

Their mother said that she did not think even the French would have aught of which to complain.

At which their grandmother turned her attention from her granddaughters and gave herself up to contemplating her daughter.

That night the two girls lay on their pallets and talked about the future. They were both sad, yet excited. It was hard to imagine life without each other—yet Berengaria had gone and they scarcely missed her now.

'I wish,' said Blanca, 'that we did not have to grow up.'

'And there are years and years ahead of us,' sighed Urraca, 'if we are going to be as old as our grandmother.'

Then they talked of what they thought it would be like at the Court of France and Blanca was sad for she said that all the excitement would be Urraca's and it is easier to accept change when it is exciting.

'But your turn will come, Blanca. I wonder whom they will find for you?'

'Of one thing we are certain: it cannot be such a grand match as yours.'

In the next few days they saw a great deal of their grandmother, who made a point of being with them and drawing them out. Blanca had always been quicker than her sisters to grasp a point; her mother had told their father that it was because of her youth and she felt the need to keep up with her sisters. However she had often surpassed them and this sharpness of wit quickly became apparent to Eleanor of Aquitaine.

When she walked in the gardens she would select Blanca on whose arm to lean. 'Come and walk with me, child,' she would say. 'I need an arm on which to lean.'

Then she would ask about life in Castile and what their tutors taught them; and she would shoot questions at Blanca and sometimes was amused at the answers she received. After supper when the candles with their cotton wicks flickered in the sconces she would ask Blanca to sing for her; and sometimes she would join in the song. She had a firm voice which belied her years.

'Your mother has taken a great fancy to Blanca,' said Alfonso to his wife.

As the days passed it was clear that the old Queen grew very thoughtful. She would sit watching the girls, her brows knit, a strange expression on her face, as though she were trying to solve some problem.

It was late one night, after the household had retired, that she went to that chamber shared by her daughter and her husband and told one of the guards in the passage outside that she wished to speak to the King and Queen of Castile. She would go to them; all she needed was for them to be prepared for her coming.

Her daughter was not as astonished as she might have been.

'My mother has never acted as others did before,' she explained to Alfonso. 'Many considered her actions strange. But it must mean that she has something important to say to us, since she comes thus by night.' She then ordered the servants to light more candles and she and Alfonso, wrapped in night robes, awaited the coming of the Queen.

She came in, as though there were nothing unusual in this nocturnal meeting.

'I have the solution,' she said as she seated herself on a stool. 'It has been puzzling me almost since the day I arrived here, because it was clear to me that the future Queen of France should be Blanca.'

'But how can that be . . .' began Alfonso.

The old Queen held up her hand and said: 'It can well be. Instead of my taking Urraca to France, I shall take Blanca.'

'But it is Urraca . . .'

'The French King will welcome my granddaughter to France to marry his son. There is no stipulation as to which granddaughter. The girl's *name* is of no importance . . . yet in a manner it is of the utmost importance. That is my point. The French will never accept Urraca. What can they call her? With a name like that she is doomed to remain a foreigner all her life. Blanca. That is different. They will call her Blanche and make her one of them—and with her wit and drive she will be a worthy Queen of France. That is what I have come to tell you, my son and daughter. Blanca shall go to France. We must find another suitor for Urraca.'

Alfonso said: 'My lady, we understand well your thoughts and intentions, but we should need time to think of this matter.'

'There is not much time,' retorted the old lady brusquely. 'But you may have two days in which to decide and I shall now make my preparations to leave with Blanca. I think from now on we should begin to call her Blanche.'

The weeks that followed were quite bewildering to Blanca— or Blanche as she must now think of herself.

She had been summoned to the presence of her parents and

grandmother and briefly informed that plans had been changed. She, not Urraca, was to go to France in the care of her grandmother in order that she might marry the son of the King of France.

Poor Urraca had been quite shocked; and, although she had wept at the thought of leaving her home, she now wept because she was going to stay in it a little longer. Blanche understood her feelings and tried to comfort her.

'My grandmother has done this,' cried Urraca. 'She did not like me from the start. You were her favourite.'

Blanche shook her head. 'How could anyone know to whom such a person would take a fancy? Oh Urraca, I don't want to go. I don't like any of it. It is so . . . undignified . . . it makes us so unimportant . . . don't you see? Just like counters. You can have one of them . . . this one or that one . . . it doesn't matter which.'

'If you can change your name, why couldn't I have changed mine?'

'Mine is not really a change. It's just the translation. You can't translate Urraca.'

'I wish our grandmother had never come here. I'm not surprised her husband put her into prison.'

'Poor Urraca,' said Blanche. 'Don't fret so. It may well be the time will come when you will see this as a stroke of great good fortune for yourself.'

Urraca looked solemnly at her sister and then threw herself into her arms. 'I don't want anything bad to happen to you, sister.'

'Perhaps it won't. In any case I shall do my best to stop it.'

Urraca looked at her sister intently. 'I think you will,' she said. 'I believe I understand now why our grandmother chose you to go to France.'

The old Queen rode much of the time in her litter, for the journey was long and arduous, and even her indomitable will could not command her bones not to ache or the exhaustion not to overcome her. Blanche rode close to the litter on her white palfrey; and there were frequent halts for rests. They stayed at inns and castles and the Queen would lie on her pallet and have her granddaughter sit beside her that they might talk together.

It was an education for Blanche and she was sure she learned more about the world in those weeks of travel than she had done during the whole of her childhood. Queen Eleanor awakened her to a new world, a world of excitement, adventure and danger; far far away was the sunny court of Castile where her fond parents had guarded her and her sisters from the world.

Eleanor talked of her own childhood when she had graced her father's Court with her sister Petronilla. What a Court that had been! The prevailing passion had been music and the greatest poets of the day and finest composers and singers had flocked there to delight the company. Eleanor remembered summer evenings in the scented gardens while the strains of music filled the air and all listened entranced to accounts of unrequited or fulfilled love—whichever it was the poet's fancy to indulge. And at this Court Eleanor had reigned supreme. There, she had been the most beautiful of women— that was credible, for in spite of the ravages of the years she retained that exquisite bone structure which even time could not change; and as she talked she glowed with an inner fire so it was not difficult to imagine that her picture of herself was not entirely without foundation.

'There are women in this world,' she said, 'who are meant to rule. You are one, Blanche. I saw it in you from the first day. Urraca! A pleasant creature—she has some beauty, grace, charm . . . yes. But not the power to rule. How angry I used to be, how frustrated to have been born a woman. When I was young I used to fear that my father would remarry. If he had got a son that puling infant would have come before me. Before me! I, who ruled that Court. And I did, Blanche, I do assure you. I ruled that Court and because I was a woman, if my father had had a son . . . who would have been years my junior . . . he would have come before me. He did not. But that made me none the less resentful. Why should a woman be debarred from rule when she has all the qualities to make a ruler?'

Blanche agreed that there seemed no logical reason for this.

'I have made it my affair to learn something of your future

husband. I have a feeling that he is not unlike his grandfather and if that be so I can tell you much about the boy who is to be your husband, for his grandfather was once my husband. Yes, I was Queen of France and my husband was Louis VII. Yours will be Louis VIII. My Louis . . . oh I was fond of him in the beginning. He was a good man, but good men can exasperate, granddaughter. He should have been a churchman. He was made to have been a churchman; he studied for it and would have been if his brother had not been killed by a pig. Yes, a pig, who ran under his horse and threw it so that he died . . . and that left my Louis to be King. How small things affect the fate of nations. Never forget that, my child. A pig changed the fate of France! Poor Louis, God was unfair to him. . . . He gave him France and me.'

'But you loved him at first, my lady.'

'Oh yes. I loved him because I could do what I wished with him. Then we took the cross and went to the Holy Land—for as I said Louis was a very religious man.'

'And you too, my lady, for you went with him . . . you a woman.'

'I have told you, child, that a woman is capable of doing most that a man can, and I did not go for religion but for adventure. And adventure I had. Oh, I could tell you . . . but I will not . . . not now. There are more important things to discuss. And I am tired now and would sleep.'

Blanche was disappointed. She would have liked to hear her grandmother's account of those fantastic adventures in the Holy Land.

On another occasion Eleanor told of her marriage to the King of England.

'He was younger than I . . . a fact he never let me forget when there was conflict between us. It was good in the beginning though. He was so young . . . different from his father. Geoffry of Anjou was one of the handsomest men I ever met. Henry didn't take after his father . . . in any way. All he had from him was his name, Plantagenet. He had much of his great grandfather, William the Conqueror, in him and a bit of his grandfather too—perhaps a dash of his Mother Matilda for he could rage in his fury at times as she could. But he was a

King. . . . You knew that as soon as you met him. It seemed then that he was the right mate for me . . . and so he was . . . in a way. If only he hadn't been such a lecher. . . . Now, my child, you have to grow up fast. There is a feeling in the world that it is fitting for a man to roam from his marriage bed and take what mistresses he will, but if a woman should likewise stray that is criminal. I never did accept these differences. I pray that you will have a faithful husband. It may well be. My first, Louis, was a faithful husband. My second, Henry, the biggest lecher of his day. Odd that I cared more for Henry. You will take Louis as a boy for he is no older than you . . . perhaps a month or two but that is nothing . . . and if you can keep him a faithful husband you will have achieved much, for it is in bed at night that promises are given and sometimes kept. Try to make sure that those promises are given to you. I talk to you beyond your understanding perhaps, but you will learn in time.'

'You are teaching me much, my lady.'

'Experience is the best teacher,' replied the Queen, 'but can be a harsh one. Yet it is so much easier to learn from one's own experiences than from those of others.'

On they rode through Castile towards the mountain barrier of the Pyrenees. There the passes were narrow and the cold intense. Blanche became anxious about her grandmother, for the old lady was clearly feeling the strains of the journey.

Blanche was already fond of her and looking forward with immense pleasure to their conversations. She was growing up fast; she was no longer a child; and she realized that what her grandmother was doing was preparing her for her new life.

On one occasion they stayed in a small dwelling in the mountains; the snow was falling and it was necessary for them to stay there for several days. There Blanche noticed how the cold exhausted her grandmother and how difficult it was for her to breathe.

Eleanor did not seem disturbed as long as Blanche was at her side.

'You must not fear for me, child,' she told her. 'My end is not far off. I know that well. Why bless you, I have been close to my end—so it was said—for the last ten years, and as

I go on, still it recedes and will not let me catch up. I shall finish this journey. I shall go back to Fontevrault. There I have to pray and be pious for I have many sins to expiate. Nothing would have brought me from my refuge except the needs of my family. I fear for my family, Blanche, oh, I fear greatly. But since I lost my son . . . my beloved son . . . there is not so much to live for.'

'Pray, Grandmother, do not speak thus.'

'Ah, there is something between us two, is there not? 'Tis a pity I am so old and you are so young. The gap is too great for that understanding between us to grow big. Still, 'tis a hardy little plant and it gives me pleasure to contemplate it. Blanche . . . you are indeed of my blood. But Richard is gone for ever. My son . . . the son I loved best in all the world. I wish you could have known Richard, Blanche. He was so beautiful. The Lion Hearted they called him. He had no fear of anyone . . . not even his father. Henry knew it. But he always hated him. It was not only because I loved him better than anyone in the world. Henry couldn't forgive that either. No one must come before him. But he had taken the Princess Alice . . . daughter of my first husband Louis. . . . He had had her sent over when she was a little more than a baby to be brought up in the Court and to be Richard's bride. But that lecher . . . my husband, the King, Henry Plantagenet, took that child to his bed, defiled her and would not give her up. He kept her . . . his secret mistress while she was betrothed to Richard and he hated Richard and flouted him in every way . . . because he wanted to keep Alice for himself. There, I have shocked you now. But you will know of these things in time. That was my husband. The man I hated . . . and loved . . . and who felt similarly for me. The man who captured me when I would have led my sons against him and made me his prisoner . . . for years and years.'

'My poor poor grandmother.'

'Poor! Don't use that word to describe me, child, or I shall say you have learned nothing. Say poor Henry! Poor Louis! But not poor Eleanor. I always got the better of them . . . as a woman will . . . for see I am alive to tell the tale . . . and they are dead . . . cold and dead in their tombs. Henry lies at Fontevrault . . . and Richard with him . . . at his feet. And one day I shall lie there with them. And when I return to the Abbey which I shall do when I say good-bye to you, I shall go to their tombs and look at their effigies and I shall speak softly to them both and it will seem as though they answer me.'

Blanche took her grandmother's hand and kissed it.

'And perhaps,' went on Eleanor, 'there is enough time left to me to see you crowned Queen of France. That is what I should like. Though Philip Augustus is not an old man—he is hale and well, I believe, and may live for years. But bide your time. It will come, I promise you. And because you have my blood in you when your time comes, you will be a great Queen.'

The weather improved and they were able to leave the mountains and take the road north towards the Loire.

There were many conversations between them and when Eleanor talked and Blanche listened the girl knew that her grandmother's aim was to prepare her for the great role she must play; and the fact that she had been chosen in place of Urraca made her determined not to disappoint the old Queen.

Sometimes Eleanor was very sad.

'I fear,' she said, 'I greatly fear for my family. There is too much conflict. My grandson Arthur . . . my son John . . . both claim the throne of England.'

'Who should have it, my lady?' asked Blanche.

'John has it and must keep it. How could young Arthur be King of England? He is but a boy . . . he speaks no English and is unknown to the English. They would never accept him. Yet . . . some would say he has the greater claim.'

'But you say John, my lady.'

'John is my son. He was brought up in England. I tremble to think what conflicts there would be if Arthur took the throne. Half the people would not accept him . . . a boy and foreigner. I never could abide his mother—and we should have her setting herself up as Queen. No, it had to be John.'

'And it is, my lady.'

'Yes it is. But the people of Brittany will not accept it. There is going to be war . . . when has there not been war . . . and I fear the King of France may well support Arthur. Then you and I would be on different sides, my dear.'

'I should never be against you, my lady.'

'Nay, child, you will be on the side of your husband and he being but a boy must support his father and his father ever had his eyes on Normandy as has every King of France since one of them was forced to give it up to Rollo, the invading Norseman. You can be sure, child, that while Normandy belongs to the King of England no King of France is going to be contented. That is something we must accept. Let us hope that John can keep a hold on his continental territories as his predecessors managed to do. If only Richard had lived, he would have held everything together.'

'You told me that he was scarcely ever in his realm.'

'That was so. He had this urge to win Jerusalem for the Christians. He never did but he came near to it. Even so he made a reputation as the finest soldier in the world . . . the greatest warrior that ever was. How the Conqueror would have been proud of him, but he would have chided him for not staying at home, I doubt not, to look after his own kingdom. And then there was the time when he was prisoner in Austria and we did not know where he was until Blondel de la Neslé discovered him through a song they sang together . . . and we ransomed him and he came home. Oh, those days are past and now there is John—and I greatly fear what will come to England . . . and I not live to see it. So I shall go back to Fontevrault and there commune with my dead husband whom I came to loathe and my dead son whom I shall always love better than anyone; and I shall wait there for the end. . . .'

'Unless . . .' began Blanche.

And Eleanor laughed. 'Unless something happens to take me from my refuge. Unless my family need me.'

'Then, dearest Grandmother,' said Blanche, 'you would be there.'

'As long as these poor limbs could carry me,' she answered.

They went on northwards and the spring was beginning to show itself. Buds in the hedgerows and clustered blossoms on the elms, the small pink petals of the crane's bill and marsh marigolds by the brooks showed that the spring was coming and the harsh winter was being left behind. But the clear light showed up the furrows on the old Queen's brow and her skin seemed yellowish in the sunshine. It was clear that the rigorous journey had had its effect on her and while the change of season invigorated Blanche it tired Eleanor.

And so they came to the Loire and here the road divided— one way to Fontevrault, the other to Paris.

They rested in a castle close by the river where the castellan was delighted to receive such honoured guests, knowing that the beautiful young girl was the future Queen of France and the old one the redoubtable Eleanor, Queen of England.

It was here that Eleanor came to a decision. She had heard that the Archbishop of Bordeaux was in the neighborhood and she asked him to come to the castle as she had a great desire to see him. While she was awaiting his arrival she sent for Blanche.

Blanche came and kneeling at her feet took her hands and kissed them. The affection between them had grown with each passing day and Blanche now felt that she knew her grandmother better than she had ever known anyone—even her parents and her sisters. In the Court of Castile life had been easy and comfortable with only the bold Saracen to haunt them now and then, and he was like a ghost on the stairs, talked of but never seen and therefore without reality. It had been a happy childhood; she appreciated the love and care of her parents, the comradeship of her sisters. But it had been like looking at a picture with what was unpleasant blotted out and the rest coloured up to make it prettier than it actually was. With her grandmother she had seen real life . . . life as it would be lived by people like herself. There would be occasions when she would have to face the truth and that might be unpleasant.

Her grandmother had prepared her for that. It was as though she had given her a suit of armour—such as knights wore—so that when she went out to face the world, her protective armour would be the knowledge she had acquired from a lady who had lived more adventurously than most.

'My dear child,' said Eleanor, 'I have much to say to you, for we are soon to part.'

'We are not yet there, my lady.'

'Nay, but I shall leave you here.'

The dismay in the girl's face both hurt and pleased the old Queen. She was aware of how much Blanche had come to rely on her. Bad for the child, but pleasant for the old woman, she thought, but I am glad all the same, for this child has brightened my last days.

'You see me thus,' said Eleanor. 'I am too old for such journeys. I have seen nearly eighty winters, child. Can you imagine such an age. I am weary. My old bones demand their rest. I cannot travel with you to Paris for if I did I should die on the way . . . back. I must go now to Fontevrault, which is not far from here, and when I reach that place of refuge I shall take to my bed and there rest until I am revived or leave this world altogether.'

'Pray do not talk so, my lady.'

'We must always face the truth, child. I came to you because I wanted to see the bride who would be Queen of France. I am glad I did. For if I had not it would be your sister who was on her way to Paris . . . and I knew as soon as I saw you that it must be you. But now, all is well. You are almost there. I have sent for the Archbishop of Bordeaux and I shall put you in his charge. He will take you to Paris and look after your interests. And I shall say farewell, my dearest granddaughter, and go to Fontevrault.'

Blanche lowered her face and wept; and there were tears in the old Queen's eyes too.

'Do not grieve,' she said, 'that which has passed between us has been good. I shall think of you for as long as I am on earth and when I die—if I go to Heaven, which is uncertain, I admit—I shall look down on you and guide you if that is possible, for I know this, that Queen Blanche of France will make her mark on the history of France and be remembered as a great good Queen.'

'If she is it will be due to the wise tutoring of her grandmother.'

'Nay, she has much to learn. She will grow in wisdom, I promise you that. All I have done is set her feet on the path along which she should go. Remember me for that. Now I hear sounds of arrival. It may be that the good Archbishop of Bordeaux is here.'

\*   \*   \*

The next day Eleanor said good-bye to her granddaughter, and the old Queen and her party went on to Fontevrault while Blanche, in the care of the Archbishop of Bordeaux, rode north towards Paris.

# Blanche and Louis

BLANCHE was now desolate. She missed her grandmother even more than she had believed possible and the Archbishop of Bordeaux was no substitute for her. His sermons and his heavy advice were very different from the colourful homilies on life presented by her grandmother.

She now began to think with great trepidation of what lay before her. Very soon she would meet her bridegroom—the one with whom she was to spend the rest of her life. He was six months older than she was, she had heard, having been born in September 1187 while her birthday had been in March 1188. So they were both twelve years old. To think of his age comforted her a little, for it seemed possible that he might be dreading meeting her as much as she was dreading meeting him. She would remember her grandmother's words about women being as important as men in the world, for after all if she had been selected for him he had been selected for her and he had had no more say in the matter than she had.

So perhaps she should not be afraid. They would both have to obey the King of France, and she imagined him benign and like her own father. She would come through her ordeal and it might be that she was unduly anxious.

It was a few days since they had parted from the old Queen's company when the Archbishop told her that they were not going first to Paris. They were travelling to Normandy where she would be met by her bridegroom.

'But that will lengthen our journey surely,' cried Blanche.

'It is the orders of the King of France,' answered the Archbishop.

'It is very strange,' she said blankly. 'I understood I was to go to France . . . to Paris and be married there. Surely the future Kings of France are married in Paris.'

'It is the King's wish that the ceremony should take place in Normandy.'

She was very puzzled and uneasy. How she wished that her grandmother was with her. There was something strange about these arrangements and she began to wonder whether the King did not wish her to marry his son after all.

The Archbishop was silent for some time. Then he said: 'You need have no fear. The Queen, your grandmother, put you into my charge, and you may rest assured that having given her my word, I will look to your welfare as certainly as she would herself.'

Blanche nodded but she continued uneasy and at length the Archbishop seemed to come to a decision.

'There seems no harm in telling you for you will know soon enough. The marriage cannot take place in France because the country is under an Interdict from Rome which means that no church ceremonies can be performed while this state of affairs exists.'

'You mean he has displeased the Pope.'

The Archbishop nodded. 'He has put away the wife he married and taken another woman to his bed and the Pope insists that this woman is no true wife to him. The King defies him declaring that she is and that his marriage to Ingeburga of Denmark was no true marriage.'

Blanche was aware of what the Interdict from Rome could mean. She had heard it spoken of in Castile as one of the worst calamities that could befall a man or woman; but in the case of a King it would apply to the whole of his kingdom.

'And why has the King put away his wife?'

'The Church says because he has no fancy for her. He says because she was too nearly related to his first wife and therefore the marriage is null and void on the grounds of consanguinity.'

'And where is she now?'

'She goes from castle to castle and convent to convent while the King lives with Agnes, the woman he calls his wife, and is so deeply enamoured of her that he will not listen to the Pope, and so the country continues to suffer under the Interdict.'

Blanche was silent. It was disconcerting to learn that if a King did not like the bride who had been chosen for him, he could put her away from him on grounds of consanguinity. Royal families had inter-married throughout the centuries and it seemed it would hardly be an impossible task to discover blood ties between any of them. She was thoughtful as the cavalcade made its way into Normandy.

At last they had come face to face. He had ridden out to meet her and eagerly they had taken stock of each other.

He was not tall, nor was he short; his features were good and his expression kindly. He was fair and there was about him an air of delicacy which immediately won her heart and filled her with a determination to protect him.

She was about his height, fair and strong, with a hint of her Norman ancestry in her looks which had no doubt been noted by her grandmother when she had been certain that Blanche must be the future Queen of France. That strength in her appealed to Louis; it was reassuring to his own weakness; and from the moment they met there was a harmony between them which augured well for the future.

They rode side by side to Port-Mort and he told her how he had looked forward to her coming and that the marriage would be celebrated without delay so that they could return to Paris together.

It was easy to talk to him and in the castle close to the Abbey they sat side by side at the top of the table while the company feasted and he told her a little of what she must expect.

'You know that I am twelve years old as you are. We have still to study; and for me life will go on much as it did before . . . except that I shall have a wife.' He smiled charmingly, implying that this fact pleased him; and she glowed with pleasure which was partly relief. He told her how he lived in his father's castles and palaces; how he had to study for a number of hours a day and his tutors had told him that when he married his wife would share his lessons. He wondered what subjects she had studied in Castile. Those she studied in

France would probably be the same. They would ride a great deal. Did she enjoy riding? He meant really enjoy it apart from the fact that it was a necessary part of one's life. He loved horses. He glowed with enthusiasm when he talked of his stables and he discussed his favourite horses as though they were human. She had not cared for them so much, but determined to from henceforth.

She would not be lonely at the French Court, he told her, apart from the fact that she would always be with him once they were married, for there were so many people there. There were his little half-brother and sister and the sons and daughters of noblemen of whom his father was the guardian.

'You must not be afraid of my father.' He frowned slightly. 'People do not always understand him. But he really does care about young people . . . particularly his family. He will love you as he does the others, for he is very eager to see me married.'

Louis looked a little embarrassed and conversation with her grandmother enabled her to realize the reason which would have escaped her before her encounters with the old lady. Now she knew that Louis meant the King of France wanted them to produce an heir to the throne.

The thought would have alarmed her but there was something entirely reassuring about Louis and she dismissed the matter.

She asked him questions about little Philip and Mary, his half-sister and brother and discovered they were the children of Agnes, the lady on whose account the King had been excommunicated.

She told him of Castile and her sisters and how she had believed, almost until it was time for the journey to begin, that it would be her sister who was coming to France.

Louis touched her hand lightly.

'I am glad,' he said, 'that it was you who came.'

A few days later the marriage ceremony took place in the Abbey Port-Mort. It was as grand an occasion as it could be, considering that the King of France was not present to see his son married. Many people thronged the Abbey however and although there was much shaking of heads over the quarrel of the King of France with the Pope, all agreed that the bridal pair looked suitably matched—a good-looking youthful couple with a look of happiness in their faces which indicated that, young as they were, they were happy to be united.

There was to be no consummation. The King of France had indicated that that was to come about naturally which it would if the young people were often together.

And so Blanche of Castile was married to Louis of France and together they left Normandy for Paris.

As they rode along by the Seine, Blanche was conscious of a silence in the villages and little towns. It would have been natural to suppose that when the heir to the throne passed through with his bride there would have been some sign of rejoicing; it was surely customary to ring the church bells to announce such a joyous occasion.

'It is the Interdict,' said Louis. 'The people feel it deeply. All church services and benefits are forbidden by the Pope. They are longing for it to end, but it can't end until my father gives up Agnes and that is something he will not do.'

'So it will go on and on and there will cease to be a church in France.'

'They say it cannot go on, that no one can hold out for long against the Pope. The people fear that God will turn against them. As you see there is a certain sullenness in their manner. They blame all their ills on the Interdict and say that it is my father's lust for Agnes which has brought them to this state.'

'And he loves her dearly.'

'He loves her dearly,' repeated Louis. 'As you will see.'

'It is a terrible position for him.'

'They would say he should never have put Ingeburga away, for he did so before he saw Agnes. None of us know why he so turned against Ingeburga. He married her and they say seemed content enough and then the next morning he was pale and trembling—so I heard—and declared he would have no more of her.'

A faint twinge of fear came to her then. He had liked his bride before the mysterious happenings in the bedchamber. Louis liked her now but what if he should later feel towards her as his father did towards Ingeburga?

She had a momentary vision of herself being sent from convent to convent, castle to castle, without ever knowing in what way she had offended; and Louis taking another wife and her family appealing to the Pope and the Pope's saying: 'I will put the Interdict on your kingdom until you take back Blanche.'

That was folly. Louis liked her. She liked Louis. She did not know how she would come through the bedchamber ordeal, but when it came she would exert all her powers to make it a success. She was relieved that she had time to find out something about it. In the meantime she rode on through a France which resentfully suffered under the Pope's Interdict.

At last they crossed the Seine and came to the Isle of the Cité which Caesar had called Lutetia—the City of Mud—because he declared there was more mud to be found there than in any city he had known.

Louis grew voluble as he regarded the city. It was clear that he loved it and greatly admired his father.

'My father has done much for Paris,' he said. 'It has changed more in the years of his reign than it did in centuries. He told me once that when he was at the window of his palace looking down on the town—which he loved to do—he saw some peasants riding below in their carts and as their wheels churned in the mud there rose such a fetid smell that my father was sickened. The idea came to him that if the streets were paved with stone there would be no mud, so he called together the burghers of the city and told them it would be his endeavour—and they should join him in this—to rid Paris of the name of Mud Town by paving the streets so that the mud would disappear and he needed their help in the matter. They saw how right he was, for there was much disease in the city and the people had begun to realize that it could be due to the obnoxious mud the smell of which attracted flies and other vermin. There was one rich merchant—I have heard my father speak of him often—he was Gerard de Poissy and he contributed eleven hundred silver marks to the making of pavements, and now as you will see Paris is a most agreeable city.'

'The people must be grateful to your father.'

Louis smiled. 'Ah, you know how it is. When it is first done they can talk of nothing else but the change in their city and after a while they forget the foul mud and cease to be grateful for their stone pavements. My father cares greatly for his kingdom. His one dream was to enrich it and bring it back to what it was in the days of Charlemagne. So you see how he loves Agnes when he says that he would rather lose half his dominions than lose her.'

'I like him the better for loving her so much,' said Blanche.

'When you meet him you will not realize the kind of man he is. He does not show his feelings but they are there . . . for all his family. He has ever been a kind father to me. He can lose his temper quickly but he can as quickly forget his rage. And he is a great King, I tell you that. He has been to the Holy Land.'

'I know. He was there with my uncle Richard,' replied Blanche. 'My grandmother told me that at one time there was a great friendship between them.'

'That is true. He ever had a fondness for Richard, although they were natural enemies—as all kings of France and England must be . . . while England holds territory which once belonged to France.'

'Perhaps they will not always be enemies.'

'They will be until all these possessions come back to the French crown. That is something we must accept, Blanche. Look at the wall of the city. My father had that built before he went off on his Crusade. He wanted to fortify all his cities and particularly Paris. When we take our rides I will show you what he has done for the city.'

They came to the Palace of the Cité and there Blanche met for the first time her formidable father-in-law.

He was tall with a fine figure and an air of great dignity so that she would have known him immediately for the King. There was a russet tinge to his hair and beard; it showed in his eyes and suggested quick temper. There was a look of hardness about him which, she imagined, would have made anyone think twice about displeasing him.

He regarded her steadily and seemed to like what he saw. Then he embraced her and calling her daughter said he welcomed her to the Court of France. He said that he believed she would be a good wife to his son and if she was she would have nothing to regret.

Beside him was his Queen—Agnes, the gentle and beautiful young woman for whom he had placed himself and his country in a precarious position. She greeted Blanche warmly but Blanche could see that although she adored her husband she was too sensitive not to realize that she was at the core of the uneasy state of affairs which existed.

Because there were no church ceremonies it seemed a strange introduction to her new home; but the King was determined that she should receive a good secular welcome.

In the great hall he had her sit on one side of him and Agnes on his other, Louis was seated beside his wife and showed by his manner that he was eager to look after her.

The table was full of dishes of food, some of which she had never seen before; the serving men and women hurried to and fro; while minstrels played soft music throughout the feast.

Among the dishes was that rich delicacy, lampreys, in which her ancestor Henry I had fatally indulged; they were served differently here from the manner in which they were in Castile. The French used rich sauces containing herbs unknown to Blanche; there were also salmon, mutton, beef, venison and great pies the contents of which she could only guess at. Much flavouring of onions and garlic was put in the food which was new to her. She liked the cheeses and the sweetmeats and all these were washed down with wines—some drunk sweet some dry. 'None can make wine as the French can,' Louis told her.

King Philip made much of her and talked constantly to her of the customs of his country and made it clear to everyone present that he was greatly pleased with his new daughter.

She quickly adjusted herself to life at the Court of France where Louis was her constant companion. They were in the schoolroom together for Philip was a firm believer in education and was constantly reminding his son that a King must study history above all subjects, for he would in due course play a part in it; geography must be mastered too, for events in various parts of the world might well be his concern some day. Literature and music must also not be neglected, for a King should be able to express himself not only with skill but with grace.

Because they learned together they learned quickly. They were two children growing up side by side and Louis supplied the companionship which she had enjoyed with her sisters. She heard from home frequently, for her parents were eager for her to know they thought of her constantly; Berengaria also wrote to her; and she was pleased to learn that Urraca was going to marry into Portugal where she would in due course become Queen.

'I am proud of my three girls,' wrote her mother, 'and one day I know I shall be even more proud.'

There were many young children in the Palace. Philip liked children and the sons and daughters of many a noble were brought up there, for the King called them his godchildren and they lived under his roof. There was not a nobleman in France who did not consider it the highest honour for his children to be brought up at Court and beside Philip's two by Agnes, there were one or two illegitimate sons of his. He liked all children and was particularly fond of his own. It was easy to see that he doted on Louis and once when he was alone with Blanche he said to her: 'You will have to take care of Louis. He was never very strong. When he was two years old we nearly lost him, I left the Crusades before I intended to because I feared he would die. I have always had a watch kept on his health since.'

Blanche assured him that she would look after him well.

They rode a great deal together; she allowed herself to be drawn into his enthusiasm for horses and the King said to Agnes that it was always wise to let the children grow up together rather than thrust them into bed when they were strangers.

The method seemed to be working well with Blanche and Louis for each day they grew more and more fond of each other.

He liked to show her Paris. He would take her through those streets—paved at his father's orders—past the silent churches up the narrow alleys where the dyers and tanners were at work. People watched them covertly and cheered them now and then. They could not visit the sins of the fathers upon the children, they said. It was not the fault of those innocents that the land was under the Interdict and there was no church comfort to be had for love or money.

He took her to the cemetery of Paris close by the Church of the Holy Innocents and the street of St. Denis. It was enclosed by a high wall and there were gates which were shut every night.

'This is my father's work,' Louis pointed out. 'He saw that the burial grounds were treated without respect. At one time this was open land and the traders used to come here and set up their stalls between the tombs. It seemed to him profane, so he had the wall built with the gates which were shut up every night. Then there could be some privacy and respect for the dead.'

'Your father is a very good king,' said Blanche.

'I pray to God I shall be as good when my time comes, but I fear not.'

'Why should you not, Louis? You are good and kind and more gentle than your father.'

'I lack his kingly qualities.' He looked very sad, then brightened suddenly. 'But I shall have you to help me.'

'And I *will* help you.' She stood there in the cemetery among the graves of the dead and raised her hand. 'I swear it, Louis. I will stand beside you and when the time comes we shall rule France together.'

He looked at her with great love and said: 'The thought of reigning had always frightened me until you came.'

There was nothing he could have said which could have given her more delight.

They rode on through the town and Louis showed her Les Halles, the great market place enclosed by walls and again with gates which shut at night.

'My father, while he is a great commander of armies and wins many battles by clever diplomacy, has an eye for the life of the ordinary people. He thinks constantly how best to make life easier for them. He has now allowed all bakers to have their own ovens, for before he made this law the ovens which were used by the trade belonged to certain large establishments many of them religious. The people do not fully realize what a great king he is.'

'People never recognize a great king until he is dead and

they have a bad one,' said Blanche. 'And I tell you, Louis, they will have such another good king after Philip.'

'I pray so, and that it will be many years before they have a new king. My father is not old. He has perhaps thirty years left to him.'

'Thirty years!' cried Blanche. 'It is a lifetime. Just think of us in thirty years time.'

'Does it alarm you?'

'Not now I am married to you.'

They came back again and again to that satisfactory state of affairs. Those about them noticed that they were falling in love. Soon, they said, they will be lovers in truth.

The King noticed. Some members of his Court thought they should be lovers in fact. Thirteen years old. Why not? And they were both mature for their ages.

'Nay,' said the King. 'When they are ready it will come. Let us not disturb their innocent pleasure in each other.'

So the weeks passed—lessons, riding to the hunt in the forests, riding quietly through the streets of Paris, watching the progress of the mighty church which Philip was building and which would be Notre Dame de Paris, and then going to the Louvre to see how the builders were getting on with the improvements to that palace where a fine strong tower was being added.

'My father is altering the face of Paris,' said Louis, 'and who can say it is not for the better?'

Blanche, who had loved her own parents devotedly, took Louis's affection for his father as natural, not realizing how rare it was. It was true her grandmother had told her of the terrible conflict which had raged between her grandfather, Henry II of England, and his sons but she had thought that was a regrettable infrequent state of affairs.

She was learning at a great rate but she still wondered why a king like Philip Augustus who was so concerned for his people that he built walls about their markets and studied their needs should have let them suffer as they did from the Pope's Interdict, which they must endure because of his actions.

\*          \*          \*

Two young people had come to the Court. This was the very interesting handsome young Prince Arthur who was the same age as Louis, and Arthur's sister Eleanor who was a few years older.

Arthur was that Count of Brittany, son of Geoffrey, elder brother of John, about whom there was a great deal of controversy because many people believed that he, instead of John, should be the King of England. Philip was very anxious to have him there, and Louis told Blanche that his visit was in a way political and far more important than those of the King's wards who played and learned to joust and ride in the courtyards and the gardens.

'My father does not trust John,' he told Blanche. 'He may decide to help Arthur to the throne. So much depends on what happens.'

Blanche liked to hear everything that was going on and she rarely forgot anything. She told her little maid Amincia, who had come with her from Castile and acted as her personal attendant, that she too must keep her ears and eyes open and let her know what was said throughout the Court. If she was going to help her husband she must know everything that happened.

So she was particularly watchful of Prince Arthur and compared him with Louis—to Louis's advantage. Arthur might be said to be more handsome; he was indeed princely; but he was a little arrogant, a fault of which no one could accuse Louis. He might joust more flamboyantly, but she did not think he was as clever as Louis.

Arthur was a little boastful, certain that he was going to be King of England before long. He used to talk to Louis and Blanche about his prospects and he believed that he had the greater claim being the son of an elder brother of John who had assumed the crown.

'It is all due to certain men in England who have supported him,' he told them. 'But the people do not like him and they would be glad to be rid of him.'

Blanche was not so sure. Her grandmother had been in favour of John. It was very disconcerting for her to know that Philip supported Arthur's cause while her grandmother was on the side of John.

She was able to talk over her dilemma with Louis who was always fair and ready to see another point of view.

'It is not an easy matter to decide,' he granted her. 'John is the son of the late King of England, Arthur his grandson. Of course if Geoffrey had been King, there would have been no doubt that Arthur was next. But Geoffrey was never King and died before his elder brother Richard came to the throne. It is therefore difficult to give a ruling. But father has no difficulty. He would like to bring Normandy back to the Crown of France and Poitou too. Therefore he does not think of what is right but what is best.'

'And you, Louis?'

'I must think with my father if I am to be a good King of France.'

'And if I am to be a good Queen of France I must agree with you.'

It was obvious of course that Philip's motives and those of her grandmother were in direct opposition, for Eleanor was anxious to hold all that had come to the Plantagenets through conquests and alliances, while Philip wanted to bring back everything to France.

It was difficult at first to know what she should do; but of course she was married now and what was advantageous to France was so to her.

She was uneasy though when Philip took possession of several castles which belonged to Arthur with the purpose he said of guarding them for his young protégé; that was not all. He declared that Arthur was ready to receive a knighthood at his hand and because he believed that Arthur was the true heir to the crown of Richard he would invest him not only with Brittany, but Anjou, Poitou, Maine, Touraine and Normandy.

As was only to be expected Hugh de Lusignan, whose bride John had taken, immediately joined in the campaign against the King of England.

'I fear,' Louis told Blanche, 'that there will be war.'

'And if there is, will you go?'

'My father has always been anxious that I should not engage in war, partly because of his concern for me, partly because he fears I might be killed in battle and France die without an heir.'

They looked at each other covertly. The moment when they must consummate their marriage was growing nearer.

It was due to this conflict that Blanche and Isabella first became aware of each other. Philip had invited King John to Paris that they might confer together and thence he came with his bride.

Blanche would always remember that first meeting with the young Queen of England and the effect she had had on all present. As she entered the great hall by the side of her husband it was not on John that every eye came to rest. She was sumptuously clad; she glittered with jewels; but it was not that. There was something in the bold wide eyes fringed with heavy black lashes, the languorous manner, the graceful catlike movements which proclaimed Isabella apart from other women. Only to look at her was to understand why John having seen her was ready to discard poor Hadwisa of Gloucester, his long-suffering wife, to abandon his honour and give himself no rest until he had abducted Isabella and she became his wife.

She displayed great pride, a certain haughtiness which demanded homage for her rare qualities. Blanche had never seen a member of her sex quite like her.

During their stay at the palace, the King fêted the pair from England with great pomp and ceremony, because he was eager to placate John and to lull his suspicions that Philip would one day rob him of his possessions.

Isabella showed an interest in Blanche and that meant that now and then she sought the company of the girl who would one day be Queen of France.

Isabella made no effort to hide the fact that she was a little contemptuous of Blanche. Blanche was handsome enough to claim her attention but Isabella showed clearly that she was aware of her virginity and despised it.

The story was that John was unable to drag himself away from Isabella's bed and that he was restless and bad-tempered when he could not be with her even for a short time.

It seemed incredible that Isabella was but a year or so older than Blanche for she seemed wise in the ways of the world and Blanche suddenly realized that she did not want to understand what this was that Isabella managed to convey.

'You are very very young,' Isabella told Blanche. 'Yet you have a husband.' That fluttering of the eyelids, that sly secret smile, what did it mean? 'How *is* Louis?' asked Isabella.

'He is well thank you and no longer delicate you know.'

At which Isabella laughed.

'I did not mean his health. Of course he is but a boy. John is very . . . experienced, very skilled. Far more so than Hugh would have been I am sure.'

'Skilled . . . in ruling. Well so should he be. He is a King.'

'You follow me not. You are a child yet, Blanche.'

'Louis does not think so. We discuss affairs and even the King talks to me sometimes of state matters.'

Isabella nodded mockingly. 'And do they so indeed. Then forsooth I am wrong and you are no longer a child . . . in all matters.'

She turned to Louis. She embarrassed him with her languishing looks and her beautiful white hands which she would lay on his arm while she stroked him gently.

'Why, Louis,' she would say, 'how very handsome you are! I trow they will call you Louis the Handsome some day.'

'I hardly think so,' replied Louis uneasily. 'They would not call me so, for I should not merit it. I would rather be the Brave . . . or the Good.'

'Perhaps you will be all three. Who knows?'

She laughed a great deal and made allusions to matters which they did not entirely understand. She talked of her husband and how he would be seeking her this moment. 'If he saw me touch your arm like this, my lord . . . yes even your *arm* . . . he would be ready to kill you.'

'Then he would be possessed of madness,' retorted Blanche, 'and he should save his anger for his enemies.'

'He would count your husband one if he saw my interest in him.'

That she was goading them in some way, they both realized. Blanche thought she was trying to tempt Louis, and that she wanted him to admire her.

She said to him when they were alone: 'I think she wanted you to say that she was beautiful . . . more beautiful than I am.'

'That I should never say.'

'Well, she wanted you to think it.'

'I couldn't, Blanche, because you are my wife.'

She smiled at him tenderly. 'Will you always think that, Louis?' she asked.

'Yes, I always shall,' he vowed.

He took her hands suddenly and kissed her in a manner which he had not used before. It startled her and yet in a way she had expected it.

The presence of Isabella, her innuendoes and her sly allusions had changed them in some way, had awakened something in them.

It was while Isabella and John were visiting the Court that they became lovers.

Now they were no longer children. The magnitude of their new relationship absorbed them. Philip and Agnes watched them indulgently.

'They have fallen in love,' said Agnes.

'It is perhaps over soon to expect an heir to the throne,' said Philip.

'And they perhaps are over young to be parents as yet,' replied Agnes.

'My dear Agnes,' said the King. 'Princesses are old enough as soon as they are able.'

Agnes herself was sorrowful. When she rode out she saw the silent looks of the people and she knew that they blamed her for bringing upon their country this evil state of affairs. To be denied the Church was a great hardship for them; and if there was war, she wondered how Philip's armies would fare.

And there would be war. How she detested the King of England and his precocious little bride. John was a wicked man, she sensed; he was capable of any cruelty, any treachery. The manner in which he had behaved to Hugh de Lusignan was unforgivable and as for his bride—she was ready to give herself wherever there was the greater advantage.

Hugh would raise his friends against John, and Philip had

always been a man to seize his opportunities. She could see war coming close. Philip had told her that he had little respect for John. 'He is a man who will find it hard to keep a grip on a slippery crown,' he said. 'His father did not find it an easy task and he was a great soldier and clever ruler. He had had his faults and they had betrayed him. His family was against him and in particular his wife . . . and it was largely these personal relationships which undermined him. If he had had the good sense to remain friendly with his wife and sons his story would have been different. But they were a treacherous band . . . except Richard.' His face softened always when he spoke of Richard. 'Richard was never false. Yea and Nay, we would call him, for if he meant yea it was yea and if nay it was nay and he told you straight. Richard was a fool in many ways but a braver man never lived. I remember him when we were young. By God, there was a handsome man! I never saw a finer. But it is all long since and what have we now but this brother of his . . . this evil man who was not worthy to unlatch his shoe. If Richard had lived . . . Richard *should* have lived. . . . But now we have to deal with John.'

'You think he will make war?'

'He will have to defend his claims to the throne, because Arthur is going to find men rallying to his cause and Hugh de Lusignan will stand beside Arthur, I can promise you.'

'And you, Philip . . . ?'

'When the time comes I'll not stand aside. You know it has always been a dream of mine to bring Normandy back to France where it belongs. I would make my country great as it was under Charlemagne.'

Agnes said, 'I know.'

He took her hand and smiled. 'And talk of war disturbs you, and I will not have you disturbed. Come, we will be happy. I will make you happy as you have made me.'

And she thought: But not France. Our happiness in each other has not been the contentment of France.

She brooded a great deal and without telling the King she sent a message to the Pope in which she pleaded with him to withdraw the Interdict. 'I love my husband,' she wrote, 'and my love for him is a pure love. When I married I was ignorant of the laws of the Church. I believed that I was truly

Philip's wife. I beg of you, Most Holy Father, to raise the Interdict and give me leave to remain at the side of the man I call my husband.'

Innocent replied that he believed in her innocence, and that he had sympathy with her, but the truth was that Philip was in fact married to Ingeburga and for that reason while he lived with Agnes the Interdict could not be lifted.

Agnes was in despair. She wrote again to the Pope that she had two children, her young Philip and Marie, and if she left Philip she would be acknowledging those children as illegitimate. That was something she could not do. She would die with all her sins on her rather than harm her children.

The Pope's reply was prompt. He believed her to be a good and pious woman who had been caught up in all innocence in this matter. He understood her loyalty to her children and if she would leave the King and go into a convent, he would declare her children legitimate since she had believed them to be so when they were born.

But remove the Interdict he would not, until Agnes and Philip had parted.

The Palace was plunged in gloom. The King shut himself in his apartments and would speak to no one. Agnes had left Paris.

She had made up her mind that she must save France from the disaster which she was sure the continuance of the Interdict would bring her to. War was imminent. No army could believe in victory when the approbation of Heaven was turned against it.

Agnes had made the great sacrifice.

Philip pacing up and down his bedchamber knew that she had done that which was best for France. He had dreaded going into battle with an army which would have decided before the fighting began that it was defeated. And yet . . . he had lost Agnes.

He cursed his fate. He was doomed to lose those he loved. Had he loved Isabella of Hainault, Louis's mother? Not greatly but she had been an amiable spouse—a lovely creature; sometimes Louis looked very like her. She had been sixteen years old when he was born—not much older than *he* was now and she had died when the boy was two. So theirs had been a brief married life; and he had mourned her. He had lost Richard Coeur de Lion, whom he had loved more passionately than he had loved Isabella. He often thought of Richard now . . . moments of tenderness, moments of anger. Love and hatred had played strong roles between them. And he had lost him. . . . But perhaps when he had almost lost his son he had suffered most. It was shortly after Isabella's death when the child had come near to dying too and he had come home from the Holy Land, leaving Richard for the sake of his child. Louis had been preserved and how he had loved the boy. He still did. He could not explain what joy it was for him to be near this son of his. That Louis was gentle both delighted and dismayed him. He often wondered what sort of King he would make. He was like his grandfather really, too sensitive for kingship. But he was a lovable boy and Philip thanked God that Blanche showed signs of strength. He would talk to Blanche some time. He would make her understand how she must grow stronger and always support Louis, for Louis would need her. Thank God they had taken to each other. He had not wanted to spoil it. That was why he had let them live innocently together until that time when they should mate naturally. If it was, as it appeared, that the time had come, he rejoiced. It would mature them both and then he could talk to Blanche and make her understand.

But now he had lost Agnes.

The Interdict would be raised and there would be rejoicing throughout the land, but to gain the contentment of France had cost him Agnes.

He supposed he could have ridden to Poissy whither she had gone, could have implored her to come back, and he knew that she would not have been able to resist him.

But a king is a king, he told himself.

He had not thought that in the heat of his passion for her. Had he not known that he was in truth married to Ingeburga and because she was a Princess the Pope would not allow her to be set aside?

Ingeburga. He shivered. Never never again. . . .

Then he thought of Agnes and wept. But there would be war.

He was going to finish John—that foolish, reckless brag-gart. Brother of Richard . . . son of great Henry! God in Heaven, how did Eleanor of Aquitaine and Henry Plantagenet get such a creature?

But thank you, God, for bringing him into this world. Thank you for making him King. This is my chance. I shall bring back all that France has lost. I shall be as great a King as Charlemagne. And Agnes, dearest Agnes, I could not have done it with you beside me.

And while the King of France made plans for war, in the convent of Poissy Agnes wept and tried to forget the past. This was the best . . . for the King her lover, and for their children. This was the sacrifice demanded of her.

She grew listless. She could eat nothing. She spent hours in prayer.

There was no happiness left in life. She longed for the peace of Heaven. She prayed for it.

'Oh Holy Mother of God, my life is over. There is nothing left to me now. In your mercy let my sorrows pass away. In death I shall find peace.'

Her prayers were granted. A few months after she had entered the convent at Poissy, Agnes was dead.

The Interdict was lifted but Philip refused to have Ingeburga back. That was one thing he stood firmly against. The Pope might have parted him from the woman he loved but he could not make him live with one he loathed. So Ingeburga contin-ued her peregrination from castle to castle, convent to con-vent; she might go where she pleased as long as it was not where Philip was.

To soothe his unhappiness he plunged into preparations against John, for John was gathering enemies fast which was a matter for rejoicing; and the prospects for France had never looked so bright. Philip was not an old man—not yet forty. He had time before him and he wanted to leave a flourishing country for Louis.

He liked to talk with his son, to train him, as he called it, for future kingship, and at the time of Agnes's death he grew closer and closer to his son.

He walked with him in the gardens and there he would

speak to him as he said in secret, which made a pleasant intimacy between them.

He studied Louis anxiously. Ever since that terrible illness he had been concerned for his health. He set his doctors to watch his son without letting Louis know it. 'For,' he said, 'I do not wish him to imagine he is ill, which he is not. But in view of the fact that he has a delicate constitution, I want to be absolutely sure that if he should need attention it be promptly given.'

It was important for France that the heir be strong, he was often telling himself. And if anything should happen to Louis he could see great conflict, for Agnes's boy would not be accepted by some even though the Pope had made him legitimate. He knew in his heart that one of the factors in the case from Agnes's point of view had been the legitimization of young Philip, for if she had remained with him, it was certain that the Church would have upheld the point of view that the child was a bastard.

Philip was angry with fate, the Pope and the circumstances which had led to his marrying Ingeburga before he had found Agnes. But it was no use. Louis was left to him and he had to guide him in his role; and he fervently hoped that before long Louis would give him grandsons and he could thankfully know that the line was secure.

Now, in the gardens, he talked to his son of the need to recapture all that France over the centuries had lost.

'We shall never be truly at peace,' he said, 'until Normandy is ours. William the Conqueror brought it to England . . . or England to Normandy which you prefer. But before his day there was strife between us. The Franks should never have given that part of France to the Norsemen. It happened centuries ago and who knows it may be our glory to bring it back. We have a heaven-sent opportunity in John. Think of him. You have seen him. What is your opinion of him, Louis? Would men ever follow such a one? Only those who sought their advantage . . . and a few to whom loyalty to the Crown is a way of life. Nay, son, there never was such an opportunity as now lies in our hands and we shall take it.'

Louis listened intently, but he was not a warrior; that much was clear. He reminded Philip very much of his own father

. . . another Louis, and a good man, a man who was pestered by his ability to see two sides to every question, a man who was haunted by the cries of innocent men and women slaughtered during the course of a battle. Philip respected such men, but did they make good kings?

He went on: 'The time is at hand. The Lusignans are ready to rise against him. He took Hugh's bride.' Philip laughed. 'There is a woman for whom men would go to war. I thank God that our dear Blanche is not of her kind. Isabella will bring John to ruin, I don't doubt. Though his own nature will do that and it will only be necessary for her to help the process. The Lusignans are a powerful clan. They are waiting to get at him. Then there is Brittany. Arthur and his adherents believe that he should be on the throne.'

'Do you believe that, Father?'

'I shall support Arthur, my son, because he is against John and my eyes are on Normandy. Your wife Blanche has a strong claim to the English Crown, you know, Louis.'

Louis smiled. 'But John is the King and he will have children.'

'From what we hear he is making every effort to get them,' retorted Philip. 'Kings lead precarious lives, Louis. If John should die in battle and Arthur too, why then who would be next in the line of succession? What of Blanche, daughter of Eleanor, sister to John and Richard—the Kings of England?'

'There is of course the connection but it is unlikely that John will die before he gets an heir and then there is Arthur. And do you think the people would accept Blanche?'

'With France behind her—yes. Think of it, Louis. The whole of France in our hands—and the Crown of England thrown in.'

'How should we hold such vast territory?'

'That is what we would think of when the time comes. It is a King's duty to take the events as they arise, but if possible to be prepared for them and to act one step ahead of his enemies. You will work with me closely on this campaign.'

'You mean I am to go into battle.'

'God forbid. You are far too young. I would not dream of allowing that. But this will be a war of strategy—as all wars are; and it is the man who is cleverest at that wily game who is more likely to defeat his opponent, even though the latter has the bigger army. That is something Richard Coeur de Lion never realized. He was the greatest, bravest fighter in the world but no strategist. If he had been, with his courage and generalship he would have brought Jerusalem back to Christendom and, given time, conquered the world. Now I never cared for battle as I did for strategy. It is a wise policy, for countries perpetually at war grow poor, the people dissatisfied and prosperity elusive. So we should try to let others fight our wars.'

'Is that what you propose to do?'

Philip nodded. 'As far as I can. I want John brought low, and because he is as he is, I do not think it will be an impossibility. His enemies are numerous. The Lusignans are raring to get at him. Arthur believes he is the rightful King of England. I shall give them my support—my moral support. Though of course if necessary I shall have to offer practical help. But let them work for us first. I am going to offer your half-sister as a bride for Arthur.'

'Marie. She is but a child.'

'That's true. But she is legitimate. The Pope has agreed on that. Marie is not ready for marriage. As for Arthur he is but a boy . . . your age, Louis. He can wait for Marie—and if he has the Crown of England by that time I shall be happy to see my daughter Queen.'

'Does Arthur know?'

'I have whispered to him that I propose to offer him my daughter. He is beside himself with joy. It means that I give my support to his claim.'

'He will be going soon.'

'Any day. The time to strike is now, Louis. Talk of these matters to Blanche. It is well that she should learn with you how affairs of state are conducted.'

'I will talk to her,' said Louis.

Arthur and his sister Eleanor were in mourning, for their mother had died. Eleanor shut herself away to brood in solitude, but Arthur was constantly conferring with the King; messengers were coming to and from Paris and there was always something to discuss, some preparations to be made that there was little time for grieving.

Blanche, aware of what was going on, saw how the excitement of coming events helped Arthur over his sorrow, just as plunging himself into the affairs of his country had helped Philip in his anguish over the loss of Agnes. It was a good lesson learned.

With rulers, she inferred, the good of the country must come first, and personal grief could be and must be set aside for the sake of duty. She wondered how she would fare if she lost Louis whom she was loving more every day; and she thought of the deep affection which had been so obvious with her own parents and she was sure meant more to them than anything on Earth—and it had indeed made a happy home for their children. Her mother wrote to her regularly telling her what was happening at home in Castile and spoke often of her father's health. The bond between them all would never be broken, but she had a new life now. Louis was more important to her than anyone, and France was her home.

Arthur rode off to place himself at the head of an army and it was with dismay that Blanche heard that her grandmother had left Fontevrault to go to the aid of John.

Louis tried to soothe her.

'But,' she cried, 'your father, you, and therefore myself, are supporting Arthur, and my grandmother is against Arthur and for John.'

'It happens so in families sometimes,' Louis answered.

'But this is different. You see we travelled together. We became very close to each other . . . we understood each other.'

'Then she will understand now that you must be on different sides.'

Blanche shook her head in grief.

And this was intensified when the news reached the Court that Arthur and his supporters had attacked the castle in which the old Queen was staying and had actually dared take her prisoner; but John had arrived, rescued his mother and captured Arthur as well as Hugh de Lusignan.

'It was a bitter defeat for Arthur and victory for John,' declared Philip and he doubted not that the result had been brought about by the old Queen for little success could be expected from John.

But it was a temporary setback. Moreover Arthur was in the hands of John and who could say what the outcome could be.

John gave expression to his venom and derived great pleasure from humiliating Hugh de Lusignan by forcing him to ride in chains in a bullock cart while Isabella, his lost love, witnessed the spectacle; but then he released him, much to the astonishment of all. It was just a sign of John's unpredictability; and as all his emotions at this time were governed by his feelings for his Queen, it appeared that in releasing Hugh he was showing her his contempt for him as an enemy.

But he was not so foolish as to release Arthur, and that was the end of the young Prince. It was not certain what exactly had happened to him, but in a few months he was to disappear from the world, leaving behind him a mystery which added to the rapidly growing evil reputation of his uncle.

Blanche often thought of her grandmother during the next two years. She knew how desolate she must be living out the last months of her life in gloomy speculation.

She would have loved to go and visit her, to tell her that although they were on opposing sides the affection between them was in no way diminished and she would never forget their journey from Castile to the Loire when they had forged the bond between them which nothing could sever.

Eleanor had conveyed to Blanche how proud she was of the Plantagenet line, how deeply she had loved Richard and how greatly she had feared for John. And rightly so, for if ever a king brought about his own ruin that king was John. Now he was losing those possessions which had belonged to his family since the days of great Rollo. One by one the castles were falling into the hands of his enemies. There were constant murmurs of 'Where is Arthur?' and gruesome stories were told of the young man's end. That he had been murdered by his wicked uncle seemed evident and his enemies—chief of them Philip of France—were not going to allow that to be forgotten.

When Château Gaillard was lost to him that seemed the end of his hopes of holding Normandy, for the castle was the

gateway to Rouen and had been known as the strongest
fortress of its time.

If he could lose that, he could lose everything.

While the Court rejoiced, Blanche could not do so whole-
heartedly for she must think of the sorrowing old lady in
Fontevrault.

At least she could send messengers to the Abbey to enquire
about her grandmother and it was thus that she heard of
Eleanor's decline.

It seemed that she had grown listless when she had heard of
the continual defeats of her youngest son and that when
Gaillard fell they tried to keep the news from her. But she
was imperious to the end and realized that some major catas-
trophe had occurred so she insisted on being told. And when
she had, she covered her face with both hands that none
might see her grief.

'It is the end,' she said.

And they were not sure whether she meant of John's hopes
or her own life.

She took to her bed and when a fever overtook her she did
not seem to care whether it left her or not.

She lay in bed, sometimes murmuring of the past and it
was noticed that Richard's name occurred very often.

She died quietly in her bed and in accordance with her
instructions was buried in Fontevrault beside the husband
whom she had hated and the son she had loved.

Blanche's grief was great; she could not forget her grandmother; and although the people around her were rejoicing at
the manner in which the King of England was losing his
dominions and gloated on the importance of this to France,
she was filled with melancholy, knowing full well that that
which delighted those around her had brought great sorrow to
the old lady whom she had learned to love.

Then something happened to divert her thoughts from her
grandmother's death.

She discovered that she was pregnant.

The King was delighted. Blanche was not yet seventeen
and there were years ahead of her for childbearing. Philip
congratulated himself that it had been wise not to hurry them.

They were in love and it was charming to see them together; Blanche was growing into a beauty and a woman of good sense, and that she was also going to be a mother was a matter for the utmost rejoicing.

Everything must be done for her ease. Her parents and sisters wrote of their delight and pleasure on her account and from her mother came advice on how to care for herself.

Great preparations were made throughout the Court and when the time came for the child's birth it would seem as though, as Blanche said, no one had ever had a child before.

But this child was the heir to France.

There was a certain disappointment that it should be a girl, and a delicate one, and when all the preparations, all the care, all the taken advice had proved futile, for within a few days, the child was dead, Blanche was desolate. Louis consoled her. 'We are young,' he reminded her. 'There will be others.'

'There must be,' declared Blanche. 'I fear that the King's disappointment will be great.'

She was right; but he did not allow her to see how great. He comforted her and told her that it often happened so—in royal families particularly.

'I believe,' he said, 'that so greatly do we desire heirs that perverse fate denies them to us. But this is but the first. Perhaps you are too young, my daughter, for you are young you know. It has ever astonished me how a chance encounter with a woman who has pleased for a day or so will result in a healthy child. There is my own Peter Charles whose mother was a fine young woman I found in Arras and there is Philip whom I named Hurepel because of the way his hair stands up. Where would you find two more sturdy boys? And bastards both! But you will have healthy sons . . . great sons. I know it. You were made to be a mother of Kings.'

Blanche thanked the King and told him that he had done much to soothe her melancholy; but in her sadness memories of her grandmother came back—she who had outlived all her sons, save John, and had little joy brought to her by him.

She would have another child soon and when she did this would become just a sad memory.

In the gardens Philip walked with his son. He wanted him to promise him something.

Louis was a little puzzled until his father went on: 'I do not want you to take an active part in a joust, and I wish you to promise me that when you attend these tourneys you will go as a looker-on.'

'But, my lord, how can I?'

'You can do so by making sure that you do not attend in armour. If you are simply present in a light mail jacket without a helmet, all will know that you have no intention of riding in the lists.'

'It will be noticed that I do not enter, Father. It will be said that I am a coward.'

'Let them say that to me! None shall say it twice, I promise you. And you and I will know that you are no coward, for it may well be that it will need greater courage to abstain from the lists than it would be to enter them.'

'Do you mean that I am not to joust ever. . . .'

'I mean that for a while I do not wish you to.'

Louis understood. He and Blanche had had a daughter who had not lived. He was the heir to the throne—the one on whose rights to inherit the crown none could throw a doubt; and until he had produced a son, he must live.

Jousting could be dangerous, for although a tourney was supposed to be a mock battle it often became realistic. Poor sad Arthur's father had ridden out to do mock battle but when he had been surrounded by his opponents he had fallen from his horse and been trampled to death. Yet it was but a mock battle.

Louis had always been aware of the responsibilities of kingship, but he had never realized them so thoroughly as he did at that moment.

Four years passed before Blanche was able to give France the hope of another heir. Meanwhile John was losing his grip even on his English possessions. His barons despaired of him and there was a growing conflict between them; he was still enslaved by his wife Isabella but that did not prevent his infidelities. He became more and more cruel as his power was stripped from him; his enemies were legion and recklessly he added to their number with every passing year.

Philip had dreamed of recovering all the French territory.

That was almost accomplished, and now he was turning covetous eyes on England itself. Why not? His daughter-in-law had a claim through her mother. There was no salic law in England; he did not see why Blanche should not one day be Queen of England and Louis King. France and England under one crown. Even Charlemagne had never been King of England.

And now Blanche was pregnant.

If this child be a healthy boy, it is an omen, said Philip. 'Oh God, give me a grandson and I will be ready to depart in good heart and spirits whenever You see fit to call me.'

Great was the rejoicing when the child was born—a boy, a healthy heir to the crown of France.

The King's eyes shone with affection for his daughter-in-law and pride in his grandson.

'There have been few days in my life happier than this one,' he declared.

As he kissed her hand, Blanche said: 'If it pleases you, I should like to call him Philip.'

Those were the years of triumph for France. Philip had his spies everywhere and nowhere were they more important than in England. That John was a feeble ruler, a man destined to fail, was becoming more and more obvious to everyone except John, who boastfully declared he would regain all that he had lost.

When John came into conflict with the Church he was excommunicated; and the Pope implied that the claims of France did not displease him.

Calling his son and daughter-in-law to him, Philip told them that the time had come to prepare for invasion. He believed that ere long Blanche would have her heritage.

Four years before, when Blanche was expecting her son Philip, Louis had been presented with his spurs by his father at Compiegne. This ceremony, which was always conducted with the utmost pomp, had been witnessed by even more than usual because on this occasion the heir to the throne would show the company his right to the honour and after that Philip could not longer prevent his son from taking part in the jousting tournaments. Moreover now he had his namesake and grandson who appeared to be growing into a healthy man; and although Blanche was a little slow in producing more grandchildren, the King always consoled himself with the observation that she was young yet.

At this time with four-year-old Philip a delight in the royal nursery, and King John excommunicated and clearly growing less and less able to hold his kingdom, Blanche was once more pregnant.

She was larger than was usual and Philip was convinced that she would be delivered of a fine boy.

She was twenty-five—no longer so young, but her intelligence delighted him; and what was most gratifying was that the affection between her and Louis did not wane as it grew more mature. Louis took after his grandfather, that other Louis, and he never looked at other women, which was very rare. Philip himself had had many loves in his life—not all women, but Louis was a serious young man; anxious to rule well, and with the aid of Blanche to win glory for his country, it never occurred to him to be other than a faithful husband.

When Blanche's twins were born dead, the euphoria of the Court was darkened for a while. It was not the first mishap which had befallen Blanche. It was true young Philip thrived in the nursery but recalling how easily young children were carried off by death, the King's uneasiness returned.

Shortly afterwards however she became pregnant again and hopes rose high.

Philip heard it whispered that there could be no continued real good fortune at the Court while his Queen, recognized to be so by the Church, was shut out and robbed of all her royal dignity.

Philip retired to his apartments and communed with himself and God. None knew what it was he so loathed in the woman he had married, and why he still shuddered to have her near him. It was a secret he was not going to divulge to any. But clearly in his private apartments he wrestled with himself. He was King of France, and perhaps more than anything he cared for France. His greatest desire was to make France great again. It seemed to him that God had answered his prayers by putting a reckless fool like John on the throne of England. Each week came news from England and he could see, perhaps more clearly than John could, the storms gathering over his head. His barons were in revolt against him and he had lost precious lands overseas. Very little of Normandy was left to him; and never had France been in a position so advantageous.

God had selected him to be his country's saviour, but he was denying him what he wanted most—a safe nursery. He had young Philip—and his heart filled with joy at the thought of the child—but he lived in terror that some fatal illness would overtake him. He feared for Philip as he had feared for Louis. He did not want the boy to ride too frisky a pony; he was terrified of his taking part in rough games which could result in accidents. Philip would have been the first to admit that this was no way in which to bring up a boy.

Now if there were three, four or five boys in the royal nursery, it would not be so imperative to guard one.

Blanche had lost the twins. Poor girl, she was very sad. She must get boys. It was the only way.

And if God were punishing him there was only one thing he could do and that was bring Ingeburga back.

She came eagerly. Her peripatetic days were over and she was received at Court with all the ceremony of a Queen.

Philip watched her with smouldering eyes; the revulsion was as strong as ever. She knew this and instead of being hurt as she had been all those years ago there was a certain defiance in her attitude.

She had won the battle between them since he had been forced after all these years to take her back, and she was going to enjoy her triumph to the full.

Everywhere they went she was beside him. The people rejoiced for they believed that Heaven would smile on France now that its King no longer offended by exiling his Queen. He showed the utmost concern for her in public but in private he rarely spoke to her; nor could he endure to have her near him.

It was a sad time for him, for she reminded him—by her very difference—of sweet Agnes, and he mourned her afresh.

His children by Agnes flourished and so did his two bastards whom he kept at Court—Peter Charles and Philip Hurepel.

He kept an ever watchful eye on that other Philip and prayed that Blanche's next would be a boy.

That year was one of mingling joy and sorrow for Blanche. In April, her child was born and to the great delight of all, was a boy. They called him Louis after his father and he flourished.

'I knew it would come,' cried the King. 'Now we have two boys whom God preserve. There shall be rejoicing throughout France. Te Deums shall be sung in all the churches. My dearest daughter, this day you have made me a very happy man.'

He believed, and so did most of his subjects, that having brought back Ingeburga and restored her to her rightful place, God was rewarding him with the grandson he so desperately desired.

'Two of them now,' Philip exulted. 'Philip . . . Louis . . . Kings' names for two little Kings.'

He would not feel that they must be guarded quite so closely. Let them play their games, ride their horses, grow into strong men.

Blanche had been having news from Castile which filled her with apprehension. Her mother wrote that her father had developed a fever which had left him weak and which kept recurring. It gave her great anxiety for when he was in the grip of this, she greatly feared for his life.

Nursing her young son, Blanche would brood on what was happening in Castile and was constantly on the alert for news.

She would sit with Amincia, the baby in his cradle beside them, while they stitched on beautiful garments for him. Amincia could do the most beautiful Spanish embroidery and this adorned many of the baby's garments. Together they would remember long summer days in Castile where the troubadours had played their lutes and sung their love songs. Amincia had a pretty voice and would sing some of them, taking Blanche right back to those days. Sometimes Amincia called her Blanca which was yet another reminder.

The singing of troubadours was something she greatly missed in France, for although there was much music at the Court, it was not as it had been in the Courts of Southern France and Spain. There was more talk of war and what was happening in England and what was about to happen there and the part France would play in it.

There came to her notice a boy who must have been some ten years younger than herself. He was handsome, a poet with a beautiful voice. He was proud of his royal blood for he was the grandson of Marie, a daughter of Eleanor of Aquitaine and Louis VII. He had been one of those children who had played in the palace gardens and was under the patronage of the King's household. He therefore considered himself as a member of the royal family and as such enjoyed certain concessions which meant a lapse of ceremony.

He was very attached to Blanche and many were amused by the young boy's devotion. He had started to refer to her in the songs he wrote. It was all rather charming for he was such a handsome, gracious boy.

So often he sat at the feet of Blanche while she with Amincia and others of her women stitched the garments they loved to make for little Louis. Young Philip often joined them; he was five years old, healthy and sturdy, the delight of the grandfather whose name he bore; and it was a very happy nursery over which Blanche presided.

The children, the satisfaction of the King, the harmonious relationship with Louis made up the happiness of that year. But sorrow was to come and was brought to her by messengers from Castile.

Her father had taken a turn for the worse. This time he had not been able to throw off the fever. He died in August when baby Louis was four months old.

Blanche shut herself away; she wanted to see no one. She was back in the past in that happiest of families where there was only the Saracen to threaten them. She remembered the occasions when her father had come home from the wars and what rejoicing there had been through the castle. She remembered the joy in her mother's face and the warm glow which had wrapped itself around them all. She and her two elder sisters with their mother would be down in the courtyard to welcome him, and he would seize first their mother and cling to her as though he was never going to let her go. Their turn came next. Happy, happy days—far away but never to be forgotten and to be relived again and again throughout her life.

'My mother will be quite desolate,' she said. 'The love between them was their life. She will be heart-broken. All her daughters have gone and there is no one. Louis, I must go to her.'

Dear kind understanding Louis, who always wanted to make her happy, said she must go at once. Would it help if he came with her? He understood the relationship between them for did he not enjoy a similar one with his own dear wife?

They made preparations to depart but alas their journey was unnecessary. Two months after Alphonso of Castile had died, Eleanor followed him. They said that she died of a broken heart because she could not go on living without him.

It was discovered that they had left instructions that they were to be buried side by side and they chose the monastery of Las Huelgas which was one for which they had a particular fondness as they had founded it together.

Thus, said Blanche, they who were so close in life will not be parted in death.

The memory of them haunted her and even the happy nursery which contained her two fine boys, and the devotion of Louis, so like that her father had felt for her mother, could not entirely comfort her.

# King and Queen of France

ALTHOUGH the situation across the Channel was growing more and more disruptive, there were troubles enough for the French. Philip's dream of invading England was baulked by one encounter at Boulogne where the English fleet, which was superior to his, sunk and captured more than half his ships. This had proved so costly that Philip had been obliged to put off thought of another attack for a while. It was not as though the field was clear. There were other commitments in Flanders and Poitou.

He had been inclined to imagine himself facing unwise and reckless John; but there were men in England who would remain loyal to the crown however worthless the wearer of it. Two such as these were William Marshal and Hubert de Burgh, and while such men worked for John his defeat would not be an easy matter.

But it was not long before the position changed.

The barons of England had risen against John and had forced him to sign a Charter at Runnymede, which restored rights to his people and mitigated the pernicious forest laws. There were sixty-three clauses, all designed to curb the power of the King and respect the rights of the people of England.

It was not difficult to imagine with what reluctance John had signed such a charter and how insecure his position must be for him to agree to do so; but it was hardly to be expected that he would not try to break his word, for more than a charter would be needed to make him mend his ways and behave with wisdom and justice. Even so Philip had not expected the English barons to play so completely into his hands. When the messengers came to him and told him what was in their minds he could scarcely believe them.

He sent at once for Blanche and Louis, for this was going to be of the utmost concern to them.

When they came he dismissed everyone that he might talk to them in the utmost secrecy.

'There is a most unexpected turn in events,' he said. 'You know how matters are in England. John cannot keep the Crown much longer.'

'But now that he has signed the Charter,' began Louis, 'the barons will keep him in order.'

'It is not possible to keep such a man in order. He is rapacious, sly, untrustworthy and reckless. He has every quality to make him a bad and evil ruler and nothing will ever eradicate one of them. The barons know it. That is why they have made this extraordinary suggestion.' Philip looked at Blanche. 'You have a claim to the throne, my dear, and Louis has through you. The English barons are offering you the Crown of England if you will go and take it.'

'Impossible!' cried Louis.

'Nay, my son, when you go you will be warmly welcomed. The barons want you there . . . they want a strong ruler who will rid them of John.'

'Louis to go to England!' cried Blanche aghast.

'It is Louis who must go,' said Philip firmly. 'He will claim your inheritance and with you rule England. Who would have believed it possible that there should be a strong contingent of men in England who would actually welcome you to their shores?'

'Could it be some trick?' said Blanche anxiously.

'I am assured it is not. These men are at war with their own King. They will have no more of him. They believe that the only way to make the country strong and bring about a return to law and order is to offer the Crown to the next in succession.'

'But there is a son,' said Louis.

'A child!' retorted Philip. 'Imagine. John deposed. A minor on the throne. Would that solve anything? No, the majority of the English barons want John out of the way and this is the way they choose to do it. Do not look so puzzled. It is a wise decision. Almost the whole of their possessions in France have now been lost to them, and many of these barons see the possibility of the return of their castles and lands. It may well be a concession they will ask and we shall grant it. We want peace between our two countries—one ruler for both. What could be better? And we shall achieve little by harsh treatment of those who have made the way easy for us. They know this. They know my rule. They know you, Louis. They compare us with John and they are inviting us to rule them.'

After they had left the King, Louis and Blanche discussed the matter together. It made Blanche uneasy.

'I like it not that you should be the one to go,' she told him. 'Would it not be wiser for your father to lead the forces?'

Louis shook his head. 'Nay,' he said. 'This crown comes to us through you. I am your husband. I shall be the King of England, you the Queen. My father is right when he decrees that I shall be the one to go.'

In the early part of the year 1216 Louis sailed across the Channel and marched on London, in which city he received the homage of those barons who were eager to displace John.

As it was natural that John, with a few who had remained loyal to him—among them those worthy men William Marshal and Hubert de Burgh—should not give way meekly, Louis had to expect resistance and it came. But the more towns he took the more people were ready to accept him. John was antagonizing the entire country through his cruel manner of taking what he wanted from the towns through which he passed and showing no respect for the religious houses. Misfortune dogged him. Crossing the Wash his baggage, including his jewels, were lost; and coming to Sleaford he died somewhat mysteriously. Some said he had been poisoned by a monk from Swineshead Abbey, where he had stayed for a few nights, and where he had seen a nun whom he had attempted to ravish. Sickness, lassitude and the ingenuity of the monks had saved the nun, but afterwards John had died through eating fruit which it was suspected was poisoned.

So he died violently as he had lived and the nightmare which he had created passed with him.

When Philip brought the news to Blanche, they rejoiced together.

'Now matters will run smoothly,' said the King. 'Louis will be crowned and we shall settle down to peace.'

'But what of his sons? I believe there are two of them.'

'Boys . . . nothing more.'

Blanche was thoughtful, thinking that if by some chance Philip and Louis both died and her own Philip, aged seven, was suddenly King, would she stand by and let a foreigner take the Crown? Indeed she would not. She would have him crowned without delay.

Then she thought of Isabella whom she had met briefly soon after her marriage. Languorous, sensuous and very beautiful she had been then. Was she still? She had married John and had seemed to feel few regrets for Hugh, and when one considered the handsome, upright lord of Lusignan and John, surely any woman would have preferred Hugh?

The fact was that although John was dead, there remained Isabella. Would she stand aside and allow Louis to be crowned in place of her son?

She mentioned this to Philip, who shrugged it aside. 'Isabella!' Philip laughed. 'If the tales one hears about her are true it would seem she would be more concerned with her lovers than her son's inheritance. You know she was more or less John's prisoner. He hung her lovers over her bed, so they say, which is characteristic of him. I do not think we need concern ourselves with Isabella.'

'I have a strange feeling,' said Blanche, 'that we shall always have to concern ourselves with Isabella.'

'Nay,' replied Philip. 'God is clearly with us.' He was sober thinking of the price God had asked for his help. Take Ingeburga back. Well, he deserved the luck of being asked to come to England and John's dying at precisely the opportune moment. Philip was sure that God had set the comely nun in John's path and put the idea into the monk's head to poison him.

But it was Blanche's deduction which proved correct.

Isabella *was* concerned with her son. Isabella was a very ambitious woman and she was not going to have her rights thrust aside for a foreigner.

Moreover she had two strong men beside her, William Marshal and Hubert de Burgh.

In a short time after John's death young Henry was crowned
and it became clear that those barons who had invited Louis
to come and rule them had only wanted to be rid of John.
God had removed him and now they would have their rightful
King on the throne and if he was but a boy of nine he had
strong loyal men beside him.

It was obvious that Louis was no longer welcome in England. He had a choice. He could remain and fight a bloody
war, and such a war fought away from home on foreign soil
would be an almost certain failure—or he could go home.

He chose the latter.

So the English adventure was over. There was a young
King on the throne and as strong men were there to support
him, law and order was restored to England. True, John had
lost most of his possessions on the Continent ('And we must
keep it so,' said Philip) but at the time there was nothing to
be done.

And while Louis had been away Blanche had given birth to
another child—another boy to delight his grandfather.

He was called Robert.

Three boys in the nursery. That was a number to make a
King happy.

While Philip was exulting in the possession of his three
grandsons, tragedy struck the nursery. The eldest and the
King's namesake, who had been out hunting in the best of
health one day, on the next was too sick to leave his bed.

At first it had seemed some indefinable childish ailment but
as two days passed and the child developed a fever there was
anxiety for his health and doctors were called from all over
the kingdom.

The King sat by his bed with Blanche and Louis, and
anxiously they watched together, but the child who had seemed
so full of health and high spirits did not rally.

'What more could I have done?' Philip demanded. 'I gave
up Agnes, I took back Ingeburga.' A cold fear came to him.
Was God asking him to live with her as her husband? Oh no!
That was asking too much. God could not be so cruel. And
while he tormented himself he watched his beloved namesake
die.

There was deep mourning at Court. Young Louis was the important one now. He was a fine upstanding little fellow, a child of whom a King could be proud—but then so had Philip been. Alive and well one week and dead the next! It looked like the hand of an avenging God, for no one could suggest for a moment that the child had been poisoned.

As though in compensation Blanche almost immediately became pregnant and in due course gave birth to another boy. She wanted to call him Alphonso after her father, but this was not a French name. However, Philip was so delighted that there should be another boy in the nursery that he agreed providing the French form of the name—Alphonse—was used. He was delighted, he said, that she showed how deeply she cared for her father that she wished her son to be called after him.

Philip admitted to himself that few kings could be as content with their heirs as he was with his. He thought of his beloved Richard Coeur de Lion—who had had none—and Henry, Richard's father, who had watched his sons—one by one—turn against him.

Louis would never do that. He could say without reservation that in Louis he had the best of sons. He remembered how, long ago, he had forbidden him to ride into the tourneys and not once had Louis disobeyed him; although the decree had put him into a difficult situation and might secretly have earned him the name of coward in some quarters.

Louis, Robert, Alphonse and then John all following each other and taking as little time as possible to do so. Four healthy grandsons. How Philip gloated! God could not have been displeased after all.

News reached the Court of France which astonished all those who heard it. Queen Isabella, widow of King John, had arrived in Lusignan with her daughter Joan who was betrothed to Hugh de Lusignan, but having set eyes on Isabella he had decided to marry her instead.

Philip laughed heartily.

'I remember her well. When John made off with her they called her the Helen of the thirteenth century. To see her was to understand why. I believe quite a number of men were completely bewitched by her. John certainly was. As for Hugh de Lusignan he waited all these years for her. But I doubt not that he has married trouble.'

'I doubt it not either,' said Blanche.

Philip looked sideways at his daughter-in-law. She would be remembering her meeting with Isabella; and she would feel that natural antipathy to her which he supposed most women would feel towards one who must put them all in the shade.

He wondered whether Isabella had lost any of her allure. He doubted it. Women like that kept it to the end of their days and the fact that Hugh had taken her instead of her young daughter suggested that she still retained that potent power to attract men.

Blanche was uneasy yet she could not understand why the thought of Isabella's being near should make her so. She had felt an inexplicable revulsion when they had met and in spite of what most people would think, it had nothing to do with envy of a blatant ability to attract men.

'I trust Hugh will be happy with her,' she said to Louis.

'He has never married and it is almost as though he waited for her, so he must be sure of his feelings.'

'I would suspect that she brought her daughter to Lusignan with the idea of marrying the bridegroom herself.'

Louis did not really believe that was possible, but then he was a very innocent man.

When news came to the Court that Hugh refused to send her daughter back to England until Isabella's dowry was sent out, the comment was that this would be Isabella's doing. For all his valour Hugh was a quiet man.

'Depend upon it,' said Philip, 'she will lead him by the nose.'

'I wonder how she likes being the wife of a Count when she has been a Queen,' murmured Blanche.

'I'll wager you she does not like it at all,' said Philip.

'Then,' replied Blanche, 'the chances are that she will attempt to do something about it.'

'What can she do?' asked Philip. 'She married him of her own free will. She is back to what she would have been if John had not seen her riding in the forest. At least Hugh won't hang her lovers over her bed.'

'It is to be hoped that she will not take any and be satisfied with her husband.'

Philip shrugged his shoulders and Blanche's uneasiness persisted.

For some time Philip had been plagued by the Albigensians against whom, because they were in the South of France, the Pope had commanded him to campaign. To go into battle with them was going into battle for the Church and it was an opportunity for a man to receive a remission of his sins where, before this sect had arisen, he would have to make the long, tedious and dangerous journey to the Holy Land to achieve the same purpose.

The Albigenses, so called because they lived in the diocese of Albi, were a people who loved pleasure, music and literature; they were by no means irreligious, but they liked to indulge in freedom of thought. Their great pleasure was to discuss ideas and examine doctrines and the Pope, recognizing in this a danger, sent men of the Church to preach to these people and point out the folly and danger of their discourse. The result was what might have been expected. The preachers were listened to at first and when it was discovered that they had not come to develop ideas but to prevent the discussion of them, were ignored.

The Church was watchful. It feared that irrefutable arguments might be put forward against it. Seventy or eighty years earlier Peter Abelard had been such a danger. His rationalistic interpretation of the Christian doctrines had caused him to be branded a heretic and St. Bernard, the Abbot of Clairvaux, had thundered against him. His love affair with Heloise, who became Prioress of Argenteuil and Abbess of the Paraclete had been of use to Bernard and Abelard had been defeated.

St. Bernard had visited Toulouse which was the centre of this unrest which had been brought about by the interference of the Church. The people of Albi had no wish to interfere with existing Church lore, merely to have the freedom to discuss and worship in their own way.

There had been attempts to carry out persecutions but these had come to little. Raymond, Count of Toulouse, was an easy-going man. He did not want trouble with Rome, nor did he wish to antagonize his subjects. When he died his son Raymond, the sixth Count, reigned in his place. He proved to be pleasure-loving, musical, cultured and was even more lenient than his father had been. At his Court religion was freely discussed and he himself became interested in the new ideas.

With the coming of Innocent III to the Papal Throne the persecution of the Albigensians broke into a cruel war, out of which had grown what was known as the Holy Office or the Inquisition. The Church was determined to stamp out heretics and was prepared to go to any lengths to do this. Those who disagreed with the doctrines as laid down by the Church were tortured in various barbaric ways and if they refused to change their views—and sometimes even if they did—were burned alive at the stake.

Innocent had found a man useful to him in Simon, Count of Montfort-l'Amaury. This man had belonged to a family which, from small beginnings, had in a few generations enriched itself. The first Lord Montfort had adopted his name and title simply because he owned a small castle between Paris and Chartres. Marriage brought them wealth and standing and the earldom of Leicester, but the Count had quickly realized that the chances of advancing himself with John were not good and that he would be better under Philip of France, so he came to his Norman estates and lived there.

He saw a chance of making his name and fortune in the war against the Albigensians and as he had qualities of leadership and was also a fierce Catholic, he was soon renowned as the leader of the crusade.

In a short time he became the Captain General; and he was noted for his fierceness in battle, his genius for leadership and his fanatical cruelty.

Philip did not like de Montfort and deplored the campaign against the Albigensians. He was not deeply involved with religion and practised it out of a desire to placate the heavenly powers rather than out of piety. He had a strong sense of justice and from his father he had inherited a belief in moderation; and as the Counts of Toulouse were vassals of his he objected to the armies of the Pope fighting there.

Innocent had sent word to him that as a true Christian he owed it to his conscience and his God to fight with the army of the righteous.

'The army of the righteous!' cried Philip. 'Who is to say which is the righteous? What harm have the Albigensians ever done to anyone but themselves if they are indeed heretics? And surely God is capable of dealing with those who defy His laws . . . if indeed they are His laws. But it may be that His Holiness has made a mistake in interpreting them.'

He wrote to the Pope. 'I have on my flanks two terrifying lions—the Emperor Otho and King John of England—who are working with all their might to bring trouble upon the Kingdom of France.' He had no inclination, he said, at that time to march against the Albigensians nor to send his son but he had intimated to his barons in the province of Narbonne that they might march against disturbers of the peace.

That was an oblique enough command, for who was to say who was disturbing the peace? It was more likely to be the foreign armies than the people of Albi whose simple determination to maintain their freedom was responsible for the trouble.

In the year 1213, Simon de Montfort won the battle of Muret and Philip sent Louis to look on while the crusaders took possession of Toulouse.

Louis came back horrified by what he had seen. The town laid waste was the smallest part of it. Every refinement of cruelty had been perpetrated on the citizens of the town.

Philip took Louis to his private chamber and there they talked. Louis was in his twenty-sixth year at that time—sensitive, brave enough, but liking war even less than his father. He said that he would never forget the fearful atrocities he had seen that day.

Philip clenched his hands and said: 'I hope before long Simon de Montfort and his men will die at their work, for God is just and their quarrel is unjust.'

However, when the victories of de Montfort were decisive he was forced to accept him as his vassal in place of Raymond but when he died he refused to recognize his son. But by that time Raymond and his son had recaptured much of the territory lost to them and in the year 1218 (two years after the death of Innocent himself) a shower of stones falling from the ramparts crushed de Montfort to death, when he was trying to recapture the castle of Toulouse.

So Philip was pestered by the Albigensian question, for like all kings he lived in some awe of the Pope and he knew from recent experience over the trouble with Agnes and Ingeburga how uncomfortable popes could make a king's life.

Now he brooded on the matter. It was not that he was ready to endanger himself or his realm through a sense of righteousness; he had ever been guided by expediency and his discretion had always been a strong point in his favour. He had governed well, he could assure himself; there was evidence of that everywhere; he was a king to be respected, and this was due to his conduct over the years of his sovereignty. He had come to the throne young—a boy of fifteen. He had reigned for nearly forty years and during that time he had learned chiefly when to act and more important when not to act. This was one of the reasons why he had been able to keep moderately aloof from what he considered to be a barbaric war of dubious justice, and at the same time not offend the Pope enough to bring about reprisals.

He had begun to be affected by recurrent fever and his doctors did not know the reason for it. When it attacked him he found it necessary to take to his bed.

There he brooded on the state of the country and often he sent for Blanche that he might talk to her. He found he could do so with absolute frankness. He was concerned about Louis.

He loved his son. 'He has never willingly caused me a moment's anxiety,' he said. 'He is a good man, but good men can easily be the victims of evil ones, as you well know. My daughter, I rejoice in the day your grandmother brought you to us. It may well be that one day you will stand beside my son and rule this land.'

'That day, I pray, is a long way off,' said Blanche fervently.

'Oh, I am a young man yet,' replied Philip. 'Perhaps I shall live for another fifteen years . . . and a few more . . . what is that. Young Louis shapes well. And there are the other boys. Young Robert loves his brother Louis well. I hope that affection continues through their lives. As for the others they are too young as yet to show us what they will become. But it rejoices me that you have filled our nursery with good strong boys. As I could not have wished for a better son I could also not have wished for a better daughter.'

Blanche was deeply moved. She said: 'I have a feeling that once more I am to be *enceinte.*'

'Praise God,' said Philip. 'And if this time it should be a girl we will bless our good fortune.'

In due course the child was born. He was called Philip, but because his parents were reminded of that beautiful boy who had died in his ninth year, they wished to distinguish between the newcomer and his dead brother and they added Dagobert to his name, so that he was always known as Philip Dagobert—it was considered to be an unusual name at this time though many Kings had borne it in the seventh century. Blanche pointed out, so that it was a pleasant idea to revive it, while naming the child after his grandfather.

The King was feeling ill and in no mood to leave his bed when news was brought to him that the Pope had called a council which would take place in Paris.

Philip who was resting at his palace at Pacy-sur-Eure grimaced when he heard the news. The fact that the meeting was to be held in Paris meant, of course, that he was expected to be present. He would like to see the whole matter of this trouble cleared up, but was uneasy because the Church, deciding with great determination to stamp out heresy, was instituting this Holy Office which Philip felt was a dangerous invention. He foresaw that no man would be safe from it, and bearing in mind the Church's constant need for money, he wondered whether those who possessed it might be selected as victims, as in addition to torturing the so-called heretic they confiscated his wealth which of course went into the coffers of the Church.

Trying to look ahead into a future which he was beginning to think he would not be there to see, he could visualize dangers in this Holy Office or Inquisition. He even wondered whether it would bring good—even if it brought gain—to the Church. He could see men of substance moving away to those countries where it was not upheld. Perhaps he would put these ideas forward at the conference. Perhaps not. It was not for him to concern himself with what went on outside France. It was because he had always followed that belief that France was now in a far better position than she had been when he came to the throne.

So he would go to the conference, speak discreetly, neither condoning nor condemning. He was adept at such manoeuvre.

He felt limp and weak, but nevertheless he was determined to attend. One so often feigned an illness and offered it as an excuse that when one was genuinely sick one was not believed.

He rode on but the heat was too much for him, for it was July and the sultry weather did not suit him.

When they reached Mantes he said he would rest for a while. He took to his bed and it occurred to him as he was helped there by his servants that he might never rise from it.

During the night he awoke and felt the fever was increasing. It had the effect of making his mind hazy and yet as he grappled to keep hold on his consciousness he was aware all the time that this was the end.

His mind went back to those days which followed the capture of Acre when he had made up his mind to leave Richard and return to France. It was a great decision . . . the right decision. He had made it for the good of his country. He could remember vividly the excessive heat . . . the fearful plagues, the mud, the scorpions, all the discomforts on which Richard had seemed to thrive.

France first . . . that had been his motto. And it had brought rewards. He was leaving Louis a well-governed land; much of that which France had lost for years was now returned. One day, the English should have no claims in France. It was not quite so as yet . . . but that would come.

Wise government . . . that was what was necessary. War only when there is no other way. Justice for the people so that they would accept hardship when need be.

Oh, Louis, he thought, you will have Blanche to help you. I pin my hopes on Blanche, my son, for although you are the best of sons I doubt you will be the strongest of kings.

Ingeburga would not mourn very much. She would be a fool if she did. Now Ingeburga would come into her own. There would be nowhere where she would not now be received with honour. The Dowager Queen of France. He shuddered to remember that first night and only night with her. She had bided her time. In a way her methods were like his own. She had refused to relinquish her hold and had quietly submitted to indignity. He had paid dearly for that hasty marriage. It had cost him Agnes . . . dear sweet, uncomplaining Agnes. And it was Ingeburga who had won in the end.

Louis the King and Blanche the Queen. They were thirty-five years old, mature and with a fine nursery of sons. Young Louis was nine years old. Well, that was a good age with a father who was only thirty-five. Louis had a long life before him yet and Blanche would train young Louis in the way he must go.

Philip could close his eyes and say: 'Lord now lettest thy servant depart in peace.'

He had arranged everything and it augured well.

Louis was bewildered. His father ill . . . possibly dying. He could not believe it.

He went into the death chamber and threw himself on to his knees. He took his father's hands and looked at him appealingly as though begging him not to die.

Philip said: 'All will be well, my son. Is Blanche there?'

She came to kneel beside her husband.

'Blanche, dear daughter, I thank God for you. Look after Louis, the King of France . . . very soon now. Into your hands I commend him . . . and the young Louis . . . my grandson. And Louis, weep not, my son. My time has come as it must for us all. Beloved son, you never caused me grief. I marvelled that it should be so. God's blessing on you. Blanche, Louis . . . my beloved children . . . I thank God I leave you each other. I have put France before aught else in my life. Perhaps I was wrong. But I served my country well and it was God who gave me the task when He made me the son of a King . . . as He now puts that burden on you, my dear Louis.'

They sat beside his bed and that contented him.

He was smiling as he died.

Blanche deeply regretted the death of the King. She loved her husband; he had never been anything but faithful to her and had shown her every kindness and consideration, but a woman as forceful as herself must know that he could never be a great king as his father had been. As a Prince of France, with his father to guide him, he had been admirable. She knew that it would be different when he stood on his own.

She was determined to bring up her sons herself so that when the time came for them to take the throne, they would be prepared. Had Philip faltered with Louis? Perhaps. That obsession with his health and safety was understandable, for he was the only legitimate son, but such coddling care was bound to have its effect. Louis was no coward but he was no strategist either. There was weakness in him, a lack of ruthlessness, which however pleasant in the personal character was no good for a ruler.

During that splendid ceremony at Rheims she was uneasy, although there was great rejoicing throughout the land and a prosperous reign was prophesied. When his father had married Isabel of Hainault who was in the direct line from Hermengarde, daughter of Charles of Lorraine, the last of the Carlovingians, the rival claims of the dynasties of Charlemagne and Hugh Capet had come together; and Louis was the fruit of this. No one now could dispute his absolute right to the throne.

All was set fair, said the people. It was a long time since France had been so prosperous. The English had been defeated as never before. Philip, that master of strategy, had held aloof from the Albigensian war. He had lived on affectionate terms with his son and they had never been anything but the best of friends.

'Oh Fortunate France!' said its people.

Ingeburga had assumed a new importance. She was affable and kind and took a great interest in the royal children. The death of Philip had naturally brought her closer into the family circle and none could understand what had been the cause of Philip's aversion to her. She lived in state and dignity and the children were fond of her.

For a few months after the coronation there was rejoicing, but if Louis believed this would continue, Blanche did not.

The first intrusion into their peace came from Lusignan.

Blanche immediately remembered the sly-eyed Isabella who

had made such an impression on her when they had first met, the memory of which had been revived by her marrying the man selected for her daughter a few years before.

When the messengers arrived from Lusignan with letters from Hugh, Blanche guessed there would be trouble, and when they read them they were not surprised.

Hugh, who had, Blanche was sure, written at the command of his wife, pointed out that King John had assigned certain lands to Isabella and it was her right to reclaim that land.

'I feel certain,' said Blanche, 'that that woman will lead Hugh by the nose and if you would have him as your ally you must placate his wife.'

'Nay,' said Louis, 'he is an ambitious man. He wants his wife's land. I hear that Isabella has a son now—Hugh after his father.'

'Let us hope,' retorted Blanche, 'that she is a better mother to him than she has been to her children by John.'

'She was wise enough to get young Henry crowned with the utmost speed.'

'Because it was to her own advantage to do so. With the same speed she took her daughter's betrothed and married him. Louis, we must be watchful of Isabella of Angoulême.'

'My dearest, we must be watchful of all.'

'We are in agreement on that, but with such a woman we will need to exercise more than usual care.'

Louis smiled benignly but she knew that he did not understand.

It was necessary to go on a tour of certain towns and he would visit, with his army, those where he might expect trouble. Blanche had agreed with him that it would be well to show that while he was prepared to be reasonable, the people must not imagine that he was going to be any less strong than his father.

They travelled first to Lusignan for Hugh was a man too powerful to ignore either as an ally or an enemy and with all the unrest which invariably followed a new reign, Louis would have to be watchful. He was expecting the English to make an attempt to retrieve their losses in Normandy.

With them rode, among other vassals to the Crown, Thibaud the fourth Count of Champagne, that very handsome though somewhat corpulent troubadour who considered himself royal because his grandmother was the daughter of Louis VII, the father of King Philip Augustus, thus making him a kinsman of the King.

He had never ceased to sing of his admiration for Blanche and had become known as Thibaud Le Chansonnier; and that royal arrogance he assumed sometimes disturbed her. There was often a suggestion in his looks which she refused to accept for what it was. None would dare insult the Queen, who was known to be as loyal to the King as he was to her; but there were some who noticed that the Count of Champagne was obviously enamoured of Blanche and would give a great deal to be her lover. A vain hope, said most; but there were some who liked to look wise and murmur that women were unaccountable, that Blanche was a strong healthy woman and Louis scarcely lusty. It was considered by some that a man who must absent himself from his wife as frequently as Louis did and be as faithful as he was, was in some way lacking.

As for Blanche she conveyed the impression that the Count of Champagne was nothing to her but a vassal and a connection of her husband's through their grandfather.

The King and Queen and a few of their chosen followers were given a loyal welcome at the Lusignan castle and the King's men were in the town or encamped in its environs.

It had seemed right to come thus, for it would show Hugh de Lusignan—if he was of a mind to be intransigent—that the King was ready to enforce his commands.

Hugh showed no sign of a lack of loyalty and Isabella did not curtsey but opened her beautiful black-fringed violet eyes and smiled at the King as she bowed her head. Blanche was watching, though hoping none saw how intently. The beautiful eyes had no effect on Louis.

Now it was Blanche's turn. Isabella bowed, every gesture implying: If you are a Queen, so am I, for once a Queen always a Queen and I was longer Queen of England than you have been Queen of France.

'We are greatly honoured to receive you,' said Isabella, and she and Hugh led them into the castle.

Hugh walked beside the King, Isabella beside Blanche.

'How desolate you must be,' said Isabella. 'I know well how you loved the late King. And your responsibilities have become great.'

Her eyes were on Blanche's gown of blue velvet which was becoming; it flowed to the ground and the sleeves were long and tight after the fashion of the day and over them she wore a supertunic and a mantle; her wimple was made of fine silk, blue to match her gown. She was beautiful. But Isabella was complacent. Without effort she could outshine any other woman she had ever met.

Her own gown long flowing with similar tight sleeves was of scarlet—flamboyantly rich and demanding attention; her hair flowed about her shoulders and about her brow was a gold circle which glowed with a single ruby.

Blanche thought: She has changed very little. If anything she is more wily because she is older.

When the royal party was refreshed there was a feast in the great hall. On the dais was a table smaller than that in the main hall and at this small table sat Hugh with Isabella, Louis and Blanche. At the great table in the centre of the hall sat the most noble of the King's followers and those of Hugh and below the great salt-cellar, those of lesser rank.

Blanche was conscious that Isabella was eager for them to realize that, although they were vassals of the King of France here in Lusignan, in England she had been a Queen and if she returned to that country would be received as the mother of the reigning King.

The table was laden with good food—venison, beef, mutton and pies of all descriptions and the wine which was produced in the nearby vineyards was of the best.

As the company sat drowsy from good food and wine the *jongleurs*, or minstrels, arrived. These were those men who travelled the country and came in search of castles and great houses where their performances would be rewarded by food and a night's shelter.

The company was always eager to see and hear them perform and they would pass judgment on the songs, which some of the minstrels had composed themselves, and pay accordingly. They were a sad company for they were despised as strolling players and it was not unknown that after having heard their performances the masters and mistresses of the big houses would begrudge their payment.

But this would not be the case on this night for they would sing before the King and in great castles such as this one, payment could be relied upon.

So it was a happy band of minstrels who performed for them.

They sang of their travels and stressed that they were poor minstrels in great company.

> 'But I know how well to serve a knight
> And of fine tales the whole sum
> I know stories; I know fables,
> I can tell fine new tales.'

The company listened to the tales and fables—mostly concerning the hopeless lover's plaint for his mistress; and the applause was led by Isabella, whose beautiful eyes sparkled as she listened.

> 'I am a minstrel of the viol
> I know the musette and the flute
> And the harp and the chifonie
> The gigue and the armonie
> And the salteire and the rote
> I know well how to sing a tune.
>
> I know many fine table tricks
> And from prestidigitations and magic
> Well know how to make an enchantment.'

Isabella clapped her hands and Hugh looked at her indulgently.

'Good minstrel,' she cried, 'tell me how *you* make an enchantment.'

'With my song, my lady,' was the answer. 'But not as sure as you can make them with your beauteous eyes.'

Then he made a song on the spur of the moment—he implied and it could well have been one which he had in readiness for ladies whom he knew would enjoy it—which told of the fatal beauty of a lady which exceeded that of all others in the world.

Blanche looked on a little cynically and thought that here was one minstrel who would not go unrewarded.

Then Isabella declared that there had been enough of the minstrels and they should be taken to the kitchens and there given food for they had done their work well; and they would play the game of questions and commands and she would claim the privilege, as lady of the castle, of asking the first question.

She walked into the centre of the hall and called to one of her women to tie a silken kerchief about her eyes. Then she stood there with her arms outstretched looking so beautiful that none of the men—Blanche noticed—could take his eyes from her. Even Louis watched her with indulgence.

She put a white bejewelled hand to her lips as though she were thinking, then she said: 'Alas ladies, our lords must often leave us and when they leave us are they faithful to us? We know their natures, ladies. Should we be blamed if we, sorely tempted and alone, fall into temptation such as they find irresistible?'

There was a hushed silence in the hall as Isabella began to move forward, her arms outstretched, feeling her way towards the tables. Ladies held their breath as she passed them and Blanche knew at once that she would be the one on whom Isabella would lay her hands and who, according to the rules of the game, must answer.

It was not a game. It meant something. Whatever peace should be made between their husbands, it was war between Isabella and Blanche.

Nearer to Blanche came Isabella and the outstretched white hands came to rest on the shoulder of the Queen of France.

'This is the one who will answer me,' said Isabella. 'If she be a lady I trust she is wise for we hang on her words.'

Of course she could see, Blanche knew. She would have arranged that with her woman. She knew on whom she had laid her hands.

'If whoever I have touched does not wish to answer,' said Isabella, 'that knight or lady must pay a forfeit.'

Blanche stood up and said coldly: 'There is an obvious answer to such a straightforward question.'

Isabella tore the kerchief from her eyes and pretended to be overcome with embarrassment.

'It is the Queen!' she stammered. 'My lady . . . I most humbly beg. . . .'

'There is no need to beg humbly or otherwise,' said Blanche briskly. 'The answer is that if the husband is so foolish as to ignore his marriage vows no good would come of his wife's repeating the folly.'

There was applause throughout the hall. Blanche felt her usual calmness desert her. She did not know what it was about Isabella that affected her so strongly. It was as though all her senses warned her against the woman. The question was meant to imply that Louis was necessarily often away from her and could not be expected to be faithful and it was a sly way of asking whether she, Blanche the Queen, took the occasional lover. We know, thought Blanche fiercely, that Isabella Queen of England was not averse to the practice since her first husband was known to have hung at least one of her lovers on her bed tester.

She said: 'I believe the rule of the game is that I am the next to be blindfolded. Pray bind my eyes.'

So she went to the centre of the hall and her eyes were bound as Isabella's had been and she made sure that the kerchief was so loosely bound that she would grope her way forward until she came to a rich scarlet skirt and then she would lay her hands on the owner of it and ask her question.

She spoke clearly: 'Should a parent put the welfare of his or her child before personal desire and pleasure?'

She was aware of the depth of the silence. Everyone would know this was a criticism of Isabella's conduct in taking the man her daughter had come out to marry and sending the child back to an unknown fate.

All present shrank into their seats fearing to be asked such a question, for the obvious answer that self-sacrifice must be made would be a deliberate slight on Isabella who had thought differently.

But Blanche picked her way carefully and there was a deep sigh as her hands rested on Isabella's shoulders.

Isabella burst into laughter. 'Why, my lady, see whom you have chosen. How strange it is, for I picked you and you have picked me. I will not pay the forfeit for I will answer the question. My lady, there is only one answer. We must all do what is best for our children no matter what the cost to ourselves.'

Everyone applauded with relief and none dared smile behind their hands for Isabella had sharp eyes and she could be vindictive.

'I shall ask no more questions,' she declared, 'so shall pass on the kerchief to another. Ah, Hugh, my husband, let me bind your eyes.'

The game went on—questions were asked and answered. Isabella smiled at Blanche. 'A childish game, is it not?' she said. 'But it would seem to amuse some. I should like more singing and then we will call the *jongleurs* back to do tricks for us. If that is your wish, my lady?'

Blanche said that she thought the game somewhat childish and that the most amusing were usually the first questions; after that it could pall.

So Isabella clapped her hands and declared that she would name some of the knights to play for them and perhaps sing if they could and that she had heard that the Count of Champagne was a very skilful songster. Would he enchant them with his music?

The Count rose from the table and bowing low declared his pleasure.

He then sang of the beauty of one whom he had long admired from afar. She was beyond his reach but so fair was she that he could find joy in no other.

It was a song which, it was whispered, he had written to the Queen; but she being so virtuous had not been aware that it was written of her.

Everyone applauded when he had finished and none more fervently than Isabella.

'A beautiful song, my lord,' she cried, 'and well sung. I am sure if your lady heard you sing with such feeling she would be unable to deny you.'

'Ah, my lady,' replied Thibaud, 'if she did my song would have no meaning.'

'Then you could write another,' declared Isabella, 'and I'll swear it would be even more beautiful.'

She then called the *jongleurs* back and they performed acrobatic feats of great dexterity to the delight of all; and so passed the night.

In their bedchamber Isabella, her hair loose about her shoulders, her eyes blazing with excitement, was laughing with Hugh.

'Dear, dear Hugh,' she cried, 'I believe I shocked you greatly tonight.'

'My love,' he replied reproachfully, 'the Queen was put out.'

'The Queen. I hate that woman. Haughty, cold, reminding all that she is the Queen.'

'She *is* the Queen, my dear.'

'She is the Queen of a few months. I have been a Queen for years. I will be treated as such. In marrying you I am but the wife of a Count but I am a Queen none the less.'

'Blanche is a reigning Queen.'

'Poor Louis! He has to do as he is told. And poor little Louis, the son . . . and the rest of them. I tell you she is a woman who will be obeyed.'

'Some women are,' replied Hugh.

She laughed at him and running to him put her arms about his neck. She pulled him to the bed and lay down with him. She could always bring him to her way of thinking at any time . . . but it was easier thus.

'They have different methods. Can you imagine Blanche and Louis like this?'

'Never.'

She laughed. 'My beautiful Hugh,' she said, 'you don't know how often I thought of you when I was with that odious John. And you love me, do you not? You would do anything to please me. What should I make you do, Hugh? Go to the royal chamber and take a cushion and hold it down over that haughty face until it is still and cold. . . .'

'Isabella, what are you saying!'

'Nothing of importance. How could you do that? And to

what purpose? But they must do what *we* want, Hugh. They are afraid of us.'

'I think not, my love. Louis is the King, Blanche the Queen. You have seen the army they have encamped around.'

'But why do they come here thus, if they are not here to placate you? Why should they come here . . . first to you. Louis is recently King and he says, "I must go and speak with Hugh de Lusignan." They are afraid of us, Hugh. We must keep them afraid.'

'Nay, I am but Louis's vassal.'

'Vassal! say not that word to me. I hate it. I will not be married to a vassal. Listen to me, Hugh. We may have to pretend to pay homage. You may . . . I never will. But my son is the King of England. Do you not see what that means? We are in a powerful position. Henry will not desert his mother. He is a good and docile boy . . . and so young. Louis is afraid of you. No, Hugh, you and I will put our heads together and use them both. Do you understand?'

'My dear, there could be war. . . .'

'Well, there will be war and if there is war Louis will be more than ever afraid of the Lusignans. Henry will want us to be on his side too. You see how well you did for yourself when you married the Queen of England. Hugh, will you leave this to me?' He did not answer and she pouted. 'I should be a little angry . . . even with you, Hugh, if you did not.'

He smiled at her and put his lips against her hair.

'You looked beautiful tonight, Isabella.'

'Do I not always?'

'Always, but tonight there was something wild about you . . . something. . . .'

'Irresistible?' she asked.

'Always that.'

'Except to two men . . . Louis and the Count of Champagne.'

'Louis has little time for any woman but his wife.'

'The virtuous husband! Are you faithful always to me?'

'Always, but for far different reasons than Louis is to his wife.'

'What reasons?'

'After you none would do for me. Louis feels no strong impulses.'

Isabella laughed aloud.

'And Champagne?'

'He is fixed on the Queen. Poor fellow, it will do him no good.'

'She is an icicle, that woman.' Isabella sighed and opened her arms. 'Very different from your Isabella.'

The Queen paced up and down the apartment which had been prepared for her and Louis.

'I don't trust that woman,' said Blanche. 'I don't trust Hugh de Lusignan either . . . now that he is married to her.'

Louis said: 'You have allowed her to upset you. The question you asked. . . .'

'I meant mine for her. I hope she remembered how inhumanly she treated that poor daughter of hers. I have heard that the child loved Hugh, who would be good and kind I am sure, were it not for that woman who seems to have bewitched him.'

'It was strange that you should have picked her out after she had picked you.'

Blanche looked at him with fond exasperation. Louis was a very innocent man.

'We must be watchful of them, of course,' Louis went on. 'They are going to ask for concessions. We must be very wary of granting them.'

'The Lusignans have always been a family to reckon with. Don't forget that Hugh is the head of a house which reigns over a large part of France from the valleys of the Creuse and the Vienne in the east to Lusignan in the west. They hold many castles in Poitou. They could be a danger. . . .'

'Either to us or to Henry should he decide to come over and try to regain that which his father lost. And Isabella is his mother.'

'That woman would have no feeling for her son,' said Blanche firmly. 'I fancy she would use him—as she did her daughter—to suit her own ends.'

'I am not sure. She is clearly in love with Hugh and he undoubtedly with her. It may have been that their emotions overruled their sense of duty.'

'As expediency would do as easily as love,' replied Blanche cynically. 'So we must take care.'

'Never fear, we shall. They are claiming Saintes and Oleron which Isabella declares were promised as her dower lands.'

'And you will grant them possession of these, Louis?'

'We cannot afford to have the Lusignans against us. Don't forget, Hugh commands a large army. If he were with us, if he were our ally, we could leave the south in his hands and return to the north where we may well be needed.'

Blanche saw the wisdom of this. 'If Hugh had not married that woman, I would trust him.'

'He has ever been a man of honour.'

'Now he is married to Isabella you will see a change in him.'

'Nay, Blanche. You are obsessed by the woman. She is a very fascinating creature and it is clear that Hugh is bewitched by her, but he is a soldier and a man of honour, and nothing can change that.'

'Isabella could change it.'

'You attribute too much power to her.'

'You say I am obsessed by her. She is obsessed by power. And if Henry of England should come against us . . . and she his mother. . . .'

'Henry is a boy yet. We must be prepared for action, yes. That is why we are here in Lusignan. If I can be sure of Hugh I can feel reasonably confident.'

'To be sure of Hugh, yes. . . .'

'He is a man I trust.'

Blanche sighed wearily. What was the use of trying to explain to Louis? When he looked at Isabella he only saw the most fascinating of women. He did not see the calculating schemer who would stop at nothing to get what she wanted.

They left during the next day. Louis had promised Hugh possession of Saintes and Oleron, and had discussed plans with Hugh for the capture of Gascony and the whole of

Poitou and promised Hugh the town of Bordeaux when it was in their hands.

Hugh and Isabella watched the royal cavalcade depart. Hugh would make ready for war to carry out his part of the bargain. He was gratified that the King had realized the wisdom of strengthening their friendship. Louis was pleased too. He was sure it was a move of which his father would have approved.

Only Blanche was uneasy as they rode away.

# ENGLAND
## 1223–1226

# Royal Brothers and Sisters

IT was rare that Henry and his brother and sisters were gathered together and this seemed to him a very special occasion. Richard, who was not quite two years younger than he was, had come to court from Corfe Castle where he was being brought up under the stern tutelage of Peter de Mauley, for Hubert de Burgh had said: 'It is getting near the time when something must be done about your brother.' Richard was at that time fourteen years of age. 'For,' went on Hubert, 'if something is not done for Princes they have a way of attempting to do something for themselves.'

Henry, who hung on Hubert's words, agreed immediately that they must send for Richard and he duly arrived at Court, where the two brothers confronted each other with a certain admiration and suspicion. Henry had acquired a regality since he had ascended the throne; as for Richard he had always been aware that he had been named after his uncle Coeur de Lion and as he had often been reminded of this he had developed a determination to be like that warlike hero. He naturally thought it was a pity that fate had been so unkind as to make him the second-born instead of the first, but the second son of a King was of great importance, so he was looking forward now to dispensing with the tiresomeness of childhood and coming out into the world to make his name.

Hubert had said to Henry: 'In a year or so when your brother is sixteen, it will be necessary to knight him, and present him with land and titles. It is important for there to be complete amity between you. A good brother can be of inestimable value; a bad one, the greatest menace a King can know.'

Henry was remembering this as he received Richard and it

191

was easier than he had believed, for Richard was delighted to be at Court. The brothers had seen each other only once since the death of their father and that had been at the time of Henry's coronation three years before. A boy grows up a great deal in three years and this was particularly so in the case of Henry.

They rode together and talked of the old days which Richard could not remember well, but Henry reminded him of how their mother had hastened him to be crowned with her throat-collar because there was no crown. That was why it had all to be done again in a proper manner four years later.

'How strange,' said Richard, 'that our mother should have taken Joan to Lusignan and then married the man Joan was betrothed to.'

'We don't like it,' said Henry importantly. 'You see, Hubert and many of them think that if the King of France persuades Hugh de Lusignan to fight for him, our mother will be with her husband, not with us.'

'Does Lusignan matter so much? He is only a count. We can fight him.'

'He owns a great deal of land and is the overlord of many. Our father, you remember, thought it wise to marry Joan to him to secure his allegiance.'

'Well, if we have secured it through our mother, what difference? Poor Joan. So she lost her husband.'

'I found another for her, so what matters it?' said Henry.

Richard looked at his brother with amusement. *He* found a husband for her. I'll wager, thought Richard, he was told whom Joan should marry.

'How likes Joan her new husband?'

'You may ask her.'

'She is coming here?'

'She is on her way with her husband from Scotland, so you may ask her yourself. She must be content, for she has brought about an alliance between us and the Scots. And as Hubert married Alexander's sister Margaret, we have very good relations with that country.'

'It is said that Hubert de Burgh knows how to feather his own nest.'

'Who says that?' demanded Henry fiercely.

'Oh, I have heard it said. And you must admit that marriage with the sister of the King of Scotland is somewhat higher than a . . . commoner should look.'

'Pray do not speak of Hubert in that way. He is a great man. There is no one of more importance to me in the whole of my kingdom.'

'Yes,' said Richard, 'that is what I have heard. The King is in leading strings to his Justiciar.'

Henry flushed scarlet. 'Have done,' he shouted. 'I'll not have such accusations made in my hearing.'

Oh, thought Richard, very much the King! *He* should have been the first-born. It was obvious.

'If I were King,' he said, 'I would rather such things were said within my hearing than outside it.'

Henry hesitated. There was wisdom in that. It was galling, though, that his younger brother should have to point it out to him.

He changed the subject. 'I have decided,' he said, 'that it would be good for you to make a pilgrimage. You have recently been in bad health and need perhaps a little humility and forgiveness of your sins.'

'My ill health was due to the cold of Corfe . . . not to my sins.'

'Are you so virtuous then, brother? This is what I wish to tell you. Alexander, your brother-in-law, is going to Canterbury to pray at the shrine of St. Thomas, and I think it would be an excellent plan if you accompanied him.'

*You* think, was Richard's inward comment. You mean Hubert de Burgh thinks.

But the idea was not displeasing to him.

He had spent too long away from affairs and it would be interesting to meet his brother-in-law.

It seemed strange to Joan to be back in the schoolroom in the Palace of Westminster. Two years had passed since her marriage with Alexander. She had then been eleven years old—a child in years but her stay at the castle of Lusignan had brought her abruptly out of childhood and had taught her the emotions of an adult.

She felt very experienced compared with her sisters: Isabella who was now nearly ten years old and Eleanor who was nine.

They had greeted her warily. Poor little girls, thought worldly-wise Joan. What did they know of life?

She had a husband of two years standing. Alexander. He was not unkind and he had made her a Queen. He was twelve years older than she was, an experienced warrior at the time of their marriage; he had frightened her a little at first, with his rather sharp features and the tawny tinge in his eyes and hair. But she was beautiful, she knew; and seemed to grow more so when her mother was far away. Everyone commented on her charm and that pleased Alexander. He was glad too of the alliance with England which she represented.

When he found that she was intelligent he talked to her a little about state matters. He was a man who while he excelled in battle was yet a lover of peace, and he told her he wanted a prosperous Scotland and no country was prosperous in war, and though he would defend his boundaries with his life he preferred to make them safe through marriages such as theirs than through battle.

She could agree with him on this and as she had learned meekness at Lusignan she accepted her lot.

He was not Hugh, of course; and she supposed she would go on thinking of Hugh all her life. He would always live on as an ideal of what one had failed to achieve sometimes did.

She did not want to think of her mother with Hugh. She had now become aware of what such a relationship meant, for she would be expected soon to provide Scotland with an heir. She was not too young for that; she had been sickened when she had heard that her mother had already given Hugh two children. She supposed in time she would get used to the idea. Often she pictured them together. Of course she had subconsciously known that there was something different about her mother when compared with other women. She would never forget the way in which Hugh's eyes had followed her as she moved around and now that she knew the meaning of those smouldering looks which passed between them she understood a great deal. She would remain here while Alexander took the journey to Canterbury in the company of her brother Richard. She remembered Richard but vaguely. He had been more forceful than Henry, always trying to push himself forward and pretending that although he was the younger he was the more important.

Her sisters Isabella and Eleanor wanted her to tell them about Scotland. They looked at her with awe—their elder sister who was widely travelled. First she had gone miles away to Lusignan and then she had come back and had a marriage. This made her a very important person.

But Eleanor, the younger of her sisters, had very special questions to ask.

'Tell us what it is like to be married,' said Eleanor.

Joan was embarrassed. 'My dear sister, you will discover soon enough.'

'Very soon,' said Eleanor. 'Did you know, Joan, that I am going to be married?'

'When?' cried Joan. 'You are far too young.'

'It is true, is it not, Isabella?'

Isabella nodded gravely. 'I heard Margaret Biset talking about it.'

'Margaret Biset had no right to talk before you,' said Joan.

Isabella was quick to defend her nurse–governess. 'But she did not know she was talking before me for I was hidden where she did not think to look for me.'

'Eavesdropping. Oh Isabella!'

'It is to be forgiven,' retorted Eleanor, 'when plans are made for us and we are not told for a long time.'

'And what did you hear?' asked Joan.

'That someone called William Marshal is claiming me,' said Eleanor.

'She means he is going to marry her,' said Isabella.

'Why, you are not nine years old yet!'

'He had another child wife, Margaret said,' put in Isabella. 'She said he must have a fancy for them.'

The two young girls giggled but Joan stopped them.

'You are being foolish. Tell me all you know of this.'

'It is just that William Marshal was promised Eleanor and is now claiming her. She will go away to him as you went to Lusignan. But you came back, did you not, Joan?'

Joan nodded.

'But not for long. Then you went to Scotland.'

'Your Hugh married our mother instead. He wouldn't have been able to do that if our father had been alive,' said Eleanor.

'Of course he wouldn't, you foolish girl,' put in Isabella. 'Do you remember him?'

Eleanor nodded. 'He used to shout,' she said, 'and scream.'

'Margaret said sometimes he fell on the floor and chewed the rushes. It made him less angry doing that. I tried it when I was cross. But it didn't make me less cross and the rushes were horrible.'

'You chatter too much,' said Joan severely, 'and you must stop hiding yourselves so that you can hear what people say. It's bad manners.'

'It's interesting,' observed Isabella.

'One day you might hear what you would rather not.'

'I'd rather not have heard I have to go to William Marshal,' admitted Eleanor fearfully.

'Well if she has to go it's best to know about it, is it not, Joan?' asked Isabella.

'Perhaps,' said Joan.

Then she turned to Eleanor and saw herself as she had been what seemed like an age ago when she had heard she was to go to Lusignan. Had she looked as young and defenceless as Eleanor now looked? And Lusignan . . . how beautiful it now seemed looking back. How she hated the harsh Scottish winter when the snow came quickly and stayed. She thought of the lush pine forests and riding with Hugh. Her mother had taken all that away from her because she was in a way a witch and made spells so that she was the most beautiful woman in the world and all men—even those betrothed to others—wanted to marry her.

She shook off these thoughts and gave her attention to Eleanor.

The poor child was more frightened than she would have them know.

It was not easy to be alone with Henry. He was so important now. It was hard to realize he was one of those brothers with whom she had played in those days which now seemed so long ago.

He had been their mother's favourite—if she could be said to have had a favourite for she did not greatly care for any of them, Joan knew now. It had been such a strange life they had led in Gloucester Castle. It seemed now as hazy as a dream. Vaguely she remembered her terrifying father; he was enough to make any girl afraid of marriage. Fortunately her mother had never been afraid of him although Joan had since heard terrible tales of their life together.

Henry, who was now King, seemed very different. Perhaps it was because he was so young. He was three years older than she was and at their age that was a great deal.

She had to speak to him about Eleanor, for she must try and reassure her young sister. It would not be long before Alexander and Richard came back from Canterbury and then she would have to return to Scotland with her husband.

She did find an opportunity when he came in from riding and she waylaid him in the hall and asked if she could have a word with him in private.

He signed to his attendants to leave him and took his sister into a small antechamber where he bade her sit on one of the stools while he took the chair. It was almost as though he were reminding her that he was the King. He did that a great deal, she noticed. He will change though, she assured herself. It is just that now he has to keep reminding people in case they forget it.

'I have little time, sister,' he said importantly. 'I have promised to see Hubert de Burgh very shortly. Peter des Roches gives me much trouble. He is continually trying to put me in conflict with Hubert.'

'There is much envy there, I doubt not,' she answered.

'Indeed yes. Peter would be Justiciar,' laughed Henry.

'And rule England himself . . . as Hubert does.'

'There is only one who rules England, sister, and that is the King.'

'I know it, but I doubt not you listen to Hubert de Burgh and Stephen Langton now and then.'

'A king cannot be everywhere in his realm at once. He must have those to work with him.'

'And you are the admiration of your subjects, I hear.'

That placated him and softened his mood.

'I wanted to speak to you about Eleanor,' she said.

'What of our sister?'

'She has heard talk of her being given in marriage to William Marshal and that disturbs her.'

'Where did she hear of such matters?'

'You know how it is. People are indiscreet. The young are curious . . . particularly when what they hear concerns themselves.'

'Indiscreet indeed. . . .'

'But this marriage, is it not common talk to all except the child it most concerns?'

'Child! You say that as though something cruel is proposed. Our sister is of marriageable age.'

'She is not yet nine years old.'

'Well, of course, the marriage would not be consummated as yet.'

'That would be left to the bridegroom's decision, I dareswear.'

'As it must be.'

Joan shook her head.

'You know nothing of these matters, sister.'

'Begging your royal pardon, I know a great deal. You forget it happened to me.'

'But our mother was of great use to you, was she not? She took your place.' The King laughed.

'So you find that amusing, Henry?'

'Far from it. They are giving us great concern over their demands for a dowry. But Hubert says it is not such a bad thing, for my mother will be able to persuade the Lusignans to stand by me against France more easily than you could have done.'

'Then it was well that it happened so,' said Joan wryly. 'And why is Eleanor to be handed over so soon?'

'Because, my dear sister, she was promised to William Marshal. You know the importance of this family. His father helped me to the throne. He and Hubert stood beside me and William would be there now if he had not died.'

'His son was not always so faithful, was he?'

'No. That is why he was promised Eleanor.'

'A reward for treachery.'

'Oh come, my dear sister. You are a princess. You know how we must work for our country. If a marriage is advantageous then it must be made.'

'No doubt ere long *you* will be making an advantageous marriage.'

'No doubt,' said Henry.

'But I'll swear you'll have more say in whom you'll take than Eleanor has.'

'Eleanor is only a child.'

'That is my point. Must this marriage take place?'

'It must. William Marshal says the time has come for us to honour the promise.'

'Was he not married before?'

'Yes, to Alice, Baldwin de Bethune's daughter. She was but a child.'

'He would seem to have a fancy for children.'

'Understand, Joan, that these marriages are made for good reasons.'

'Good reasons being not the affection of the partners but the advantages to accrue to their sovereigns.'

'Do you learn such ideas in Scotland? I am surprised at Alexander.'

'I have a mind of my own. I reason things out.'

'Then be sensible. Eleanor will be well cared for. And she will ensure the loyalty of William Marshal.'

'Why was Eleanor affianced to this man?'

'A very good reason. Marshal was proposing to marry a daughter of Robert de Bruce. It was not good for England that one who has shown himself a friend of France, should put himself in the position of having influence in Scotland.'

'I see. So Eleanor must marry him.'

'Yes. Cheer up, sister. You will not stay with us long. Let us be merry while you do. The signs are good. Our mother married in Lusignan, you in Scotland and Eleanor shortly, with the Marshal.'

'You have still Richard and Isabella to barter with.'

'Their time will come,' smiled Henry.

'And yours, brother?'

'And mine,' he repeated. 'Now I must leave you. State matters call me, sister.'

Joan looked after him when he had gone and her thoughts went back to Hugh and her fear of him when they had first met, which quickly changed to an emotion she must not think about.

# The Adventures
# of William Longsword

HUBERT DE BURGH was waiting for an audience with the King. He was feeling gratified by the way in which events were moving, but he would not have been the experienced statesman he was if he had not known that there was no occasion for complacency. Since he had achieved such high office there never would be.

He knew there was whispering against him. His old enemy, Peter des Roches, Bishop of Winchester would keep that alive. It was a battle between them and it could only end in the elimination of one of them.

Hubert felt he had the greater chance of winning because he had the King's affection. He was not a man of the calibre of William Marshal, first Earl of Pembroke, who had on more than one occasion risked his life to uphold what he felt to be true. The character of the second earl had yet to be proved, but he had already shown that he could change sides if he thought it the wise thing to do. Marshal the younger would have argued that when he had gone over to the French it was because he had believed that England must be rid of John at any price, and perhaps there had been good sense in such a conclusion but the fact remained that he had deserted the sovereign to whom he had sworn allegiance—something his father would never have done. Little harm had come to him through that disaffection and he was now going to get the King's sister for his pains.

Well, Marshal was a name to be reckoned with and the marriage would mean his loyalty was firm. He would be the King's brother-in-law; and there was a certain charm about

William Marshal which had already had its effect on the somewhat impressionable young king.

So when the marriage had taken place William Marshal would be established in the royal circle. Not that Hubert could complain. His wife Margaret had brought him his aura of royalty; he was the husband of the King of Scotland's sister and that gave him a kinship with the King of England.

He had come far since the days when King John had sent him on a mission to Falaise to put out the eyes of Prince Arthur and castrate him. He had been a different man then. Rashly he had acted and out of emotion—carelessly, recklessly risking his life. Yet it was an act which, cynical statesman that he had become, he never regretted. If he had carried out John's orders, he had said at the time, he would never after have slept peacefully in his bed. The same applied now.

Hubert knew that the murmurings around him were growing. It was said that although he had been a wise counsellor to the King he had feathered his own nest in doing so. And why not? Did they blame birds for making good nests for their young?

Two events had recently occurred which had set people's tongues wagging. William Earl of Arundel had recently died and Hubert had been made guardian of his young heir. The death of Arundel had been shortly followed by that of Hugh Bigod Earl of Norfolk and his son and heir had been put in Hubert's charge.

As these two young men were the heirs to considerable fortunes and were of the highest families in the land, Hubert's wealth and above all his power was largely increased by his handling of their affairs; moreover he could have a great effect upon their future by leading them in the direction he wanted them to go.

No wonder it was being said: 'Hubert de Burgh is in fact the ruler of England.'

He must be watchful and he would be particularly careful of Peter des Roches. Stephen Langton had brought about a reconciliation between them but it was an uneasy one.

When he was in the King's presence he told him at once that the King of France was ignoring his demand for the restoration of Normandy and moreover had brought in the Count of Lusignan and Henry's mother to work with him.

Henry was amazed. 'My own mother!' he cried. 'How could she possibly work against me!'

'The King of France would have made special concessions and the Count, I doubt not, thought it would be more gainful to work for Louis. And of course there is the irksome matter of your mother's dowry.'

'Perhaps we should send it,' suggested Henry.

'My lord, we must not show weakness. There is only one thing we can do. We must prepare for war.'

Henry frowned. 'I want above all things to keep the country peaceful.'

'So do all those who wish you well, my lord, but there are times when a display of strength is necessary and unless you are going to allow the French to take everything—God knows there is little left to us—we cannot stand aside. If you do, it will be said that you are another such as your father.'

'Let us prepare for war,' said Henry firmly.

It was easy to plan but not so easy to carry out. Extra taxes must be raised. Hubert suggested that one fifteenth part of all movable possessions should be demanded from both the clergy and the laity, and as was to be expected this aroused murmuring throughout the land and was responsible for a wave of unpopularity for the King. It was demanded that Henry confirm the Charter which his father had been forced to sign at Runnymede. This he did, as he pointed out, of his own motion and good will.

While these preparations were going on Eleanor was married to William Marshal, who was immediately appointed Justiciar of that turbulent country Ireland which meant that his stay there could be a lengthy one. The married pair left each other happily—William going off to his duties and Eleanor left behind to devote herself to the business of growing up.

So there she was back in the nursery with Isabella and being married made no difference to her way of life.

Joan was delighted for her and said that she had heard that William Marshal was a good man, and by the time he came back from Ireland perhaps Eleanor would be ready to live with him.

Joan herself returned rather sadly to Scotland and her brother Richard remained at Court, for as Hubert had pointed out, he was now getting too old to be ignored.

As he had reached his sixteenth birthday Henry gave him his knight's sword and invested him with the Earldom of Cornwall and as the plan was to send him to France to lead the expedition under the care of the old Earl of Salisbury, he was also given the title of Count of Poitou.

The young Earl, eager to prove himself, set out with great enthusiasm. His co-commander, William Longespée or Longsword as he was more generally known, was Richard's uncle, for Longsword was a natural son of Henry II by Rosamund Clifford. He had acquired great honours—for Henry II had genuinely loved Rosamund Clifford and had done everything possible for her sons—and Longsword had married the Countess of Salisbury and through this marriage he attained his earldom. His career had not been exactly glorious for he had been a close companion of his half-brother John and, reckoned to be one of his most evil cousellors, he had been involved in many acts of cruelty for which he showed a certain relish. One of the chief of these was the affair of Geoffrey of Norwich, a very able cleric who withdrew from his office when John was excommunicated. John's retort was to send Salisbury to seize Geoffrey. It was true he did this on John's command but all said at the time it was one from which any humane man would have shrunk. The unfortunate Geoffrey was put in prison in Bristol where a heavy lead cope was placed upon him and he was left to die in agony.

Longsword, however, went from strength to strength and he supported John against the barons, but changed sides when it seemed that Louis of France had come to stay. When John died Louis—whose ally he now was—sent Longsword to Hubert de Burgh to attempt to persuade him to relinquish Dover Castle. Hubert, despising him for his lack of loyalty to his nephew the young King, berated him soundly: something Longsword was not going to forget. However, as soon as the French had left the country, Longsword immediately joined the King, declaring that he would win forgiveness for his defection by going on a crusade to whichever spot the Legate should see fit to send him.

He had proved himself to be a good soldier—though a ruthless man capable of great cruelty—and he seemed to Hubert a good choice to accompany the inexperienced young Earl of Cornwall on his first military venture.

Richard showed the makings of a good commander and his enthusiasm allied to the experience of the old Earl proved a match for Louis whose dreams of conquering Gascony had to be temporarily abandoned because Bordeaux refused to surrender to the French and as a result Gascony was saved for the English and Louis had to think again.

Leaving Richard behind, Longsword set sail for home. It was now autumn and very rough seas were encountered. There came a time when death seemed inevitable. The vessel was tossed on the heavy seas as though it were made of parchment and when all the goods on board were flung overboard, every man believed that his last moment had come.

Longsword clinging to the rail was haunted by all the evil deeds of a lifetime and he prayed aloud to the Virgin to save him, reminding her that ever since the day he had been knighted he had never failed to set a light to burn before her altar.

Then what Longsword believed to be a miracle happened. He and the sailors swore they saw a figure at the masthead. It was a beautiful woman whom they were convinced was the Virgin Mary. She had come at his hour of need, Longsword thought, to thank him for all those lighted candles.

From that moment the ship, though listing badly and at the mercy of the wind, began to drift. They came to an island and scrambled ashore.

'Saved,' cried William Longsword, 'by the Blessed Virgin.'

Hubert told the King that the news was good. They had shown the King of France that they would defend their rights. The days of John were over. A new King was on the throne and—let Louis remember—he had wise men to counsel him.

'What next?' asked Henry eagerly. 'We must continue. Everything that my father lost must be regained.'

'A campaign will need careful planning,' Hubert reminded him. 'We will wait for the return of William Longsword and hear what he has to tell us of Louis's defences.'

'Louis's army cannot have been very good for we have defeated it.'

'One victory does not win a war, my lord,' warned Hubert. 'Let us employ a little caution. We will wait for Salisbury's report.'

A few days later Henry fell ill and Hubert feared for his life. What now? he asked Stephen Langton. There could be trouble. They must bring Richard back without delay. The country was enjoying only a superficial peace and Peter des Roches would be watching for his opportunity.

Stephen Langton declared they must employ patience. The king was young; he was not a weakling. They would do everything in their power to bring him back to health and they would not let anyone know how uneasy they were.

Richard, the new Earl of Cornwall, had certain qualities of leadership which perhaps his brother lacked, but he would be difficult to handle. Fortunately he was there to follow if need be but they would hope and pray that Henry would recover.

He did and no sooner was he well again than he began to talk of preparing for the campaign for France. If they were going to win back their possessions, Henry wanted the glory. He was not going to let Richard claim it on the strength of one campaign.

Louis then made a strong decision. Whether he feared the forces which had come against him, or whether he had some premonition, no one knew; but he suddenly decided that he was going to join the Church's forces against the Albigensians. This meant that he had undertaken what was tantamount to a crusade. It had the effect which perhaps Louis had desired. The Pope sent a command to the English King that he was not to take up arms against the King of France who was now engaged on a holy war.

Henry was furious, but as Hubert pointed out, he could not go against Rome, for this could result in the dreaded Interdict, and everyone knew what disaster that could bring.

Henry must therefore bide his time. There would be opportunities in the future.

Meanwhile nothing had been heard of the Earl of Salisbury except that some time before he had sailed from France.

When Hubert considered the rich estate of Salisbury and that William Longsword had had a countess who could not be more than thirty-eight years old and who would now be a widow, he decided that it would be a good idea to bring the Salisbury fortune into his family.

He had a nephew, Reimund, who was looking for a suitable wife. What better, thought Hubert, than for Reimund to marry Ela, the Countess of Salisbury. She had brought rich estates to William Longsword. Why should she not bring them to Hubert's nephew? The family would know how to take care of them.

He approached the King cautiously.

'It is a sad matter about Longsword for he must now be reckoned as dead. Poor fellow, he was cruel and his sins must be great, but he was a great soldier and a valiant man.'

'It is true,' said Henry, 'but like all bastards he was cursed with the need continually to proclaim his royalty.'

'Well now he has died. He has left a widow.'

'That's true,' said Henry, 'and one who brought him great wealth.'

'And not an old woman by any means. She cannot be more than thirty-eight and still capable of bearing children. She should have a husband.'

Henry nodded.

'Er . . . my nephew, Reimund, is looking for a wife. He is a good steady fellow, ever loyal to his King. He would care for the Countess and look after her estates. How would you feel—if he should succeed in winning her—about giving your consent to the match?'

'If she consented I would be willing enough,' said Henry.

It was all Hubert needed. He lost no time in summoning his nephew and sending him off to begin his wooing.

If the Virgin Mary had saved the Earl of Salisbury from the sea that marked the end of her help for, although he and some of the survivors from the broken vessel were washed ashore, their refuge happened to be the Island of Ré which belonged to Louis.

They were, however, able to find shelter in the abbey of the island and as they were in such a sorry state were not immediately recognized. They had come near to death and were in urgent need of rest and nourishment and this was afforded them.

But the Earl could not hope to remain unrecognized for any great length of time and in due course one of the monks realized who he was.

Being a man of religion the monk did not betray him because he knew that the Earl was as yet unfit to make another voyage. So the secret was kept while Salisbury made plans for escape.

More than three months had elapsed since he left the coast of France so it was logical to believe him to be dead; and when in time Salisbury had managed to procure a boat and returned to England a great shock awaited Hubert.

The Earl at once discovered what was happening. His wife being wooed, believing herself to be his widow. And her wooer was no other than a nephew of Hubert de Burgh!

Incensed, the Earl went straight to the King.

Henry declared himself delighted to see his uncle returned from the dead. 'For,' he said, 'that is what we feared. It is so long since you set sail.'

'It is a shock, my lord, to return and find my wife all but married to another man.'

'My dear Longsword,' replied Henry, 'she is not an old woman and because of my nearness to you I wished to see her in good hands.'

'And my estates?' cried the Earl. 'I doubt not that those good hands were held out greedily to receive them.'

'My dear uncle, we had every cause to believe you dead. That you are not is a matter of rejoicing. I will send for Hubert and his nephew and they shall welcome you back and make their apologies to you, if you think they should. But, I do assure you, we acted in the good interest of your Countess.'

'Then, my lord, I thank God—and the Blessed Virgin— that I was brought home in good time.'

The King kept his promise to send for Hubert and his nephew and in a few weeks there was a meeting between them and Longsword over which the King presided.

Longsword glared at Hubert and declared: 'I understand well your motives, my lord.'

'They grew from our concern for your Countess, my lord Earl,' Hubert tried to assure him.

'And for her estates I doubt not.'

'My lord, I assure you that my nephew had a genuine affection for the lady. Is that not so, Reimund?'

'It is indeed so, my lord.'

Longsword was purple with rage. 'You dare stand there and tell me that you have an affection for my wife and would marry her.'

'My lord . . .' began Reimund, but Hubert cut him short:

'My lord Salisbury,' he said soothingly, 'my nephew *had* an affection for a lady whom he believed to be a forlorn widow. Now that he knows her to be a wife his feelings have changed.'

'He changes his feelings as men change a suit of mail,' snarled Longsword.

The King intervened. 'Uncle, I would have you make peace with Hubert. I believe his motives to be as he says and I find these quarrels irksome. You have had a miraculous escape. Methinks you should be thanking God that you have emerged from this disaster at sea and arrived home in time to save your wife from a marriage which would have been no marriage.'

Salisbury bowed his head. 'What's done is done,' he murmured, 'but I shall not forget. . . .'

'Now, Hubert,' said Henry, 'you shall invite him to a banquet and there all will see that you truly repent of your mistake and that my uncle understands full well how it came about.'

'With all my heart,' said Hubert and somewhat ungraciously the Earl of Salisbury accepted the invitation.

It was a very grand banquet. The King was present and the Earl of Salisbury sat on the left hand of Hubert de Burgh. They talked amicably together and all said that the unfortunate incident was over and it appeared to have brought these two men—who were not natural friends—together.

Salisbury was a great soldier. With the young Earl of

Cornwall he had achieved victories in France and he had shown the people that the humiliating days of John's reign were behind them. People had feared him in the past; he had been noted for the cruelties he carried out in the name of John; but a well governed country meant the return of law and order and with such a state of affairs Salisbury would dispense with his cruelty and be the good soldier ready to lead his country to more victories.

But when he reached Salisbury Castle, he was overcome by violent pains which were followed by a high fever and was forced to take to his bed, where his condition did not improve.

In a few days he was so weak that he feared his end was near.

'Bring Bishop Poore to me,' he said, 'for I must confess my sins and receive the last rites.'

As he lay in bed awaiting the coming of the Bishop memories came back to him. He wondered how many men he had murdered in the name of King John . . . and not only in his name. He remembered the thrill of sacking a town and the needless suffering he had inflicted on its inhabitants—not because such conduct furthered the progress of the war but because he considered it good sport and enjoyed it.

Agonized faces haunted him from every corner of the room. He could hear the cries of mutilated people as they were deprived of feet, hands, noses, ears and their eyes were put out.

Any amount of candles to the Holy Virgin could not save him. He had to face the fact that he had led a wicked life.

He deserved to hang—the death of a common felon was not too good for him.

He should have been warned when he was shipwrecked. The Virgin had given him another chance but he had not taken it. He should have spent the last weeks in preparing for a crusade rather than furthering his quarrel with Hubert de Burgh over the Countess.

He rose from his bed and stripping off all garments but a loin cloth, he called for a rope which he put about his neck, so that when Richard le Poore, Bishop of Salisbury arrived, he found him thus.

'My lord,' cried the Bishop, 'what has happened to you?'

'I am the worst of sinners. I fear eternal damnation.'

'Oh, perhaps it is not as bad as that,' replied the Bishop comfortably. 'There is time for you to repent.'

'I shall not rise from the floor until I have confessed my sins to you—as many as I can remember. I have been a traitor to God. I must receive the sacrament without delay.'

Before the Earl died, the Bishop did all that the Earl required of him and eased his conscience considerably.

Poison, was the verdict. Of course Hubert de Burgh poisoned him. It was at the banquet, for would he not know that his conduct over the Countess and his nephew would always be remembered? The Earl would be Hubert's enemy for as long as he lived—and Hubert was a man who could not afford powerful enemies.

This suspicion was stored away in people's memories to be brought out when required. There was no danger of its being forgotten. Men such as Peter des Roches would never allow that.

As for Hubert he realized that Reimund could scarcely go wooing the Countess of Salisbury after what had happened. She should be left well alone.

But his indefatigable efforts on his family's behalf procured another rich widow for his nephew and shortly after the death of the Earl of Salisbury, Reimund married the widow of William Mandeville, the Earl of Essex, who brought as much to the family as the Countess of Salisbury would have done. Another nephew became Bishop of Norwich; and as his brother Geoffrey was already Bishop of Ely, Hubert could congratulate himself that he had his family well and strategically placed, which was what all ambitious men realized they must do.

His enemies continued watchful, but Hubert felt strong enough to defy them.

# FRANCE
## 1223–1227

# The Amorous Troubadour

BLANCHE was uneasy. She felt very much the responsibilities which had been thrust upon her since the death of Philip Augustus. There was one secret anxiety which was something she would not have discussed with anyone and scarcely liked to admit to herself. Louis was not a great soldier; in her heart she doubted whether he was a great King. She herself had been endowed with the qualities of leadership but Louis had not been so fortunate. Louis was a good man and—so rare a quality—a faithful husband and a loving father. His children adored him as he did them. If he had been a minor nobleman, his castle situated in some quiet part of the country where he need not trouble to defend himself, with his family about him and those dependent on him to work for him, he could have been a happy man.

Such had been his grandfather. The tragedy of their lives was that kingship—which so many men would have risked their lives to possess—was not desired by them, for the simple reason that, being men of deep intelligence, they knew their inadequacies to meet its demands.

But Louis had a wife.

'Oh God,' prayed Blanche, 'help me to act for both of us.'

She was supervising the upbringing of her children with the utmost care—particularly that of young Louis. How she loved her eldest son! She was fond of the others—without doubt—but she could sense in young Louis the making of a great King. When his time came—and she trusted that it would not be for many years—she must see that he was ready.

She was preparing him; but his sovereignty was innate. Moreover he was possessed of striking good looks. His features were clearly chiselled; his skin fine and fair, glowing

215

with good health; he had a mass of blond glossy hair which he had inherited from the beautiful Isabel of Hainault, his paternal grandmother. He was kindly like his father but there the resemblance ended. Louis was good in the schoolroom, for he had a lively interest in all subjects, but he also liked the outdoor life; he enjoyed all sport and in particular hunting and he loved his dogs, horses and falcons. He was all that a healthy boy should be—but there was more than that. He was careful in his dress displaying an elegance even at his age.

If ever a boy was born to be king, that boy was Louis.

Yet she was fearful. She would not coddle him as Philip Augustus had tried to coddle his son Louis. She wondered what young Louis's reaction would be if she attempted to. She doubted he would take it without protest as his father had. Yet he was a good and dutiful son. She could not forget the loss of her boy Philip at nine years when death had suddenly risen to smite him spitefully as though to be revenged on the boy's parents.

But Philip had lacked the qualities of his younger brother Louis, so perhaps fate had struck him down because Louis was destined to be King.

Such thoughts were unprofitable. Philip was dead and Louis was the eldest son. They were indeed fortunate to have such a family. She must be grateful and not fret because she feared for her husband's health and strength as a ruler. She should thank God for giving her such a wonderful son; and for having endowed her with qualities—which it would have been foolish and falsely modest to deny—which made her competent to guide him and shoulder his responsibilities.

Louis was fighting with more success than she had dared hope for. With a satisfied Hugh de Lusignan on his side they were bringing victory to France. In various towns the citizens had surrendered to him without a fight, believing that they could not stand out against the French.

However Bordeaux stood firm for the English and since the newly created Earl of Cornwall had arrived with the veteran Earl of Salisbury, there was little news, which Blanche sensed meant there were no more easy victories; and perhaps this was at the root of her anxieties.

While she was awaiting an account of Louis's activities

Joanna the Countess Flanders arrived at Court. She had come, she said, to ask the Queen's help.

Blanche was wary. Louis was not on good terms with Flanders and at this time Joanna's husband, Ferdinand, was imprisoned in the Louvre where he had been sent more than ten years before by Philip Augustus. The trouble between them had flared up in the year 1213. This was at the time of King John's excommunication when Philip Augustus had thought it was opportune to make an attempt to seize the crown of England to which he asserted Blanche had a claim. Philip had summoned his vassals to meet him at Soissons that they might prepare themselves to aid him in his venture, but Ferdinand failed to arrive.

Philip Augustus proceeded with his project which was doomed to failure because before he could set sail John— shrewdly—had called in the help of the Pope. Instead of being a country under the Interdict which would have been so easy to attack, England was under the wing of the Pope and Philip realized that it would be folly to take up arms against Rome.

Fuming, Philip declared that the attack could not now take place as Rome instead of himself had subdued England.

In his angry mood he learned that Ferdinand of Flanders was seeking to make an alliance with John and if he could not declare war on John he could on Ferdinand. Ferdinand had grown reckless because of a prophecy a soothsayer had made in the presence of his mother-in-law, the Queen of Portugal, and she had lost no time in writing to tell him of it. The seer had said that the King of France would be defeated by Ferdinand in battle and in a dream she had seen him entering Paris where the people welcomed him with great delight.

Poor Ferdinand must have been extremely gullible to believe such a prophecy for even if the King of France had been killed, he had a son whom it seemed likely the people of France would welcome more eagerly than they would the Count of Flanders.

Alas for Ferdinand, the prophecy proved far from true. It was the King of France who was victorious and he, Ferdinand, who became the prisoner. Philip knew that a man with such grandiose ideas represented a threat and it was not long before Ferdinand found he was indeed in Paris but his lodging was a small chamber, in the Tower of the Louvre, where he had remained ever since.

Now his wife Joanna had come to Court and was begging an audience with the Queen. Blanche guessed that the Countess of Flanders was once again going to plead for the release of her husband and was wondering whether it might not be expedient to consider releasing Ferdinand. Perhaps he would be grateful to the King—after all it was not Louis who had imprisoned him. And he would know that if he was a traitor to the Crown once more it would be the end of him.

She was surprised that it was not of her husband that Joanna wished to speak.

Joanna was a strong domineering woman. It was through her that Ferdinand had inherited Flanders, and she was not one to forget it. During her husband's stay in the Louvre she had governed Flanders and had proved herself an able ruler.

Now Blanche immediately recognized her as another such as herself and felt a great respect for her.

Joanna said: 'You think I have come to plead for my husband. That I might well do, for it is many years since the last King made him his prisoner and he has paid for his follies.'

'I will speak to the King of the matter,' said Blanche. 'I am sure he will be ready to consider your request.'

'I thank you, my lady. What concerns me now is Flanders. A cheat and an impostor is trying to wrest it from me and I have come to ask your advice and help.'

'Pray tell me what this means,' said Blanche.

'You may remember that my father Count Baldwin went on a crusade to the Holy Land some twenty years ago. From this he never returned.'

'I had heard it,' said Blanche.

'He led the Fourth Crusade and was made Emperor of Constantinople. Then . . . he disappeared.'

'How so?'

'He was captured by the Saracens and it was said that he was put into one of their prisons.'

'So many Christians never again saw the light of day after they were taken by that enemy.'

'I believe my father died in his prison, but now this impostor of whom I spoke has appeared. He has a look of my father and claims that he is he.'

'But he cannot prove this.'

Joanna raised her hands in a gesture of despair. 'He tells many tales of the Holy City and his adventures there. He swears he is the Count of Flanders.'

'But you, his daughter, must know.'

'I do know. He is not my father.'

'Well?'

'My lady, there are many who believe this, and some accept it because they do not love me and resent being ruled by a woman. Many people are rallying round him. They are accepting him and rejecting me.'

Blanche thought: Yes, I can understand you would be a stern ruler. Just perhaps, but perhaps somewhat harsh. And the people of Flanders are not fond of you so they would replace you by this man even if he is an impostor.

'Well?' said Blanche.

'I want your help, my lady, and that of the King.'

'How far has the matter gone?' asked Blanche.

'Very far, I fear. You see, my lady, there are unscrupulous men in Flanders.'

'Not only in Flanders,' replied Blanche grimly.

'These men see a chance of enriching themselves,' went on Joanna, 'for to gain their support this man is giving them land and titles and promising them easy living.'

'Has he, do you think, really deceived them?'

'I am not sure. He has a certain look of my father but he is shorter by two inches and again and again he shows clearly that he is a trickster.'

'What can I or the King do for you?'

'You might ask him to Court. You might question him. I believe that he would be less arrogant in your presence. If he were asked certain questions he would most assuredly give the wrong answers.'

'Have you asked him these questions?'

'I have and he has not satisfied me, but it is believed that I so enjoy ruling Flanders that I will do anything to stop his taking authority from me.'

Blanche considered. Ferdinand was in fact Louis's uncle for he was a brother of Isabel of Hainault and she knew that Louis had a strong feeling for his mother's family. He often talked of Isabel—whom young Louis was said to resemble—although he had never known her. He had heard that she was both beautiful and gentle and he was very regretful that she had died two years after he was born and he could not remember her. He would want to help if he could; and she was certain that now the plight of Ferdinand would be brought to his notice he would want to release him.

Blanche said that she would send a messenger to Louis and let him know what was happening in Flanders and in the meantime she and Joanna would put their heads together and try to work out some plan for putting the impostor to the test.

It was Blanche who suggested that they send for Sybil of Beaujeu, who was the sister of the true Count of Flanders; surely she who had been brought up with her brother would know whether this man was really Count Baldwin or an impostor.

It seemed an excellent idea.

'I should like the disclosure to be made in the presence of you and the King,' said Joanna.

'We shall see if that is possible,' replied Blanche.

Louis was not sorry to receive the message. He had little feeling for war. It had been different when the towns had fallen easily to him, but now that Henry had sent his young brother and the Earl of Salisbury against him he was glad of a respite.

He sent back a message to the effect that he would be at Péronne and that Blanche and Joanna might meet him there. He had then sent a message to Sybil asking her to come to him there and a similar message to the man who called himself the Count of Flanders.

The latter came with all haste for he believed that the King's summons was for him to do homage to him as his liege lord which he would only ask if he believed him to be the true Count.

Blanche was delighted to have Louis with her again. She suspected that she was pregnant and when she told Louis he was delighted.

He confessed to her that he had always felt a sympathy

with the stamping out of heresy and that he had long considered the Albigensian movement to be a dangerous one.

'Moreover,' he added, 'I have heard that the King of England is planning to send over a large army, which is what I expected he would do. He is going to make an attempt to regain what he has lost. I fear a long and wretched war, Blanche.'

'Yet you would go to war against the Albigensians.'

'That is a holy war. The Albigensians are not a well-equipped army. Depend upon it, this war will not be nearly so deadly nor so costly as war against England.'

'The Albigensians are a people fighting for their beliefs, Louis. Such people are apt to be fierce fighters.'

'I know it, but if I take up the Cross and go against the Albigensians, the Pope will forbid the English to make war on me.'

'You mean that war against the Albigensians is more to your taste than war against the English.'

'I want no war,' said Louis, 'but if war there must be I had rather it was a holy war.'

Blanche made no attempt to dissuade him, but she was deeply concerned for she thought he had aged considerably during the last campaign and indeed looked exhausted.

She could almost welcome this controversy over the Count of Flanders to give him some respite and with Sybil de Beaujeu they discussed how best to tackle the matter.

'Leave it to me,' said Sybil, 'I will ask him a few questions which only my brother would know.'

When the man calling himself the Count arrived at Péronne, Sybil admitted that he bore a strong resemblance to her brother, although Baldwin had never been so arrogant. His over royal manner, she declared to Blanche, betrayed him; and she was almost certain that he was an impostor.

It did not take her long to discover the truth. For when the man heard that he was to be brought face to face with Sybil he was clearly disturbed. He found the questions she fired at him quite disconcerting and he declared that he was in no mood to be treated so discourteously by his sister and he would answer no questions that night, but in the morning he would answer all the questions to her satisfaction and he would ask that first of all he might be granted the courtesy of a bed and his supper.

The end was in sight for the bogus Count. The next morning it was discovered that he had fled during the night. The game was up. Although he could pose as the adult Baldwin— having probably been on a crusade to the Holy Land and possibly in Baldwin's company for he had scars on his body to show the people and these could certainly have been inflicted by a Saracen sword—he had no knowledge of Baldwin's childhood.

Joanna was delighted. The impostor was eager to get as far away as possible from Flanders. He was later discovered and brought to the Countess Joanna who had no compunction in having him publicly hanged.

So the affair was satisfactorily settled from the Countess's point of view and at least it had given Louis a short respite from the wars.

Blanche who had been expecting a child gave birth to a girl. After five boys it was pleasant to have a girl but when Louis suggested the child should be called Isabella she felt an immediate revulsion because she was reminded of Isabella de Lusignan, the woman whom she hated more than any other.

Isabella was a royal name. Louis had wanted it, and when she had said that she did not care for it he had immediately remarked that it was because it reminded her of the Queen Mother of England.

He smiled at her almost teasingly. 'You hate her, don't you. Why? She's a very attractive woman.'

How could she explain that it was not because of her attractiveness that she hated Isabella. Yes, hated her, for hate was not too strong a word to describe her feelings. How could she explain that some premonition warned her and she disliked being reminded of her.

A sensible woman such as Blanche of Castile, Queen of France, must not have odd fancies.

'What nonsense,' she said lightly. 'I do not dislike the name so much. Isabella. Yes, it's a pretty name . . . a worthy name. Let us call her Isabella if it is what you wish.'

'It was the name of my mother,' said Louis quietly.

'Then you wish it and it shall be.'

So the little girl was Isabella after all.

Before Louis left Blanche was once more pregnant.

Thibaud of Champagne was sighing over the poem he was writing. He was prepared to spend his life in sighing, for the lady he loved was unattainable and his poet's heart told him that her desirability was in a measure enhanced by the fact that she was out of his reach.

There he was—not unhandsome in spite of too much weight, about which he had been teased all his life. Perhaps that was why he had turned to the pen. He could write glowing verse of his longings, his aspiration in the field of love, and find great satisfaction therein, for he was beginning to be recognized as one of the finest poets of his day.

Surely this must impress the Queen who had been brought up in a cultivated court. Her parents had loved the troubadours and had always encouraged them. And he was a royal troubadour, Thibaud le Chansonnier. He was eager for that not to be forgotten. His great grandfather Louis VII was the King's grandfather. Just a little twist of fate and he might have been King. If his great grandmother Eleanor of Aquitaine had borne a son . . . instead of a daughter . . . well, it would not have been Louis who was on the throne but Thibaud, and Blanche of Castile might have been his bride instead of Louis's.

What bliss that would have been. And because Fate had been unkind Louis was her husband; it was Louis's children she bore, the children of France—and he was merely Thibaud, the troubadour Count of Champagne.

So he must sing his songs and he had made of Blanche an ideal and she being the woman she was had shown him so clearly that there was never a hope of her becoming his mistress. She liked his songs though. What woman would not enjoy hearing herself so honoured.

Adoring Blanche he had come to despise Louis as being entirely unworthy of her. Louis had always been a weakling, physically. His father had feared for his health. Of course he was just and lacked the cruelty of so many men; there was no doubt that he had certain good points but even if he could be an acceptable King, he was not worthy to be Blanche's husband.

And while he sat at his table, murmuring to himself the words he was turning over in his mind, a messenger arrived with a command from the King.

Louis reminded him that he was his vassal and that as such he could be called to serve the King in battle for forty days and forty nights. He was therefore ordered to join the King's army without delay, bringing with him his men at arms, for the King was laying siege to the town of Avignon in the fight against the Albigensians.

Thibaud felt a burning resentment. He had no desire to go to war. He was not out of sympathy with the Albigensians. They had been foolish perhaps in trying to pit themselves against Rome, but he was all in favour of the easy comfortable life they had so enjoyed. Raymond of Toulouse was a man of culture and a friend of his. Raymond was more interested in music, literature and discussion than in war.

And he, Thibaud the Troubadour, was being asked—nay, commanded—to leave the comfort of his castle and go to war.

And he must . . . because he was a vassal of the King and the King commanded him.

With something less than a good grace Thibaud set out for Avignon, but as he rode along he sang one of his latest compositions, the subject of which was the beauty of a lady whom he could not get out of his mind—and all knew that that lady was Blanche the Queen.

He would have liked to sing of a rare passion between them which both admitted to in secret, but it was not true and might even be considered treason. He could imagine those cold blue eyes on him if he hinted at such a relationship between them. She would banish him from Court and he would never see her again. So he had to be careful.

So to Avignon—that rich and beautiful town which owed its prosperity to its clever trading and the peace it enjoyed with the neighbouring Counts of Toulouse. The people of Avignon shared a desire with those of Toulouse to live in peace and comfort, they loved music and welcomed the troubadours of Toulouse and with them shared the new ideas and found great pleasure in discussing them. Avignon was not going to give in easily.

Thibaud arrived in a mood of discontent which was certainly not dispersed by the sight of the grey walls of the town which looked impregnable and the soldiers encamped outside them weary and disillusioned for they had come expecting a quick victory.

When Thibaud went to the King to inform him of his coming and to pay his respects, he was shocked by the sight of Louis whose skin was yellowish and his eyes bloodshot; he was a sick man, concluded Thibaud.

He asked after the King's health and received a short reply that there was nothing wrong with it.

An opinion I do not share, Sire, was Thibaud's inward comment, but he bowed his head and said he was glad to hear that was so.

'The town has some strong defences,' Thibaud ventured.

'That's so,' replied Louis. 'But I shall take it . . . no matter how long I stay here.'

Thibaud thought: A vassal owes his lord but forty days and forty nights. I am not prepared to stay here longer.

They studied each other—the Queen's husband and the poet who declared his love for her in his verses. My verses will outlast you, my lord, thought Thibaud.

'I am glad you came,' said Louis. 'It reached my ears that you were reluctant to do so and had you disobeyed me I should have been obliged to take measures against you.'

'My lord, I came to your command. I have sworn allegiance, and when you call me to battle I owe you forty days and nights of my service.'

'I should have been forced to make an example of you, Thibaud,' the King warned him, 'by laying waste the lands of Champagne.'

Thibaud thought: You would have found stout resistance, my lord, and you are in no position to wage war against those who would do you no harm if you left them in peace. You have mighty enemies. The English will soon be at your throat. You need friends, Louis, not enemies. You poor creature. *Her* husband. I know I am over fat, too fond of good food and wine; but for all that I am more of a man than you are.

He said: 'It is not good, my lord, for there to be dissension in your own ranks. So I am here to fight with you in a cause which has no great concern for me.'

The King dismissed him and Thibaud left his camp to mingle with others of his kind who had been called to honour their vows. He was not surprised that many of them expressed a similar discontent. They were ready enough to fight for their lands; they would have gone into a battle against the English; but even though this war had the backing of Rome and they were said to win Heaven's forgiveness by taking part in it, their hearts were not in it.

'Forty days and forty nights—well I dare swear it can be endured,' said Thibaud.

'Do you think the siege will be over by then?' was the reply. 'They have food and ammunition within those walls to hold out for a year.'

Thibaud shrugged his shoulders. 'But I, my friend, have given a vow to serve only forty days and nights.'

The weary siege went on. The people of Avignon were truculent, believing that in time their friends of Toulouse would arrive to save them.

The heat was intense; men were dying of disease and Louis ordered that their bodies be disposed by throwing them into the river. It was not the best of burying grounds but at least it was better than having rotten corpses lying around.

His own deteriorating health was noticed.

'My God,' said Philip Hurepel, 'the King looks sick unto death.'

Philip Hurepel was disturbed. He was fond of the King as well as being a loyal servant. They shared the same father for Philip Hurepel was the son of Philip Augustus by Agnes, the wife he had taken after he had declared himself divorced from Ingeburga. The Pope had declared Philip Hurepel legitimate as a concession to his mother, but it was not everyone who accepted him as such. However, Philip Hurepel had never shown any desire to assert his right. He was a Prince of

France and loved by Louis; in return he gave his affection and loyalty.

He discussed the King's condition with a group of friends, among them Thibaud.

'The King has fits of shivering which I like not,' he said. 'I fear they are a symptom of something worse. He finds it hard to keep himself warm. I have told them to put furs on the bed. But no matter if he be weighed down with furs he is still cold.'

'What he wants,' said Thibaud, 'is a woman in his bed to keep him warm.'

Philip Hurepel looked with distaste at the troubadour.

'As a poet,' he retorted, 'your thoughts leap to such matters. The King has ever turned his back on such amusements.'

' 'Tis an old custom,' said Thibaud. 'I merely mention it. When an old man cannot keep warm at nights there is only one remedy. I have seen it work again and again.'

'Such talk is disloyalty to the King,' said Philip sternly.

'Thibaud is right,' put in the Count of Blois. 'A naked girl of sixteen years . . . that is what he needs.'

Philip ran his hand through his shock of hair which his father had remarked on and from which he had acquired his nickname. 'Louis would be furious,' he said.

'He would have to admit that the remedy proved to be a cure.'

'I have been close to the King for many years,' said Philip, 'and never have I known him to take a strange woman to his bed.'

Thibaud folded his hands together and raised his eyes. 'Our King is a saint,' he said with a hint of mockery in his voice. There was a great deal of mischief in Thibaud. The King was ill—sick of a fever. It might well be that he was a little delirious. What would he do if he awoke in the night and found a naked girl in his bed? Would he think it was the incomparable Blanche?

He had ever been faithful to his Queen. He loved her; but so did Thibaud. Perhaps they had different ways of loving. Thibaud was romantic; he had to admit he enjoyed this saga of unrequited love. Louis would never indulge in such fantasy. Why should he? He had the reality.

It was no use trying to arrange something with Hurepel. He would just tug his bristly head and say the King would be horrified.

But why not? It was a well tried custom.

He talked to Blois and Count Archibald of Bourbon who was a great friend of the King and was very worried about his state of health.

It was a chance, Thibaud pointed out. It could do no harm.

It was amazing how easy it was to persuade them. They were men who took amorous adventuring as part of life; the King's abstention had always made him seem a little odd and Thibaud knew that men who indulged in what might be called a little vice, liked others to share in it too. Nothing could be more depressing for a man who enjoyed the occasional peccadillo to be with one who never did, but continued to live in virtue and was a pattern of morality.

Even the King's best friends would like to see him commit one little act of indiscretion; and it could always be covered up by the assertion that the girl was put there just to keep him warm.

Thibaud found the girl. She was barely sixteen, plump, smooth-skinned and experienced.

All she had to do was slip into a bed and warm up the poor man who lay there, really very sick, and she might use whatever method she considered best. She must understand that all they wished was to warm the man, for he shivered with cold and there was nothing else which could keep him warm.

Louis lay between sleeping and waking—the dreadful shivering fits taking possession of him periodically.

'I am so cold,' he had complained, and more rugs had been found; their weight was heavy but it could not get him warm.

He wished that he was in his castle with Blanche. He thanked God for Blanche and young Louis and the rest of his family. It was only three years since he had been crowned a king—and he feared not a great one. He hated war and he constantly prayed that he could bring peace to France, but it seemed that God had decided differently. Philip had been so confident when John had come to the throne that soon the English would be driven out of France and the reason for this perpetual strife would be over. But it had not been completed. That was the trouble. If John had lived a little longer, he could have become King of England. . . .

But it was no use. It had not happened that way.

He was aware of whispering voices in his room and he closed his eyes, having no desire to speak to anyone. He merely wished to lie still.

They were at his bedside.

Someone was in his bed. He roused himself. He was looking at a naked girl.

He must be in a delirium. But why should he dream of a naked girl? He had never desired naked girls. He was not a man to indulge in erotic dreams.

He cried out: 'What means this?' The shock of seeing the young woman had shaken off the lassitude brought on by his state. Standing by his bed, watching him, were several of his men. He recognized the Count of Blois and Thibaud of Champagne.

'My lord,' said a voice soothingly, and he recognized that of Archibald of Bourbon. 'We but thought to bring some warmth into your bed.'

'Who is this woman?'

The poor girl looked crestfallen.

'She is one who will know how to keep you warm, Sire,' said Thibaud quietly.

A dislike of the man rose within Louis.

He raised himself. 'Who dared bring in this woman?'

'Sire,' began Thibaud.

'You, my lord,' said Louis coldly. 'Take her away. I have never yet defiled my marriage bed nor will I do so now. You mistake much, my lords, if you think I am of your kind. I shall remember this.'

The girl stared from Louis to the men about the bed in bewilderment.

Archibald signed to her to go. When she had left he began to explain: 'My lord, we feared for you. Your body was so cold and we could think of no way to comfort you.'

'Leave me,' said Louis, 'and if ever one of you again

attempts to dishonour me, remember this: you will incur my deepest displeasure.'

They slunk out. Thibaud, inwardly convulsed with laughter, but the others deeply disturbed.


The affair seemed to have some effect on Louis, for he recovered from his bout of illness and the next day left his bed.

He looked ill however and was deeply depressed by what he found in the camp. The heat was trying; the flies and insects an added affliction; nothing seemed to go right for his army and it was hard to believe that God was on their side. They had made an attempt to scale the walls at their weakest point; they had managed to throw a bridge across the river to the castle walls but this had collapsed and several hundred men had been thrown into the river. Many of them had been drowned, many more injured. It was a tale of disaster.

As he inspected his camp he came upon Thibaud of Champagne and he felt extremely uneasy, remembering that scene in the bedroom when he had awakened to what he had thought must be delirium to find the naked girl in his bed and the Count of Champagne watching him in a manner he could only describe as sardonic.

This was the poet who dared write verses about Blanche. He told the world in his songs how he longed to make her his mistress. It was too much even for the most lenient and peace-loving King to accept. Blanche—thank God—was a virtuous woman. She had been as faithful to him as he had been to her. She had shrugged aside the impertinence of Thibaud but what would her reaction be if he told her the fellow had tried to put a naked girl in his bed?

Dislike for the man overcame him and it showed in his manner.

Thibaud was inclined to be truculent. He had had enough of Avignon. The siege was nowhere near over. He would like to remind Louis that he also was royal, a descendant from Louis his grandfather and the renowned Eleanor of Acquitaine. Why should such as he have to take orders from a cousin— for their relationship was something like that.

'They continue to hold out, Sire,' said Thibaud, who should

have waited for the King to address him. 'If you ask my opinion, they're good for many more weeks yet.'

'I did not ask your opinion,' replied Louis coldly.

'Ah, then I withdraw it, my lord.' The ironic bow. The gleam in the eyes, the mischief. He was thinking of that naked girl.

Whatever could have possessed Blois and Bourbon to do such a thing? They might have known what his feelings would be. They had been urged on by this man who had too great an opinion of himself and who had dared to cast eyes on Blanche.

'We shall stay here,' went on Louis, 'no matter how long the people of Avignon hold out.'

'Your vassals, my lord, owe you but forty days and forty nights.'

'My vassals, sir, owe me their complete loyalty.'

'They vowed but forty days and forty nights. That was in their oath. I have been here thirty-six and my time of service is coming to an end.'

'Yet you will stay here until we have the town.'

'I promised forty days and the nights that follow them, Sire.'

'You will not leave us nevertheless. If you did, I would raze Champagne.'

'You would find strong resistance, my lord, if you attempted to do that.'

'Yet I will not suffer traitors about me.'

Thibaud smiled that insolent smile which angered the King even more than his words.

'I am sure you will consider such an act well before you undertake it,' said Louis. 'It could bring great misfortune to you.'

Then he passed on.

The news spread through the camp. Thibaud is preparing to leave.

Philip Hurepel remonstrated with him.

'You must not go now,' he protested. 'They cannot hold out much longer. The King will be your enemy for as long as he lives if you desert him now.'

'I have served my forty days. Why should I stay longer?'

'Because if all deserted him now it would mean defeat for him.'

'What rejoicing there would be in Avignon.'

'Be sensible, Thibaud.'

'I am weary of this siege. I promised the King forty days and nights and I have given them to him.'

'If you go you will regret it.'

'You think only of your brother, Philip.'

'Is he not your kinsman too?'

' 'Tis a fact he rarely remembers.'

Others came to him and pointed out the folly of leaving. There were some who scorned him for suggesting such a course of action. Thibaud was surprised how many supported the King when they were all weary of the siege and were certain that the besiegers were in a more sorry state than the besieged.

Thibaud realized that opinion was against him. He knew that the King must in time subdue the town; he knew that if he left now it would be remembered against him and could bring him harm. And yet he could not resist the impulse.

Louis was unworthy of Blanche and Thibaud longed to be her lover and he would never feel completely happy with any other woman because he had set himself this unattainable ideal. And Louis had been married to her without effort— simply because he had been heir to the throne.

He had to fight Louis. It was against his impulsive, reckless, not always logical nature not to do so.

It was dark when he gathered his knights together and prepared to slip away.

'You will regret this,' Philip Hurepel told him angrily.

'I have met my dues. I will give nothing to Louis.'

'You fool,' said Philip.

'You loyal brother,' mocked Thibaud. 'Who can tell how much my desertion will cost me and what the rewards of your loyalty will be? Adieu, Hurepel. I doubt not we shall meet again ere long.'

Then Thibaud and his company rode back to Champagne.

\*    \*    \*

'Traitor!' cried Louis. 'I ever found it hard to tolerate that fat man. Though I must admit he is a good poet and I have enjoyed some of his work. What think you, Blois, Bourbon, Hurepel . . . will others follow?'

Philip Hurepel said stoutly that the King had enough good friends beside him to enable him to take Avignon.

'I doubt it not,' replied Louis. 'But I like it not when traitors desert.'

'Thibaud is too fat to be a good soldier,' said Bourbon. 'He is more adept with the pen.'

'The pen can be a mighty weapon,' said Louis, and he wondered whether those poems about Blanche had engendered his hatred of the man.

As he feared, Thibaud's departure had increased the dissatisfaction of the men. The people of Avignon had been well prepared. Never it seemed to those outside the walls had there been a city so well equipped to withstand an army. Louis's health was failing again and his friends watching him with anxiety wondered if it would not be wise after all to raise the siege and abandon Avignon.

August had come—sweltering hot. Never, declared the soldiers, had the sun shone so fiercely; dysentery increased. Men were dying all around them.

'It would seem that Louis will be one of them if we don't get out of this place,' said Philip Hurepel.

Bourbon was of the opinion that the King would never give in.

'Perhaps, after all, Thibaud was the wise one,' suggested the Count of Blois. 'At least he escaped this.'

'He will repent his folly,' said the loyal Philip.

It was only a few days later when the governor of the town sent a messenger to the King. The town was ready to make peace, for it could hold out no longer.

This was victory—but a dearly bought one.

Louis had no wish to send his soldiers to rape, murder and pillage. He shrank from such procedure. He could not but respect such valiant men. He therefore decreed that the people should be spared but it would be construed as weakness if some punishment were not meted out to a town which had cost him so much in men, arms and money.

He ordered that the walls of the city should be demolished but the townspeople unharmed.

His work was done at Avignon. It could be carried out by others whom he appointed. He could go back to Paris.

Blanche would be waiting for him and there he would enjoy a time of recuperation in her soothing company.

He needed it.

So he began the journey.

The siege had ended at the close of August but there had been a great deal to arrange and it was the end of October before he could begin the journey back.

He felt very tired and a day spent in the saddle often exhausted him so much that it was necessary for him to rest the following day.

It was when he reached the Castle of Montpensier that he took to his bed and found, when he attempted to rise the next day, that he was unable to do so.

'Alas, my friends,' he said, 'I fear I shall be obliged to rest here for a few days.'

Blanche called the children to her . . . her adored Louis, who grew more handsome every day, Robert, John, Alphonse and Philip Dagobert. Isabella was too young of course; she must remain in the nursery where another little one would soon join her.

'Your father is coming home,' she told them, 'and we shall all go to meet him and give him welcome. That will give him as much pleasure as his victory.'

Young Louis said: 'What will happen to the people of Avignon, my lady?'

She looked at him sharply. There was compassion in his voice and she wondered why it should have occurred to him first to ask after the defeated.

'Your father will know best how to treat them.'

'He'll cut off their hands perhaps,' said Robert, 'or their feet. Perhaps put out their eyes.'

'Our father will do no such thing,' declared Louis.

'He will punish them for having a siege, won't he?' demanded Robert.

'It is their leaders who were to blame,' pointed out Louis.

'The people should not be punished for that should they, my lady?'

'When your father returns,' said Blanche, 'you may ask him what happened to the people of Avignon. Then you will hear that justice was done.'

'Is our father always right?' asked Robert.

'Your father always does what God tells him is right,' answered Blanche.

'God does not always answer,' Louis pointed out.

'But He guides, my son,' replied Blanche. 'You will understand one day, when you are King. That will not be for many many years. First you will have learned from your father how best to reign.'

How proud of them she was as they rode out together. It was fitting that they should be there to greet him after the victory at Avignon. How glad she was that it was over, for there had been a time when she had feared that the siege might have to be abandoned and that would have been bad for France and for Louis.

As they came near to the castle of Montpensier she suggested that Louis with his party should ride on ahead so that he should be the first to greet his father.

This the young boy was eager to do. At twelve years old he already had the bearing of a hero. His blond good looks and his regal bearing attracted men to him for his bearing was enhanced by a certain gentleness. Blanche did not think it was disloyal to Louis to notice that his son was the more kingly of the two. Louis himself had remarked on it.

The young boy rode a little ahead of his attendants in his eagerness to see his father and he had not gone very far when he saw a party of horsemen coming from the château.

He pulled up and cried, 'Where is my father? I have come to greet him.'

'My lord,' said the leader of the group, 'where is the Queen?'

'She is a little way behind. I rode on ahead. She wished it.'

'Will you return to your mother and tell her to come with all haste to the château?'

'But my father. . . .'

'It would be well, my lord, if you would come with your mother.'

Louis turned and rode back.

When she saw her son a terrible fear came to Blanche. She spurred up her horse and galloped to the castle.

Philip Hurepel was waiting for her there. There were tears in his eyes and she knew before he said: 'My lady, the King is dead. Long live Louis IX.'

Blanche was in command now. The new King was a boy of twelve and, though possessed of great gifts, a boy.

She must set aside her personal grief. There was no time for it. Later she would think of Louis, the understanding between them, the affection, the respect they had always had for each other, the happy married life—almost as felicitous as that of her own parents; but now she must think of the future.

When a King died and left an heir not of an age to govern, there was always danger.

'The King is dead. Long Live the King.' It was an old cry; but that King was not truly recognized as King until he was crowned.

So before she sat down to grieve, she must get Louis crowned. And then she knew that there would be little time for grief. Louis was too young; he would need guidance. She had good friends and Louis would have loyal subjects, but on her would rest the main burden.

From Philip Hurepel, the Counts of Bourbon and Blois she heard the story of Louis's last days. He had exhausted himself before Avignon; they had known he was ill but not how ill—and could be said to have died fighting for a holy cause, so they need have no fear for his soul.

'I never had fear for his soul,' cried Blanche. 'He was a good man. There are few as good in this world or in the next, I assure you.'

The men bowed their heads and said: 'Amen.'

'Indeed we need have no fear for him,' said Blanche. 'He is at peace. Now we must think what he would wish us to do. We have a new King, Louis IX. He is a promising boy . . . but a boy. My lords, the late King would wish us to make sure that he is crowned without delay.'

They agreed that this was so.

'Then, my lords, let us see that this is done.'

She should rest a day at the château, Philip Hurepel told her. 'You need your strength to support him. *You* must not be ill.'

She agreed to rest there and in her room her grief and desolation swept over her.

Dear, good, kind Louis . . . dead! She could not believe it. Never to speak to him again. She needed him now . . . so much she needed him.

Her women came to her and found her seated on her bed staring ahead of her, the tears slowly falling down her cheeks.

'My lady,' said one, 'is there something we can do for you?'

She shook her head. 'There is one thing I would you would do for me and that is bring a sword and run it through my heart.'

'My lady!'

'Oh, that is foolish is it not? But if I could make a wish it would be to be lying in a tomb beside him. He has been my life. We have been together in love and understanding. Do you realize what that means?'

'To have seen the King and you together, my lady, was to understand.'

'I have no wish to live without him.'

'There is the young King, my lady.'

'Yes, the young King. Could it be that others could guide him better than I?'

'None can guide him as you can, my lady.'

'I know that to be true and it is for this reason only that I wish to live.'

'You must live, my lady. You must not harm yourself with grief. You must remember, the young King needs you.'

'It is true,' she said. 'Send the King to me.'

Louis came and throwing himself at her feet gave way to weeping.

'My beloved son,' said Blanche, caressing those shining blond locks, 'you have lost the best of fathers, I the dearest of husbands. But we have work to do. We must not forget them.'

'No, my lady, I do not forget it.'

'His death which has made me a sorrowing widow has made you a King, He would want you to be worthy of him, my son.'

'I will be. I promise you, my lady. I will never do anything that would make him ashamed of me.'

'May God bless you always.'

They were silent, weeping together.

Just this night, thought Blanche. Just this little time to mourn him. Then there will be work to do. My dear young King—so beautiful, so vulnerable—it will not be easy for you.

But he would have her beside him—and she knew she would be strong.

# Isabella Schemes

SIX years of marriage had not had the effect of lessening Hugh de Lusignan's passion for his wife—rather had it increased it. Uxorious, adoring, he had allowed her gradually to take over his life; he rarely made the most insignificant decision without consulting her and if she disapproved of it, that was an end to it.

His reward was a life of such eroticism as would have been beyond his belief had he not known her and the knowledge that—as far as it was possible for her to love anyone—she loved him.

In many ways she was not discontented with her life. She was close to her native Angoulême, and indeed spent much of her time there; she had children without much difficulty, although she did deplore the mild discomfort that must be endured before their arrival. She was very faithful, which seemed natural in view of her insatiable sexuality, and she accepted her children with a certain amount of pleasure. Children could be very useful. In six years of marriage she had had five; and she guessed there would be more. Hugh, the eldest, was a fine boy who was very like his father in appearance and manners—a child as yet but one of great promise. Then there was Guy, only a year younger, and Isabella, William and Geoffrey. Four boys—all strong, all healthy. And a girl was useful. Young Isabella was a charming creature but Hugh declared she would never have the beauty of her mother. But then whoever had and whoever would?

But there was one thing Isabella could never forget and that was that she was a queen. It was all very well to be the centre of Hugh's life and domain, to be admired wherever she went, to have every whim respected, but in Lusignan she was merely the Countess of La Marche. With John she had been Queen of England and even when she was his prisoner, that fact had remained. In England she would still be Queen—though Queen Mother. She grimaced at the expression, but still with a son who was young and had not yet found a queen of his own she would have had considerable standing.

So there was always the need to remind everyone that she was a queen, to bestir Hugh to actions which would let everyone know how important he was.

Of course he was the lord of a great deal of territory. There were many who owed allegiance to him; but one fact remained and it irked her more than anything she had ever known—and that was that Hugh must swear allegiance to the King of France.

How she hated that cold-eyed Queen who had regarded her with such distaste. She would like to see her brought low, her and her stupid Louis who doted on her. He was completely faithful to her. People were constantly commenting on it. Well, he was scarcely a man—and what of her? Did she have lovers? Although no scandal had touched her, all knew that the fat troubadour made songs about her. Isabella despised them all—Louis, Blanche and Thibaud of Champagne.

Messengers arrived at the castle with letters for the Count. She had gone down to the hall with Hugh to receive them, and when she saw that they came from the Queen she could not conceal her impatience.

She dismissed the messenger to the kitchens where he would be refreshed and said: 'Let us go to the bedchamber where we can be quite alone to read what this means. It is important. Rest assured.'

She took the packet from Hugh, who meekly allowed her to do so, and when they were in the bedchamber it was she who broke the seals.

He came and looked over her shoulder.

'My God!' he cried. 'Louis . . . dead.'

'Always a weakling,' she said. 'You know what this means. *She* will be the sovereign now.'

'It is young Louis. . . .'

'Young Louis! A boy of twelve. This is what Madame Blanche has been waiting for.'

Hugh was well aware that Blanche would be desolate at the death of her husband and no woman as wise as she clearly was would want to see her son of twelve years on the throne, but he had learned not to contradict Isabella.

'She is the mistress now.' She turned to Hugh. 'It is to this woman that *you* will have to bow the knee.'

It was a familiar theme and Hugh would like to ignore it.

'Why look,' he said, 'We are summoned to the coronation.'

Isabella's eyes were narrow. She was thinking back to ten years before when the news had been brought to her of John's death and she had then been in a similar position to that in which Blanche found herself now. What had she done? She had instinctively known that her young son must be crowned without delay. Blanche was realizing the same thing now.

'We must make ready at once,' said Hugh. 'There is little time.'

'Hold!' said Isabella. 'I am not sure that we are going to this coronation.'

'Isabella, my dearest, this is a command.'

'Hugh, my dearest, you married a Queen. She does not take orders from that woman . . . even though she also is a Queen. We are equal in rank and she does not command me.'

'She commands us as Count and Countess of La Marche and as such we are the vassals of France.'

'Oh Hugh, you madden me sometimes. It is well that I love you. If I did not I should quarrel most surely with you and leave this place and go back to England.'

Hugh turned pale at the thought of such a disaster.

'Now, my love. What are we going to do?' she asked.

'Prepare to leave. If we are going to be in Rheims. . . .'

'We are not going to be in Rheims.'

'Isabella, what do you mean?'

'We are setting out at once to call on our neighbour of Thouars.'

'He too will be summoned to Rheims.'

'Then we must reach him before he commits the folly of going there.'

Hugh stared at her aghast. She put her arms about his neck and laid his cheek against hers. 'My dearest husband,' she said, 'where would you be without me? I am going to make you the most powerful man in France.'

'Isabella, the King. . . .'

'That soft-cheeked infant. Do not talk to me of him. My Henry is a man in comparison. You see, my love, you are in a very good position. You are the husband of the mother of the King of England. I have been thinking for some time that we might be happier supporting him than this woman who now sets herself up as our ruler.'

'But I have sworn allegiance. . . .'

'Oaths! What are oaths? Oaths are for vassals. . . . We should not allow ourselves to be fettered by such.'

'Isabella, much as you mean to me, I have my honour, my duty. . . .'

She laughed softly. 'And I would not have you other than you are. But before we go to Rheims I want you to come with me to visit our neighbours. I will send a messenger immediately to Thouars and Parthenay to tell them we are on our way.'

'This is the coronation of our King. . . .'

'Oh come, Hugh. There is no time to waste. That child is not ready to be crowned. He will merely be the mouthpiece for his mother.'

He made a mild effort to detain her; but laughingly she thrust him aside, and the next day they set off for northern Poitou.

Guy de Thouars, Hugh and the Lord of Parthenay were the most powerful lords of this part of the country and they had begun to realize that linked together they were a formidable force.

Guy received them eagerly when they arrived. Hugh by this time had allowed Isabella to override his doubts and had convinced himself that what she had suggested was indeed the truth.

Louis had been no friend to them; there was now a king who was only a minor; and Isabella was convinced that Blanche worked deviously against them.

It was Hugh who began the explanations. Isabella had

primed him in what he had to say and she knew that Guy and Parthenay must be convinced that Hugh was not merely up-holding her views.

Hugh pointed out that the late King had not served them well. He had suddenly decided to fight in the Albigensian war instead of continuing to wage war against the English. As soon as the Earls of Salisbury and Cornwall had shown they were not without military skill he changed wars.

'Now,' said Hugh, 'we have a child as our King, and we know full well that our true ruler will be the Queen.'

'It seems likely,' agreed Guy.

'She will have able counsellors,' put in Parthenay.

Isabella interrupted them: 'We know the Queen, my lords; she is not of a temper to consider advice. She will have her say and expect all to follow her wishes.'

'It would seem,' said Hugh, glancing at Isabella, 'that we should offer our allegiance elsewhere.'

The two men looked aghast, and Isabella said quickly: 'I am not without influence in other quarters. I happen to be the mother of the King of England.'

'My lady . . . my lord . . .' began Guy.

'Yes,' said Isabella. 'I can promise you lands and riches. When my son comes here and regains that which has been lost to England, he will not be ungrateful to those who helped him. I can promise you that.'

'We have sworn an oath of allegiance. . . .'

'To King Louis VIII,' cried Isabella. 'He is dead.'

'His son is now our King.'

'His mother hastens to crown him, to have you all kneel before him and swear allegiance, but you have not done that yet, my lords. Will you be foolish enough to go to Rheims and mildly bend the knee to the Spanish woman?'

'The coronation of our King is to take place on the twenty-ninth of this month.'

'But three short weeks after the old King's death! Well, we will say this for the lady. She knows how to move fast.'

'I would say,' put in the Lord of Parthenay, 'that the Queen will be an able Regent with good men to help her. We shall not find her ill-prepared for the task.'

Isabella was stung into sudden fury. Little enraged her more than to hear praise of Blanche.

'Prepared! Indeed she is prepared. I'll vow she was waiting most impatiently for this day. She . . . and her plump paramour.'

'Isabella!' cried Hugh. The others regarded her with amazement.

'Oh come,' cried Isabella. 'We know of these matters, do we not? She is a woman . . . for all that she shows a frozen face to the world. Have you read those verses written to her by her fat Count? They are the words of a lover, my friends, a satisfied lover. Should we blame her? Louis was scarce a man. She has her needs, like the rest of us. If she took him openly I could like her better. It is this mock purity which galls me.'

'My lady,' said Guy, 'you speak of the Queen.'

'I speak as one Queen of another.'

'This must not go beyond these four walls,' said Hugh uneasily.

Isabella laughed shrilly. 'My dear husband, my dear friends, it has already gone to the four corners of France. Are you so innocent that you do not know that tongues are wagging about our lily white Queen? *He* is not silent. He might as well stand at the turret of his castle and proclaim his mistress to the world. He does more than that. He writes it in songs which are sung throughout France. Who does not know of the guilty passion of these lovers?'

'Champagne writes of her as the unattainable,' said Guy.

'You are a soldier, my lord. You do not read into those poems what is there to be seen. He is mad with love of her. Louis dies suddenly. Did you expect him to die? Come, confess it. Was it not a shock to hear that the King was dead? But I tell you this: the Count of Champagne quarrelled with him. He left before the walls of Avignon . . . and soon after we hear the King is dead. Of a fever, we are told. Of drinking bad wine. Who gave Louis bad wine to drink? The Queen's lover was there was he not . . . and Louis died!'

'But it was weeks after he had left that Louis died,' Parthenay pointed out.

'Those who are clever with poisons may choose the time

they work. I tell you this, my lords, I call it strange that Thibaud of Champagne should write so of his love, and that he should be with the King before he dies. And the Queen . . . what of her? What does she say: "I must get my son crowned without delay." In fact there has been such little delay that one might be forgiven in thinking that it was planned beforehand.'

There was a deep silence. With her glittering eyes and flushed cheeks Isabella presented a sight of such beauty that none of them could take his eyes from her. If there was something evil in her undeniable loveliness, that did not make it the less fascinating.

Hugh was undoubtedly uneasy. 'There is no proof of this . . .' he began, 'but. . . .'

' 'Tis better not spoken of,' put in Guy quickly.

'But we must think of the future,' said Hugh.

The two men nodded.

'Nothing rash should be done,' went on Hugh.

'Do you mean,' asked Parthenay, 'that we should not take our oath to the King?'

'If we are not at Rhiems we cannot do so,' said Hugh. 'In the meantime let us consider the friendship which must exist between my house and that of the English King. He is showing himself to be a King now . . . I do not think he would want to work against his mother and her friends.'

There was a deep silence in the hall. A young King; a woman to rule. It was not a good prospect. And was it not just the time when the King of England would attempt to regain the lands his father had lost?

He would need help. And who better to help him than the lords of Poitou and Lusignan?

Hugh was smiling quietly. Isabella is right, he thought. They are beginning to realize it. There is more to be gained from England and France. It was unwise of course to talk so of Blanche. Perhaps it is true. Why should it not be?

As usual he was beginning to believe what Isabella intended he should.

Then he thought suddenly: But by God, how she hates Blanche.

\*   \*   \*

Thibaud of Champagne sang blithely as he made his way towards Rheims.

The King was dead and Blanche a widow. He thought of her constantly and now that she was a widow she had seemed to come a little closer to him.

As he rode along he was composing new songs to her. She was the White Queen now, for as was the custom she must go into mourning for her husband and mourning was white.

The Queen with a name as fair as her beautiful hair and the white mourning of a widow. Even her name was appropriate. Blanche, The White Queen.

He sang a little and he was enchanted with the words he made to fit the melody.

And now to the coronation at Rheims.

He had sent his sergeant-at-arms on ahead to make sure than an adequate lodging was found for him. It must be one worthy of his rank and loyalty. A coronation was a time when a new king must be reminded of his blood relations.

Rheims! What a fair city, situated boldly there on the Vesle river. It was becoming one of the important towns of France since Philip Augustus had been crowned there and Louis after him—and now young Louis the new King would share that experience. It seemed that a precedent was being set for the crowning of Kings.

Thibaud was wondering whether he might present himself to the Queen immediately after the ceremony or if he should wait awhile.

He would make it clear to her that he would put his heart and everything he possessed at her feet.

'You have but to command, Queen of my heart. . . .'

He imagined the gratitude in her eyes. She would be glad of a protector now. She would have her enemies, for there were always those self seekers who would be looking for advantages now that she was a widow. He would make her understand that she could rely on him absolutely.

He could see the towers of the cathedral. Many people were coming into the town. Knights with followers, all the highest in the land.

As he made his way through the streets to the lodging

which he believed would be waiting him he was recognized by several people.

They cheered him somewhat mockingly. It was due to his size. He was known and recognized at once as the Fat Troubadour.

He acknowledged their greeting and broke into song. That silenced their mockery. They must be aware of the beauty of his voice and the merit of the songs he sang which were his own.

This put him in good spirits, and he rode along happily rehearsing what he would say to the Queen.

But where was his lodging? Where were the pennants fluttering in the breeze to tell the townsfolk that this was the temporary residence of Thibaud, Count of Champagne—a kinsman of the young King, and of royal blood?

His sergeant-at-arms was waiting for him at the house which was to have been honoured by his occupation, his expression woebegone, as he gesticulated wildly in explaining to his master what had happened.

'My lord, I arrived here. I took up residence. I had your standards flying and the mayor and some of his men came to the house and demanded that the standard be removed . . . ay, and that I remove myself and all our servants from this place.'

'God in Heaven,' cried Thibaud. 'I'll have his blood.'

'My lord, he pleaded that he acted on orders.'

'On orders! Who would dare give such an order?'

'The Queen, my lord.'

'It can't be so. Does she not know . . . ? Why I am the most faithful of her servants.'

'Her orders were that you were to have no lodging in Rheims and that your servants were to be turned into the streets when they came to prepare one for you.'

'But I am to go to the coronation.'

'The Queen's man said that the presence of one who had deserted the King's father when he was in dire need, would not be welcome at the coronation.'

Thibaud was silent.

Then he clenched his fists. He realized he had allowed

himself to dream too wildly. She was as remote as ever she
had been.

A great rage possessed him.

'We will go then,' he said at length. 'Doubtless there will
be some who welcome us if the King does not.'

It was a moving sight when the boy King rode to the
cathedral on a large white horse. The women among the
spectators wept for him. He looked so young, so defenceless
with his thick blond hair free of any covering, and so handsome were his beautifully chiselled features and his smooth
fair skin.

One of the monks assisted him to alight and led him inside
the cathedral. There was great dignity about the boy which
was immediately noticed and commented on. Blanche, watching her son, was proud of him. He looked so vulnerable; he
would need her guidance.

Had she been wise, she wondered, in refusing Thibaud of
Champagne permission to attend? She was unsure now. A
rumour had reached her that some were saying he was her
lover and the thought had filled her with such anger that she
had allowed her personal resentments to take precedence
over her common sense.

The prospect of seeing that fat man at this time, when
she was feeling her loss of Louis so acutely, was more
than she could endure. But she did understand that the last
thing she must do was antagonize any of the powerful lords
who could make her position—but mainly that of her son—
untenable.

A young King, a Regent Queen . . . that situation was
filled with dangers. She would have to act carefully and
quell her personal feelings in the future. Merely because
the foolish troubadour had mentioned her in his songs in
such a manner that she was immediately recognizable, people
had started to circulate this slander. If she could discover
the source she would let someone feel the weight of her
anger.

In the meantime she must curb her feelings. It was disconcerting to contemplate that already she had acted recklessly.

She turned her attention to the ceremony. The Abbot of Saint-Rémi was approaching the platform on which young Louis sat and he carried the sacred oil with which the King would be anointed before he was crowned.

'Oh God keep him,' prayed the Queen. 'Long may he reign and well.'

He sat there on the platform before the chancel where all could see him, and gathered about him were the most important noblemen of France who had come from far places to assist at the coronation and afterwards to give the oath of allegiance.

They were dressing him now in the long purple hose which were decorated with the fleur-de-lis and then the tunic and cloak which also bore the golden lilies of France.

How beautiful he looked. All must agree to that. It was not merely that she saw him through a mother's eyes. He was going to be a great King—a greater King than his father, a greater King than Louis or Philip. People would mention his name with that of Charlemagne.

Was that a premonition, a hope, a plea to God? She could not be sure. She could only say with fervour: 'God save the King.'

The Bishop had placed the crown on his head and he was mounting the steps to the throne now; he sat on the silk encovering which was embroidered with the fleur-de-lis.

There could have been few in the cathedral who were not moved by the sight of their young King.

The Bishop came first to kiss him and then followed the noblemen in order of precedence . . . there to kiss the King and give him the oath of allegiance.

Thibaud of Champagne was missing. Others were missing too.

Where were Hugh and Isabella de Lusignan and their neighbours?

Suddenly the thought struck Blanche that the source of the rumours concerning her and Thibaud of Champagne could have come from Lusignan.

She could clearly picture the mocking evil eyes of Isabella.

And as she listened to the cheering as the little King rode

through the streets of Rheims, she knew that, although there were many loyal men to support him, he would have powerful enemies.

As soon as the coronation was over the Queen must give her thoughts to the imminent birth of another child. This proved to be Charles.

She had believed that it would be a difficult birth, for she had received such a shock during her pregnancy, but the child arrived promptly and in good health and she herself, knowing that a quick recovery was essential, made one.

At the coronation many had been moved by the appearance of the beautiful young King, but how many of them, she wondered, would remain faithful to him if they thought they could best serve their own interests by being otherwise.

That was something she would soon find out.

She was still a little weak from her confinement when Brother Guérin came to see her. His gravity alarmed her, for she knew Guérin to be a man of unswerving loyalty. He had given a long and trusted service not only to her husband but to Philip Augustus before him and both had recognized his worth. This man, a hospitaller, who lived humbly, though because of his position at Court could have amassed great wealth, had had one desire: to serve France well. Philip Augustus had singled him out for his confidences and had appreciated his skills. Louis VIII had made him his Chancellor, and Blanche's one anxiety about him was that his health might fail, for he was old.

So when he came to her and his concern was obvious, Blanche knew that he did not bring good news.

She received him in a private chamber and there he came straight to the point of his visit.

'There are certain to be ambitious men who seek to profit from a situation such as that in which we now find ourselves—a young King who is not of an age to govern, and there will be those who wish to take the reins of government into their own hands.'

'Such as myself?' she asked.

'My lady, you are the Queen and the King's mother. It is fitting that you should place yourself at the head of affairs.

There are many loyal men and women who appreciate your worth.'

'And you are one of them, Brother Guérin?'

'I am indeed, Madam.'

'Then I feel great comfort,' said the Queen.

'But, my lady, you are surrounded by enemies. Some of them are strong and very powerful. . . .'

'I know that Hugh de Lusignan is my enemy.'

'I regret it,' said Brother Guérin. 'It would not have been so but for his wife.'

'Ah, Isabella. She has been responsible for much mischief. I would to God, she had never decided to bring her daughter out to Hugh. If she had stayed in England methinks we should have been spared much trouble.'

'You must know, my lady, that much discontent has been fermented.'

'And she is at the bottom of it. You do not have to tell me that.'

'Lusignan and Thouars have been joined by Peter Mauclerc,' said Brother Guérin quietly.

Blanche put her hand to her head and groaned. Peter Mauclerc was a troublemaker. It was a great misfortune that he was related to the royal house and had descended from the Count of Dreux, one of the sons of Louis VI. As a younger son he had not been so well endowed as his brothers. How much trouble came from impoverished sons whose parents had had more of them than goods to share out! This always seemed to have a bad effect on the person concerned. John Lackland, King of England was an example—and even when such people gained possessions their characters seemed to remain warped and for ever rapacious.

Peter Mauclerc had acquired his nickname because at one time he had been in holy orders. He had long left that behind him, but it was remembered and since he was noted for his ill deeds he became known as Peter Mauclerc.

Since a marriage had been arranged for him with the heiress of Brittany there had been a rise in his fortunes. His Countess had died leaving him three children—John, Arthur and a girl, Yolanda.

As soon as he had Brittany he began making the reputation

which had earned him his name; and all knew that he was a man who must be watched for he was capable of deception, self-advancement and any villainy that he could think up to further his own ends.

So when Peter Mauclerc's name was mentioned Blanche was prepared for trouble.

Well she might have been.

'His first claim is to the throne,' said Brother Guérin.

'To the throne. He must be mad.'

'Perhaps merely puffed up with pride,' admitted Guérin. 'He declares that the first Count of Dreux was not the second son of Louis VI but his first son.'

'What nonsense. He had been he would have been King!'

'His theory is that that Robert of Dreux was passed over because his father considered him to be less clever and capable of governing than his brother Louis who, though younger, was made out to be the elder and as Louis VII inherited the crown. In which case he, as one of the descendants, claims the throne.'

'But this is absurd. Even if it were true he has elder brothers who would come before him.'

'He reckons that if he fights for the crown it will be his. He is preaching that no good can come to a country which is governed by a boy and . . . your pardon, my lady . . . but I tell you what he says . . . a boy and a woman.'

Blanche laughed derisively.

'When a minor comes to the throne there will always be such nonsense. We could send troops to capture this man. What he talks is treason. He should be in prison.'

'I am of like mind,' said Guérin. 'But he has acted promptly.'

'In what way?'

'He has allied himself to powerful men. Thouars, Lusignan, and I hear that Thibaud of Champagne has joined the malcontents.'

Blanche put her hands over her eyes. What a mistake to turn Thibaud from his lodgings! She had expected that he would be faithful to her. What a fool she had been! He was a poet. What he wrote in his verses meant nothing to him. He chose words for their beauty more than their meaning.

She noticed that Brother Guérin was watching closely. Oh God, she thought, does even he believe these rumours?

'Hugh de Lusignan is the most to be feared,' she said.

'He was once a tolerant man.'

'Oh, but he married,' she cried, 'and since then has no mind of his own. He is one who does what he is told. It is not Hugh whom we must consider but she who guides him in all things. That woman! She will lead him to disaster in time. I know it.'

'At this time,' said Guérin gently, 'they are to be feared. I have not told you all. Mauclerc has betrothed his daughter Yolanda to the King of England.'

'Brother Guérin,' she cried, 'pray tell me all quickly. The situation becomes more and more gloomy as you proceed to give me disaster piecemeal.'

'That is all I have to tell you, my lady. I think you will agree that it is a situation fraught with foreboding.'

'I do. Powerful barons rising against the King. And one of them allying himself through marriage with England.'

'Forget not that Isabella is the mother of the King of England. Her sympathies will be with him.'

'And where hers are so are her husband's'

' 'Tis true. If the English King were to choose this moment to attack us, he would find strong support here.'

'And these are the traitors we know. How many are there who keep their secrets, Brother?'

'One day we shall find out unless we can put an end to this.'

'The last thing I wish is for my son to be plunged into war so early in his reign.'

'The position is dangerous, my lady, as it always is when a young king mounts the throne. He has not yet proved himself. He is but a child. Ambitious men are waiting to seize power.'

'I do not wish to go to war,' said Blanche.

'There is only one other alternative.'

She nodded. 'Negotiations. That is the alternative I intend to use.'

'Mauclerc's claim . . . ?'

Blanche gave an impatient exclamation. 'That is the least

important. Who will take that seriously? It is the Lusignans who are making the trouble. From the day Isabella of Angoulême married Hugh de Lusignan I expected it. She saps his spirit. She makes him go the way she wants him to.'

'It is perhaps natural that she should support her son.'

'There is nothing natural about that woman. She is obsessed by herself.'

'How will you overcome her obsession?'

'Perhaps by offering her something better than she could get from her son.'

'You will buy her loyalty?'

'She has no loyalty to give to any but herself. I can perhaps buy her withdrawal. For if what one must have for the safety of the realm cannot be given there is only one alternative and that is to buy it.'

'What will you use for currency?'

'I will consider, Brother, and inform you of my decision. There is one bright hope in this sorry business and that is that those with whom we have to deal will give their allegiance to the highest bidder—for as long as it can do them good of course.'

She would speak to him again later, she told Brother Guérin. Then she prepared to have done with her convalescence.

There was work to be done.


She must lose no time. The rebels were gathering against Louis. They were asking why France should be governed by a woman—a foreigner at that. Even those who wished to remain loyal to Louis did not want a foreigner ruling them—and a woman.

Forces were gathering at Thouars; they would attack in the Spring. But she must stop the fighting. There must not be civil war in France.

'Have we not enough to do to defend ourselves from the English?' she asked. 'How long will it be before they attack us?'

Brother Guérin said that he believed that Hubert de Burgh was urging the King not to think of regaining French possessions just yet. They had not enough men and ammunition to make it a success. It was true that the King's brother, the Earl of Cornwall, was still in England and they must pray that he would not join up with the rebels.

She set out and travelled south towards Thouars and set up her camp between that town and Loudun. She then sent messengers to Thouars and asked that one of their company should meet her that they might discuss their differences.

Then she waited in trepidation. So much depended on this meeting. Would they take her seriously? They must have known that her husband had taken her into his confidence, that she was as much a statesman as he had been, and how often he had benefited from her judgment. They must know that—foreigner though they called her—her one desire was for the welfare of France, that country of which her son was now the King.

Who would come? she wondered. Would it be Hugh de Lusignan? His wife would surely not be with him. How could she be in the camp! But he would know her wishes and be afraid to act against them.

It was not Hugh who came as the enemy's ambassador.

She felt a flutter of excitement tinged with apprehension and a certain annoyance when he was brought to her, for the man who was bowing before her was Thibaud of Champagne.

So they were face to face—the heroine of his fantasies and the man who had told the world that above all things he longed to be her lover.

He was prepared, for he must have begged to undertake the mission, while she was taken completely by surprise; but it was she who was in complete control.

'So you come here as my enemy, Count,' she said briskly.

He lowered his eyes and murmured: 'My lady, that is something I could never be.'

'Let us keep to the truth,' she retorted. 'It will avail us nothing to reject that. You have joined those who stand against the King and they have sent you here to parley with me.'

'My lady, I begged for the chance of doing so.'

'That you might receive my scorn for you all in person.'

'Nay,' he said, 'that I may have the joy of seeing you.'

She shook herself impatiently. 'My lord, have done. Let us

be sensible. You have come here to parley, have you not? To make terms with me that you and your fellow rebels may not harm the King and his lands.'

'I promise you, my lady, that I will serve you with my life.'

That made her laugh.

'So it seems, my lord! Pray keep your flowery phrases for your verses.'

'You have read my verses, my lady?'

'A few of them. When they have been brought to my notice.'

'I will tell you the truth,' said Thibaud, 'for in your presence I could do nothing else. When I was banished from Rheims I turned to your enemies.'

'Before that,' she said. 'I remembered how you had deserted the King and for that reason would not have you at the coronation of his son.'

'I warned him. I had served my time. I was a loyal servant of the King but I had no love for him. That was impossible.'

She ignored the implication.

'And now what have you to say? What threats have you come to offer against the King?'

'Now that I have seen you, my lady, I could do nothing but serve you with my life.'

'Even though that meant serving your King to whom you owe allegiance?' she asked cynically.

'If that were your command.'

'It is.'

'Then it shall be.'

'You change sides quickly.'

'I was never on any side but yours, my lady. I suffered momentary pique. I had planned to offer myself to you completely. To be your humblest slave if you so wished. And then I was turned away. . . .'

'I see that I acted unwisely in that. I ask your pardon for it.'

His face was illumined with a joy which almost made him handsome.

'My lady, I swear I shall serve you with my life.'

'At this time all I ask is that we make some agreement with the King's enemies.'

'They are powerful, my lady. Peter Mauclerc is bent on mischief. Hugh de Lusignan is in leading strings to his wife. Her son, Richard of Cornwall is now in France; these rebels are planning to join with him.'

'I know it well. And you are one of them?'

He said quickly: 'No longer so, my lady.'

'Are they bent on war?'

'They could be. Mauclerc's daughter is betrothed to the King of England. He must need support here badly to have agreed to that. But 'tis my belief that before that marriage becomes a fact the King of England will find reasons why the marriage shall not take place.'

'But at this time Mauclerc believes it will.'

'Mauclerc is not with our camp in Thouars at this time. It would be well to make a treaty before he joins it.'

'Would that be possible?'

'My lady, we could make it possible.'

'How so?'

'You have good bargaining counters, my lady. Ah, forgive me. It is not meet to speak thus of the children of France. There is nothing like a betrothal, an alliance, between families to bring them together.'

'You believe this would be acceptable?'

'If my lady would try, she would see. And no harm done if it failed. If it succeeded time would be won . . . time to let the young King become not so young . . . time to prepare for any conflict that might follow later. . . .'

'You give good advice, Count.'

'I would give everything I possessed to you, my lady, and ask nothing more than that you allow me to your presence.'

'Thank you,' she said.

'I will return to my camp now,' he said. 'And you will see that I shall serve you with all my heart.'

When he had gone she sat brooding for some time. Her thoughts were in a turmoil. He disturbed her. He really was enamoured of her—this strange plump poet who did not look in the least romantic yet wrote such beautiful verses.

In some ways she hated to make use of him. Her impulse was to dismiss him, to tell him that she wished to hear nothing of him.

But that would be folly. She had seen how her actions at Rheims had been disastrous.

She must use the devotion of the Count of Champagne as well as she could. It was most important to make a truce with the rebel barons in order to strengthen her son's hold on the Crown.

Isabella came to Thouars where Hugh had asked her to join him. She knew that something important had happened and that he was afraid to make a decision without her.

The rebels were conferring with the Queen of France and her advisers. Blanche must be alarmed to condescend to do so. She must be learning that she could not flout the mighty knights and barons of France, Queen though she might be.

'What news?' she demanded imperiously when she was alone with Hugh.

He looked at her lovingly and wonderingly. 'You are even more beautiful than I have been remembering,' he said.

She laughed, pleased but impatient.

'That is good hearing,' she replied, 'but it would please me even more to hear that we had got the better of our enemy.'

'We have been negotiating.'

'Ah, and I trust have good terms. You must have realized the strength of your position since mighty Blanche herself has come to see you.'

'I think the terms are excellent . . . for us. Blanche has offered her son Alphonse for our Isabella and our Hugh for hers.'

'Our daughter is a child yet!'

'But she will grow up. The King's brother for our little Isabella and Hugh for the King's sister. What think you of that?'

Isabella nodded slowly. 'Fair enough,' she said.

'Mauclerc's daughter Yolanda is for the King's brother John.'

'She was to be betrothed to my son Henry of England.'

'Blanche fears us. That much is clear. Since she is ready to take Yolanda for her son to save her from an English alliance.'

'And these are the terms of the treaty?'

'They are, my dearest, and I think we have come well out of them.'

'It is a good match for our Hugh,' she admitted.

'And for Isabella.'

'These matches have a way of never being made.'

'We shall see that they are.'

'Will you, my strong warrior?'

'I swear it.'

'You see what she has done, do you not? She is making it impossible for us to side with my son. She is winning us to her side with these alliances.'

'My dear, this is our home. Henry is far away. Do you not think we have more to gain from France than from England?'

'That we shall discover. For the moment, it amuses me to see the Queen of France begging our favours. How was she when you spoke with her?'

'I did not. It was not I who was the mediator.'

She turned on him fiercely. 'It should have been you.'

'We thought it better that it should be the Count of Champagne.'

Isabella stared at him; then she broke into loud laughter.

'The fat troubadour! The Queen's lover!'

'You must realize that he is not that, Isabella. Blanche is a virtuous woman. She has always been.'

'You believe that . . . like the rest. And you sent him to her.'

'It was well. He made good terms.'

'How I should love to have seen them together. How she must have laughed when he arrived. Mayhap it was a ruse on their parts . . . to be together. It may be that they sweetened their parley with other matters.'

'You are quite wrong about the Queen.'

She turned a cold malicious glance on him. 'So you think I am a fool.'

'Never that . . . but . . . the Queen you know is . . .'

'Let me tell you this, Hugh. I know the Queen's sort. They are no different from the rest of us. Thibaud of Champagne has told us of their love affair has he not? What if he murdered Louis to rid her of him?'

Hugh was clearly aghast.

'Oh, she could not be involved in that, could she?' went on Isabella. 'She is too good . . . this pure white Queen.'

Hugh could not answer, nor could he completely hide his horror; but there must be no disagreement with Isabella. He did not want the time they could be together spent in quarrelling.

Blanche considered what she had done. The trouble had been thrust aside and there was peace temporarily.

That was what she had sought. Just a short respite while Louis grew up a little and understood what it meant to be a King.

Marriage-alliance with the family she hated since Isabella of Angoulême had become the head of it. Such betrothals, she consoled herself, so often came to nothing.

My children marry hers! She felt sickened by the thought of that. What if they had inherited their mother's ways!

But there could be no question of any of these marriages taking place for years. She was safe. Before then she would find reasons why they never should.

She needed all her wits to keep the peace; to keep the kingdom intact until that time when Louis should be old enough to take over, and whatever was needed she would do, even if it meant feigning friendship with her enemies.

She heard that when Peter Mauclerc was told of the terms of the treaty he had cursed. He wanted war, that man, because he was going to make an attempt on the Crown.

They did not tell her exactly what he had said but when she knew that he had declared vengeance on Thibaud of Champagne for betraying them, she knew too that he had coupled her name with that of the troubadour.

It was such as Peter Mauclerc who would sow the seeds of scandal all over France. Men such as he was; women such as Isabella. Such were her real enemies. Not men like Hugh who was led this way and that by a wife who had bewitched him.

But for a while there was peace. She must not be lulled into a feeling of security. She had to be ready. She knew that sooner or later the threat would come . . . if not from her enemies here, from those across the Channel. Henry would be furious. His mother was ready to support the French! His promised bride Yolanda was to go to a Prince of France!

It could not be long before the enemy from across the Channel decided to make war. When he did, could she rely on those men with whom she had just made her treaty?

Who could say? All she could do was be prepared.

# ENGLAND
## 1226–1242

# Hubert in Danger

RICHARD, Earl of Cornwall went straight to his brother at Westminster on his return from France. They embraced with real affection. Richard had proved himself an able general and he immediately told Henry that this was but a beginning. He had had some success and now had experience to know that everything would not be won back in one short campaign.

He studied his brother carefully. Henry was now nearly twenty years old—very conscious of his position and determined that everyone should be aware that he was the King. Richard could not help thinking that he himself would have been more suited to the task. Henry was too easily persuaded and if rumour did not lie he was completely in the hands of Hubert de Burgh, the Justiciar.

They talked of troubles in France and of the family. Joan was apparently content in Scotland with Alexander. There had been one or two matters of contention on the Border but thanks to the alliance nothing serious had developed.

'There is no heir then?' asked Richard.

'None.'

'There surely should be by now.'

'She is young yet—barely seventeen. She complains a great deal about the Scottish climate. It is a pity she ever went to Lusignan. She seemed to pine for the warmth after that.'

'A pity she did not stay there and marry Hugh.'

'Oh, our mother will watch over our interests better than Joan ever could.'

'I am not sure of that,' said Richard. 'She has another family now.'

'Hugh's. But that does not mean she will forget us. I am the King remember.'

'I heard that Hugh dotes on her and that it is she who makes the decisions.'

'So much the better for we can rest assured that we have a good friend there. I am all eagerness to get over there and I shall do so as soon as we are ready.'

Richard felt mildly annoyed. Was his brother suggesting that he only had to cross to France and immediate victory would be his? If so, he would have a rude awakening.

'And Isabella and Eleanor?'

'Isabella is with the Court. Eleanor is with her husband.'

'Is William Marshal a good husband to our sister?'

'I have heard no complaints. But I doubt she is a true wife to him yet. She is but twelve years old, you know.'

'I suppose ere long a husband will be found for Isabella.'

'Negotiations failed with the King of the Romans. I would prefer a marriage between her and the young King of France.'

'A fine match. That would put an end to our wars. Why if our sister's son inherited Normandy how could you fight him for it?'

'Before our sister would be of an age to get a son I intend that the whole of Normandy shall come back to the English Crown.'

Richard looked sardonic. This brother of his had no idea of the difficulty of that task. Their father had done such disservice to the Crown of England that it was doubtful whether it would ever be put right.

It was no use trying to explain what it was like over there to Henry. He would have to find out for himself.

Richard would go off and see his sister Isabella and tell her about his wonderful deeds in battle. He would frighten old Margaret Biset out of her wits with his gruesome tales. She had always tried to protect her charge from the world. It was no good when poor Isabella would very shortly be shuffled off somewhere to be the wife of a man she scarcely knew.

It had happened to Joan and it had happened to Eleanor. It was only due to chance that young Isabella remained in the nursery with Biset brooding over her.

Hubert de Burgh, Justiciar of England, who had the complete confidence of the King, came to see him in some dismay. It was some months after Richard's return from

France and after a brief stay at Court he had gone to his estates in Cornwall of which he was very proud, for the tin which was found in the mines there had made him rich.

Hubert de Burgh was not discontented with his lot either. He had succeeded in persuading the King to banish his great enemy Peter des Roches from the country and Peter had joined Frederic II, Emperor of Germany, on a crusade to the Holy Land, so he was well out of the way. Since then Hubert had consolidated his position and although Henry was striving to be more independent he could not govern without Hubert, so Hubert was becoming richer and more influential every day. He knew that resentment against him was rising among those who sought to take his place; but that he recognized as the inevitable result of power. He must accept it, while being wary of it. But with Peter des Roches so happily disposed of, he had begun to feel very confident.

Now he came to the King with a complaint against Richard of Cornwall and he had no doubt that his advice would be acted on.

Richard was becoming truculent and too sure of himself since he had led an army. Hubert did not doubt that it was in truth his enemy, the now defunct Earl of Salisbury, who had been the genius behind that campaign.

'My lord,' said Hubert, 'I have to bring to your notice the conduct of your brother who has acted in a manner which I know will give you little pleasure. You may not remember that your father gave to Waleran le Tyes, the German, a manor for his services. Waleran fought well for your father, and although he was but a mercenary the King wished to reward him. Richard has now seized this manor.'

'For what reason?' demanded Henry.

'He says it once belonged to the county of Cornwall and as Earl of that county it is in fact his.'

'I will tell him to give it up without delay. Send for him, will you, Hubert?'

Hubert said he had already anticipated the King's feeling in the matter and had sent a messenger to Richard commanding him, in the King's name, to present himself at once.

Henry frowned slightly. Now and then people hinted to him that Hubert de Burgh took too much upon himself. One had actually said: 'Does he think he is the King?' But he did want Richard to come to him, so how could he complain?

Hubert was quick to notice the expression which passed across the King's face and he said: 'I am sure, my lord, that you will deal with this matter in the right way.'

'I intend to,' replied Henry.

'I do not know, my lord, whether you consider your brother has perhaps become too much aware of his importance and feels that his relationship to yourself should give him especial privileges.'

'I think this may be so.'

'Ha, you will know how to deal with that,' said Hubert.

When Richard arrived at Court Hubert was with the King and when he asked if the King would wish him to leave, Henry had replied: 'No, you may stay.'

Richard looked haughtily at his brother and demanded to know what all the bother was about.

'This manor which you have taken from the German . . .' began Henry.

'It belongs to Cornwall,' retorted Richard, 'and therefore belongs to me.'

'I command you to give it back,' said Henry in his most regal manner.

Richard hesitated for a moment while he regarded his brother through half-closed eyes. Henry, thought Richard, not quite two years older than he was and imagining he had the right to command him! What a tragedy that he had not been the first-born. And what was Hubert de Burgh doing there? Was Henry afraid to move without his wet nurse?

Richard spoke coolly and calmly. 'That I shall not do. The manor is mine by right.'

'But *I* command it,' cried Henry.

'Then there is one thing for me to do. I shall take the matter before King's court and the magnates whose judgment must be in my favour. Only if they decide against me would I consider giving it up.'

Henry saw this as a direct insult to that which he was eager to stress, his royal dignity.

He clenched his fists and approached his brother. He was

beginning to betray a hot temper, Hubert noted, which could rise suddenly and result in somewhat impulsive actions.

'You will either give up the castle or leave the country,' he said.

'So you would banish me! You give yourself airs, Henry.'

'Airs. *I* the King.'

'There was a charter, have you forgotten? Our father was forced to give his name to it. There is, as a consequence, some justice in this country. I shall go now to the barons and insist on justice and abide by the judgment of my peers.'

With that he turned and strode from the chamber.

Henry was too taken aback to speak for a moment. His rage choked him.

Hubert watched him and waited for him to speak. He was realizing that Henry was not so easy to handle as he had once been, and he himself would have to tread carefully. Those sudden rages were alarming and if he could turn so on his brother for whom he was supposed to have some affection, how much more easily he could do so on his Justiciar.

At last Henry spoke. 'Well, Hubert de Burgh, what think you of that?'

'I think you have decided that the Earl of Cornwall must be dealt with in a manner he may not like.'

Henry was relieved. He had thought for a moment that Hubert might consider Richard had right on his side.

'You think I was over harsh?'

'I think you were just, which is what a King should be.'

Henry looked with affection on Hubert. 'Well,' he said, 'what now? What if he takes this matter to the Court? What if it is decided that he has right on his side?'

'In one matter he has no right on his side. He has behaved in a manner towards his King as no loyal subject should, and though he is your brother he is your subject. For that he deserves to be taught a lesson.'

'What lesson?'

'He should be seized and kept in confinement. Perhaps that will show any court that you will brook no insults.'

'You are right, Hubert.'

'Shall I send a troop of men out to take him?'

'Pray do so. When he is my prisoner he will have time to cool his temper.'

The command was given, but by the time a guard was sent in pursuit, Richard had already escaped.

He was on his way to William Marshal, his sister Eleanor's husband, and the man to whom those who thought the power of Hubert de Burgh was too great, were beginning to turn.

Richard rode with all speed to Marlborough, where he expected to find William Marshal. He was not sure what Henry's reaction would be when he had time to recover himself. Henry was very unsure of himself—that much was certain, but when Hubert had told him what to do, he might take some revenge.

It was a good idea to go to Marshal because Richard knew that there was a growing resentment in the country—not so much against Henry whom they all regarded as little more than a boy, as against Hubert de Burgh. Hubert was far too rich and powerful—and getting more so; and it was obvious that in this matter of the Cornish manor Hubert was on the King's side. Therefore he would be against Richard.

It was bad luck that when he arrived at the castle William Marshal was not there. But Eleanor, his sister, was and how delighted she was to see him.

She flung herself into his arms and clung to him. She was thirteen years old and a wife; but a virgin still, Richard guessed.

It was amusing to see her as the châtelaine, and he was mildly touched because she was so very young.

She told him that her husband would shortly be returning to the castle. Perhaps that very day. His sister, Isabella, and Isabella's husband Gilbert de Clare, were staying with them, and though Gilbert was with William, Isabella was in the castle.

They would be delighted with his company.

Eleanor commanded that a bedchamber be prepared for him and he sat with her and talked while this was made ready.

He had recently been at Court. How was their sister Isabella? And he must have been with Henry.

He told her that Isabella was well and that old Margaret Biset was the same as ever.

'Have they found a husband for Isabella yet?' she asked.

He told her they had not but the King was feeling his way on that matter.

'I hope she finds a good husband and does not have to go overseas.'

'We cannot all be lucky like you, little sister.'

'*You* will be. Men always are. They do not have to go away—and they have more choice in the matter of marriage.'

'But you have been fortunate, little sister?'

'I did not see my husband for a long time. He was in Ireland, you know. Now he is home. . . .'

She looked a little bewildered, but not, Richard was glad to note, altogether alarmed.

He wished William would come back. He had so much to say to him and if he did not return soon he would have to ride on and find some other whom he knew would be sympathetic.

But there was something solid about Marshal which came from the present one's father, the first Earl of Pembroke, who had served Henry II, Richard and John and, before he had died some eighty years before, had been responsible for helping young Henry to the throne. He had been recognized throughout the kingdom as a most honourable man and one in whom those who worked for the right could put their entire trust. This William, young Eleanor's husband, the second Earl had not yet been tried, but he stood reflected in the bright glow of righteousness which came from his father's reputation.

As he talked to Eleanor he was aware of someone coming down the stairs. He turned and was looking at a woman of great beauty. She was not young but that did not take anything from her charm. Her thick dark hair hung in a plait and she wore a blue gown embroidered with white silk.

'My brother has come, Isabella,' said Eleanor.

Richard rose and going forward bowed low.

Isabella de Clare extended her hand which he took and kissed.

'This is a happy meeting,' he said.

She smiled and said: 'My husband will be pleased that we were here when you came.'

'Not more pleased than I,' he said.

She came and sat at the table with Eleanor and Richard and he told them of his adventures in France and that he supposed he would go again one day.

As he talked he watched Isabella. He thought she was the most beautiful woman he had ever seen.

A servant came into the hall and Eleanor rose, enjoying her role of châtelaine.

'This means that your chamber is prepared for you, brother,' she said. 'Shall I take you there?'

'Later,' said Richard, and went on talking to Isabella.

A few hours after Richard had arrived at the castle, one of his servants rode up. The man had travelled at great speed.

'I must see the Earl of Cornwall without delay,' he cried and when he was taken in to Richard's presence, he said: 'I come to warn you, my lord. The Justiciar is looking for you. He had advised the King that you should be made a prisoner and kept in restraint, he says, until you are brought to reason.'

'This man dares say that?' cried Richard.

' 'Tis so, my lord. I have it straight from two who overheard it. And it is a fact that the Justiciar's men are searching for you.'

'You did well to come here.'

'Oh I knew, my lord, that you would come first to the Earl of Pembroke.'

'Let us hope that others did not share your knowledge.'

' 'Twas what I feared my lord, and 'tis why I have ridden here with all speed that you may be warned.'

'I am warned and shall know what to do if any should dare try to take me. I have a good sword as well as good servants. You shall remain here until I have decided what shall be done.'

His rage was great. To make him a prisoner! The King's brother. It was not to be endured.

William Marshal returned to the castle in the early evening. He was not entirely surprised to find his brother-in-law there. He had heard a rumour that there had been a quarrel between the King and his brother and he had remarked to that other brother-in-law Gilbert de Clare, that trouble between the King and the Earl of Cornwall was inevitable sooner or later.

Richard explained to him what had happened and said that he was quite prepared to have his case tried, which was surely the just thing to do. And for this Hubert de Burgh would put him in prison.

'Hubert de Burgh is a man who has grown foolish through power,' declared Marshal. 'He is like a man who drinks too much of an intoxicating liquor. He develops grand notions of himself. It is time an end was put to his posturings.'

Richard was relieved. William Marshal was on his side. So was Gilbert de Clare, husband of the most beautiful woman he had ever seen. Richard was somewhat susceptible to beautiful women and he had a fancy for those who were a little mature. Richard's quarrel had been with his brother but somehow it had turned into a condemnation of Hubert de Burgh. After all it was Hubert de Burgh's idea that he should be kept in confinement.

'There comes a time,' said William Marshal, 'when injustice must be faced and put a stop to. I think this may well be the moment to deal with Hubert de Burgh.'

De Clare pointed out that the King thought a great deal of him, had an affection for him and had more or less banished Peter des Roches, Bishop of Winchester, because of him.

'All of which,' said William Marshal, 'has so puffed up the pride of our Justiciar that he has become intolerable. He decides when the Earl of Cornwall, who is as royal as the King, shall be made a prisoner.'

'What do you suggest we do?' asked Richard.

'That we make at once for Chester. There we will meet the Earl who, I know, will be our very good friend. I will send for the other Earls, who have had enough of this Justiciar of yours. Warwick, Hereford, Ferrers, Warenne and Gloucester.'

'You can be sure of the support of these men?' asked Richard incredulously.

William assured him that he could.

There is indeed a conspiracy against Hubert de Burgh, thought Richard. I wonder how loyal these men are to the

King if they so hate one whom the King has raised up and admires so certainly?

They left for Chester and when they arrived, found that the five Earls were waiting for them there.

The King was deeply disturbed. After his first bout of anger against Richard he began to think he might have acted a little rashly to have allowed Hubert to threaten his brother with imprisonment. After all, it had merely been a quarrel, and he and Richard had quarrelled often when they were young children.

While he was thinking thus he received an ultimatum from an unexpected quarter. He could not believe it when he read it. A large force was collecting at Stamford and this was composed of disgruntled Earls and their followers. When he looked at the names of those Earls he was alarmed: Marshal, Gloucester, Ferrers, Hereford, Warenne, Clare, Warwick and Chester. Some of the most formidable in the land. Richard had added his name to theirs.

So this was due to a foolish quarrel about a manor house. It need have been no more if Hubert had not absurdly threatened him with imprisonment.

The Earls reminded the King that he had recently annulled the Charter of the Forest, an act which was extremely unpopular with the people. He would remember his father's conflict with the Barons and their fight against repression such as the cancelling of the Forest Charter. If the King did not want to see the country plunged into similar disruption, it would be well for him to meet the Earls—without Hubert de Burgh in attendance—and then perhaps these unfortunate matters might be settled in a manner satisfactory to all sides. They considered Hubert de Burgh to be at the root of the trouble and would not meet the King if he were present. The alternative would be civil war.

Henry was in a quandary. While he consoled himself by blaming Hubert, at the same time he wondered how he would meet his challenge without him.

He made a decision. He would meet the Earls; he would consider their demands; he would show them—and Hubert—

that he was capable of taking command without the aid of his Justiciar.

They met at Northampton. It was a subdued Henry who faced these rebels; but he was glad to notice that Richard was a little shamefaced to find himself on the side of his enemies.

Marshal was spokesman. He pointed out that he was aware that Hubert de Burgh had led the King astray and the entire blame must rest on the Justiciar. Henry became stubborn about dismissing Hubert and the Earls did not press the point, for Marshal had agreed that it would take a little time to dislodge him from a position in which he had become so firmly entrenched. Hubert could wait awhile. The point of this encounter was to bring home to the King the fact that the Barons were as powerful now as they had been in the reign of his father; and the fact that, through the Justiciar, his brother was alienated from him and on the side of the Barons, was a significant point which he must realize.

He must be watchful of the Justiciar, he must reissue the Forest Charter and if he wished to take the Cornish manor from Richard he must compensate him with something greater than that which he had taken.

Henry was overawed. Without Hubert he could not barter. He could see great trouble ahead with strife in England when his great desire was to regain the lost possessions in France.

He gave assurances and he would bestow on Richard his mother's dower which included the lands in England which had been owned by the Counts of Brittany and Boulogne.

Richard had come well out of the affair and he was glad for he hated quarrelling with his brother.

He was fond of Henry and his only real grudge against him was that he had been born before him.

They embraced.

'It is as it was before between us?' asked Henry.

Richard agreed that it was.

'It was Hubert de Burgh who caused the trouble,' said Richard.

Henry said nothing. He knew he could not do without Hubert . . . just yet.

\*       \*       \*

Christmas was spent at York. Joan, Queen of Scotland, was delighted as she always was to be with her family. It gave her great pleasure to be back in England; she confided to Isabella and old Margaret Biset that Scotland could never be home to her.

'It always seems cold,' she told them, 'even in summer. The draughts are bad for my cough.'

'There are enough of them here in York,' grumbled Margaret, 'and I am constantly scolding my lady here because she will not wrap enough against these icy winds.'

'Oh, Margaret, you coddle me,' said Isabella.

'And look at her for it,' cried Margaret proudly. 'Is she not the picture of health?'

Joan agreed and Margaret thought: It is more than I can say for you, my lady of Scotland.

Margaret shivered. She did not believe in these royal marriages. She would have liked her little ones to have married noble lords of the Court so that she could flit about between them and look after their babies when they came. She lived in terror that ere long they would find a husband for her remaining charge. She stoutly told herself that if they tried to marry her pet to some old man—king of a remote country—she would tell the King she would not have it. Merely bravado of course. How could she prevent it?

Joan wanted to know if Isabella had seen their sister Eleanor recently.

'Yes,' said Isabella. 'She came to Court with the Earl of Pembroke.'

'Is she . . . happy?'

'Poor mite,' said Margaret Biset. 'Little more than a baby . . . and to be a wife.'

'It happens to us all, Meg,' said Joan.

'But my little Eleanor . . . she had no notion of it at all . . . and there she was married to that man. Now you, my lady, went off to foreign parts first and lived in that strange place.'

'Yes,' said Joan wistfully.

'It gave you a little foretaste, you might say.'

'Yes, Meg, you're right.'

'And your mother took your place.' Margaret's lips were

tightly pressed together. And good riddance, she was thinking. 'And a big family she's providing I hear.'

'Yes, our mother had a great many children,' said Isabella.
'I wonder how it feels to have two families.'

Margaret made a clucking sound which might have indicated contempt or indifference. She loved those she called her
children the more because they had had such unnatural parents.

She was going to make a posset or two for Joan and see
what she could do about that cough before the child went
back to that unnatural place above the Border.

They were like children together—Isabella and Joan. Margaret was glad Joan had been able to come here for the
festivities. It was company for Isabella and it gave Margaret a
chance to look after Joan. It was a pity Eleanor couldn't be
with them, but there had been some trouble between Eleanor's husband and the King and although the quarrel had been
patched up, there was this difference which fermented
underneath.

I hope we're not going to have *that* sort of trouble, thought
Margaret. Why couldn't people live in peace and why did
there have to be all this juggling with the young people to
make this and that alliance?

Her girls had a right to be happy—as happy as she had
always made them in her nurseries.

Now they were indeed like two children together discussing
their gowns for the Christmas celebrations—Isabella forgetting the ever-present menace of a foreign marriage and Joan
refusing to remember that soon she would have to go back to
the bleakness of Scotland. Margaret listened happily to their
chatter.

Joan would wear a wimple of gold tissue and Isabella one
of embroidered silk. Perhaps they would let their hair hang
loose or perhaps wear it caught up in a coil of gold thread.
Joan as Queen would be more sumptuously clad than Isabella.
She would wear a circlet of gold jewels about her head. She
showed it to Isabella, who tried it on, and as she did so said:
'I wonder if I shall be a Queen too?'

Margaret watching was saddened, for she thought it very
likely that before long her last remaining charge might be
snatched from her.

There were the customary Christmas celebrations with dancing, singing and games which included *roy-qui-ne-ment*, in
which a King who did not lie was chosen to ask questions and
comment on the answers—whether they be true or false. This
was a great favourite, for everyone sat in trepidation lest they
should be called upon to answer truthfully a question when it
might be an embarrassment to do so. What the penalty was if
a lie was spoken, no one was quite sure; it was never referred
to; but most of those who played the game believed it would
be swift and terrible. The enjoyment of this game seemed to
be the shivering terror in which the players sat throughout and
the relief when it was over.

Then there were the usual jugglers and sword dancers,
morris dancers with their bells, sticks and hobby horses;
vaulting, tumbling and even wrestling.

Beside the King sat his brother Richard of Cornwall and
Hubert de Burgh. There had been a certain coolness between
the King and Hubert, and Hubert and Richard after the meeting with the Earls, but that had seemed to have passed away
and they talked amicably.

The King looked on at the performers with pleasure, obviously enjoying the manner in which everyone deferred to
him.

The pleasures of kingship were a delight at times such as
this when there was nothing to think of but entertainment and
everyone looked to him to begin the dance, to give dismissal
to the dancers, to choose the king or queen who does not lie.

He thought how much more powerful he would have been
if his father had not plunged the country into civil war and all
that rich land in France belonged to him. But it should not
prove an insuperable task to get it back. A young King on the
throne, guided by his mother it was said; and there had been
trouble with the barons there as there had in England. Spies
over there reported that Hugh de Lusignan, Guy de Thouars
and the Count of Champagne had joined forces against the
young King and his mother. Naturally Hugh would. Why,
Hugh was his stepfather and his mother would be unnatural
indeed if she sided with the French against her own son.

Why this delay then? He had thought the French possessions would be in his hands by now.

He turned to Hubert and said: 'Next year I intend to take an army into France.'

Hubert looked dismayed. 'My lord,' he said, 'that would be a big undertaking.'

'A big undertaking. What do you mean? Have not my ancestors taken armies into France ever since it came into our hands?'

'It would need preparation. . . .'

'Well, we will prepare.'

Richard was listening intently. Having been in France he considered himself far more knowledgeable than the King or Hubert de Burgh.

'The time is ripe,' he said. 'Louis is young . . . completely tied to his mother's apron-strings. She is not popular with the French. She is a foreigner and the French do not fancy being ruled by a foreigner. And rule she does. Louis does everything she tells him to.'

'There, you see,' said Henry.

'There could be dissension in the country,' said Hubert, 'but you will see that if the English came against them, they would join ranks and stand against us.'

'Hubert is determined to kill the enterprise before it begins,' said Richard.

'Nay, my lord,' protested Hubert, 'I am as eager as you to bring back what is ours by right. I merely say that the time is not yet.'

Henry looked sullenly at his Justiciar and many noted it.

'The time will be when I say,' said Henry.

Hubert was silent. He did not want an argument at the table.

Later he contrived to be alone with the King and raised the matter of taking the war into France during the year which was about to begin.

'I would beg of you to consider, my lord, the low state of the treasury, which is the main reason why an expedition to France would not be wise.'

'I will raise the money,' declared Henry.

'More taxes! That would not please the people.'

'I shall not wait on people's pleasure.'

'It would be wise to.'

'Listen to me, Hubert. When I say I shall go to war I mean I shall do so.'

Hubert bowed his head.

No good purpose could be served by a quarrel. He would have to try to find other means of preventing the King from attempting to go to war until he was well equipped to do so.

This proved to be impossible. Henry had made up his mind.

He was going to take an expedition to France at Michaelmas and no matter how Hubert tried to dissuade him he would not listen.

Hubert was in despair. He asked himself again and again how they could equip an army without money; how could they even procure the ships to transport that army overseas? Henry was childish, completely unable to grasp practical details. When Hubert tried to explain and Henry showed signs of losing his temper, Hubert was uneasily reminded of the King's father.

There was nothing he could do but stop pointing out the inadvisability of continuing with the preparations, yet they went on apace.

Henry would have to learn by his own bitter experience Hubert realized, and it was going to be a costly matter.

In due course they were ready to sail for France and Henry at the head of a large army rode down to Portsmouth, Hubert beside him, and that hardened warrior, the Earl of Chester, was at the other side of the King.

Henry glowed with pride. This was how a King should be, at the head of his troops going into battle. He felt noble and brave. He wanted to impress his brother who had already been engaged in battle and who thought he had inherited some special quality from his uncle Coeur de Lion as well as his name.

But when they reached Portsmouth it was realized that there were not enough ships to take the soldiers across the sea, and Henry fell into a violent rage.

'Why so? Why so?' he kept shouting. 'Where are the ships? Why is it that there are but half of what we need?'

'My lord,' began Hubert, 'I warned you that we would

need a great many ships. The cost of supplying them was so great that your treasury could not meet it.'

Henry turned white with rage. 'So it is you who have done this. You would teach me a lesson, is that it? You would let me bring my troops here to find that there is not enough transport for them. You traitor . . . you old, sly traitor. I believe you are in the pay of the Queen of France. Is that it?'

There was a shocked silence among the beholders. Hubert was suddenly afraid. The Earl of Chester was thinking that the end of the Justiciar's rule must be in sight.

'You jest, my lord,' began Hubert. 'You never had a more loyal subject than I. And you will remember I persuaded you to wait until you were properly equipped. . . .'

This was adding fuel to the fires of rage.

With a gesture worthy of his father, Henry drew his sword and would have run it through his Justiciar if the Earl of Chester had not seized Hubert and dragged him away.

'My lord,' said Chester, placing himself between Hubert and Henry, 'you do not mean to kill the Justiciar.'

Henry glowered at them all and Chester thought: Is he going to be such another as his father?

Chester wanted to see Hubert's decline but not in this manner. If he were not careful this Henry would soon be emulating that other of his name who had done penance at Canterbury for the murder of Thomas à Becket. They did not want Hubert to be made into a martyr.

'He has deliberately done this,' spluttered Henry.

'Nay, my lord,' said Chester. 'He but warned you that the enterprise will be costly and so shall it be. We need more ships, but the way to get them is not by thrusting your sword through the heart of your Justiciar.'

Henry regarded Chester steadily. He was not sure what to do. His anger had cooled. He knew he had acted foolishly for Hubert had truly warned him that it would be too expensive to provide all the ships they needed; and he was really angry with him because he had been proved to be right.

Chester went on: 'Should we not use what ships there are and then when we have transported all they can carry they can return for the rest?'

'It would seem there is nothing else to be done,' said Henry sullenly.

He did not look for Hubert. He had slipped away; he would tactfully keep out of the King's sight for a while, and when they met the incident would appear to be forgotten.

But it would never be. There had been too many to witness it; and in the thoughts of many was the notion that this was the beginning of the end for Hubert de Burgh.

It was as Hubert had thought it would be. They met again in France and there the King behaved as though that scene had never occurred.

Hubert thought: The thought of war has gone to his head like too strong wine. He is a boy in truth. But I should act more warily in future.

Henry knew in his heart that he had behaved foolishly and in an ungrateful manner. If the Earl of Chester had not stopped him in time he would have killed Hubert. It was a most unwise thing to do—and he regretted it; but this made a rift between him and Hubert; he could not feel the same towards his Justiciar again, for he could not forgive him for having made him act so foolishly.

The many enemies of Hubert had exalted in that display of royal anger and ingratitude. This was the beginning of the end for Hubert de Burgh, they thought. Metaphorically they began to sharpen their knives.

Nor was it in Hubert's favour that his warning had proved to be right.

The expedition to France was quickly proved to be a failure, and an extremely costly one.

The English returned, chastened with the knowledge that conquest was not going to be easy.

Hubert had been right. It had taken place too soon.

The King was fully aware that he had turned his back on Hubert's wisdom, but his knowledge did not make him love Hubert the more.

# The Love Match

AMONG those who lost their lives in that ill-conceived campaign was Gilbert, the seventh earl of Clare and husband of William Marshal's sister Isabella who had made such an impression on the King's brother, Richard of Cornwall, when he had met her at Marlborough.

Isabella was in the castle near Gloucester when she heard the news of his death. Gilbert had been a good husband and she had been a worthy wife, bringing him rich estates and during the years of their marriage six children—three sons and three daughters.

Her father the great William Marshal who had been responsible for putting the young King on the throne and until his death in 1219 had, with Hubert de Burgh, Justiciar, governed the realm, had arranged her marriage with Gilbert when he had taken him prisoner at the battle of Lincoln, Gilbert at that time having been fighting on the side of the French. As a prisoner Gilbert could scarcely refuse to accept her father's terms among which was the condition that he should marry his daughter.

Isabella had docilely submitted. Like all girls she had been brought up to believe that a marriage would be arranged for her and that she had no alternative but to accept the man whom her father had chosen for her.

So they were married and the marriage was tolerably happy and certainly fruitful. Amicia the eldest child was betrothed to Baldwin de Redvers although she was but ten years old; and good marriages would be arranged for Agnes and Isabel. Her eldest son Richard was eight at this time and he had two brothers, William and Gilbert.

They were with her when news of their father's death was

brought to her and solemnly she went to the schoolroom to tell them of it.

They listened quietly, but of course they had seen little of Gilbert and it was clear that his death did not touch them deeply. It was different when his body was brought to Tewkesbury and they attended the ceremony of his burial. There was genuine mourning among those attached to the Abbey for he had been one of its greatest benefactors.

After the ceremony they returned to the castle and Richard asked her what would happen to them now. She told him that she doubted not that they would go on as before. The arrangements made for them by their father would be carried out and Richard must work harder than he had been doing because now he was the head of the family.

It was not long before her brother came to see her.

He took her hand and kissed her warmly for there was affection between them.

'Well, Isabella,' he said, 'how are the children and you yourself after this shock?'

'We continue as before,' she answered calmly.

'My dear Isabella, you were always noted for your good sense. Even our father remarked on it.'

'You can rest assured that I shall know how to manage my household.'

William saw the children at dinner and talked to them reassuringly, as though he had taken the place of their father, to which they responded politely. Afterwards he talked alone with Isabella and when he pointed out that she was still young and very handsome, she knew what was in his mind.

Their father had been one of the richest men in the kingdom and they had been well endowed; so what he was saying was that Isabella the widow was in a position to make a very good marriage.

'Ah,' said Isabella, 'I knew you were coming to that. I have always thought that a woman who has married once for the sake of her family should the second time marry for the sake of her own.'

'My dear sister, you are a woman of great fortune. You could be deceived by one who sought to share it.'

'I am not a young girl, William. I believe I should recognize a fortune hunter.'

'There are some clever rogues about. If one should take your fancy I could not give my approval to your marriage.'

'William, my good brother, my husband is recently dead. Give me time to recover from that before you talk about replacing him.'

'Assuredly,' said William. 'But even though we do not talk of the matter, it may rest in our minds.'

'I confess I had given it no thought.'

'Then it shall be laid aside . . . for a while. We will return to it later.'

'Shall we say that if I should decide to marry again I shall return to it.'

William smiled affectionately. She had a strong will, this sister of his. Well, it was what one would expect of the daughter of William Marshal.

He had done his duty and departed, and after he had gone, Isabella began to remember a day in Marlborough when Gilbert had been visiting her brother and there had come to the castle a bold young man, of kingly bearing, who had shown a marked interest in her.

She must be a fool to have cherished memories of that time. He was the King's brother, and several years younger than she was. But he *had* admired her. He *had* shown his pleasure in speaking to her and sought to detain her in conversation and walk with her in the gardens even though at that time he had been deeply concerned with his quarrel with his brother.

What foolish thoughts! She, the mother of six children—and a young boy! For Richard, Earl of Cornwall, was little more.

It was most unseemly. But William had been right when he had implied that, however unsuitable, one could not help one's thoughts.

The old year was passing. It was three months since the death of Gilbert. Then the New Year came and Isabella concerned herself with the arrangements to set up a memorial stone to her husband in Tewkesbury Cathedral.

It was in the spring when her brother sent a message to Tewkesbury that he was about to visit her with a friend. She went down to greet them and she was taken aback to see that the man who came with her brother was Richard of Cornwall.

He held her hand and looked into her face.

'By my faith, lady,' he said, 'you are more beautiful than ever.'

William was quite clearly pleased and as she led them into the castle a wild thought occurred to her, but she dismissed it at once as impossible.

She would never forget that brief stay of the visitors to the castle. She went about her duties as châtelaine in a state of excitement for which she could only reproach herself. She was behaving like a foolish frivolous girl instead of a serious-minded widow.

She rode out with the men and Richard often contrived to be alone with her—and in this she was aware that her brother was his willing ally. Did William really think. . . . He was ambitious she knew, and he was married to Richard's sister Eleanor.

Richard was courteous, charming and always admiring.

He told her of his life at Corfe under the stern Peter de Mauley and the equally severe Roger d'Acastre. He made her laugh by recounting the pranks he had played on his tutors. Then he told her of his adventures abroad as though he were trying to impress on her that although he was twenty-one the life he had lived had made him mature.

She felt that she should remind him of the difference in their ages and constantly she referred to her six children. His reply was that she must have some secret power because she had the looks of a young girl.

'Perhaps you have not known any young girls,' she answered. 'It would seem so since you confuse a matron such as I with them.'

He told her that he was far from inexperienced and it was due to this that he was able to appreciate her.

'It surprises me,' replied Isabella, 'that being a man of such wide experience you have not yet married.'

'That is easily answered. Nor has my brother married—

because we are of a mind to make our own choice in this matter.'

This sounded significant, but she continued to refuse to believe it possible.

When they rode away she felt melancholy. Their brief stay had been one of the happiest times of her life, which was a sad confession for a widow to make. But what was the point of lying to herself? She had never been in love with Gilbert and if the choice had been left to her she would not have married him. How different he was from this royal prince.

And herself? A matron, yes, the mother of six children, but still handsome. Had she not been known as one of the most beautiful girls in the country before her marriage? She still was beautiful, and her good looks had become accentuated by an inner radiance which she heard came from being in love.

There! She had confessed it. She was in love with the King's brother.

Richard was the most impatient of young men. He knew what he wanted and determined to get it.

He told Henry: 'I am going to marry Marshal's sister.'

'What! Gilbert de Clare's widow?' cried Henry.

'None other.'

'You must be joking. She is an old woman.'

'Indeed she is not.'

'What? The mother of how many children is it?'

'She is beautiful. You would never guess that she has borne six children. It is an added virtue. She will give me sons.'

Henry was thoughtful. He knew that if he raised objections Richard would thrust them aside. He had no desire to quarrel with him again.

'Well?' said Richard.

Henry shrugged his shoulders. Marriage was a sore point with him. It was time he had a wife, but he seemed cursed in this, because every time a suggestion was made for him, there was some reason why it was impracticable. Marriage negotiations had a way of petering out. A marriage with the daughter of Leopold of Austria, another with the daughter of the King of Bohemia; then marriage with Yolanda daughter of Peter of

Brittany . . . nothing came of them. At one time he had been ready to consider the daughter of the King of Scotland, but the Archbishop had pointed out to him that as the Justiciar had already married the elder daughter, the King could scarcely marry the younger. Hubert again! He was beginning to feel more and more resentful of him.

And now Richard wanted to marry his mother of six. Well, let him. Richard was a fool and would soon realize that. It would do him good; it would show him that he was not always so much wiser than his brother—which Henry was beginning to suspect he really thought.

'It is your affair, brother,' he said. 'If you asked my advice, I would say it is folly but if you wish to act so, pray do so. She is rich and handsome you tell me, and Marshal's sister, and he already has *our* sister for a wife. One thing, it should assure Marshal's loyalty to us and that has at times been something I have been led to doubt.'

'It will indeed,' agreed Richard. 'In fact, brother, it is an alliance which will do us much good.'

'And you are looking for the good it will do you. Go then and marry your widow.'

Richard was pleased, although had Henry been against the match he would have made it all the same.

He went at once to William Marshal, who delightedly agreed to ride with him down to Tewkesbury.

Isabella was in a state of excitement as she welcomed them and Richard lost no time in coming to the point. William left them together and Richard immediately asked her to marry him.

It was an unusual situation. How many women in her position had ever received a proposal of marriage? It was the general rule that she should be told by her family that she was to make such and such a marriage and she would be obliged to fall in with their wishes. This was most romantic, but she wished she were younger, at least a little nearer to his age.

Richard told her that he had fallen in love with her the first time he had met her. Then of course she had had a husband and he could not declare himself, but now that obstacle had been removed there was no impediment to their happiness.

She attempted to protest. 'I am so much older than you.'

'You do not look so. Nor would I want a younger and foolish girl. You are to my fancy—and what more could I ask than that?'

Still she hesitated. 'I am the mother of six. . . .'

'Another of your virtues. You have been so generous to de Clare, you will be so to me. We will have a nursery full of boys.'

Still she shook her head. 'Now perhaps you feel it will be good. But in a few years time the difference in our ages will be more apparent.'

He kissed her and immediately she was ready to throw aside all her objections. Even if in time he grew tired of her, why should she not be happy for a while?

They were married in April—a beautiful month thought Isabella with the trees full of buds and the joyous birdsong in the air.

Young Eleanor, her sister-in-law, Richard's sister, was with her and the two were very happy together.

Eleanor was sixteen years old and certainly not in love with her elderly husband, but she was aware of the happiness which Isabella was experiencing and perhaps a little wistful. To choose one's husband! That must be wonderful and Richard was such an attractive adoring lover that it was an experience to watch them together.

'I wonder,' said Eleanor, 'if it will ever be like that for me.' Then she realized that for it to be so, William would have to die, and she was ashamed to have spoken. But all her shame could not stop the thoughts in her mind. It was unfair to William who had been a kind husband and happy to be married to her—though largely she was knowledgeable enough to realize it was because she was the King's sister.

Isabella prepared for her wedding, discussing with her young sister-in-law the clothes she would wear. The gold mesh snoods, the wimples of silk, the embroidered gowns, they were all a delight to see. Isabella was like a young girl and even her own children scarcely recognized their mother in this gay bride.

It was wonderful, thought Eleanor, that while the bride and

groom were so happy in each other, everyone said what a good match it was; and nobody could have been more pleased than William.

The marriage was celebrated. William gave away the bride; and Richard and Isabella were left together while Eleanor with William rode back to Marlborough.

William was somewhat exhausted by the journey, and she was glad when it was all over. He went straight to his bed for he said he felt very tired.

Like the good wife she had been taught to be Eleanor looked to his comfort. She herself prepared the possets. She sat by his bed and he told her how delighted he was by this marriage, for it bound their families even closer together. Eleanor said yes indeed, and if Henry failed to have children, Richard would be King and the son he might have by Isabella would follow him to the throne.

William smiled at her. 'That is so, little wife,' he said. 'My father would be pleased by this match.'

'It is a rare match,' said Eleanor, 'for not only is everyone pleased but the husband and wife also.'

William looked at her a little sadly. She was such a dainty child—and beautiful too. All the daughters of Isabella of Angoulême had had some beauty—though none could compare with their mother. When he rose from his sick bed they must give themselves to the matter of having children.

She herself had always seemed to him such a child that his efforts in that direction had not been many. He had promised himself that there was time.

He was mistaken, for a few days later he died, and sixteen-year-old Eleanor was a widow.

# Persecution

THE relationship between Hubert de Burgh and the King had never regained its old footing since that unfortunate episode at Portsmouth. It continued to rankle with Henry who had displayed a violence in his nature which he had been ashamed of, and he could not forget that Hubert had proved him to be in the wrong when the expedition failed. Instead of being grateful to a wise man who had been frank with him, so unsure of himself was he that it irritated him to contemplate he had been less than wise himself; and he imagined that Hubert was remembering it too.

Hubert's enemies were aware of what was happening and they sent a message to his old enemy Peter des Roches, Bishop of Winchester, to the effect that it was time he returned to England.

Meanwhile trouble flared up between the Archbishop of Canterbury and Hubert over the town and Castle of Tonbridge which Hubert had been holding for the young Earl of Gloucester, since he had been put into his charge. The Archbishop declared that they did not belong to the Earl but should be held by the See of Canterbury. The Archbishop, Richard Grant, took the matter to the King who gave the ruling that they were held through the Crown and that the See of Canterbury had no claim on them.

Incensed at this verdict Richard Grant set out for Rome to set his case before the Pope, and as the Archbishop was one of Hubert's greatest enemies he decided to make the most of the occasion by bringing more complaints against the Justiciar.

Hubert de Burgh, he told the Pope, governed the country and tried to set the King above Rome. This was obvious because he had encroached upon the rights of Canterbury.

Moreover he had married the daughter of the King of Scotland who was too closely related to his previous wife, Hadwisa, who had been the first wife of King John, and repudiated by him in order that he could marry Isabella of Angoulême. Hubert was a much married man, pointed out the Archbishop. He chose wives from that quarter which could bring him most good. His first had been Joan, daughter of the Earl of Devon and widow of William Brewer; his second Beatrice, daughter of William of Warenne and widow of Lord Bardulf; his third Hadwisa, divorced by John. So it would be seen that he had had a fondness for those who had been previously married providing they were also wealthy. Then he had turned his attention to the daughter of the King of Scotland, whose royalty doubtless made up for her lack of a previous husband. But His Holiness would see that this was a man who seized every opportunity. The closeness of the ties of Hadwisa and Margaret of Scotland therefore made this last marriage invalid.

The Pope listened to Richard and the King was obliged to send his proctors to Rome to defend his cause. The Pope, nevertheless, sided with the Archbishop which was upsetting for Henry. He disliked being at enmity with the Church.

Having made his point the Archbishop decided to return to England, there to engage in argument with the King and his Justiciar, but on the way passing through Italy he fell ill in Umbria where he had paused to rest for a night at the convent of the Friars Minor.

Within a few days of arriving at the convent he died.

He was buried in his Archbishop's robes wearing jewels and after his burial thieves came in the night to rifle his tomb. It must have been a grisly scene, but unabashed the robbers proceeded to strip the corpse; but when they tried to remove the ring from his finger they could not do so although it appeared to be quite loose. Conviced that this was a sign of divine displeasure they took fright and ran away, leaving the opened tomb and the jewels they had taken from the dead man scattered around him.

The next day he was buried again and news was sent to King Henry of his death.

It was not long before people were saying that the Archbishop had been poisoned. And who was the most likely man to be responsible for that dark deed? Why Hubert de Burgh, the Justiciar, of course—acknowledged to be his enemy. It mattered not that Hubert was in England and nowhere near the Archbishop when he died. Had he been near the Earl of Salisbury when *he* had died. No, but old Longsword had died soon after he had quarrelled with Hubert de Burgh and such a man would have his spies and servants everywhere.

Peter des Roches was entertaining the King at Winchester and never had Henry been so lavishly treated. The Bishop who, when Henry had been but a young boy, had been inclined to lecture him and to adopt a tutorial manner which secretly had made him turn away from Peter to Hubert, now behaved as though Henry were the fount of wisdom.

Henry enjoyed that.

It was Christmas time and the Bishop had determined that this should be a festivity which the King would never forget. The gifts he lavished on the King won the admiration of all. He had brought home jewels from the Holy Land and silks and wines from abroad, and he implored the King to take his choice of these.

Peter had changed. He had ceased to be the stern priest and was an amusing companion. Of course he had had many adventures which he described vividly and wittily so that Henry could believe himself on the spot. He had met the French King and his mother as he had passed through France and had succeeded in making a peace treaty between England and France which was to last for three years.

He had shown himself to be a good servant of the King. Moreover he had won the approval of the Pope and came to England with his blessing to show the King of England how he had been led astray by guilty advisers.

It was not difficult to realize to whom he referred. During those Christmas festivities he had the King's ear, it was said. Into it he poured his venom and it was all about the misdeeds of Hubert the Justiciar.

His treasury was always empty, complained the King.

But of course it was, replied Peter. As fast as his subjects filled it with their taxes, Hubert directed it into his own coffers. Had the King noticed how all his friends and relations had wormed their way into the important positions in the land? Hubert had had the temerity to marry into the royal house of Scotland. Did the King know that he had seduced poor Margaret of Scotland—and in such a manner which some might call rape—so that the poor girl could do nothing but implore her brother to allow her to marry the man who had made it impossible for her to marry anyone else?

This was startling. The King had not known. But he did know that his treasury never seemed to contain what he thought it should.

He began to think that it would be well to be rid of Hubert. Whenever any controversy arose between them, he fancied he could see in Hubert's eyes that he was recalling that disastrous expedition to France.

As soon as Christmas was over Henry dismissed Hubert from his office and told him that he would not have it back until he had produced an account of all the payments he had made from the treasury during his reign and that of his father.

This was an impossible task. Henry knew it and so did Hubert. It was tantamount to telling him that he was out of favour and there was no longer work for him to do in his old post.

Peter des Roches was delighted. He came to the King and congratulated him on his wisdom.

'But, my lord,' he said, 'you will see at once that this is not enough. There are certain charges which all righteous men wish to see brought against Hubert de Burgh for it is only just that he should answer them.'

'What charges?' demanded Henry.

'It was he who prevented an alliance between you and Margaret of Austria.'

Henry looked bewildered and Peter went on: 'Your expedition to France would have been successful but for him. It was he who delayed preparations so that there were not enough ships to take your men to France. And later, so I hear, when you were there, he had friends in France, who saw that the expedition did not succeed because he had said it would not—and it suited his friends, the French enemies of England, that it should not. He is supported in this by the treasurer

Ranulf de Brito—a man chosen by him. Dismiss him from the post and appoint Peter of Rievaulx in his place.'

The King promised to consider this and quickly agreed to the replacement turning his mind from the fact that Peter of Rievaulx was the nephew of Peter des Roches.

When Hubert heard of this he knew that the battle had begun in earnest. He was immediately called upon to relinquish Dover Castle and other properties and at the same time he was told that the wardship of the young Earl of Gloucester, whose estates had been the cause of the controversy with Archbishop Richard, was to pass to Peter des Roches.

The Londoners had never forgiven Hubert for the death of Constantine FitzAthulf and were ready to give their support to any move against him.

Peter des Roches came gleefully to the King and told him that now he himself had acknowledged the villainies of Hubert de Burgh others were joining with him and there was a demand throughout the country that he be brought to trial.

Henry was unsure but had no wish to appear so. He had only wanted to dismiss Hubert and had had no intention that matters should go so far. But it was difficult to hold back now that Peter des Roches had set the case against Hubert in motion, so he agreed that a date should be fixed when Hubert be brought to trial to answer charges against him.

Hubert could not believe what was happening. So often he had been aware of enemies but he had so far managed to get the better of them.

His wife was very anxious and he tried to soothe her.

'Why,' he told her, 'I knew that as soon as the Bishop of Winchester returned to the country there would be trouble. It is he who is making an effort to destroy me.'

'He is more powerful since his return,' replied Margaret. 'And now he is ever with the King.'

'Henry will tire of him.'

'I hope so, before it is too late.'

'I should never have advised him against going to France,' said Hubert sadly. 'I should have flattered him and told him his judgment was wise. He blames me for the failure of that expedition. How can one deal with a man who is headstrong, acts unwisely and then blames those who tried to advise him against such conduct?'

'He blames himself in secret, Hubert.' said Margaret, 'but refuses to see it. He is angry with you for knowing this.'

'He has not yet grown up.'

'It is time he did. He is of an age now to govern and how can he govern a kingdom if he cannot govern himself?'

'What we have to consider is your position. Dismissed from your post, your lands and castles taken from you, these ridiculous charges. . . . What will the outcome be?'

It was while they were talking that his friend Ranulf de Brito came to him in great haste to warn him that he was going to be brought for trial and preparations were going ahead to take him prisoner.

'You know what the verdict will be,' said Ranulf.

'It is already decided that I am guilty,' answered Hubert.

'God knows what they will do. Hubert, they will brand you traitor.'

'I cannot believe the King will allow it.'

'The King sways this way and that. He is so anxious that none shall believe he is unsure of himself. I would not put my trust in the King.'

'You must go from here,' said Margaret. 'You must not be here when they come to take you.'

'Where?' said Hubert. 'I have begun to think that there is no way out.'

'There must be a way out,' said Margaret. 'Think of the dangers you have faced throughout your life—and you have always defeated your enemies.'

'Yes,' said Hubert. He thought then of how he had defied King John over Prince Arthur. Then it would have been understandable if John had destroyed him; but he had come through that dangerous situation. But now he was fighting a different battle. He had done nothing but serve his King, and his enemies were calling for his blood while the young King who had stood amicably beside him had suddenly changed sides.

Margaret said: 'You must not stay here. They will be here soon to take you.'

'There is nowhere else to go, lest it was sanctuary.'

'Sanctuary! That is the answer,' cried Margaret. 'You must go into sanctuary. None would dare harm you there and in time the King will come to his senses and see that the traitors are those who now call for your blood.'

'It *is* the answer, my lord,' agreed Ranulf. 'You must leave at once. Any delay could be dangerous.'

'I see that you are right,' said Hubert.

'Merton Priory is the nearest,' added Margaret. 'You must go there.'

Within half an hour Hubert was on his way.

When the King was told that Hubert was taking refuge in Merton Priory he was angry. He had heard then that he was about to be arrested and was either guilty or he did not trust the King's justice—Henry preferred to believe that he was guilty.

'He shall see that it is useless to attempt to hide from justice,' he declared; and he pondered as to what he could best do.

The Londoners had hated Hubert since the riots when he had ordered their leader and his nephew to be hanged and had caused to be mutilated those who had been taken prisoner. The dead might have been forgotten, but there were so many men living minus a limb or their ears that the grievance was kept alive.

Henry sent out a proclamation.

Hubert de Burgh, traitor to the country, was hiding in Merton Priory. Londoners who had long been aware of his perfidy and had good reason to remember his villainy should take him from his refuge and bring him to the courts.

The Londoners were on the march to Merton.

There was one among them—a merchant of deeply religious leanings who raised his voice at this order and asked whether it was fitting to violate a sanctuary. The law of the Church was that any man—however wicked—could find refuge, if only temporarily, in a holy place. He knew that the King had ordered this but the King and the Church were not always in agreement and they must remember that the King was young and the Church was old.

'What then?' cried the crowd. 'Tell us what then.'

The merchant was a respected man among them known for his pious ways and just dealing, and considering this the mob was halted in its madness to get at Hubert.

'The Bishop of Winchester is lodged nearby,' said the merchant. 'We could ask him if it is fitting for us to take the Justiciar from a sanctuary when it is the command of the King.'

'To the Bishop,' cried the crowd; and instead of going to Merton they made their way to the Bishop's lodging.

Peter des Roches was amazed to find them gathered at his gate.

He addressed them from a window.

'What would you have of me, good people?' he asked.

The merchant was the spokesman. 'My lord Bishop, we have had a command from the King to go to Merton and take Hubert de Burgh that he may be brought to justice. Should we obey the King?'

'Are you good subjects?' replied Peter. 'If you are you know full well that you should obey your King.'

'My lord Bishop, he is in holy sanctuary.'

Peter des Roches hesitated. The merchant was a moderate man, that much was certain. Not so those who gathered about him. There was the blood lust in their eyes. They hated Hubert. They were bent on revenge. They blamed Hubert for the hanging of Constantine and the mutilation of so many of the citizens and they wanted a scapegoat. Hubert was known to be severe because he believed that it was the only way to keep law and order in the country.

The fate of Hubert, as he saw it, could rest on the next few seconds. If he came to court, he might well prove himself guiltless. After all he had governed the country well. Peter des Roches knew that. But if this mob got at him, he would never have a chance to do anything. In their present mood they would tear him apart.

'We would ask your guidance, as a man of Holy Church,' went on the merchant.

Peter made his decision. This was an easy way of getting rid of Hubert—once and for all.

'The King has given you an order. You must obey your King.'

There was a shout from the mob.

'To Merton,' they cried. 'The blood of Hubert de Burgh.'

The Earl of Chester had seen the mob marching to the Bishop's house and had heard their bloodthirsty shouts.

He had believed that the Bishop would advise them to disperse and was astonished when they came from his house shouting, 'To Merton.'

He went at once to the King.

'My lord,' he said, 'the mob is on the march.'

'To Merton,' replied Henry. 'I have asked them to bring me Hubert de Burgh.'

'Bring him to you! They will murder him first.'

Henry did not answer and Chester went on: 'My lord, it is dangerous to rouse the mob. They will murder Hubert . . . horribly, doubtless. I have seen these men. It is a fearful sight to see a mob on the march. I beg of you to disband the mob while there is still time. It is not good for the people to see that it is possible to get what they want by force. I implore you, my lord. Command them to disband while you still have the power to do so.'

Henry hesitated. He knew that Chester was an enemy of Hubert. That was why he could believe him. He was suddenly afraid. He knew what had happened when the barons had risen against his father. Retaining the Crown depended to a large extent on the goodwill of the people. The terrible story of his father's reign was a lesson to him.

'What must I do?'

'Ride out with me now. We can catch up with the mob. You must command it to disband.'

So the King rode out with Chester and when they had caught up with the marchers Henry spoke to them.

He had not meant them to go thus to Merton. They knew that Hubert de Burgh was resting in sanctuary. It was against the laws of the Church to take a man from such a refuge. He had spoken rashly and they were in no way to blame or would not be if they disbanded quietly and returned to their homes.

The merchant who had doubted the wisdom of breaking into sanctuary was clearly relieved. He spoke for the mob and said they would return to their homes. They knew that the King would do what was necessary and that Hubert de Burgh would be brought to justice in due course.

When Peter des Roches heard what had happened, he was furious. Not only was Hubert still alive but he had been exposed as giving advice which was contrary to the rules of the Church.

He presented himself to the King and told him how wisely he had acted. He had been confronted by the mob, he explained, and he had told them that they must at all costs obey the King, which was what he believed good subjects should do; and Henry, who realized how foolish he had been in giving the order in the first place, was quite relieved to accept this explanation.

'What do you propose to do in this matter now, my lord?' asked Peter.

'It is a matter for consideration,' murmured Henry.

'I doubt not that you will decide that he should have a list of the charges against him and be told that he is to prepare his answers.'

'That had been in my mind,' said Henry, looking eagerly at the Bishop for more suggestions.

'And perhaps a safe conduct from the Sanctuary to some place of his choice.' Then taking him would not present the same difficulties.

'It is what I had been considering.'

The Bishop retired well pleased. It was gratifying to his self-esteem to be able to guide the King so effortlessly.

When Hubert received the safe conduct from the King he and Margaret went to Brentwood—a house which belonged to Hubert's nephew the Bishop of Norwich. He could rely on the help of the Bishop who owed his present position to him. But feeling it unwise to stay in the house he took refuge in the Boisars Chapel close by that he might once more find sanctuary.

As soon as Henry heard where he was he sent guards to take him and bring him to London.

When Hubert realized the perfidy of the King who had

promised him time to prepare his answers against the charges, he tried to defend himself, but was soon outnumbered.

His captors, however, were afraid he would escape and sent for the local blacksmith to make chains that he might be fettered. The blacksmith, however, knew who he was and he declared that he wanted nothing to do with the matter. If the troops wished to fetter the Bishop's uncle they must find some other to do it. Hubert decided that if ever he came into power again he would remember that blacksmith. His captors were not to be beaten however; they would do without chains and would bind him with ropes.

So he was bound and set upon a horse and brought to the Tower of London, and there he was lodged to await his trial.

The Bishop of London, hearing that he had been taken from the Boisars Chapel where he was in sanctuary and brought in fetters to London, went to see the King and pointed out to him that it was against the law of the Church for a man to be taken from sanctuary. No matter what a man's crime, he was immune.

The Bishop was a little stern, implying that the King had forgotten the law of sanctuary which was that any man, be he the most hardened criminal, was entitled to refuge under the roof of the Church. For forty days and forty nights he should be safe there and any who dared touch him defiled the Church. At the end of that time he was bound to leave the country and should be guaranteed freedom from molestation while he made his way to the coast.

This law, the Bishop pointed out, had been ignored in the case of Hubert de Burgh and the men who had dragged him from Boisars Chapel.

Henry was once more in a quandary. The Bishop of London was very stern and although he referred to the soldiers who had taken Hubert as the offenders, he meant of course the King. Henry, who liked to think of himself as a deeply religious man, hated the thought of conflict with the Church; so he immediately agreed that Hubert should be taken back to the chapel where he would be guarded by two sheriffs. His servants might be with him to provide his food and any comforts they could.

After that, he could leave England, according to the laws

of sanctuary, or if he failed to do this he would go to prison as was fitting for one who had proved a traitor to his King and country.

Hubert decided that he would leave England for a short period during which time he would prove his innocence, but it was discovered that he had a large quantity of jewels and gold and when these were found his enemies declared that these were in fact the King's property and here was the proof they needed that he had enriched himself at the King's cost.

It was no use Hubert's protesting that the goods had been honestly earned during a lifetime of service. His enemies, led by Peter des Roches, advised the King that Hubert deserved to die.

Henry agreed and it appeared that the end was in sight. But it was not so, for Henry's conscience began to worry him. He remembered scenes from the past and how Hubert had been there in many a crisis and that when the French were over-running the country at the time of his father's death, it was Hubert with William Marshal who had arranged for his coronation and had made the people see that with two such men beside him, supporting him, it was possible to drive the French out of the country.

Peter des Roches came to him and he could not hide how exultant he was. Henry took a sudden dislike to him and began to ask himself why he had allowed himself to be led by him.

'We have cornered the wolf,' said Peter des Roches. 'His days are numbered. Nothing can save him now.'

Was this a man of God, to rub his hands in glee, to lick his lips in anticipation because a man's blood was to be shed?

Henry said: '*I* can save him.'

'My lord, what mean you?' cried the Bishop.

'I mean,' said Henry, 'that I am unsure of what will happen to Hubert. I have always heard it said that from the time he was a very young man he served my uncle Richard and my father very well. I used to think he served me well too.'

'My lord, he is a cunning man.'

It was the wrong approach. It was suggesting that Hubert's cunning had deceived Henry because he was less wise.

'I have decided what shall be done,' he said regarding the Bishop of Winchester with a certain coldness of expression. 'I shall restore some of his castles and he shall be lodged at Devizes. I shall appoint certain lords to watch over him and his fetters shall be removed.'

Peter saw that it would be unwise to press for a favour he was determined to ask. That was that he should be appointed custodian of Devizes Castle; and if he were it would not be long before Hubert died of some vague sickness which perhaps gullible people might believe had been brought on by all he had suffered.

Life had become like a nightmare for the once powerful Justiciar. At least he had some faith in the King who swayed this way and that and could not seem to make up his mind.

Hubert understood. Henry was young; he was unsure; he was unable to form his own judgment and was so eager that none should guess that he changed his views according to the person who influenced him most at a given time.

He may grow up into a strong King, thought Hubert, but he doubted it. Perhaps Richard of Cornwall would have been the better one.

The fact that the King had released him and placed him here in this castle, showed that he was not listening completely to those who were determined to destroy him. There was a spark of honour in the King. If only he could get near enough to ignite it, he might win back Henry's favour.

In the meantime he must lie low at Devizes and hope that would satisfy his enemies; and perhaps in due course the King would see him and he could talk him into reason.

He was distracted when one of his manservants—a loyal man whom he could trust—came to him in some agitation.

'One of the servants of the Bishop of Winchester has come to the castle. He did not immediately tell us for what purpose, but a little good wine loosened his tongue. He has come in advance to make ready for his master. The Bishop of Winchester has prevailed upon the King to give him the custodianship of Devizes Castle.'

'God help me,' cried Hubert, 'this is the end. You know his purpose.'

'It is to murder you, my lord, I would say. We should retire once more into sanctuary.'

'You are right, my good fellow.'

'We have made ready. Two of us will come with you. We will take food and warm robes and there we shall be when the Bishop of Winchester arrives in Devizes.'

It was night when they made their escape from the castle, Hubert creeping out disguised as one of his servants.

They spent the night in the church but when those who had been set to guard him discovered Hubert's disappearance they were so alarmed because they had let him escape that they decided they would rather face the wrath of God than that of the Bishop of Winchester, so they went to the church and brought Hubert and his servants back to the castle.

It was the old pattern. The Bishop of London this time protested at the violation of sanctuary and Hubert went back to the church.

Henry had now swayed back again and was listening to the Bishop of Winchester.

'What can I do?' cried Henry. 'Whatever happens he slips through our fingers. He is now once more in sanctuary. There is nothing to be done but leave him there.'

'There is something,' said the Bishop. 'If no food is allowed into the sanctuary how can he stay there for his forty days? You could starve him into submission.'

'That I will do,' cried Henry. 'I can see there will be no peace for me while this man lives.'

He gave the order and it seemed to Hubert that this really was the end. There was no church law regarding the refusal to allow food into sanctuary, and the grim choice lay ahead for Hubert. Stay there and starve or come out and face the charges.

Hubert knew that in time he would have to give in. He would have to come out and allow them to take him back to the Tower of London. Who knew that he might yet be able to confute his enemies. Those who would comfort him told him that the Bishop of Winchester was losing his hold on the King. That was a comforting sign, but Peter des Roches was not his only enemy.

It was one night when the decision seemed imminent.

Hubert was cold and hungry. He could delay little longer and perhaps the next day he would walk out and give himself up to the King's men.

Darkness had fallen. The church door opened silently. A man was standing there looking for him, he knew. Hubert could see him but he could not as yet see Hubert.

Hubert called out: 'Who are you?'

The man came over to him and two more seemed to materialize in the gloom.

'Do you want your freedom, Hubert de Burgh?' said a voice.

'I do.'

'Come with us then.'

'Who are you?'

'Enemies of the Bishop of Winchester.'

Hubert hesitated and the man said: 'Stay here and die or come with us. Take your choice . . . only we might decide to take you whether you wish to come or not.'

Hubert had spent a lifetime making quick decisions, but he had never made one more quickly than this.

'I will come.'

'That is good. There are guards outside and if you did not come of your own accord a fight might result.'

'Where will you take me?'

'You will see.'

Weak with hunger, Hubert rose unsteadily. He crept out of the chapel and mounted a horse which was waiting for him.

'Away,' said the man. 'We'll stop soon to feed you, for you are near to starving I see. Can you ride a little?'

'Since my life would appear to depend on it, I believe I can.'

'Wise man. Ride . . . and then soon you shall eat.'

They turned their horses in the direction of Wales.

The new Archbishop of Canterbury, Edmund Rich, had been watching the rise to power of the Bishop of Winchester and his protégé, Peter de Rievaulx, with misgiving; and he decided that he must warn the King that the violation of sanctuary which had occurred more than once had indicated a lack of respect for the Church and this must be stopped without delay.

He called together certain barons—many of them those who had risen against John and forced him to sign the Charter and with them the leading bishops who shared his anxieties.

The King received them with great courtesy for Edmund was a man who was beginning to be called a saint. He was known for his piety and austere living. It was said that he had not lain on a bed for many years but took a little rest now and then sitting or on his knees. His clothes were rough worsted and he submitted himself to self-inflicted torture with knotted ropes. He gave money to the poor so that he had very little of his own, keeping back only enough to provide the small amount of food he allowed himself.

Among churchmen who looked for land and favours and made a habit of promoting their friends and relations to those posts where they could do their benefactor the most good, Edmund was a rarity.

But his habits did mean that he was regarded with awe, and Henry, who had a greater respect for the Church than any of his predecessors since Edward the Confessor, would not have dreamed of treating him with anything but the utmost respect.

Thus when he called a meeting Henry responded with alacrity.

'My lord,' said Edmund, 'there is much anxiety in the country. Hubert de Burgh has fled and is in the company of the enemies of the Bishop of Winchester, Richard Siward and Gilbert Basset. They are laying waste to the Bishop's lands and have saved Hubert de Burgh from his evil intentions. Twice he and his followers have violated the laws of the Church, yet he remains in your favour.'

'My lord Archbishop,' protested Henry, 'the violating of sanctuary was not done at my command.'

'You ordered the people of London to go to Merton,' said the Archbishop sternly.

Henry quailed. Saints were uncomfortable people, for no matter how they were threatened they showed no fear. How could you threaten a man who tortured himself and cared nothing for the comforts of living?

'I ordered them not to afterwards.'

'That is true. When the folly was pointed out to you by the Earl of Chester you realized what you had done. But the same fault was committed once more. My lord King, if you do not dismiss the Bishop of Winchester and Peter de Rievaulx and their foreign adherents I shall have no recourse but to excommunicate you.'

Henry turned pale at the prospect.

'My lord Archbishop,' he stammered. 'I . . . I will indeed do as you say, but. . . .'

'Then that is well. There should be no delay. You do well, my lord, to remember what happened to your father.'

'Yes,' said Henry, 'I know full well.'

'Never forget it. It should be a lesson to you and all Kings that follow. Kings govern through justice remembering the good of their people and their allegiance to God.'

'I know it well,' said Henry. 'I shall dismiss the Bishop and those who are with him.'

'You should recall Hubert de Burgh and make your peace with him.'

'That I will do, my lord Archbishop.'

When Henry was alone he trembled with fear to think of what might have happened if the Archbishop had brought about his excommunication.

In a short time Hubert came back into power. He had aged considerably; and he had grown wiser too in as much as he would never be at ease with the King again, for he would never trust him.

# The Princess
# and the Emperor

ISABELLA, wife of Richard of Cornwall, was expecting a child and her sister-in-law Eleanor, who had been widowed at the death of William Marshal, was with her.

Eleanor knew that all was not well with Isabella. Nor had it been for some time. Poor Isabella, she had been so happy during the first year of her marriage, even though she had talked now and then of the disparity between her age and that of her husband.

It had been so pleasant then at Berkhamstead where they had been living at the time. Eleanor had been comforted in an unexpected way. Perhaps it was because Isabella had like herself been married when but a child, had become a widow and then found this great happiness. Isabella had said: 'A woman must marry first to please her family; then she should have a chance to please herself.' It had been the case with Isabella. Would it happen in that way with Eleanor?

The two had become good friends. Richard was away from home a good deal which was necessary, of course. He became more and more important and great homage was done to him as the King's brother; and the less popular the King became, so Richard's prestige rose. His quarrel with his brother and his friendship with the barons had made him one of the most important men in the country.

Isabella used to talk to Eleanor of his greatness and she admitted in the utmost confidence of course and behind closed doors—that she believed he was more fitted to be the King than Henry was. Eleanor was inclined to agree with her.

But there was one thing Eleanor had noticed and which she

308

did not mention to Isabella for a long time. It was a matter which—if Isabella wished to discuss it—she must raise herself.

Richard's visits had become less frequent. When he did come to them he seemed less exuberant than before. Isabella was uneasy and not the same and she was becoming more and more preoccupied with her appearance in a frightened kind of way.

This was ridiculous for Isabella was a very beautiful woman.

Her hopes at this time were centred on the child she would bear, and Eleanor knew that she prayed for a son because she believed that the souring of her relationship with her husband was her inability to get a son.

Early that year Richard had come to Berkhamstead and stayed with them. It was clear that he had something on his mind. Isabella did not mention this but Eleanor was sure that she was aware of it.

And during that visit Richard, much to Eleanor's surprise, had talked to her about his wife and tried to explain the cause of his uneasiness.

She had walked in the gardens with him, for he had requested her to do so and she believed afterwards that he had suggested this to prevent their being overheard.

'Eleanor,' he had said, 'you are much with Isabella.'

'Oh yes, brother. We are finding pleasure in each other's company.'

'It is good for you to be here, for you are sisters twice over. Through your late husband and through me you have a kinship with Isabella. I doubt not you chatter together over your needlework and suchlike occupations which you share.'

Eleanor admitted that this was so. 'Isabella says I am company for her during your absences which are frequent.'

'Necessarily so,' he said quickly.

'Indeed we have not thought otherwise.'

'We?' he said. 'You mean you and Isabella. Eleanor . . . what I wanted to say to you is this. . . . Do you think Isabella would be very unhappy if . . . if . . .?'

Eleanor's heart began to beat very fast. She was no longer a child and she understood something of the relationship between these two. In the beginning it had been all romantic passion. That it was now something less, she was well aware—

not on Isabella's side but on Richard's. She now began to suspect that the emphatic manner in which he had asserted that his absences were necessarily frequent meant that they were not and the reason that he did not come often was because he did not want to.

'What are you telling me, Richard?' she asked.

'Well, sister, you will understand that my marriage had not turned out as I hoped.'

'Isabella loves you dearly.'

'You see, I need a son. I must have a son.'

'You have had children. . . .'

'Neither of whom have survived—little John dying soon after he was born and our Isabella living exactly one year. It seems that we are doomed not to have children. Isabella is not a young woman.'

'Oh but she is not old, not beyond childbearing. You will have children yet, Richard.'

'I am not sure. I am uneasy. You know Gilbert de Clare has a blood relationship with me.'

'Oh, not a close one, Richard.'

'In the fourth degree.'

'But almost everyone one thinks of is connected with us in some degree.'

'Such closeness is frowned on by God.'

'Oh, I can't think God would frown on your marriage with Isabella. She is such a good person.'

'Eleanor, you talk like a child.'

'What . . . are you going to do about it?'

'If you will promise me not to tell Isabella . . . as yet . . . I will tell you.'

'Yes, I promise.'

'I have sent to the Pope asking him whether I should seek a divorce.'

'Oh Richard . . . it will break her heart.'

'Better that than offend the Almighty. He is displeased. That much is obvious. Otherwise why should our children die?'

'Many children die, Richard.'

'But a man in my position must have sons.'

'Many of them don't.'

'It is said it is because of some past misdeed. If one has sinned in some way and incurred the wrath of God the only thing to do is to rectify that sin.'

'You have not told Isabella what you have done then?'

'No. I will await the Pope's verdict.'

'And if he agrees to the divorce?'

'You will comfort Isabella, Eleanor.'

She was too disturbed to speak. She wanted to be alone to think.

She went to her bedchamber and lay on her pallet. The beautiful romance—for which she had envied Isabella—was over. It was like the castle built on sand and the first rough winds had swept it away.

Isabella had been right. She was too old for him. He realized it now, although at the time he had been the one so sure that it was not so.

He was making excuses to be rid of her. When he said he had a fourth degree of kinship with her late husband he was really saying he was tired of her.

So much for love! So much for choosing one's own husband the second time!

No one had thought it a very suitable match—except Richard and Isabella. He would leave her soon and marry someone else. Perhaps he already knew whom.

Poor sad Isabella! She would be in need of comfort.

Richard left the following day and in due course and before Richard received news from Rome, Isabella discovered that she was pregnant.

When he heard the news, Richard came with all speed to Berkhamstead.

Eleanor was surprised at his pleasure in the news. He was kind and gentle to Isabella but he said at once that he could not stay long.

Eleanor had an opportunity of speaking to him alone and she asked him if he had heard from Rome.

He admitted that he had and that the Pope was against a divorce. He thought that he should continue in matrimony, but if Isabella failed to give him a son, added Richard, he would not let the matter rest there.

They were quite gay during that visit.

'Oh let her bear a son,' prayed Eleanor.

She was glad that Isabella did not know how much depended on her getting a healthy boy who lived.

Isabella did notice that *she* had changed. 'What is it, Eleanor?' she said. 'You are different.'

'In what way?' asked Eleanor.

'You are less . . . soft . . . less innocent . . . perhaps. There are times when you are even somewhat cynical.'

'I suppose I am growing up,' said Eleanor.

'One day they will be finding a husband for you.'

Eleanor's face hardened. 'I have no wish for marriage,' she said firmly.

Isabella smiled. 'Oh it is the happiest of states. There are disappointments, of course. I thought my heart was broken when my babies died. But now you see I am expecting again and all is well.'

Is it? thought Eleanor sadly.


On one of his journeys Edmund Rich, Archbishop of Canterbury, called at Berkhamstead.

Isabella was delighted to see him; she wanted to give him a banquet but that was not to the Archbishop's taste; nor did he want the best chamber in the castle prepared for him.

He would be on his knees for most of the night, he told her, and perhaps he would sit on a stool where he would meditate for the rest of the time. So he needed no bedchamber, only a plain, quiet room.

Isabella asked him to bless her and her child and he readily did so adding that it was the blessing of God she needed, not that of his servant.

The humility of the Archbishop was the wonder of all and Isabella told Eleanor that to have this saintly man under their roof at such a time was a sign of good fortune. She knew that her child would be a boy—and live.

The Archbishop indicated to Eleanor that he wished to see her and she went to the room in which he had slept. It was almost bare apart from the crucifix on the wall which had been put up by his servants.

She knelt with him and prayed with him and he asked after the health of Isabella.

Eleanor told him that it sometimes gave her cause for anxiety.

'Tend her well,' he said. 'It is important that the child she bears shall live.'

Of course the Archbishop knew of Richard's plea to the Pope, which would be passed on doubtless through him; and she knew that he was anxious for Isabella's welfare because of this.

'My lord Archbishop,' she said, 'I promise that I will care for her in every way.'

'Stay with her until the child is born—and after. She will need you to rejoice with her . . . or to help her if aught should go wrong.'

'I had intended to do that.'

He did not look at her; the palms of his hands were pressed together and he looked ahead at the crucifix. Her eyes were also on the crucifix and she stared at it unable to do anything else.

'My child,' he said, 'it may be that ere long your brother the King will find a husband for you.'

She thought of Isabella and Richard and she cried out: 'No.'

'The married state is not to your liking?'

She shook her head.

'You were a young wife once. Has that made you feel that you would not wish to enter into marriage again?'

'Perhaps, my lord, what I have seen of marriage makes me feel I should be happier without it.'

There seemed to come to pass an understanding between them, for he knew that she was thinking of the romantic passion of Isabella and Richard and how quickly it had changed.

'It may be, my daughter, that you would wish to take your vows of chastity.'

'Yes, my lord.'

'Ah. Then in due course you must do so. You are sure it is what you wish?'

She looked at the crucifix, which seemed to glow with an

inner fire, and it was as though some stranger spoke through her.

'It is what I wish,' she heard herself say.

The Archbishop took her hand.

'You have given yourself to God,' he said. 'You have made your promise to me. You are not ready yet but the time will come. Now you must stay here with Isabella, care for her. She needs you and you can best serve God by looking after her at this time. But the time will come. . . .'

'Yes, my lord,' she said.

Edmund Rich left that day. When he had gone she began to feel uneasy. There was something mesmeric about his presence. He had made her feel she wanted to shut herself away from the world, but now she was not so sure.

In November Isabella's baby was born and, joy of joys, was a healthy boy.

The whole household rejoiced and everyone was smiling and happy. They called the baby Henry.

Richard came. He was wildly happy. His little son was healthy in every way. He cried lustily, smiled, was bright and happy even in the first month of his life.

Richard seemed to have fallen in love with Isabella all over again and everyone was happy.

Eleanor thought: To marry, to have children. What a happy state.


Margaret Biset was alarmed. It could not go on thus, she knew. The day would come when a husband was found for her charge and then there would be separation. Margaret could not imagine herself apart from the Princess Isabella. It had been a wrench when the others had gone but it seemed fate was on their side for the marriages arranged for Isabella—as were those for the King himself—always came to nothing.

Margaret at times felt illogically indignant. What did they think they were doing, bargaining for her darling—and then these fine gentlemen daring to change their minds.

But Isabella was now in her twentieth year. Unless they had decided not to marry her off at all, they would have to do something soon.

Therefore she was not entirely surprised when Isabella was sent for by her brother the King.

Isabella shared Margaret's apprehension and it was with misgivings that she bowed to her brothers—first to Henry, then Richard—for Richard was at Court at this time.

Henry was no longer so young, being twenty-seven years of age and still without a wife himself. Richard and Joan were the members of the family who were married—and Eleanor of course, who was now a widow.

Henry said: 'Good news, sister. Let us pray that this time our hopes will not be foiled.'

Then she knew that the dreaded thing had happened and they had found a husband for her. She waited.

'A very great match for you,' said Henry. 'The Emperor of the Germans, Frederic II, is asking your hand in marriage.'

'The Emperor of Germany!'

Henry smiled. 'You see, Richard, our sister is overcome by the honour. Well, it is a good match for you, Isabella, although doubtless the Germans will consider that their Emperor has done very well in securing the sister of the King of England.'

'He does indeed,' said Richard. 'I have had it from his own lips. He is eager that there shall not be any delay.'

Isabella felt dizzy. Of course he was in a hurry. He was an old man. It was nearly ten years ago that she had been betrothed to his son.

'He will be kind to you,' said Richard. 'He is experienced in matrimony. You need have no fear, Isabella.'

'You mean he has been married more than once.'

'He has been twice widowed and so enchanted is he by the thought of another marriage that he will hear of no delay.'

'When . . . am I to go?'

Richard came and laid his hand on her shoulder. 'Ah, your eagerness matches that of your bridegroom. There will be certain matters to be arranged. The Emperor says that he will send the Archbishop of Cologne and the Duke of Brabant to escort you to Germany. They are already on their way.'

Henry said: 'You do not look as pleased as I thought you would.'

'It is a big undertaking to leave one's native land.'

'I know it well,' said Henry. 'But it is the fate of princesses. Would you wish to spend your life in the company of Margaret Biset?'

'My lord,' cried Isabella, 'may I ask one favour? I could only go if Margaret came with me.'

The brothers exchanged glances and Richard nodded his head. 'Why not?' he said. 'You will take some attendants. If you choose to take your old nurse, why should she not be one of them?' Henry was beginning to look annoyed, and knowing him well Isabella said quickly, 'It is for the King to decide. Henry, I beseech you. I know you have a kind heart. To leave here without Margaret would break mine.'

Thus appealed to, Henry's good-humour was restored.

'My dear Isabella, of course Margaret Biset may go with you.'

'She must make sure not to offend the Emperor or he might send her back,' warned Richard.

'She will not offend him, knowing what is at stake.'

'Now there is much to be done,' said Henry. 'Go back to Biset and tell her that you will ere long be leaving.'

Isabella left them and ran to the old nursery where she flung herself into Margaret's arms.

'There,' cried Margaret. 'What is it, my love? What did they say to you?'

'You are coming with me,' said Isabella. 'My brother has promised it.'

'Then we can face the rest. Where is it?'

'Germany . . . to the Emperor.'

'An old man! Well, it is not so bad as I feared. Old men can be kinder than young ones . . . and we shall be together.''

'If they had tried to separate us, Margaret, I should have refused this marriage.'

Poor child, thought Margaret. And what would that have availed!

But it was well that she had the royal consent to accompany her charge.

After Isabella had left them, Henry said: 'Let us hope that I have found a husband for her at last.'

'Poor Isabella. It has been a string of disappointments for

her—though I doubt she sees it as such. If Joan hadn't come home in time she might have been Alexander's wife. How is Joan?'

'Not well. She declares that she never has been since she went to Scotland. The harshness of the climate is not good for her. Each winter she is ill.'

'Poor Joan! She would have been better in Lusignan.'

'But our mother decided otherwise.'

'Our mother! Little she has done for us. She is more loyal to her family by Hugh than to that by our father.'

'Well, she hated our father, did she not? And who could blame her? She seems to have some affection for Hugh—because he allows her to lead him where she would have him go. Our father would never have had that.'

'One of these days, Henry, we are going to win it all back.'

'I have vowed to do so,' agreed Henry.

'Alliances help.'

'It was a pity you chose to marry as you did.'

'It was a mistake, I grant you.'

'A woman so much older than yourself.'

'Isabella is one of the beauties of the day.'

'*Was*, brother. She is an old woman now.'

'Still an attractive one . . . and not so old. We do not seem very fortunate in our matrimonial adventures, Henry. Joan in Scotland . . . that is not bad, except that her health suffers. Eleanor a widow. . . .'

'And you married to an old woman!'

'And you not married at all.'

Henry's lips tightened. He wanted to marry. It was time he produced an heir to the throne. What was wrong that all his efforts to do so came to nothing? Was he not the King of England? One would have thought that every ruler with a marriageable daughter would have been eager to present her to the King. Yet every attempt had come to naught. People would be saying soon that there was something wrong with the King of England.

'Eleanor should be brought back to Court,' said Henry. 'We should find a husband for her.'

'Isabella and she are good friends.'

'Eleanor has a role to fill in life other than that of keeping your wife company while you go off on other adventures.'

'If it is your command,' said Richard with a bow.

'Let her come back then. I will send for her. And there is another matter. I myself intend to marry soon.'

'You could not do better. You owe it to the country.'

'I know that well. I have spoken to the Archbishop.'

'And the lady?'

'The daughter of the Count of Provence. His daughter Marguerite, as you know, is already married to the King of France.'

'Why, brother, it is a stroke of brilliance. I am sure your choice will win approval. The Count will be sore put to it to give his allegiance to France when one of his daughters is the Queen of England.'

'A similar situation would arise if he thought of giving it to England.'

'It will render him neutral, brother. And think of the harm he could do our cause.'

'It seems to be a wise choice and I intend to give the country an heir at the earliest moment.'

'Let us pray that you will do so.'

'The first thing is to get married. Which I shall do as soon as satisfactory treaties have been drawn up.'

'May you have luck in your marriage, Henry,' said Richard.

'Better than you had in yours I hope,' retorted Henry, not without a certain gratification.


It was a beautiful May day when the Princess Isabella travelled with her brothers and her sister Eleanor to Sandwich.

Through Canterbury they passed, calling at the Cathedral to ask the blessing of St. Thomas and then on to Sandwich where Isabella, in the company of the Archbishop of Cologne and the Duke of Brabant, would set sail.

Margaret was beside her so she was not unhappy. Margaret pretended to be in high spirits but Isabella knew that they were a little false. Margaret was wondering what sort of man her darling was going to and if he would be a good husband. They watched orange-tipped butterflies sporting among the ladysmocks and cuckoo flowers along the banks; they smelt the scent of hawthorn blossom on the air, and Isabella said sadly: 'It is a beautiful country to be leaving.'

'It may be, my love, we are going to a more beautiful one.'

'More beautiful than this! Impossible!'

'Your native land is always the sweetest. But Germany will be our home, dearest child; and we'll grow to love it.'

'I have thanked God every morning on rising, since I knew, that you are coming with me.'

'Your gratitude was no more fervent than mine.'

They were together so it was not too sad an occasion.

Eleanor rode side by side with a young man who appeared to be about six years older than herself. He was handsome, charming and lively in his conversation and she had rarely enjoyed anyone's company more. She was beginning to think that she was shut away from the pleasures of Court life with her sister-in-law and there was a great deal that she was missing.

The young man told her that his name was Simon de Montfort and that his father was that Simon de Montfort l'Amaury who had made a name for himself in the war against the Albigensians.

The King had been good to Simon and had restored to him all the lands which had belonged to his father, and he had what he had long sought, a secure position in England and the favour of the King.

Eleanor was delighted to hear that Henry was his friend and she told him freely of her marriage to William Marshal and how she was a widow of some years standing.

He had said that he was surprised she had been allowed to remain so for so long.

'Oh,' she answered, 'I had no inclination to remarry. Not that the decision would rest with me.'

Simon de Montfort looked at her rather quizzically and said: 'Do you know, I believe that if you were so inclined you are of a nature to insist that the decision should be yours.'

That remark impressed her deeply.

Was it really so? She had always been so meek with William Marshal. But then she had been but sixteen at the time of his death.

Simon de Montfort had made her realize something. She was growing up; her character was forming and it was going to be that of a strong-minded woman.

Isabella and Margaret Biset said good-bye to those who had escorted them to Sandwich and set sail for Antwerp.

The four days at sea were far from pleasant and during them Isabella thought little of what was awaiting her. Of one thing she was certain: nothing could be worse than being at sea.

When finally they did land it was to find friends waiting for them to tell them that there was a French plot afoot to capture Isabella and prevent her marriage to the Emperor. They stayed at an inn, where Isabella was said to be a young noblewoman travelling with her governess, and under cover of darkness they left the town. It was several days before they could be assured that they had outwitted their would-be kidnappers and by the time Frederic had sent a strong guard to protect and bring her to Cologne.

There was a halt in that city. It was dangerous to proceed because the Emperor was at war—strangely enough with his own son who at one time had been put forward as a husband for Isabella—so she and Margaret had six weeks respite during which they began to learn the ways of the country.

In due course the Emperor arrived to greet his young bride with great rejoicing. He exclaimed at her charm and beauty and declared himself to be absolutely delighted.

He embraced her warmly and told her that he was determined to care for her and make her happy. Margaret clucked with delight. She was glad they had not given her charge to some brazen young man. From the Emperor she would receive tenderness and consideration.

The wedding celebrations were magnificent and continued through four days, for the Emperor wanted his subjects to know how delighted he was with his bride.

Isabella found that her marriage was not nearly as distasteful to her as she had feared it might be. The Emperor, delighted with her youth and freshness, was anxious not to frighten her. He told her that he had loved her from the moment he had seen her and her beauty exceeded all reports of it. She was his treasure, his sweet young bride; and his great desire was to please her.

However he did propose to send back all her English attendants and when she heard this she was filled with fear.

She threw herself at his feet and wept bitterly and when he raised her and asked what was wrong she burst out: 'Margaret Biset and I have been together all my life. I cannot let her go. If you send her away I shall never be happy again.'

Then he kissed her and said that although he had wanted all her English attendants to go and she to become his little German wife, he would show his love for her by allowing Margaret to stay with her for as long as she needed her.

At that Isabella dispensed with all ceremony, threw her arms about his neck and kissed him fervently.

'It seems that you love the old Emperor then?' he asked.

'I do,' she answered fervently. 'You are so good to me.'

'And you can be happy here?'

'I can be happy if you do not take Margaret away from me.'

'So Margaret remains.'

The Emperor grew so enchanted with his wife that he wanted nothing but to be with her all the time. He took her to his palace at Hagenau and surrounded her with all the luxury he knew of. The furnishings of her apartments were as rich as anything she had ever seen. He brought her more jewels than she could possibly wear. There were silks and fine clothes for her servants to make into any garments she fancied, and there were rich meats and wines to suit her taste. But he could not bear that anyone should see her lest they take her from him.

She and Margaret were together as they had been at her brother's Court; and the Emperor's fondness for her was remarked on throughout the land.

In due course she was pregnant and merchandise was sent to her that she might choose what she fancied for her child. Margaret liked to make most of the garments herself and it was their pleasure to sew and talk together of the child.

It was pleasant to be so petted by her loving husband; and at this time Isabella was content to be shut off from the world in her silken cave. Margaret was with her and they played the guessing games they had played during her girlhood. It was all so like her childhood—apart from visits from the Emperor— that she did not feel in the least like a prisoner.

When her child was born it was a girl. If the Emperor was disappointed he did not say so, but she knew he would have preferred a boy. When she jokingly told Margaret that she would name the child after her and mentioned it to Frederic he made no protest. If that was what his little darling wanted, so should it be.

So the child became Margaret and so did the nurse dote on her namesake that Isabella declared the baby was taking her old nurse away from her.

'What nonsense!' cried Margaret. 'There's enough love in this old body of mine for you both.'

So the pleasant life went on—except that one cage was changed for another. The Emperor had to visit his Italian subjects so he moved her to Lombardy and there she with Margaret and her baby and the few maids who attended on their needs lived once more in a luxurious palace, with their beautiful gardens—high-walled where no one came but the Emperor.

He rarely let anyone see his bride.

And there Isabella's son was born. She called him Henry after her brother. And the Emperor said he had never known such joy.

It was a strange life, but one which was not unhappy.

The old ageing Emperor and his beautiful young wife had become something of a legend in the land.

# Eleanor and Simon de Montfort

ELEANOR was in love.

The most interesting, exciting man at her brother's Court was Simon de Montfort. Henry liked him, she was glad to notice; but he had many enemies. She lived in terror that one day they would harm him.

He had said to her once: 'I am considered to be French by the English and English by the French. It does not make either side over fond of me.'

When she rode out with a party she would invariably find him beside her; and on one or two occasions, greatly daring, they would slip away from the others. How she enjoyed those rides, galloping over the grass with Simon a little behind, allowing him to catch up, when he would say: 'Halt a while, Princess. I would talk with you.'

Then they would walk their horses and talk. It was mostly about themselves.

He was an adventurer, he said. She was the King's sister. Was it not strange that they should have so much to say to each other, such understanding?

'I am an adventurer too, I sometimes think,' she told him.

'You . . . a princess!'

'Why should a princess be doomed to a dull life?'

'Not all princesses are,' he reminded.

'I am determined to live my life as I wish.'

'I knew there was something unusual about you from the moment I first saw you.'

He told her about his life and she told him about hers.

If his grandfather the lord of Montfort and Evreux had not married the sister and co-heiress of the Earl of Leicester he would never have come to England. 'Think of that. But for that marriage you and I would not be riding together here now.'

'I am glad of that marriage,' said Eleanor.

He laughed; his eyes gleaming with pleasure. It seemed to her that there was deep meaning behind everything they said to each other.

'Their second son, Simon, led the crusade against the Albigensians and to him came the title of Earl of Leicester and half the estate.'

'And you are the son of that crusader.'

'I am he. My brother Amaury resigned his rights in the estate to me and I came to England to claim them.'

'It seems you have not been unsuccessful here.'

'Your brother has been good to me.'

'He took a fancy to you. I understand why.'

'The fact that his sister understands why means more to me than the King's favour.'

'Then I must change my opinion of you. You are not as wise as I thought.'

'That, my dear lady, remains to be seen.'

'How long must we wait for this revelation?'

'I hope not long.'

Eleanor was exultant. What could he mean. She knew her feelings. What were his?'

'Your brother has given me a pension of four hundred marks,' he told her. 'When I recover my estates I shall be rich. But I shall not forget the help I have received.'

'My brother's pension must be of great importance to you.'

'Not so important as the sympathy I see in his sister's eyes.'

'Surely to a man of good sense a pension should be of more use than sympathy.'

'Nay, not so,' he contradicted. And it was at moments like this that she spurred her horse and galloped away because she had never been so happy in her life before and she knew that it meant she was in love.

She tried to explain to him what her life had been.

'As a child I was married to old William Marshal. It had to be, because they were afraid he would go over to the French.

I was only a child. After the ceremony he went away to Ireland.'

'Poor little girl!'

'I stayed in the palace with my sister Isabella and our old nurse Margaret Biset. Isabella is an Empress now and Margaret is with her.'

'They will find a husband for you.'

'I will not take him . . . unless he is of my choice.'

'Ah, when the moment comes shall you be strong enough, think you?'

'I know I shall be strong enough.'

'Kings, archbishops, barons, lords . . . they can be very strong.'

'I can be strong too. A princess who marries once for state reasons, has the right to take her second husband when and from where she pleases.'

'You think that would be permitted?'

'I should decide.'

'Oh you are a bold princess as well as a beautiful one. You have the qualities I admire most in women—beauty and independence.'

'I am glad that I please you, my lord.'

'I hope that the pleasure I find in our company will never give you cause for regret.'

No one had ever talked to her in this way before. She knew that he was telling her he loved her. Was it possible for her to marry a man without a fortune? For he had none and had still to regain his estates. All he had at the moment was a claim to them. What else had he? The King's friendship; the love of the King's sister.

And yet because he was Simon de Montfort it seemed that he had a power within him to accomplish what would have been impossible in another man.

She wondered what Henry would say and do if she told him that she wished to marry Simon de Montfort.

Henry would be more inclined to be lenient now because he had a bride of his own. This time he had actually achieved marriage and there was a Queen at Court. Eleanor—named as she was—was very young and very beautiful and had come from Provence to be Henry's Queen. She was a little spoilt and petulant, demanding her own way, but Henry was so delighted to have a bride and so enchanted by her beauty that he had mellowed considerably and because of this would have some understanding and sympathy for his sister.

It was when they were in the forest and had evaded the rest of the party—a habit which was becoming too frequent not to go unnoticed—that Simon broached the subject.

There could not be many men at Court who would dare suggest marriage to a princess, but Simon of course was no ordinary man. He had complete confidence in himself. He was going to make his mark in the world. He was so distinguished. That was clear to himself and Eleanor. So he could therefore do what other men would never dare to.

He said: 'You know that I love you.'

She was too forthright to pretend. 'Yes,' she said, 'I know it.'

'And you love me,' he stated; nor did she deny it.

'When people love as we do there is one thing they must do, and that is marry. Do you agree with me?'

'I do,' she answered.

'What then?' he asked.

'We should marry.'

'Would you be ready to, Eleanor?'

She held out her hand and he took it. How his eyes gleamed. He was looking at the future.

'Then one thing is certain,' he said. 'We *shall* marry.'

'That is certain,' she agreed.

'How I love you!' he said. 'You and I were meant for each other. We are bold, are we not? Ready to take what we want from life?'

'It is the only way to live,' she answered.

'Well, what next?'

'We marry.'

'Secretly.'

'I could sound the King.'

'Would he agree?'

'I think he might . . . if we were careful. We must not let others know. There would be objections.'

'Simon de Montfort and the Princess,' he said. 'They would tell me I was unworthy.'

'We know otherwise. I will discover from my brother what his feelings are in this matter. He is inclined to be lenient with lovers just now.'

'The uxorious husband loves his Eleanor . . . but not as I love mine.'

'How can you know?'

'That child! What does she know of life?'

'She knows how to get what she wants of Henry. But then it would not be difficult for a woman to get what she wanted from Henry.'

'Even his sister?'

'I will sound him.'

It was Christmas time and they were at Westminster. The King was very busy with preparations, eager to show his new Queen how lavish they could be.

Eleanor hesitated to approach him because if he would not help her he could make it impossible for her to marry Simon. Possibilities occurred to her. He could even imprison Simon, have him mutilated, murdered. . . . Not that Henry had ever showed any signs of behaving in such a cruel manner. He was not like their father. Henry was more of a man of peace. And yet she was taking a risk. Talking to Simon, she had felt so bold and brave; when she was not with him she found herself facing realities.

She made up her mind that there was one person whom she could safely consult and that was her sister Joan who had been with the Court since September when she had gone on a pilgrimage to Canterbury with the King and her husband Alexander. Alexander had now returned to Scotland but Joan had made an excuse to stay on in England for a few weeks longer. That stay had extended.

So to Joan went Eleanor and contrived that they should be alone together.

Concerned as she was with her own affairs, Eleanor could not help noticing how wan her sister looked. Poor Joan seemed to be wasting away. She made excuse after excuse to stay in England and so far she had remained. She had spent several weeks in her bedchamber when the weather was cold and seemed to be better for it, but she dreaded returning to Scotland.

Beside her Eleanor looked blooming, knew it, and was a little ashamed of it.

She asked with tenderness after her sister's health.

'It is better,' Joan told her. 'It is always so in England.'

'Poor Joan.' Eleanor was thoughtful. No matter where Simon went she would gladly follow. Joan clearly did not feel the same about Alexander.

'I want to talk to you, Joan. It is secret . . . very secret. I want your advice.'

Joan smiled at her sister. 'I shall be pleased to help if I can, you know.'

Eleanor nodded. 'I am in love and want to marry.'

Joan looked concerned. 'It so much depends with whom. Is he what would be considered suitable?'

'To me he is the only one who could possibly be suitable.'

'That is not what I mean, Eleanor.'

'I know it and I suppose he is what would be called completely unsuitable.'

'Oh, my poor sister.'

'Not so, Joan. I refuse to be called poor when Simon loves me.'

'Simon?'

'Simon de Montfort.'

Joan wrinkled her brows. 'Is he not the son of the general who fought the Albigensians?'

'He is the same. We are going to marry—no matter what anyone says. If we have to go to France, if we have to escape . . . we shall do so to be together.'

Eleanor raised her eyes to her sister's and saw that Joan's were shining with admiration.

'You are right, Eleanor,' she said. 'If you love . . . and he loves you . . . then let nothing stand in your way. You married once for state reasons. Now freedom of choice should be yours.'

Eleanor went softly to her sister and took her in her arms. She felt uneasy because of Joan's frailty.

'I did not think you would understand,' she said.

'I do understand, Eleanor,' answered Joan. 'I loved once

. . . I am glad that I did, although it did not bring me happiness.'

'You, Joan . . .!'

'It was long ago, oh long long ago it seems.'

'You were sent away when you were a child. Sent to Lusignan.'

'To the man who was to be my husband,' said Joan. 'I was frightened and I learned not to be. I grew to know him. He was so good . . . so kind.'

'You loved him!' cried Eleanor. 'And he married our mother.'

'Do you remember her, Eleanor?'

'But little.'

'She had some allure. I cannot explain it. I never saw it in any other woman. It was a kind of magic. Not good, not kind, but she bewitched people with it. She bewitched Hugh. So I came back and married Alexander.'

'My poor, poor Joan!'

'Oh, it is too long ago now to talk of, and here I am the Queen of Scotland.'

'A poor compensation, you are telling me, Joan.'

Joan held out her thin hands on which blue veins were painfully visible.

'I am telling you that if you have a chance of happiness you should take it. You do not want to spend your life regretting.'

'So that is your advice, Joan?'

Joan's answer was to put her arms about her sister and kiss her gently on the brow.

'Sound our brother,' she said. 'But carefully. It may be that at this time he will feel tender towards lovers.'

Henry regarded his sister with mild affection. He was very contented with his marriage. His bride was very young, the second daughter of the Count of Provence; and her elder sister was already the bride of Louis IX of France. Not only was she beautiful, she was accomplished too. She was noted for the verses she wrote and she could sing and dance in a manner which was enchanting.

Henry was particularly delighted because his brother Richard had made the acquaintance of the Princess of Provence on his travels and had been charmed by her bright intelligence and her beauty; Henry knew he would have liked to marry her himself. No hope of that. He had his ageing Isabella, whom he had insisted on marrying. So this was one of the occasions when Henry would score over his brother.

When Eleanor came to him he was in a state of some euphoria and she, in her newly found wisdom and her awareness sharpened by her desperate need, began by telling him how delighted she was by his happiness and how enchanting the new Queen was, and how fortunate he had been to wait awhile before hurrying into marriage. Whereupon Henry began enlarging on the perfections of his Queen and the joys of the married state which made it easier for Eleanor.

'Ah, I would I had the good fortune to know such happiness!' she sighed.

'My poor sister, you were married to old William Marshal. How different that must have been from the state in which I find myself!'

'My fortunate brother! None could wish you greater happiness than I. I know that, understanding so much, you would, if it were in your power, help me to attain a similar joy.'

Henry smiled expansively. 'Dear Eleanor, I would the whole world could be as happy as I am.'

'I could be so . . . or almost, I think, if only it were possible. . . .'

Henry was looking at her questioningly and she went on: 'Henry, I am in love. I want to marry and I implore you—understanding so well—to help me in this.'

'My dear sister, what can I do? Who is this man?'

'He is Simon de Montfort.'

Henry was silent for a few seconds, while Eleanor suffered agonies of doubt and plans for immediate escape from England began to form in her mind.

Then Henry slowly smiled. 'He's a bold fellow. I always knew it. But I did not know how bold.'

Eleanor caught his hands and cried: 'Henry, you who have achieved such happiness . . . can you deny it to me, your sister, who has already suffered one unwelcome marriage and years shut away from your Court?'

Henry embraced her. 'I will help you,' he said. 'It will have to be secret for a while. . . . No one must know.'

'My dearest, dearest brother, if you consent, that is all I ask!'

Henry, smiling benignly, told her that she should have her wish. He would arrange it. But for the time being she must remember . . . secrecy.

She could scarcely wait to see Simon. There was no opportunity until they rode out with a party in the forest, for she realized the need to keep her coming marriage secret. They were not safe yet. Henry could change his mind if he were prevailed upon and it was certain that he would be if their plans were discovered. Many of the barons were envious of Simon and they would consider that marriage with the King's sister was a move he had made from ambition. They would do anything rather than see him advance.

They escaped from the party. There again—this would be noticed if they did it much more.

She told him: 'I have spoken to Henry. He will help us.'

Simon was astounded. 'Is this really so?'

'I chose my moment. He is so delighted with his marriage, I flattered him. He is always susceptible to that.'

'My God!' cried Simon, 'then ere long you will be my wife.'

'It should not be too long delayed. He could change his mind.'

'That's true enough. As soon as Christmas is over. . . . Oh, you clever Princess!'

'You will find that I shall always be clever when it is a matter of getting what I want.'

'I see I shall have a very forceful wife.'

They were too moved to say much and they rode silently through the forest.'

They came upon a chapel there and it was Eleanor who said they should alight, tether their horses and go inside to pray at the altar to thank God for His goodness to them and ask for His continued help.

'We may well need it,' commented Simon.

So they went inside the chapel and at the altar they knelt

together. And as Eleanor raised her eyes they came to rest on the crucifix and she was transported back to a time when she had knelt in a bedchamber side by side with Edmund the Archbishop of Canterbury.

She could not control the trembling which came over her. She had said on that occasion that she would take a vow of chastity. Oh, but she had spoken lightly. She had felt that that was what she had meant then, but she had not at the time met Simon.

It was not binding. It was nothing. She must not think of it.

They rose from their knees and as Simon took her arm to lead her from the chapel he said: 'Why, you are trembling.'

She answered: 'It was cold in the chapel.'

And that was all.


It was a cold January day when Eleanor stood beside her brother who gave her away, after commanding the priest to swear to secrecy, and she was married to Simon de Montfort.

She could not believe her happiness, but she wished all the same that she could rid herself of that niggling fear which had come to her in the chapel.

Again and again she reminded herself that the words she had spoken to Edmund had not been seriously meant. He could not take them in the nature of a vow . . . or could he?

She thought of that stern aesthetic face. People who subjected themselves to great self-sacrifice could be very harsh on others.

It was foolish of her to allow her happiness to be spoiled when Henry had given his consent and had actually given her away. But then he did not know of that scene between herself and Edmund. And when Edmund did. . . .

She would refuse to think of it.

As they came out of the chapel, Henry looked rather worried.

He had begun to believe that he might have acted rashly. He had been so anxious for his sister to be happy and it had given him a deep satisfaction that he could provide that happiness; but now that the ceremony was over, he was asking himself whether he had acted wisely.

He said sharply: 'None must know. You must keep your secret for a while.'

Eleanor took his hand and kissed it fervently.

'Dearest brother, most noble King, I shall never forget what you have done for me.'

That satisfied Henry. Until he began to be uneasy again.

As the weeks passed the cold was intense. The wind whistled through the castle rooms and even great wood fires could not keep the inhabitants warm.

Joan's cough grew worse and when Alexander sent messages to Westminster to know why she did not return she was very depressed, but she made her preparations.

Eleanor spent a great deal of time with her. Joan was one who knew of her marriage. It was pleasant, as Eleanor told Simon, to be able to talk to someone; and Joan was so pleased that they were happy.

Poor Joan! If only she could have known this bliss. Of course Alexander was not like Simon. It amused Eleanor to contemplate that Joan's would be said to be a good marriage, whereas hers . . . well, it was most unsuitable. Oh but happy, thought Eleanor. How wonderful life was!

She was talking with Joan in the cold room, Eleanor seated on a stool and Joan lying on a pallet covered by a fur rug because she could not get warm.

'You cannot leave yet,' said Eleanor. 'You will have to wait until the weather is better.'

'Alexander grows very impatient. I should have gone before the winter started.'

'Nonsense. Why should you not visit your family?'

'It has been a wonderful visit. It has made me so happy to see Henry and you contented in marriage.'

'Though mine is to be kept secret for a while.'

'You like that. Confess! Does it not give a zest to it all?'

'It did not need it,' replied Eleanor.

'May you always be as happy as you are now, dear sister.'

'I intend to be,' replied Eleanor. 'When we have our castles you will come and be with us often.'

'I should like that.'

Joan began to cough and could not stop, and Eleanor was

distressed and frightened. When one of those paroxysms seized her sister, Eleanor was afraid she would choke.

Joan lay back on her cushions. Eleanor saw the blood and shivered.

'Dearest Joan, is there anything I can get for you?'

'Sit by me,' said Joan.

Eleanor sat until darkness fell. And she was thinking of poor Joan's going far away to Lusignan to a husband she had never seen, loving him, and losing him.

Joan said suddenly: 'Eleanor, are you there?'

'Yes sister. What can I get you?'

'Bring Henry, will you?'

'Henry!'

'Please . . . I think he should be here.'

Eleanor went out. It was half an hour before she could find her brother and bring him to the bedchamber.

They came carrying lighted candles; and the sight of their sister lying on her cushions filled them with deep foreboding.

Henry knelt by the bed and took her hand.

'Dear brother,' said Joan. 'You know this is the end, do you not?'

'Nay,' declared Henry. 'We shall keep you here. You shall not go back to Scotland. My doctors will cure you.'

Joan shook her head and said: 'Eleanor . . . sister.'

'I am here, Joan.'

She shook her sister's hand and held it.

'God bless you both,' she said. 'Be happy.'

'We shall all be happy,' Henry assured her.

'Help me up a little,' said Joan; and Henry put his arm about her and held her thus.

'I . . . am happy to be with you . . . here in England. . . . I am glad . . . to have come home to die.'

Both Henry and Eleanor could not speak; they averted their eyes from their dying sister.

'Henry, I should like to lie in Dorset . . . in the nunnery of Tarent. . . .'

'When the times comes so shall you,' said Henry with a sob in his throat. 'But it is far off, sister.'

She shook her head and smiled.

For some time there was silence; then Henry looked into her face and slowly released her.

'She has gone,' said Eleanor, and she put a hand over her eyes to hide the tears.

It was impossible to keep the marriage of Eleanor and Simon de Montfort secret for long.

When Richard of Cornwall heard of it—and that it had taken place with the consent of the King—he was furious.

He himself was growing more and more dissatisfied with his own marriage. Every time he saw Isabella she seemed to have aged a few years. He did not realize that she understood that he no longer cared for her and this gave her sleepless nights and days of anxiety.

Simon de Montfort was one of the most unpopular men in Court circles. He was a foreigner and Henry had always had a tendency to favour foreigners, more so now that his wife was bringing in her friends and relations, and favours which should have gone to Englishmen were going to them.

The Barons were beginning to gather round Richard. He had a fine son, young Henry, and the King was, so far, childless. Henry did not have the power to attract men to him. There was a certain weakness in him which they detected and which made him act sometimes most unjustly when at others he was over eager to please.

Richard came to the King and gave way to vociferous indignation.

He would like to know why Henry should have given his consent to a marriage which was clearly displeasing to many of the most important people in the country, who should have had some say in choosing a husband for the King's sister.

'It was unnecessary for others to choose,' said Henry. 'I gave permission. That was enough.'

'Clearly it is not! It was important that you should have brought the matter to light. Instead you join in the secrecy.'

'Know this, brother,' cried Henry, 'I shall do as I please.'

'That's what our father said.'

This was the kind of remark which had been flung at Henry ever since he came to the throne. It never failed to enrage him because it frightened him.

'Have a care, Richard,' warned Henry.

'It is you who must have a care. There are rumblings of discontent throughout the kingdom.'

'There always have been and always will. There are too many men who seek riches for themselves and will make trouble hoping to get them.'

'It is no help to your cause to act like this. Our sister is a royal ward. You know what that means.'

Henry burst out: 'I had my reasons.'

'What reasons could there be for giving our sister to an . . . adventurer.'

'I will tell you this. He had seduced our sister. I thought it better to set this matter to rights by giving her to him in marriage.' Henry had turned pale. It was a lie. But if it were true—and who knew it might be?—none could blame him for getting them married.

'The scoundrel!' cried Richard, who had seduced many women in his not very long but somewhat full amatory life.

'She wished for the marriage,' continued Henry. 'Let us hope he will make her a good husband.'

'I shall seek out Simon de Montfort,' cried Richard.

'Pray do. Eleanor will not bless you. She is extremely happy with the fellow.'

'An adventurer . . . and a royal ward! Our own sister.'

'Oh come, Richard. They are fond of each other. You married of your own free will and I forgave you. Eleanor took Marshal at a time when it was necessary to prevent his going to the enemy. Let her live in peace with the man she chooses.'

'Who seduced her before marriage!'

'So thought I,' said Henry cautiously.

Richard stormed out of his presence, leaving Henry angry and at the same time ashamed.

It would seem that he is the King not I, he thought; and then he laughed inwardly to think of Richard with his ageing wife, of whom he would clearly like to be rid, and his own sweet Queen who continued to delight him.

Edmund Archbishop of Canterbury came to the King to tell him that he was very concerned to hear of the marriage of the King's sister. He had a very special reason for being so. . . .

'It was a true marriage,' said the King. 'I was present myself.'

'I have something very grave to say to you, my lord,' the Archbishop explained. 'Your sister, widow of William Marshal, made a vow of chastity to me. It would seem that she has broken that vow. This is a grave sin in the eyes of heaven.'

Henry was weary of the matter. Why would they not let Eleanor and Simon de Montfort live in peace? Did all these people so hate to see a happy married pair? Were they so envious that they must seek to destroy that happiness?

Of course Edmund was a saint. Hair shirts tormented his skin; he beat himself with knotted ropes; scarcely took enough food to keep himself alive, never went to bed and spent half the night on his knees. One could not expect such a holy man to be overjoyed by the carnal happiness of Eleanor and Simon.

But if it really was true that Eleanor had made a vow, what could she have been thinking of to break it?

'I know of no such vow, Archbishop,' he said.

'Nevertheless it was made in my presence. She has placed her immortal soul in peril.'

'I do not think God and his saints will be so hard on her. She was married to old Marshal you know when only a child, and she truly loves her husband.'

'My lord, I understand you not. Can it be that you have forgotten your duty to the Church? It is small wonder that our kingdom is in turmoil.'

A plague on these pious churchmen, thought Henry. Then he was afraid of such irreligious thoughts and fervently hoped that the recording angel had not garnered that one.

'I will speak to my sister,' said Henry.

'My lord, that will not be enough. She will need a special dispensation from the Pope.'

Henry sighed and sent for his sister.

Eleanor came in some trepidation. She had been in a state of great uneasiness ever since she had known that the news was out.

Simon had said they must hold themselves in readiness to fly from the country. He himself had gone to Richard and humbly asked his pardon. He had taken gifts and had tried to explain to his brother-in-law how he had been carried away by love for his sister.

Richard listened, accepted the gifts and said that he was in trouble with the Archbishop over some matter of a vow Eleanor had made—and that could provide even more difficulties for them.

There was a certain understanding between the two men and during the interview Richard had relented a little. He began to think that if the Barons rallied round him and it became necessary to rise against Henry, Simon would be a good ally.

He said that he understood Simon's feelings and that he knew Eleanor had grown into a strong-minded young woman. If she had made up her mind to marry Simon, then Simon had little help for it but to obey her. They laughed together and Richard was mollified.

It was not going to be so easy with the saintly Archbishop. Eleanor's knees trembled as she stood before the old man. His fiery eyes seemed to penetrate her mind and she remembered vividly kneeling with him before the crucifix.

Henry said: 'The Archbishop brings me grave news.'

Eleanor faced the old man unflinchingly—hoping he could not see how her hands trembled.

'It would appear,' said Edmund, 'that you have forgotten the vow you made to God.'

'I did not regard it as a vow, my lord.'

'So you made a vow which was no vow,' said Edmund. 'I beg of you do not add flippancy to your sins.'

'I was very young and inexperienced of the world. I said I might consider going into a nunnery.'

'Take care. Your words will be recorded in heaven.'

'I have a husband whom I love. I do not think God would consider that a sin.'

'You have broken your vow to Him. Every time you lie with this man you commit a sin against Holy Church.'

'I do not think so.'

'You . . . a foolish girl!'

'Nay,' said Eleanor with spirit, 'a proud and happy wife.'

Henry could not help admiring her. Of course he must

respect such a saint, but Eleanor did not seem to care whether or not she offended God. He almost expected the Almighty to show His displeasure by striking her dumb or blind . . . or barren perhaps. He could not tell about the last but she certainly escaped the first two.

'You give God . . . and us . . . great cause for sorrow.'

'There are so many nuns,' said Eleanor, 'and not so many happy wives.'

'You are without shame,' cried the Archbishop.

'Am I?' said Eleanor.

'You must have a care, sister,' Henry warned her mildly. He wanted an end of the scene so he went on before the Archbishop could speak again. 'What must my sister do, my lord? She is married. We cannot unmarry her. Pray give your advice.'

'A plea for dispensation must be sent to the Pope with all speed.'

'That shall be done,' said Henry.

The Archbishop regarded Eleanor coldly.

'There is only one who should be sent to His Holiness to make the plea. That is, you will agree, Simon de Montfort.'

How she hated the saintly old man. He could not unmarry them, but he could separate them . . . for a while.

It was not a bad solution, Henry decided, for with the bridegroom away, the Barons could forget their discontent with the marriage. Eleanor was angry. That could not be helped. She must expect to pay some price for her unconventional behaviour. She had the husband of her choice and in due course he would come back.

Eleanor's sorrow in the temporary loss of her husband was somewhat alleviated by the knowledge that she was pregnant. Moreover the Pope, seeing that the marriage had already been celebrated, was of the opinion that there was no other alternative but to grant the dispensation.

In due course Simon returned and Eleanor's son was born in Kenilworth Castle. Eleanor decided to call him Henry after her brother, which delighted the King.

In fact Henry himself was in a state of excitement over his

wife's pregnancy, and when his son—whom he called Edward—was born, he was overjoyed.

To show that Eleanor was completely forgiven he invested Simon with the Earldom of Leicester.

Alas, there was some trouble of a debt Simon had incurred during his stay abroad and as Simon could not meet the payment the account was sent to the King.

Then Henry was enraged. It seemed to him that his sister was using him. She flattered him when she wanted something—Richard had suggested as much. Her husband so took advantage of his elevation into the royal family that he ran up bills he could not meet. He was going to show them that he was aware of their chicanery.

He made an attack on Simon in the company of several of the dignitaries who had gathered togther for the churching of the Queen, accusing him of seducing Eleanor before their marriage, and bribing the Pope for the dispensation and then failing to meet his debts.

'If you do not remove yourself from my sight this moment you will be in the Tower before the night is out,' he declared.

Simon was bewildered. It seemed to him that Henry was behaving in a manner such as his father often did.

But he and Eleanor left the Court without delay.

'He will have recovered from his ill temper in the morning,' said Eleanor.

'What if he does not?' asked Simon. 'I did not care for the look in his eyes.'

'What then?' asked Eleanor.

'Get the child. We will leave the country for a while. It is safer so. I see that he will always remember this accusation against me and use it when it best suits him.'

Eleanor sighed; but she knew that he was right and as long as they were not separated she was reconciled to anything that had to be. A week later they arrived in France.

Isabella, Countess of Cornwall, was an unhappy woman. She knew that Richard was seeking an excuse to be rid of her. He should have listened to her when she had told him that she was too old to please him. She missed Eleanor and often envied her her happiness with Simon de Montfort. Dear

Eleanor, she deserved to be happy at last; and she would be because there was a certain strength about her which Isabella admired the more because she knew she herself did not possess it.

Richard rarely càme to see her now. He made an effort to be affectionate but it did not deceive her, for she knew that he was seeking means to be rid of her, and although the Pope had decided against that dispensation five years ago, Richard had not given up hope.

Sometimes she felt very much alone in the world. Her great father long since dead; her brother on whom she had relied now gone. All she had was her son Henry—and he was a delight to any mother's heart—but how long before he would be taken away from her? Nobly born boys were never allowed to grow up in their own homes. He would be sent away to be educated that he might become what they would call a man—the tender care of a mother being considered a handicap in such training.

She was again with child though—her one consolation, although during this pregnancy she had become easily exhausted and often felt ill.

She was fortunate to be surrounded by good servants. Those close to her knew of the sadness her husband's neglect had brought her. It was touching to see how they tried to make up for his lack of care by lavishing their attentions on her, with something more than could be expected from the best of servants.

In due course her time came and to her delight she gave birth to a son.

Richard arrived at Berkhamstead a few days after the birth.

He looked young and vital as he sat by her bed; she felt old and tired and she knew that she looked it.

'It was good of you to come to see our son,' she said to him.

'Naturally I should come to see the boy . . . and you.'

'Even more good of you to come to see me . . . when it is against your inclination.'

He shifted uneasily on his stool.

'You are not looking well, Isabella,' he said. 'Are they caring for you? I must speak to them.'

'They give me loving care, Richard. You can imagine how I appreciate that.'

'I am glad of it,' he said.

He sat in silence and she wondered whether he was thinking that she looked so ill that she might never rise from this bed.

It would save him a lot of trouble, she thought, and me a great deal of heartbreak.

It was, said her servants, almost as though she were willing herself to die.

He spoke to the most devoted of those who were with her night and day.

'Your mistress seems lifeless,' he said. 'Is she very ill?'

The old woman bridled a little and faced him coldly. Such women he knew cared for no one, however high in rank, and would fight an army of kings for the sake of their beloved charges.

'It has been an unhappy time for her, my lord,' was the brusque answer.

'A difficult pregnancy, I know.'

'Did you know, my lord? You have seen little of it.'

'But I know such things are.'

'This was aggravated by my lady's melancholy state.' The old woman bobbed a curtsey and turned away muttering: 'I must see to my lady.'

He went to see the child which lay quiet in its cradle. White and still, eyes closed, it reminded him of Isabella.

He called to the wet nurse.

'How fares the child?' he asked.

'Oh my lord, a *good* child. Never cries. . . .'

He went to his chamber thinking of poor melancholy Isabella and the child that never cried.

The doctor said the child should be baptized at once, and he was christened Nicholas just before he died.

He did not tell Isabella but she knew. She lay in her bed, listless.

Richard sat beside her.

Then she said: 'Richard, I should like to be buried at Tewkesbury beside my first husband.'

Richard said: 'Nay, you are not going to die yet, Isabella.'

She turned her head away and he knelt by her bed, taking her hand in his. He knew that he had been a bad husband. He knew that he had caused her great suffering.

Theirs had been an impulsive marriage—on his side. She had loved him though. He wished he had been better to her. If he had known her end was near he would have visited her more often during the last year. But how could he have known? And the truth was that she was ageing; she was not gay as he liked women to be; she was too virtuous, too serious to please him.

Their marriage had been a failure as she had said it would be. He could hear her voice coming to him over the years: 'I am too old, Richard.'

And how right she had been.

But now he must comfort her. He would not allow her to be buried at Tewkesbury beside her first husband. That would be construed as a slight to him. He knew what he would do, for it was a mistake to ignore completely the wishes of the dead. Her heart should be put into a silver casket and buried beside her first husband, her body in a place of his choosing.

The pressure of her clammy fingers in his reminding him that he was disposing of her before she was dead and in a sudden access of shame he said: 'Isabella, you *must* get well.'

And he promised himself that if she did he would be a better husband to her.

'Richard,' she said, 'do not reproach yourself. I was to blame. I knew all along. . . .'

He said: 'I loved you. . . .'

'You love easily, Richard. I know that now. Take care of little Henry.'

He kissed her hand. 'I promise you I shall love that boy as I love none other.'

'I believe you,' she said. 'I think it is time to send for the priest.'

So the priest came and he sat with her as she died. He wept a little and he tried to stop himself exulting because there need be no more negotiations with a Pope who raised objections. He thought of the beautiful daughters of the Count of Provence.

Free. He was free.

\*    \*    \*

In the hall at Westminster Henry had summoned all the magnates to a council meeting. Richard was present and sat beside him on the dais.

Henry addressed the assembly: 'I have a message from my father-in-law the Count of La Marche. He has promised that if we take an army across the Channel he will help us against the King of France. My lords, this is the opportunity for which we have been waiting. At last we have a chance to regain all that we have lost. The Poitevins, the Gascons, the King of Navarre and the Count of Toulouse are with him. Their quarrel with Louis has grown and they are ready to march against him.'

There was a murmuring among the assembly. If this were true, it could indeed be the chance they were waiting for, but how far could they trust the Count of La Marche?

Henry answered that question. 'The Count, through his marriage with my mother, has become my stepfather. I have always known that when the moment was ripe he would come to my aid.'

It seemed reasonable. It could well be the time. Many eyes glistened at the thought of recapturing those lost castles.

'Then, my lords,' said Henry, 'we are of one mind. We will now begin to make ready to make war on the King of France.'

# FRANCE
## 1238–1246

# The Spy from Rochelle

ISABELLA of Angoulême, Queen Mother of England and Countess de la Marche, had changed a little over the years, although she was now the mother of many children. There had been one for almost every year of her marriage to Hugh. It was said that she must have some special power—and many believed it had been bestowed by the devil—for in spite of the encroaching years and the exigencies of childbearing she had remained beautiful and maturity had not brought a lessening of her allure.

She was arrogant, demanding and could be vindictive. Her husband and her children were in considerable awe of her, yet they were devoted to her. In spite of her overbearing manner and her extreme selfishness, they were aware of that enchantment which had been with her since she was a girl; and if it was in their power to give her what she wanted, they gave it.

Hugh, her eldest son, who greatly resembled his father, was her devoted slave; he would one day be the Count of Lusignan; Guy her second son was the Lord of Cognac; William was to have Valence and Geoffrey Châteauneuf, while Aymer was to go into the church. Then there were the girls, Isabella, Margaret and Alicia.

Ever since she had married Hugh she had been obsessed by her hatred of one woman; and that hatred was perhaps the greatest emotion of her life.

Not a day passed when she did not think of Blanche, the Queen Mother of France, and when she would ask herself what she could do to make life uncomfortable for that woman. For many reasons she hated Blanche, and she knew that Blanche hated her. It amused her to contemplate that Blanche

was as much aware of her as she was of Blanche and that the
good and virtuous woman would be as ready to slip a dose of
poison in her wine as she would in Blanche's.

There was a natural antipathy which they could feel, so
strong was it, whenever they were near.

Isabella rejoiced in the troubles of the Queen Mother of
France—and they were great. For a forceful woman such as
she was it was not easy to step back and take second place
after ruling. She had been Regent of France while Louis was
in his minority and now the little Saint had become of an age
to rule himself; and was showing himself capable of the task.
He had married Marguerite of Provence—a pretty creature of
whom he was enamoured—a little to the chagrin of his mother
who had doubtless imagined she would keep her influence
with him. A situation which amused Isabella, particularly
when she heard that the poor little Queen went in fear and
trembling of her mother-in-law.

Isabella had spread a great deal of scandal about her enemy
in connection with Thibaud of Champagne, and there were
many who believed that Blanche and Thibaud had in fact
been lovers—and just a few who carried the scandal further
and suggested that Thibaud had murdered Louis in order to
enjoy more of the Queen's company.

It was nonsense. Even wild romantic unwise Thibaud would
not be such a fool. Isabella had to admit that. Blanche was a
cold woman, very much aware of her regality; and she would
never take a lover—let alone Thibaud of Champagne, the fat
troubadour, who in spite of his poetry—which those who
knew declared had great merit—was a bit of a buffoon.

She had laughed heartily when she heard the story of how
when Thibaud was presenting himself at Court in the most
elaborate garments, on mounting the stairs to enter the Queen's
presence he had been covered in curdled milk which had been
thrown on him from an upper balcony by Robert of Artois,
Louis's younger brother who, resenting the scandal surrounding this man and his mother, had decided to make Thibaud
look ridiculous.

The Queen was furious to see her admirer in such a state
and there would have been trouble had not her mischievous

fourteen-year-old son confessed that he had arranged the incident.

He had been reprimanded and forgiven; but it did show that the scandal was well spread and that even the children of the royal household were aware of it.

Isabella had done her work well.

She longed for the day when the promises made in treaty between Hugh and Blanche which had been signed soon after the death of Louis VIII would be carried out. Then her daughter Isabella would be married to Blanche's son Alphonse, and Hugh the son and heir of the Lusignans, to Isabella, daughter of Blanche.

Then their families would be linked. Blanche would be mother-in-law to her son and daughter and she to Blanche's.

That thought had sustained her through the years and now the time was approaching.

It was for this reason that she had insisted that Hugh ally himself to the King of France, which seemed unnatural since her own son was the King of England. But, she reasoned, Henry should never have allowed her to turn to his enemy. He should have been a better son to his mother and not denied her the dowry she had asked for.

The King and Queen of France with their son and daughter had offered the Lusignans more than Henry across the water ever had. Therefore he had lost his mother—and deserved to, as she was fond of telling Hugh.

Meanwhile she was waiting for these royal marriages which were going to bring so much power and pleasure to the family.

'Surely,' she had said to Hugh, 'it is time our son was married. He is of an age. And the Princess is no longer a child.'

'I have heard rumours of the Lady Isabella,' Hugh told her. 'She is growing up most pious and has expressed a wish to go into a convent.'

'Nonsense,' cried Isabella. 'How can she go into a convent when she is betrothed to our Hugh?'

'It would be possible,' replied Hugh. 'There has been no formal betrothal. I have heard that Queen Blanche is anxious for her daughter to have her will, since she could be happy in no other way.'

'We should see that she is kept to her promise,' retorted Isabella.

'She herself made no promise, my dear,' Hugh reminded her mildly.

'You annoy me,' she told him. 'You have no spirit. That girl was promised to our son. It was the price we asked for peace. Promises were made to be kept. . . .'

Hugh smiled gently. Did Isabella keep her promises? He would have reminded her how often she had broken her word when it was expedient to do so, but he would not, of course, for if he did she would fly into a fury and sulk for days—which he dreaded, for on those occasions she would lock the bedchamber door against him; and even after all these years that was a state of affairs which he found unendurable.

'Blanche will decide,' he said gently.

But the idea of that woman deciding their destinies made her angrier than ever.

She insisted that he send emissaries to the Court of France to ask when the marriage between their son and the daughter of France should take place. Hugh was reluctant. He could never forget that he was a vassal of the King of France. She had to remind him constantly that he might be, but she was a Queen and a Queen of England and therefore on equal footing with the Queen of France.

Eventually, however, he gave way and his deputy was sent.

The answer came back promptly. The Princess Isabella had no desire for marriage. She was earnestly considering a life of seclusion.

Hugh shrugged his shoulders helplessly. What could he do? He was sure that if the Pope were called in His Holiness would most certainly approve of the Princess Isabella's pious resolve.

'It is a plot,' shrieked Hugh's Isabella. 'A plot to flout us! I'll swear that ere long we shall hear that she has married elsewhere.'

'Nay,' said Hugh soothingly. 'She has always been a girl

to spend long hours in prayer and meditation. It has been remarked for a long time that she had an inclination for the religious life.'

'You talk as though she had not been promised to our son.'

'Nay, my love, indeed she was promised, but if she has no feeling for the married state and has the Pope's permission to be released from marriage there is nothing we can do.'

'Nothing *you* can do, perhaps!' cried his wife. 'Has it not always been so? Have you not ever given way to those who would force their will on you? Have I not always had to force you to take action? It is small wonder to me that Spanish Blanche believes she can do what she will with you. You are spineless, Hugh de Lusignan!'

He showed a rare spirit. 'Then I wonder that you allowed yourself to marry me.'

'Because I thought that I might put a little spirit into you . . . which I have done. Where should we be if it had not been for me?'

Hugh sighed. He might have said: Living in peace with fewer enemies around us! But he restrained himself. She looked so magnificent in her anger, and he knew that without her his life would be bleak indeed.

'I shall never forgive Blanche and her saintly Louis for this,' she muttered.

Hugh was not unduly perturbed because over the years she had often expressed her hatred of the Queen, and he knew that it had always been so intense that nothing could in fact make it more so than it was already.

There was worse to come.

Alphonse, third son of Blanche, who had been promised to Isabella daughter of Hugh and Isabella, was married to Joan of Toulouse.

This was flouting Lusignan indeed. The treaty was forgotten. All these years when Isabella and Hugh had been faithful to the Court of France—even though Isabella's own son was the King of England—had brought them nothing. This was insulting.

Isabella raged and ranted so violently that her family feared she would do herself an injury. She raved against Spanish Blanche and cried out that she would be even with her. Hugh was afraid that her invective might be reported and reach the Queen's ears.

Isabella did not care. She had never been so angry in her life. The Queen of France and her son the King behaved as though the Lusignans were the humblest vassals, of no account.

'She shall see,' cried Isabella. 'She shall see.'

She wanted Hugh to call together the nobles of the neighbourhood to march against the King, and when he pointed out the impossibility of this, she called him a coward.

He tried to reason with her but she would not listen. She was a Queen, she cried. It was difficult for those of less nobility than herself to understand. It may be that her husband was prepared to stand by and see her insulted; but she thanked God that she had enough courage left to fight for her rights.

For days she refused to speak to Hugh. Her son implored her to forget her anger. She raved against them all. They had no thought for the insults heaped upon her by that Spanish woman. Did they not see that her sole reason was to discountenance the woman she hated?

'I shall get even with her!' she cried. 'One of these days it will not be Blanche who sits and laughs at Isabella, Queen of England, Countess of Lusignan. I can promise you that.'

Her family did not want her to promise them anything but that she would forget her rancour.

When she heard that Alphonse had been created Count of Poitiers and had taken possession of Poitou her fury broke out into even greater violence.

She was sure now that Blanche's motive was to humiliate her, for Poitou had been the territory of her family for years. Richard Coeur de Lion had been the Count and at this time Richard of Cornwall, her second son, deemed himself to own it.

'A deliberate insult to my family,' cried Isabella.

And she shut herself into her bedchamber plotting revenge.

Blanche had every reason to be proud of her son.

After the death of her husband she had worked solely to protect young Louis from his enemies and to keep him on the throne, but when Louis came of age she had been able to pass over power to him with every confidence.

She had reason to thank God for Louis. He was extremely handsome and distinguished looking with his mass of blond hair and fine fresh skin, but what was most gratifying was that inherent goodness. There was about Louis growing saint-liness, something wise and gentle. Not that he was by any means aloof from the worldly pleasure. He was elegant, took a pride in wearing magnificent garments when state occasions demanded that he should; and he excelled in games and was fond of amusements such as hunting. No, there was nothing of the recluse about Louis. He was greatly interested in the way people lived and could be very distressed at the conditions of the poor. He determined to do something about bettering their conditions, he told his mother; and he liked to go out into the forest very often after Mass and would take with him some of his friends, but he made it clear that anyone, even a passing traveller, might join the company. Then he would bid them talk—of any matter which interested them. He wanted to know their opinions and not only of those who frequented the Court.

Blanche at first remonstrated with him. Was this a kingly act? she wondered. Was he not in some way besmirching his royalty by making himself so accessible?

He shook his head at this and replied: 'It is the King's duty to rule his people, and how can he do this wisely if he does not understand his people's problems?'

Blanche withdrew her disapproval. She had long before known that this son of hers was a King who would have a great effect on his country.

He had a few of the weaknesses of young men—including a fondness for the opposite sex—and she decided that it would be a good idea to get him married early, and when she suggested this to him, he raised no objection.

It was not difficult to find a bride for the King of France; and when Blanche selected a Princess who was said to have received the best of educations and was also noted for her beauty, Louis agreed to be married without delay.

So Marguerite of Provence became Queen of France, and the two young people took to each other, and when Louis had a wife he settled down at once to a sober domesticity. No more amatory adventures. No more extravagant clothes; he began to dress with the utmost simplicity; he became more reflective. He confessed to his mother that he had two great missions in life: to rule France well and at some time, when it was safe to leave the country, to go on a crusade to the Holy Land.

Blanche replied that ruling the country was his first duty and she believed that most Kings found it a lifetime's work.

He agreed but she could see the dreams in his eyes and she wondered whether he was not a little too serious. She wondered too whether he was growing away from her.

He was completely content in his marriage and Blanche, who had believed her son's welfare was her ultimate desire, surprised herself at her growing resentment. She loved this son of hers too much, perhaps. Of course she wanted his happiness, but she could not bear to lose him. Yet, as his wife passed out of her girlhood he took her more and more into his confidence; and it seemed to Blanche that, even apart from this, they had little domestic secrets in which she had no share.

For the first time in her life Blanche felt alone. Her husband had loved her dearly and greatly respected her. She had helped him make decisions; she had ruled with him; and on his death she had ruled for Louis and then with him; and now this little girl from Provence was slowly but surely ousting her from her position. It was becoming Louis and his wife Marguerite—not Louis and Blanche his mother.

Because she was fundamentally wise, Blanche reasoned with herself. It was not an unusual situation. Mothers who had greatly loved their sons frequently resented their sons' wives. The fact that, in their case, this meant a shifting of power made the situation ever harder to bear.

Marguerite became pregnant and there was great rejoicing throughout the Court. Blanche took charge and would not allow her to accompany the King on some of his journeys.

'I shall be with him, my child,' she told Marguerite. 'It is for you to rest. You must take great care of yourself.'

Louis knew what was happening. He and Blanche had been so close that he understood her thoughts completely. He loved her dearly; he was appreciative of all she had done for him; but she would have to understand that his wife must come first with him. It was something to which he would have to bring her in time, but he would do it gently, for he had no wish to hurt Blanche, for whom he had such love and respect.

Moreover Marguerite was made very unhappy by Blanche's treatment of her. Like most people she was decidedly in awe of Blanche and had tried hard in the beginning to win her approval. She saw that this was useless for the Queen Mother had no intention of allowing intrusion and could not bear to share her son with anyone.

So alarmed was Marguerite by her formidable mother-in-law that she warned her servants to let her know when Blanche was approaching so that she might have time to escape. Even Louis resorted to this subterfuge; and matters grew worse, for when Blanche was under the same roof, she made it difficult for the royal pair to be together at all.

Blanche was aware of her selfishness and hated herself for it, but she could not bear to relinquish her hold on her son. She realized that beyond anyone she loved this son; and never had she cared for any as she cared for him. To such an extent had her obsession grown that she could not endure it when his attention strayed from her; she wanted him all to herself; and gradually she had begun to look on his love for his wife as the biggest threat to her happiness.

Often she asked herself if she would have wanted him to have had an unhappy marriage. Of course she would not. What she wanted was for him to have married a nonentity, a silly pretty little wife who was good for nothing but bearing children. It had been a mistake to choose one of the most educated princesses in Europe.

In due course, Marguerite gave birth to a sickly child who died soon after and the Queen herself came near to death. Louis remained at her bedside, so much to his mother's chagrin that she came to the sick room and told him how much it grieved her to see him stay there. 'You can do no good, my son, by remaining here,' she insisted.

Louis stood up and as he did so, Marguerite opened her eyes and looking full at Blanche said with unusual spirit: 'Alas, neither dead nor alive will you let me see my lord.'

She had half raised herself in her bed and as she spoke

those words she fell back, her face ashen pale, her eyes closed, and she appeared to have stopped breathing.

There was intense horror in that room. Louis fell on to his knees at the bedside and said quietly: 'Marguerite, come back to me . . . I swear that we shall be together . . . if only you will come back.'

In those moments, when it seemed that the Queen of France was dead, Blanche suffered an overwhelming remorse.

She could not bear the sight of her weeping son kneeling by his wife's bedside; she could not bear to think of what the future would be if Marguerite died.

She came to the bed. 'Glory to God,' she whispered, for Marguerite was still breathing.

'She has fainted merely,' she cried. 'Go to the doctors, Louis. Bring them quickly. We will save her yet.'

And they did. During her convalescence it was Blanche who insisted that Louis should be with her. 'Give me grandchildren,' she told Marguerite, 'and I shall be content.'

This was as near as she could get to an expression of contrition.

It was a bitter lesson she had learned for she knew that had Marguerite died Louis would never have been close to her again.

She accepted her own selfishness. She faced the truth; she had made him the centre of her life; but she saw now that her love had been selfish. His happiness, his victories were hers, and she must learn to rejoice in his marriage to a wife whom he loved.

Released from her determination to keep her son to herself, she was happier than she had been since his marriage. Marguerite quickly became pregnant again and accepted the new relationship between them with a sweetness which was characteristic of her.

There was so much evidence that Marguerite loved Louis truly, and as a good mother Blanche began to rejoice in their happiness together.

Rumours were coming to Court constantly. There were always enemies, and she had never trusted the Lusignans. She talked of them with Louis and Marguerite.

'Hugh would be a good and loyal vassal,' she said, 'but I

would never trust Isabella of Angoulême. There is an evil woman.'

'Hugh is too powerful to be lightly put aside,' said Louis. 'He could if he had a mind to it, stir up great trouble.'

'He has no mind of his own. That should be our concern. We have to deal with Isabella, and believe me, I know from the past, she is capable of any evil.'

Blanche had always had friends who travelled about the country and reported to her what was happening. Louis knew this and was interested to hear that in Lusignan Isabella made no secret of her determination to take revenge on the King of France and his mother. She greatly resented the desire of Princess Isabella to go into a convent and Alphonse's marriage had even more infuriated her.

'I hear that she is stirring up trouble,' said Blanche.

'Is that not a perpetual state of affairs?' asked Louis.

'Never more than now. I believe the situation is becoming more dangerous there. It is for that reason that I intend to send a man there. . . . He is from Rochelle. He has no reason to love them and I believe him to be loyal to you. His duty will be to listen and to report what he hears.'

'Another spy,' said Louis.

'Yes,' replied Blanche, 'another spy.'

The French Court had travelled down to Saumur in Anjou. There the King intended to hold a great display. It would be costly and luxurious although such extravagance was alien to his nature, for his mother had impressed upon him the need for this. It was, she had explained, to show not only the wealth of the King of France, but his power.

She admitted that she had been greatly disturbed by the accounts which had been sent to her by the man from Rochelle. There could be no doubt that Isabella of Angoulême was stirring up trouble. She was impressing on Hugh the need to show the Court of France that they could not be flouted. She was in touch with the powerful lords of Saintonge and the Angoumois and impressing on them the need to hold themselves in readiness to take up arms against the King, for it would soon be necessary to do so.

Louis realized this and agreed with his mother.

'During the ceremonies,' she said, 'it would be well for Alphonse to receive the homage of those counts whose suzerain he is.'

'Which,' said Louis, 'will include those who will be none too pleased to do so.'

'All the more reason why they should.'

'Do you think Isabella will allow Hugh to pay that homage?'

'If we are watchful, yes,' said Blanche.

Louis looked quizzically at his mother and she said. 'Our man from Rochelle is a good servant to us.'

# Isabella's Revenge

IT was while Isabella had gone to her castle of Angoulême that the summons appeared for Hugh to attend the Court at Saumur in order to pay the homage required of him by his suzerain Alphonse.

Hugh could not but be relieved that Isabella was away. He knew that she would have been furious at the summons, but as a law-abiding man and one who had been brought up to study his honour and to do without question what was demanded of him in that respect, he realized that he should in duty bound obey the summons.

When Isabella was not there he could reason with himself. She was wrong, but he understood her anger. She was the Queen Mother of England and as such the equal of the Queen Mother of France, and it was humiliating for her to have to play a humble part in France. He could not imagine his life without Isabella. It had been empty of excitement before he had married her. He never regretted for one moment that marriage. Violent scenes there were, but there always would be where Isabella was. He was a man of peace, but he was only half alive without her; and the truth was he could not live without her. Virago she might be, but she was, to him, the most attractive woman in the world.

And now this summons. He knew he should obey it. It was his duty to. Isabella would be enraged. He would have to try to explain to her that it was his duty to pay homage to his liege-lord and even if he did think the title should not have been bestowed on Alphonse, it would be tantamount to an act of war to refuse to pay homage.

Through years of living with Isabella he had learned that if something should be done it was better to do it first and suffer for it afterwards, for not to do it would mean that he would be persuaded against his judgment; and in this case such an act could plunge him into a war for which he was not ready.

After a good deal of consideration he rode to Saumur and there paid homage to Alphonse.

There was no doubt that Louis and his mother were pleased to see him. They had been afraid that he would not come, but thanks to the man from Rochelle, the summons had been sent when Isabella was absent, which had meant that the sober Hugh had made his own decision, which of course, was the right one.

Hugh took part in the jousts and tourneys and even though he was no longer young, carried himself through with skill and dignity.

If he had never married Isabella, thought Blanche, how much happier we should all have been. Isabella would have remained in England to plague her son—which would have been good for us too. Alas! But at least we have outwitted her this time.

When the royal party left, Hugh was with them and as they passed through Lusignan, it was natural that they should stay at the castle there.

With what trepidation Hugh had led them through the gates.

Blanche had caught sight of the man from Rochelle among those who came out to pay their respects to the King.

The Lady Isabella was not in the castle, for she had not yet returned from Angoulême.

Blanche was amused. She was indeed scoring over her enemy. And she was showing Hugh how much easier life would be for him without his wife.

There was merriment in the castle. The minstrels sang and there was feasting; and the next day when the royal party left, Hugh rode some way with them to speed them on their way.

When he returned to the castle he was dismayed, for Isabella had returned and discovered that, not only had Hugh been to Saumur to pay homage to Alphonse, but also that the royal party had stayed in the castle.

Her fury possessed her, and Hugh feared she would do herself an injury.

She—a Queen—had been slighted. Her husband had done homage to a mere Count and that meant that she must take second place to his wife . . . a Countess when she was a Queen. It was unendurable. It was better that she was dead.

She stormed into the castle calling to her servants to do her bidding. The furnishings of those rooms which had been put at the service of the royal party must be torn down and thrown out. Everything they had used must follow. She stood in the midst of the turmoil, her hair unbound—for it had escaped from her head-dress—and fell about her shoulders in glorious confusion. The colour flamed into her cheeks seeming to add to the depth and beauty of her violet eyes. Even the humblest servant was impressed, though conscious that her fascination flowed from something evil.

'My love,' cried Hugh, 'what do you intend to do with these things? If you need them at Angoulême I can buy more. . . .'

'Out of my way,' she cried. 'I want nothing of one who so demeans himself and me.'

'Tell me,' wailed Hugh. 'Tell me what you wish.'

'I wish this,' she shouted, 'that I had never come here to be insulted thus.'

She leaped on to her horse and casting a disgusted look at the goods which had been thrown out, she galloped off.

Hugh was bewildered. Two of his sons, Hugh and Guy, came to join him.

'She will have gone back to Angoulême,' said young Hugh.

'I do not understand . . .' began his father.

'She was in a fine fury when she knew what had happened. She said she woud go back to Angouléme.'

Hugh sighed and ordered the servants to carry the furnishings back into the castle and set them up in their old places.

Then he went sorrowfully into the castle.

He tried to explain to his sons. 'There was nothing else I could do. I was duty bound to pay homage to the Count of Poitiers. Honour demands it of me.'

His sons agreed with him.

But that was small comfort. The quiet of the castle was unendurable to them all.

'I must bring her back to us,' said Hugh.

So he set out for the castle of Angoulême.

\* \* \*

The castle was barred against him.

'My lord,' said the man at arms, 'my lady has given orders that none shall be let in . . . and especially you, my lord.'

Some men might have forced their way in and subdued her. Not Hugh. He was overcome with sorrow. He heartily wished that he had refused to pay homage to Alphonse. It would have been an act of war, but anything was better than that Isabella should leave him.

He asked one of her servants to tell Isabella that her husband was at the gates humbly begging to see her.

The answer came back: 'My lady will not receive you, my lord.'

Miserably he waited outside the castle until night fell and then he had no recourse but to take a lodging in the Knights Templars' Hostel which was close by.

The next day he was back at the castle. More messages were sent in and more refusals brought out.

It was three days before she consented to see him.

She stood in the hall, her beautiful hair unbound; her gown of soft blue velvet open at the throat to show her magnificent bosom across which her white hands were folded almost symbolically as though she were withholding herself from him.

'Well, my lord,' she cried.

'My dearest wife. . . .'

'Nay,' she interrupted. 'Not your dearest wife. You cannot count me so. I am not dear to you. Have you not allowed me to be humiliated . . . insulted. . . .'

'Nay, 'tis not so. I would never allow that.'

'But you have. You have bowed the knee to my enemies.'

'I will do everything you ask of me. Only listen, Isabella. Come back to me. . . .'

She looked at him from under the thick dark lashes. 'Well,' she said, 'you will listen to reason then? And let me tell you this, Hugh: if you do not do as I wish I shall never lie beside you again. I will not suffer you in my sight.'

'Do not say such things. You are my wife. You know my feelings for you.'

'At this time I know that you have betrayed me. You will have to show me that you have *some* concern for me.'

'You are my concern . . . you are my life. . . .'

She laid her hand on his arm, her expression softened.

'So thought I,' she said. 'But that woman came . . . that Spanish woman. I wish she would come back to my castle. I would see that she never left it. I would deliver her such a draught which would send her writhing in agony . . . and this should be long lasting that she might not die easy.'

'Isabella, have a care. . . .'

She laughed loudly. 'Poor frightened Hugh! I tell you this: you will have no need of fear if you listen to me. We are going to regain that which has been taken from us. We are going to have Spanish Blanche on her knees begging before us. . . .'

'Isabella, let us plan carefully . . . quietly. . . .'

She looked at him with shining eyes.

'So you will do as I wish, Hugh?'

'I will do anything for you,' he answered. 'The only thing I cannot bear is that we should be apart.'

Gently she touched his cheek.

'I knew you would come to me, Hugh. I knew you would help me to revenge.'


Together they rode back to Lusignan. The first plan was to gather together all those Barons who were hostile to France.

They would invite them to the castle and lay their plans.

Isabella had an idea which she had decided she would not set before them. In time they would realize that she was more capable of bringing about the defeat of the French than any of them. This was her quarrel. This was obvious when the humiliating subservience of Hugh was considered. As she saw it—two women rode at the head of their forces—one was the Dowager Queen of France and the other of England. Blanche was her enemy. Blanche was the one she wished to see brought low. Blanche who had hated her but not as much as she hated Blanche. Blanche who had contrived to make Hugh bend the knee to her son—and not even her first-born—by bestowing the Poitiers title on him and thus setting him above the Count and Countess of La Marche.

This was going to be a full-scale war. No skirmishing between barons. And she knew how to make it so.

This was her secret.

Why should she not write to her son? He would be eager to come to the help of his mother—particularly when in doing so he could fulfil a lifelong ambition.

The Barons of the South would rise against the King and his mother—and meanwhile the English would land and march south.

Louis and his forces would be caught in a pincer movement. Defeat for France. Triumph for England, and the King of England would have his mother to thank. She would not let him forget it.

She would write to Henry in secret. She would tell him how many men she could raise. And when Hugh and his friends of the South realized the English were joining them, she would admit this happy state of affairs had been brought about by her ingenuity.

She sent messengers in secret to England.

The man from Rochelle was assiduous in his duties. Blanche was informed of the meetings of the Barons at Lusignan and the gist of the conversation which took place there.

A messenger arrived at the Castle of Lusignan.

The new Count of Poitiers was holding court at Poitiers and he commanded all his vassals to attend.

Hugh was shaken when he received the order, for he could only guess what Isabella's reaction would be.

She laughed when she heard it.

'What now?' asked Hugh fearfully.

'We are going to Poitiers,' said Isabella.

On the journey there she told him what she planned they should do. It was useless for him to protest that it would be an act of war. She was adamant.

'One thing I will never allow,' she said, 'and that is for you to bend the knee to this man.'

'But he is my overlord . . . as I am overlord to so many. . . .'

'If you pay homage, then that is tantamount to my doing so,' declared Isabella. 'I shall never do it, Hugh. If you do, it is the end of everything between us. I shall go to Angoulême and you shall never be admitted to my castle.'

'My dearest wife, we stand together,' answered Hugh.

In the town of Poitiers, a lodging of some magnificence, befitting their rank, had been provided for them. Isabella smiled as she studied it.

'The new Count of Poitiers is afraid of us, Hugh,' she said. 'He does not wish to offend us. Well, we shall show him our true feelings. . . .'

'In view of our plans, is that wise, Isabella?'

'We are not paying homage to him, Hugh. I have said that if you do so it is the end between us.'

'I know, I know,' said Hugh unhappily.

'Well, you know what we have to do.'

He nodded.

The time came when they must pay their respects to the Count.

Hugh's war-horse was ready for him. He was attired as for war. On the crupper behind him was Isabella in rich blue velvet edged with ermine, her beautiful hair loose.

Thus, surrounded by their men-at-arms, all of whom carried their cross-bows as though ready for battle, they rode into the presence of the Count of Poitiers.

There was a tense silence throughout. The Count stared in astonishment. Every eye was on the warlike Hugh and his beautiful wife.

Then Hugh said loudly so that all could hear: 'I might have thought, in a moment of forgetfulness and weakness, to render homage unto you. Now I swear that I shall never be your liegeman. You have unjustly named yourself Count of Poitiers, a title which belongs to my stepson, Earl Richard of Cornwall.'

The Count of Poitiers cried out in protest but by this time, having made his declaration, Hugh and Isabella and their armed men thrust aside any who would bar their progress, and galloped back to the lodgings.

There they commanded their men to set fire to the lodgings as an act of defiance and to show the Count of Poitiers in what contempt they held him.

Isabella was laughing wildly as they rode out of Poitiers.

'It was magnificent. Did you see that poor fool's face? He was never so surprised in his life. Did you see how he grew pale when you mentioned my son Richard?'

'It means war,' said Hugh soberly.

'What matters it?' demanded Isabella. 'Are we not prepared?'

And she thought of the messages she had sent to England and the reply she had received.

Her son Henry was preparing to attack the French.

So it was war.

The French had long been aware of the preparations which were going on at Lusignan and were by no means as unready as their enemies had believed.

The Barons, brought together by Hugh and Isabella, did not know that Isabella had told her son Henry that these men were eager to place themselves under the English Crown. They had no intention of doing this, their one idea being to establish their own independence.

Isabella brushed this aside. She would deal with any such arguments when they arose. All that mattered now was that Henry should come with his armies and they with the Barons bring ignominious defeat to the French. Thus should Blanche be humbled. *She* should do homage to Isabella.

She was at the coast to greet her son when he arrived.

It was an exciting moment for them both. It was years since they had seen each other. The little boy she had left in England after having him crowned with her throat-collar was a man.

He was amazed—she knew at once—by her apparent youthfulness. She shook out her long hair and laughed aloud.

'Is it possible?' he asked. 'You . . . my mother.'

'It is so, my fair son, and it pleases me that you have come to help your mother whom Spanish Blanche and her sons would eagerly trample beneath their feet. Now, pray God, it will not be as they wish. . . . It will be quite the reverse.'

Henry declared he would win back all that had been lost to England. That it should be Plantagenet country from the coast to the Pyrenees.

'So be it,' declared Isabella.

But it was not to be.

Louis was a brilliant general and through her spies Blanche had kept him fully informed so that he was well prepared.

He began by taking possession of several castles belonging to those of whose loyalty he was unsure. Their owners quickly decided that it would be wise to support the King of France.

Louis was already winning the approval of his subjects. His mother might be a foreigner but she was a strong woman. She had held the Regency while waiting for her son's majority with wisdom. Many of them remembered King John.

It very soon became clear that the easy victory planned by Isabella was not going to come about.

The French were winning. The English had their backs to the sea and it was not easy to bring stores across the sea.

Henry was disappointed. He had not found what he had expected.

He took Hugh to task about this. He had been deceived, he said. 'You promised me as many soldiers as I could wish for. You told me that hundreds of knights were awaiting my coming that I might deliver them from Louis's tyranny.'

'I told you no such thing,' cried Hugh.

'But indeed you did. I have your letters in my travelling bags and can confirm this.'

'You cannot, for I sent no letters. I would have told you nothing but the truth.'

Henry narrowed his eyes. 'Such letters were received by me. They gave me an entirely false picture. I tell you this: You have brought me here on false promises.'

'You say you have had such letters in truth. . . .'

'I say it and I will prove it. I will have them brought and shown to you.'

'And signed with my name?'

'With your name and seal.'

'May God help me,' cried Hugh. 'I understand now. It is your mother who wrote these letters. She has used my name and seal.'

Henry turned away in contempt.

'You should take better care of your wife,' he snapped.

He was angry and humiliated. He could see defeat staring him in the face. He had been promised men, arms and

368 The Battle of the Queens

support throughout the country and a weak ineffective enemy.
And what had he found? Little support, few men and a strong
French army who had forestalled him.

Everywhere the French were victorious and Henry, accepting defeat, left for England.

Blanche was exultant.

'The Count de La Marche is at your mercy,' she told her
son.

'We owe much to your spy who brought us such clear
reports of their plots,' answered Louis.

'And now our braggart Count is asking for peace?'

'And for his lands?' asked Blanche.

'They shall belong to the Count of Poitiers under the
suzerainty of the Crown.'

'Madame Isabella will like that!' said Blanche ironically. 'I
would give much to see her when she hears the news.'

Her wish was granted.

Deprived of their lands there was nothing to be done but to
go to the King and ask for mercy. Too much was at stake for
pride to intervene. Louis had confiscated most of their land
but there were some on which Hugh could hope for a grant,
but this could only be obtained through special intercession
with the King.

It was therefore necessary to present himself in person with
his wife and family.

Louis was already noted for his magnanimous nature. There
was a chance, Hugh knew, that if he was sufficiently humbled and showed himself contrite, Louis would be lenient.

Isabella realized this and much as it went against her nature
she knew that she must join Hugh.

It was a moment she would never forget.

Louis was seated on his chair of state and as she had
feared, beside him was his mother. She could be trusted to
make herself a spectator of her enemy's humiliation.

They knelt before the King; Hugh, Isabella and every
member of their family. They wept and remained on their
knees while Hugh declared that he had been ill advised.

If Isabella felt a twinge of conscience she did not show it.
In fact she was not thinking of the part she had played in this

miserable drama so much as the hatred she felt for that pale-haired complacent woman.

Like Isabella, Blanche had kept her looks and was still beautiful—calmly so, with that purity of feature and those ice blue eyes.

She is everything that I am not, thought Isabella. The only thing we have in common is hatred.

The King was playing his saint's role, she perceived. He liked not to see great soldiers so humbled, he said, and bade them rise. He bore no malice against Hugh, he said; he forgave him. If he would go back to Lusignan and remain the faithful vassal of the King, this revolt would not be held against him. The King would ask that he give up three castles as a guarantee for his fidelity; the King's garrison would be in those castles and that garrison must be maintained at Hugh's expense. Later they would review the situation and if the King had no cause for complaint the position could once more be reviewed.

Hugh kissed the King's hand and with real tears in his eyes thanked him for his mercy.

The two women regarded each other. Blanche could not veil the triumph in her heart. Angry as she was, Isabella knew that Blanche must have no notion that murder was in hers.

Silently they rode back to Lusignan.

There was the castle, its towers reaching to the sky, its grey walls as solid as ever.

'It might so easily have been taken from us,' said Hugh sadly. 'The King is generous.'

'They were prepared,' cried Isabella. 'All our plans were known to them. Someone must have told them.'

'They had their spies everywhere. . . .'

'So but for spies. . . .'

All her dreams, all her hopes were gone. She would not give up, though. She cared nothing for Louis and his godly ways. Her enemy was the woman who stood there watching her humiliate herself . . . watching her with those cold icy eyes.

She had taken from Isabella what she had most coveted: power.

Now we are reduced to this, she thought. My husband has betrayed me. First John and now Hugh. Weaklings both of them.

But no matter. There is no weakness in me. I will have my way. She has reduced me to this. How can I hurt her as she has hurt me? What does she love more than anything on earth? The answer flashed in her mind: Louis.

Spies had ruined their plans. Spies should work for her.

It was not difficult to come by what she needed. Everything could be obtained by money.

She sent for two men—villains both of them, but she needed villains for this task.

'What I wish of you is a delicate task,' she told them. 'Once it is completed you will slip away and come back to me. When I have the news I need you will be so rewarded that you will build a castle apiece and rise high above your humble station.'

'It is a dangerous task,' said one of the men.

'Only if you are caught. If you are clever it will be easy. First you will find appointments in the royal kitchens. That should not be difficult. You will then know which dishes are prepared for whom and when you see one that is especially prepared for a certain person . . . that is all you need to know.'

'It would depend on the person.'

'Do you imagine that I should offer you this reward if it were for some humble knight? If you speak of this to any . . . and I say any . . . I will have your tongues cut out. Do you understand?'

The men turned pale. Isabella had an evil reputation. It was believed by some that she was a witch, for only a woman of her years could retain her beauty if she were a witch; and the power she had over Hugh de Lusignan made all marvel.

'We understand, my lady,' they answered.

'Then take this powder. It is tasteless and will dissolve quickly. When you know that one special dish is going to the King, put this in.'

'The King!'

'I said the King. Speak of it to no one, before the deed is done and after.'

'My lady, you ask a good deal.'

'I know it and I will give a good deal when the news is brought to me that the King is dead.'

She dismissed them and settled down to wait.

She was pleased with her revenge.

At first she had thought of poisoning Blanche, but what good was that? At most a few hours torment before death. No, she wanted a greater revenge for her enemy. She wanted to deprive her of what she loved more than anything on earth: her beloved and saintly Louis.

When Louis was dead, the whole meaning of life would be lost to Blanche. Her punishment would be that she would have to go on living without him.

How long the waiting was! How quiet she was! Hugh thought: Events have changed her. And he looked forward to a peaceful life. Could it be that she had indeed learned a lesson, that at last she realized that to bow the knee to a man such as Louis was no humiliation?

Each time a messenger came to the castle she was waiting for him.

What news? What news of the Court?

But there was nothing of importance.

Often she wondered about those two villains. Had they become afraid? Had they put as long a distance between her and themselves as they could?

How far could she trust them? What if they talked of what she had ordered them to do?

What would happen then? It would be the end of everything for her.

She should have had their tongues cut out before she let them go. But then they would never have worked for her. They might have had their revenge.

This was a bold plan she had embarked on. But then she was bold. Was that not why she was so impatient with Hugh and all those who surrounded her?

Some day there must be news.

\*     \*     \*

It came. A messenger from the Court. Not the villains she had sent. But one who wished her well.

She saw the messenger coming. She went down to the hall of the castle. Hugh had seen and was there too.

'It is someone from the Court,' he said.

'My lord, my lady.' The man stood there with wide staring eyes. He was looking at Isabella and there was horror and fear in his eyes.

'Yes,' said Hugh impatiently. 'What news of the Court?'

'Two men have been taken in the kitchens.'

Isabella caught at the table for support.

'They were discovered putting poison into the King's dish.'

'What then?' she cried.

'They were hanged.'

Isabella felt floods of relief sweeping over her. It had failed then, but none knew.

But there was to be no comfort. 'First they were put to the torture . . . they were questioned. . . .' The man was looking straight at Isabella. 'They named you, my lady.'

The silence in the hall seemed to go on for a long time. It was over then. This was the end. The Spanish enemy had won.

Nothing could protect her now.

She snatched at Hugh's sword and tried to kill herself, but Hugh was there and the sword went clattering on to the flagstones.

'Isabella!' he cried.

'Let me go,' she cried. 'This does not concern you.'

Then she ran out of the hall to the stables and she seized a horse and rode away.

# *Fontevrault*

THE end, she thought. This is the end. Those fools—to have been caught! If they had not . . . all would be well.

But what to do? Where to go?

Sanctuary. Fontevrault. No one could take her there. Even Spanish Blanche could not break the rules of Holy Church.

It was her only hope, to reach Sanctuary before they took her.

She rode on, thinking of Hugh. He would come for her, fight for her, defend her. Would he? Would even he shrink from one who had planned the diabolical murder of the King who had so recently shown them so much kindness?

It was over. She realized that at last.

Her only hope now was Fontevrault.

She reached the Abbey. The nuns took her in.

They would succour her. There was refuge here for all.

They put her into a secret chamber where none could reach her.

'I am in flight,' she said. 'I have sinned greatly and I wish to pass my days in repentance.'

They believed her. They knew she was the beautiful Isabella who had been responsible for much strife throughout the land. They had not yet heard of her attempt to poison the King of France.

They left her to rest and to pray.

And she thought: So it has come to this. When a woman must spend her last years in repentance, that is indeed the end.

\*    \*    \*

Alone in her secret chamber she sat brooding on the past. What was there left to her but prayer and repentance? She thought back over her life and was afraid for her sins. It was as though her carefully guarded youth dropped from her now and the years which she had held at bay were at last overtaking her.

There were no lotions to preserve her smooth skin; no oils for her hair; no scents for her body.

If she were truly seeking repentance, she should have no need of such things.

Strange it was that she, proud Isabella, should have come to this

There was no safety outside for her. If she emerged they would accuse her of attempting to murder the King. Her Spanish enemy would have no mercy on her.

She scarcely spoke to any, and so deep was her melancholy that the nuns believed she would die of it.

They brought her news of the world outside the convent. She heard that her husband and her eldest son had been arrested on charges of being involved in an attempt to poison the King.

'Oh no, no,' she cried aloud. 'They knew nothing of it.'

Hugh defended her as she knew he would. 'They lied,' he cried. There had been no poison attempt in which his wife or any member of his family had been involved. The villains had mentioned his wife's name because of recent happenings and they thought their wicked story would be believed. He challenged Alphonse to single combat that he might defend his wife's honour.

Dear simple Hugh!

Alphonse would not fight. He declared that Hugh de Lusignan was so treason-spotted that he would not demean himself by meeting him. Young Hugh then offered to fight but his offer was refused because, it was said, with such parents, he was unworthy.

Thus they were all brought low, and since it was believed by Louis and Blanche that Isabella alone was guilty, Hugh was freed and went back to Lusignan to mourn his sad fate.

Isabella would see no one. Nothing would make her emerge from her chosen solitude.

She would take the veil and live out her life seeking forgiveness for her sins.

With the passing of the days her will to live escaped her. She sought nothing now but death.

She told the nuns that when she believed her sins were forgiven she would take to her pallet and rise no more.

There was nothing for her in the outside world. All she sought now was death.

So earnestly did she seek it that within two years of her flight from Lusignan it came to her.

They buried her, as she wished, not in the church but in the common graveyard, for she had said, 'Proud was I in life but humble in death.'

Thus passed the turbulent Isabella of Angoulême, and on her death Louis saw no reason why Hugh and he should be enemies. He had known—and Blanche had known—that only Hugh's excessive love for his wife had made a traitor of him. Such good friends did they become that Hugh accompanied Louis when he realized one of his main ambitions: to join a crusade to the Holy Land. It was on this crusade that Hugh was mortally wounded.

Six years after Isabella's death Henry, King of England, on a visit to Fontevrault, was shocked to discover that his mother lay in a common grave.

He ordered that her body be taken from it and buried beside his grandfather and grandmother, Henry II and Eleanor of Aquitaine. Then he caused a tomb to be built over it and a statue of her in a flowing gown caught in by a girdle and a wimple veil framing her face.

'I remember her beauty in my childhood,' he said, 'and when I met her later she was as fair as ever. I never saw a woman as beautiful as my mother, Isabella of Angoulême.'